DES. AFORETHOUGHT
◆ BOOK 1 ◆

DEMONS AND DEBTS

KYRA ALESSY

Copyright 2023 by Dark Realms Press

All rights reserved.

No part of this book may be reproduced in any form or by any electronic or mechanical means, including information storage and retrieval systems, without written permission from the author, except for the use of brief quotations in book reviews.

This work of fiction is licensed for your enjoyment only. The story is the property of the author, in all media, both physical and digital, and no one may copy or publish either all or part of this novel without the express permission of the author.

Cover by Deranged Doctor Designs

Also by Kyra Alessy

WRATH AND WREATHS: A SNOWED IN CHARITY ANTHOLOGY

Unwrap three volumes of snow-blanketed steam *(that's a thing, right?)*. From heart-pounding dark romance to spine-tingling paranormal encounters, these stories have everything your delightfully dark heart desires.

🌑 *And the best part? It's all for a good cause; proceeds are helping The Cancer Research Institute and The World Central Kitchen.*

Entire Set > Snowed In Charity Anthology Set

I'm Here> Snowed In Volume Two

DESIRE AFORETHOUGHT COMPLETED TRILOGY

Caught in the clutches of five formidable Incubi bikers, neurodivergent Jane Mercy navigates a treacherous world of dangerous secrets, unyielding passion, and looming threats

DEMONS AND DEBTS

When debts call for desperate measures, will a deal with demons be the path to salvation or damnation?

https://geni.us/DemonsandDebtsAudio

https://geni.us/DemonsandDebts

DEBTS AND DARKNESS

In the darkest corners of desire, will she find freedom or lose herself forever?

https://geni.us/DebtsandDarkness

DARKNESS AND DEBAUCHERY

Caught in a web of lies, betrayal, and heartache, can she conquer the darkness and reclaim her life?

https://geni.us/DarknessandDebauchery

DESIRE AFORETHOUGHT COMPLETE SPECIAL EDITION HARDBACK

When Jane Mercy's path collides with the notorious Iron Incubi MC, the threads of desire, danger and destiny begin to unravel, and in a world where demons rise and love is the ultimate debt to pay, nothing will ever be the same.

https://geni.us/DesireACompleteSeriesE

VENGEANCE AFORETHOUGHT TRILOGY

When hearts are the real treasures to be stolen, can a con-woman outwit the demons of her past?

VILLAINS AND VENGEANCE

She stole from them, lied to them, and now they're her prison mates.

In a world without exits, trust becomes the rarest and most deadly commodity.

https://geni.us/VillainsandVengeance

VENGEANCE AND VIPERS

https://geni.us/VengeanceandVipers

I was supposed to be their downfall. They were meant to be my revenge. But the chains that bound me have now tangled us all.

VIPERS AND VENDETTAS

https://geni.us/VipersandVendettas

Six seductive demons, bound by venom-laced passion, teeter on the brink of salvation and ruin.

a former slave waging a final stand for a life far beyond her darkest dreams.

DARK BROTHERS COMPLETED SERIES

In a world of darkness, the intertwining fates of fierce women and brooding mercenaries challenge the very essence of love and war.

SOLD TO SERVE

In a game of power and survival, will she be the pawn or the queen?

https://geni.us/SoldToServe

BOUGHT TO BREAK

Liberation comes in many forms... sometimes in the arms of the enemies.

https://geni.us/Bought2Break

KEPT TO KILL

When your salvation lies in the hands of beasts, will you conquer or crumble?

https://geni.us/Kept2Kill

CAUGHT TO CONJURE

Unleashing the power within, a witch's redemption, or the world's doom?

www.kyraalessy.com/caught2conjure

TRAPPED TO TAME

In the arena of love and war, who will reign - the damsel or the dark fae?

https://geni.us/Trapped2Tame

SEIZED TO SACRIFICE

With forgotten sins and unseen foes, will memory be her weapon or her downfall?

https://geni.us/seized2sacrifice

For more details on these and the other forthcoming series, please visit my website / join my mailing list!

https://www.kyraalessy.com/bookstore/

IF YOU ARE IN ANY WAY RELATED TO ME

Seriously, I feel the need to put this in every book I write. If you are a part of my family, put this book down.
Go no further!

Delete it from your e-reader and forget about it.
It'll be better for everyone.

If you do not heed this page, never EVER speak of it to me. I don't want to hear anything about this book from your lips. I don't want to hear that you're surprised that I'd write about such kinky kinkiness and I CERTAINLY don't want to know that I've unlocked a new kink *for you*.
No, thank you!

Granny, if you're reading this ... STOP IT! Where did you even *get* an ereader?

AUTHOR'S NOTE

Jane, **the FMC in this series is autistic**. The following is a fictional work of DARK romance, but the portrayal of this 'condition' is as accurate as this author can make it and is based on said author's first-hand (and personal) experiences of autism, both humorous and serious in nature.

If you believe you may be autistic following reading this book, the author suggests reading up on ASD and seeking official diagnosis as many women are not diagnosed until well into adulthood.

If you are autistic, you are not crazy and, although all of us are different, you are not alone.

It is also important to note that, *probably* due to the author's neurodivergent brain, she '<u>HATES</u>' double quotes ("") with an eye-twitching, burning passion that rivals the heat of a thousand suns and thinks it makes the page look 'too busy'.

Because she lives in the UK where single quotes are

almost always used for dialogue nowadays, she's made the executive decision to never EVER include them in any of her books no matter where they are sold and no matter who complains about how 'wrong' it is.

EVER.

Sorry, my American friends, but in the words of Montgomery 'Scotty' Scott (who I almost met in Ticonderoga once and seems like a really stand-up guy irl), 'I just can't do it!'

TRIGGERS* in this book include (but may not be limited to):

- Portrayal of autistic meltdowns / shutdowns
- Non-con
- Dubcon
- Stalker
- Kidnap
- Death outside the harem
- Mild sexual assault to FMC outside harem
- Portrayal of sex work
- Cliffhanger

*AUTHOR'S BRAIN too twisted to realize some things are triggering to 'normal' people and forgets to include them in trigger lists. Sorry.

DEMONS AND DEBTS

A NEURODIVERGENT WAITRESS BEING HUNTED.
AN INCUBI MC WHO CAN HELP.
BUT WILL THEIR PRICE BE MORE THAN SHE CAN PAY?

WHEN I WAS FOURTEEN, A WOMAN I CALLED MOM WAS MURDERED ... AND IT WAS MY FAULT.

I'VE BEEN ON THE RUN EVER SINCE, BUT SOMEONE'S CHASING ME. I DON'T KNOW WHO THEY ARE OR WHAT THEY WANT. THE ONLY THING I'M SURE OF IS THAT I NEED TO KEEP MOVING OR MORE PEOPLE WILL DIE.

THEY'RE GOING TO FIND ME AGAIN. THEY ALWAYS DO.

THE HUMAN AUTHORITIES ARE USELESS. THE SUPE COPS, EVEN WORSE. MY ONLY HOPE IS THE IRON INCUBI MC, THE BIGGEST, BADDEST, MEANEST SUPES AROUND. I'M SICK OF RUNNING AND I'M DESPERATE ENOUGH TO MAKE A DEAL EVEN IF IT COSTS ME EVERYTHING I HAVE LEFT.

OH, AND I'M AUTISTIC. MY CONDITION MEANS MY BRAIN WORKS DIFFERENTLY. I CAN KEEP IT TOGETHER IN THE DAY-TO-DAY AND MASK MY HUNDREDS OF QUIRKS WHEN I'M AROUND OTHERS FOR SHORT TIMES, BUT NOW THE FIVE HUMAN-HATING INCUBI WHO I WENT TO FOR HELP HAVE ME PRISONER AT THEIR 'CLUBHOUSE', I.E., MANSION IN THE MIDDLE OF NOWHERE.

SO, WHAT HAPPENS WHEN FIVE HOT AS SIN SEX DEMONS LOCK UP A HUMAN GIRL WHO SUCKS AT ALL THE BEDROOM STUFF, DOESN'T COPE WELL WITH CHANGE, AND DEFINITELY CAN'T MASK HER ASD 24/7

MY NAME IS JANE MERCY AND I HAVE NO F**KING CLUE, BUT I DON'T THINK IT'S GOING TO GO WELL FOR THOSE GORGEOUS-ENOUGH-TO-BE-UNDERWEAR-MODEL, MERCENARY SOBS ... ESPECIALLY WHEN MY STALKERS COME FOR ME ...

KYRA ALESSY

CHAPTER
ONE
JANE

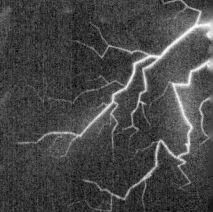

hen life hands you lemons, make lemonade!

Someone told me that once and it always stuck with me, not because it made me feel better on dark days, but because it's such a dumb thing to say. It's like a meme on your feed with a mountain background or a cute kitten and message on it saying something like 'Don't worry! You got this!' or 'Make someone smile every day, but never forget that your someone too.' (Yeah, with that 'your'.)

I don't think the people who made up these little proverbial sayings and uplifting generic messages had a group of stalkers dogging their steps either. I mean, seriously, for one thing, what kind of fucked up lemonade can you make from a scenario where people you've never seen threaten to hurt anyone you come to care about, people who never let you make a home anywhere? How do you make the best of *that* shit?

I already have my hand on the door when I freeze. I can hear a tune from an old juke box. The song it's playing is dated; not the kind of music that would be on a playlist in a crowded wine bar. There's a pool table inside. I can hear the balls knocking against each other, low chuckles, the clink of glasses, and errant, female laughter.

I shouldn't have come here. I told Sharlene the same thing, but she said these guys are the meanest and have the most muscle in town ... for a price.

I hear someone snigger behind me and voices murmuring. I glance over my shoulder to see two human guys in their leathers, standing with their bikes and sporting the patches of some MC I've never heard of. I'm not surprised they're there. This is a biker bar after all. They're watching me, talking about me. Cold, calculating eyes take in my jeans and old sneakers, the oversized thrift store jacket that I bought to keep me dry, but is nowhere near waterproof enough for the amount of rain we've been getting lately.

Not giving them the chance to say anything to me directly, I yank open the door. I don't need any trouble. I got more than I can handle as it is and that's the only reason I'm here.

My senses are hit with the force of a sledgehammer, my usual defenses crumbling like a dried-up sandcastle on the beach. I automatically keep the cringe inside. I wish I could put my earbuds in just to help with some of the louder noise, but that would look too weird now. The cacophony of sound that had been muffled before makes my steps falter. The neon signs over the bar glare at me, and the smell of smoke and stale air assails me. I almost take a step back, call this whole thing off.

But I can't. What's waiting for me if I don't do this is worse than a little discomfort.

So I push it down, wondering why it's so hazy when lighting up indoors has been illegal forever.

I survey the room, not even trying to pretend I belong

here as the second-hand smoke chokes me a little. There are quite a few people sitting around. I can see some others playing pool at the back. As I make my way over to the bar, I garner a few curious looks, but no one approaches me.

I stop and stand in front of the one and only bartender. He's about a foot taller than me with dirty blond hair just long enough, *just styled enough* to look like he simply rolled out of bed, giving the impression that he can't be bothered to go get a haircut because he just doesn't care. But I'm not fooled. Guys, just like girls, have to put in the effort to be *this* hot. It's not a natural occurrence no matter what he wants people to think. This guy is all mirage. There's nothing real about him.

Hot Guy ignores me for long enough that my waiting for him to look up becomes awkward even though he's not serving anyone. I'm standing right in front of him and he's intentionally not letting his gaze fall on me.

So rude.

This is a college town and I've gotten used to dealing with pretty boys like him in the diner over the past few months, but as the irritation mounts, I forget my usually crippling social anxiety. I push away the sensations screaming at me to go somewhere dark and quiet and just zone out for a few hours.

'Excuse me,' I say lightly, pretending I haven't even noticed his BS.

He finally looks at me and I'm caught. I'm ensnared by eyes that are the color of molten caramel with little flecks of gold that catch the lights even low as they are. My breathing stutters and I swallow hard. I've never felt anything like this.

His knowing smirk is enough to shake me out of my

embarrassing reaction and I frown at him. What was that? What is *he?*

The realization hits me, and I take a step back, my nostrils flaring on a gasp I try to keep under wraps.

Incubus.

I should have known he was one of them even though I've never actually met one of his kind before. In general, the supes move in very different circles from humans, but I know they hang out in this bar. That's why I'm here.

'You break down or something?' he asks in a lazy drawl as if I'm taking up his valuable time.

But something in his eyes makes me think that, like the rest of his appearance, this is a show he's putting on. There's something about me that's intrigued him, and I don't like it. The last thing I need is his full attention.

'I'm looking for the Iron Incubi.'

He barks out a loud laugh and I can't hide my wince. What if their gatekeeper won't even let me talk to them? What's my plan if I can't get their help?

Leave, a helpful voice inside my head supplies. *Get on the first bus out of town before bad things start to happen here too.*

But I can't do that. I need this all to stop. I'm so tired. I just want to live my life. I don't want to go to a new town, live on the streets for the first few months, get some shitty job that doesn't ask questions so I can beg my way into some hellhole apartment on the worst street. And then do it all again in a few months just like I always have to do when they track me down. They always find me. The thought of it makes me want to curl up and cry.

But I don't. I'm here so this can finally be over.

Hot Guy doesn't say anything, his gaze roaming over me, and I get the feeling I've somehow baffled him and he's trying hard to figure me out.

Who knows, maybe he's the kind of guy it's *really easy* to confuse. Even a hot incubus can't have looks *and* brains, right?

He gestures with his chin to the darker area where the booths are.

'They're in the back by the pool table,' he says.

I incline my head in thanks, grateful he's not throwing me straight out on my ass.

I walk through the smoke that's heavier back here, trying not to cough. I can make out murmured talking and the feminine giggles I heard from outside.

Grinding to a sudden halt, I have third thoughts at the juncture where the floor changes from old wooden boards to an industrial carpet; the kind with brown toned patterns to hide the dirt. It doesn't work here. I sort of don't want to touch *anything*.

If I go past this line, there's no turning back. Forcing myself to raise my eyes, I'm taken aback by the men in front of me even though I should have expected this level of good-looking.

There are more hot AF men back here. Two of them stand at the wall like sentries, one's by the pool table in the middle of a game and the other two are sitting in a lone booth with the woman whose laugh I could hear before, I realize belatedly.

'What the fuck is this?' one of them asks, putting a little snort at the end.

My eyes follow the voice to the two men leaning against the wall. The one on the left was the one who spoke, I'm sure. He's got brown hair, a shaggy haircut, and the beginnings of a beard along a jaw so chiseled I could swoon like a debutante. This one *actually* doesn't care what he looks like I'm pretty sure, but he's as gorgeous as Hot

Guy at the bar and he's got a broad set of shoulders that I can't seem to ...

I tear my eyes away.

Don't get drawn in. You know what they are. You never even notice guys like this. Pulling you in and lowering your defenses is literally what incubi do.

As I look over all the men here, I realize that four of them are even better looking than I originally thought. They could literally all be freaking underwear models if the toned arms I can see are anything to go by. The fifth one my eyes hardly land on. I don't think he's one of them.

I scrutinize the small woman in the booth that I just barely noticed. She's pressed up against one of them and I look away immediately. He's massive and he's feeding from her ... just a little and she's probably not unwilling, but her eyes are glazed over. If she was in control of herself when she came in here, she isn't now. At least they aren't fucking her at the table, I guess. Though from the sounds she's making, I doubt it'll be much longer before they are.

That'll be you if you don't get your shit together.

I silence the thought that comes after that image – that they'd never want someone like me – for multiple reasons. Firstly, I'm trying to be kinder to myself, mostly to get Sharlene off my back because she keeps saying I need higher self-esteem. Secondly, the truth is that if they're hungry, what I look like doesn't matter. They might not want to feed off a homeless drifter, but they will feed if they need to.

Kind thoughts!

The one who spoke is looking past me and I turn my head to see Hot Guy shrugging behind the bar.

'What do you want?' asks one of the guys at the pool table to my right. He sounds bored and annoyed at my interruption.

My eyes find his dark and foreboding ones. He's got a short, black beard that matches his hair and ... *I want to run my fingers through it?*

No, Jane!

'We already have enough humans to play with.'

He glances at the booth where the woman is now letting out a series of strangled moans and a couple of the guys nearby chuckle.

'Try your luck in a couple months, sweetheart.'

I cant my head at him as I try to work out what he ... *Oh! ... ME?* My eyes widen. 'Oh! No.'

'No?' he asks, the menace in that one word making me glance at the nearest exit, which happens to be past him. 'Too good for us, human?'

'I mean that's not why I'm here,' I mumble, mortified that he'd assume I thought I was better than anyone. Is that really the vibe I give off?

'Gonna have to speak up, little girl,' the other one by the wall says and I glare at him.

I'm not a loud person and my voice never seems to carry all that far.

'That's not why I'm here,' I say more loudly, putting the effort in to be heard.

The one with the dark beard walks forward slowly until he's right in front of me looking down his nose at me as I'm forced to tilt my head up. Shit, he's tall. He could probably break me in half. Sharlene was right. These are the kind of men I need at my back. I'm not leaving here until they work for me.

～

Vic

As I stare the girl in front of me down, I can't help the frown that creases my forehead. She's not the usual type we get in here; the townie girls looking for the quick high they've heard we can provide while we feed. If the girls who try their luck here could be bothered to do their research, they'd know we aren't allowed to just take humans in off the street to snack on anymore. There's an extensive process now. Interviews. Contracts.

This one's older than I first thought when I noticed the sneakers and the faded jeans. I'd have put her at around eighteen when she came in, but she's probably in her twenties. Her brown hair is scraped back into a ponytail and her matching eyes don't stay on mine, constantly moving. I stifle a snort. Yeah, she knows what we are and she's afraid she'll get ensnared by one of us.

I glance over at Sie in the booth, just making sure our wildcard isn't still starving enough to lunge at this one, but it looks like Carrie, the blond contracted to us who he's playing with at the table, has taken the edge off. He's watching the one in front of me, but he's got his needs under wraps for now. He smirks at the little brunette, doing something to make Carrie scream her release without even looking at her. I sigh, Carrie's sexual energy sating me a bit just from my proximity to the action. When I look back down at the human girl before me, her wide eyes are locked on Sie's, and I can tell my lieutenant is imagining fucking her.

Interesting. He hardly looks at humans at all these days. I practically have to make him feed.

'What do you want from us if it's not a good, hard fuck?' I ask and grin at the shock she's trying to hide.

She pulls herself together quickly though and gives me a level stare. It almost appears as if she's looking directly into my eyes, but she's actually looking at the wall past me to the side of my head. She thinks the eyes are the only way I could capture her. I bet she's never had direct contact with an incubus before. Her knowledge is second-hand at best.

Silly little human.

'I want to hire you,' she says.

I wasn't expecting that, but I don't let my surprise show.

'What kind of dumbass problems a girl like you got?' Korban sneers from his place by the wall.

She doesn't answer him, hardly even notices him. Instead, she looks at me – well, almost. She's still avoiding my eyes.

'Stalkers,' she says, and I hear a couple of the other guys chuckling low.

I don't laugh with them. The others here might not understand what a stalker can do to a woman, supe or otherwise, even if he never touches her, but I know how life-destroying it can get.

Not that I give a shit about this woman per se.

'A stalker, huh?' I look her up and down and I see her shiver a little. 'What do you have to pay with?'

I'm surprised that the first idea that pops into my head is that she has no money and she'll have to pay us with her body, and I push away the thoughts of her on her knees before us. We aren't allowed to do that shit anymore, I remind myself.

'*Stalkers*,' she corrects me. 'As in more than one.'

That gives me pause. The others too.

'How many?' asks Theo.

He's sitting in the booth waiting for his turn after Sie's had his fill of Carrie.

The girl in front of me glances over at him, and I notice

she takes pains not to look at Sie though *he's* still watching *her*. I wonder if he's going to be a problem.

'I don't really know, but there's a group of them.'

Probably some of the frat assholes from the local college.

'Payment?' I ask again.

She hesitates.

Korban pushes himself away from the wall and takes his shot, grinning from beside the pool table. 'You didn't come to the Iron Incubi without something to trade, did you, princess?'

'No,' she says quietly, and her shaking hand begins to unzip her oversized jacket.

Fuck.

I'm standing here with bated breath, hoping for a glimpse of what's underneath like a teenage boy. I swallow hard and turn away, pretending to ignore her while I play my turn. Yellow to corner pocket.

I miss, but everyone's eyes are on her anyway.

'Your body's the payment?' Korban asks as he slides closer, and I shoot him a warning look.

Feed from her before she's signed an agreement, and the supe authorities WILL find out. Unlike some, those are the rules we have to live by, and, in return, the cops mostly leave us alone. Besides, we have three girls living at the house already. We don't need another.

But she looks baffled for a second at his words, not afraid. And then she lets out an incredulous laugh.

'No.'

She pulls out an amulet and all of us look just a tiny bit disappointed. How does this girl have us all practically salivating over her? It's not usual, not even when we're hungry and that realization is enough to make me want to flip the kill switch on whatever this is. She looks, smells, feels like a normal human, but something isn't right.

She draws the necklace over her head and holds it up.

'We don't deal in jewel—' I begin, getting ready to shut her down and get Paris to boot her out the door.

And then I get a good look at the blue, iridescent stone set in a cage of silver hanging from an iron chain.

Even Dreyson, one of the human prospects, takes a step forward. 'Is that a—?'

An orc stone.

'So what happened?' I interrupt. 'You go to the wrong place at the wrong time in the wrong outfit or something?'

I sound bored, but I'm looking at this girl with new eyes.

Does this little human have any idea how much that bauble in her hand is worth in our world?

I'm guessing not and I hide the gleam in my eye. We're about to get the payday of the year and all I need to do is send one of the prospects to take out the trash.

'Something like that,' she says. 'Doesn't matter where I go. They find me. They do ...' Her eyes get a faraway look in them. 'Bad things.'

Her head gives a little shake. 'I work over at Gail's. My friend Sharlene said you might be able to help me. Can you?'

I hold out my hand and she lets the dull, cerulean gem fall into my palm. I feel the hum of power as it touches my skin and I know I'm right. How the fuck did she get an orc stone?

'We don't usually do this sort of thing,' I begin and see Theo rolling his eyes in the booth, 'but we'll take care of your little problem for you.'

Her hand clenches the thick chain hard as I curl my

fingers around the pendant. Her eyes are suddenly boring into mine.

'You'll keep me safe, get rid of the group who wants to hurt me to the best of your ability. In return, you can have this necklace, and only this necklace, as payment. The terms are final.' She says the words clearly. 'Who will bear witness?'

I give her a slow smile and watch a blush climb up her throat to her face. She's not unaffected by me even though I'm not using my power, and she's not stupid for a human either. She'll make this official through all the right magickal channels.

Unfortunately for her, those ancient laws were written by the fae. They're sly as fuck and, holy shit, are there some fun loopholes. As I look at her, it strikes me as weird that she seems to know some basic rules about our world, but not others. I frown. Is she a cop? They've tried to infiltrate us before with human prospects, but not in ages. But I'm not going to stop the deal. That orc stone is worth calling in some old favors if we get any trouble from Johnny Law.

'I'll witness,' Paris says from behind her. He's left the bar unattended, and I give him a look, but there's no one here to serve anyway.

She jumps a little as he clasps her wrist and mine in his hands and he looks at her oddly for a second before he closes his eyes and says the binding words that make the deal unbreakable ... for her anyway.

'It's done,' I say. 'Dreyson, go with her and see to her little problem.'

I'll let the others know my suspicions about our new client on the DL later. Until then, Dreyson won't do or say anything in front of an outsider anyway.

The human prospect pushes himself off the wall and

glances at Carrie. Sie's still feeding from her lust, and he looks a little disappointed since he sometimes gets to have a little fun with our contracted girls once we've had our fills.

'You prove yourself with this and that's it. You're one of the Iron I's,' I tell him.

Dreyson's face lights up at the promise. 'I won't let you down, Vic!'

'Keep it professional though, huh?'

He nods, looking a little surprised that I'd spell it out, but he's a ladies' man and this one is off-limits.

I pull on the chain that's still wrapped around the girl's fingers. She looks up at me and then at her hand as if she can't quite bear to let it go. Maybe she does know what it is, she's just so desperate that she'll give it up anyway.

'What's your name?' I ask.

'Jane,' she whispers, letting out a small breath and dropping the necklace.

With a mental high five to myself, I pocket it immediately and go back to my game without another word. As far as I'm concerned, we're done and when I look back after taking my next shot, she and Dreyson are gone.

CHAPTER
TWO
JANE

It's almost dark when I get outside the bar, and the storm clouds are rolling in. A droplet falls on my nose and I sigh as I zip the jacket higher even though it won't do me much good. At least the diner isn't too far a walk.

I check my watch. Twenty minutes until my shift starts. Enough time to get there and changed if I powerwalk. I rub my wrist, the one the barman took to seal the deal. His touch was like a brand. Must be an incubus thing, or maybe it was the magick that now binds them to fulfill their end.

I frown as I think about what I've given up. That necklace was the last thing I had of my mom, but I don't remember her she's been dead for so long. I hadn't actually thought it would be so hard to let it go.

'What did you say your name was, sweetheart?'

The human they've sent with me, Dreyson, is at my back and he sounds too close. I spin around as I take a step backward and my foot slips off the edge of the curb. I stumble and he gives me a what-the-fuck-is-your-problem look which I outwardly ignore as I give him a quick perusal.

He's in his twenties like me, about 5'9" with a buzz cut and a tattoo creeping up the side of his neck that I can't make out. Some girls would call him cute, I guess, and it looks like he knows it from the shit-eating grin he gives me as he looks me over in return. I get a feeling off him I don't like, but help is help.

'Jane.'

I turn and begin walking.

'Where you goin'?' he asks, sounding puzzled.

I sigh. 'Work.'

'Gail's you said, right? Hop on my hog. I'll take you.'

I glance over my shoulder at him and then his bike with a grimace and shake my head.

Not getting on that thing and definitely not with you.

'Nope. I'll meet you there. Shouldn't be seen arriving together anyway.'

There's a pause before he speaks again and when he does his tone has dropped a few degrees.

'I could make you.'

And there it is.

His voice is low, menacing, but it has none of the power in it that I felt inside from his boss. He's pretending to be one of them. An incubus. I'm not even surprised. Just another human trying to lap up the dregs the supes leave at the bottom of the cup. I don't usually blame people like him. If I know anything it's that life is hard down here in life's basement. But I wonder how many times he's done that to girls who don't know any better. What a prick.

I turn and level him with a hard stare. 'No, you can't.'

I start walking down the cracked, uneven sidewalk away from him, hearing him rev up his Harley and I wince at the sound. I fumble in my pockets for my earbuds. They don't play music anymore; haven't in months, but they do bring everyday decibels down to more acceptable levels, so I don't want to claw out my own brain every time I encounter something too loud.

I have my trusty buds in by the time Dreyson whizzes by me a few seconds later, way faster and closer than necessary, I guess to prove a point or maybe just to be a dick. At least it's muffled enough that I'm not forced to cover my ears and cringe away from the thunderous sputtering of his peen extension, but it does make my heart lurch in my chest.

A part of me yearns to feel that exhilaration and the wind in my hair as I watch him speed down the street, and then I see a May Bug flying around and I wonder how many of those he'll get splattered across his face on the way into Welford. *No thanks.*

The trip back to Gail's, past the strip mall where some of the most important businesses in a town like Welford reside – such as the nail salon, thrift store (my personal fav), and Marcie the Medium – is quick and uneventful, and I make my way past the dumpsters to slip into the diner through the back.

'Did you go?'

I jump with a matching yelp as Sharlene melts out of the dark where the security light blew out and Chuck hasn't bothered to fix it.

My co-worker is taller than me by at least four inches. She's got long, auburn hair that I think is dyed and she wears a small Band-Aid on the side of her neck all the time – to cover up an old tattoo she told me once. She's in her mid-forties, but the combination of too many vices and too little money has aged her prematurely as it seems to do to everyone down here on the bottom rungs sooner or later.

'I went.'

'Well, fuck.' She flicks her cigarette away and comes with me inside. 'You talked to them?'

I give her a look. 'Wasn't going there just to stare.'

She lets out a throaty cackle that turns into a cough. 'If they'd let an old gal like me through the door, I'd stare at those supe biker hotties all night long!'

I smile because I know that's what she's expecting but the truth is I'm still getting over the meeting I had with the Iron Incubi MC. It's left me feeling adrift in a way I haven't since I was ten and Dad disappeared. I don't like it; don't like feeling like a lost little girl. I'm a freaking adult dammit. I have a job and pay rent ... most of the time. I have like *responsibilities*. For myself mostly, but it still counts.

'Did you tell them about everything?'

'Yep.' *Nope.*

I haven't even told Sharlene all of it, not the worst parts. She's like a mama bear and she's got enough going on with her own kids without worrying about all my shit too.

We get inside and the smell of the Thursday special (French onion soup) hits me, making me want to gag. My watch says I have two minutes to get changed so I run through to the empty back office and close the door, pulling off my wet clothes and flinging them in a pile on the floor. I throw on my uniform and dumb little apron, forcing my feet into flimsy, black, ballet flats as I bolt back out the door to the front.

Chuck side-eyes me from behind the Formica counter, but I'm on time. He's not getting my tips tonight!

Grabbing my favorite pencil from where it lives in my apron pocket, I go to my section and start my shift. I'll be here until closing now so I try not to stare at the slow-moving hands of the clock on the wall over the front door as I take orders and refill sodas.

Hearing the bell chime as the door opens, I see Dreyson come in, his leathers appearing out of place at Gail's. He looks the place over, his eyes lingering on a table of college girls with their textbooks open, talking quietly amongst themselves. He gives me a smirk and sits in my section.

I give it a minute before I approach.

'What can I get you,' I ask brightly.

I know how to pretend to be friendly if I'm not too tired to give a shit.

He makes a show of perusing the menu for so long that my feet start to get antsy.

'I'll take a cola,' he finally says, not looking up at me.

'Coming right up.'

I leave to get his drink and the bell chimes again. My heart sinks as I recognize the raucous voices.

Oh no. Not today.

'Oh hey, it's Plain Jane! Look, guys, Plain Jane's here tonight!'

I frown at the boy in front of me. I'm here practically every night and he knows it. They all know it. The group practically leaps through the diner and sits in my section.

Of course.

I see Sharlene give me a look and she silently asks me if I want her to take them, but I shake my head. I've found it's easier to just deal with them and pretend they don't get to me. If they see a rise, they'll stay all damn night, and I don't have it in me to deal with them *and* the Iron Incubi in one day.

I hand out the menus and don't meet any of their eyes.

'Can I get you any drinks to start?' I ask in a chirpy voice that I hope hides my inner anxiety.

A menu slides to the floor.

'Oops.'

Plastering a smile on my face, I bend down to retrieve it, but as soon as I do, another one slides down.

Oh, this game. Great.

Sniggers ensue as I get on my knees to pull that one out from under the table and I glance at Sharlene who's staring at Chuck with a 'are you really gonna let these assholes get away with this shit *again*' look that he completely ignores. He doesn't care how the customers treat us as long as they pay their bill when they're done.

'Hey, Plain Jane, do you have any waffles?'

Cue their stifled laughter at some joke at my expense that I don't understand, and I fight the urge to roll my eyes while inside, beyond the bravado, I begin to tense up. I really don't have the energy to deal with their crap right now, and I can't have a meltdown here. Not here!

Another menu wafts to the floor and I pin them with a look.

'Oooh! She's getting angry, guys!'

I sigh and try again with the smile. 'Yes, we have waffles tonight. Can I get you any drinks to start?'

Thankfully, one of them orders a soda and the others follow suit. I guess bothering me makes them thirsty. I leave the table to get their drinks and see Dreyson's eyes following me, his expression taunting. Glad he finds my life so amusing, I think as I duck into the hallway where the bathrooms are and close my eyes, holding my ears.

Just a moment, I promise myself. That's all I need and that's all I get before the bathroom door opens and one of the frat boys comes out. I didn't even know he'd left the table.

'Aw, Jane. Having a bad night, babe?' he asks me in a pouty voice.

I don't say anything, just turn on my heel and go behind

the counter. I start filling glasses. I don't understand why they're like this. Why is torturing a waitress like me so entertaining?

'I can take 'em if you want,' Sharlene says in a low voice from next to me.

'No, it's ok. I got it.'

'Rich little assholes,' she mutters under her breath.

I survey the diner and notice Dreyson's table is empty. *Guess I'm paying for his soda.* I shake my head as I put the drinks on a tray and take them slowly over to the frat guys.

I put the glasses out on the table and they're blessedly silent, all looking at their phones.

'I didn't order that.'

Yes, you did.

'Oh, I'm sorry. What did you order?'

The blond one clears his throat. 'Yeah, you did, Ford.'

He looks up and I wonder why he stood up for me. This is new and I like it even less than their bullying crap.

'Are you guys ready to order?'

He throws the menu down on the table, eyeing me oddly as he takes a gulp of his drink.

'I think we'll go somewhere else,' he says.

'Sure,' I say sweetly and quickly tally their drinks bill. 'Here's your check.'

He pulls out a wad of cash in a money clip like he's a fucking high-flying businessman, or something. My eyes flick down to it nervously. As it stands today, I don't have enough to make the rent this month and even one of those hundreds would basically set me up for the week.

His eyes don't leave mine as he takes the money out of the clip and makes a point of unfolding it slowly. He takes out a ten to cover the bill and then a twenty. He holds it out to me, and I hesitate.

'For such good service,' he drawls.

I reach for it and at the last second, he pulls it away.

'But wait what am I thinking? You girls split tips, don't you? There's two of you working the tables tonight. One bill isn't fair.'

He tears it in half.

'There you go. Now you and your friend can share.'

He and his friends start laughing.

Swallowing my pride and my fury, I sink to the floor to pick up the pieces. I need them.

'Would you look at that,' Blondie says. 'The bitch is already on her knees, and I only gave her a twenty!'

They're practically rolling on the floor as I stand up, gripping both halves of the bill in my fist, wishing I could bury them in his fucking face.

Starting to feel numb, I'm pushed back as he gets out of the booth, his knuckles brushing against my breast in what must surely be an accident, I think. I turn away without another word and catch one of them murmuring about how weird I am to his friend as they leave.

The rest of my shift is relatively quiet. The frat boys don't come back and neither does Dreyson. I'm out the door at midnight and walking for the bus. I catch the last one and give the driver a half-smile. It's empty as usual and I take the seat I always do, settling in to stare out the window while at the same time looking at the reflection of the interior.

There is someone else in the back, I realize, my heartbeat picking up as I surreptitiously stare. Male. Slumped over like he's drunk. I keep an eye on him, but he doesn't move in the half an hour it takes to get to my stop.

The driver stops without me having to pull the cord. He knows where I get off.

I murmur a good night and step out into the dark street. He shuts the door, but he always waits until I get inside the building, which makes me feel a little better when I get back late in this neighborhood.

Unlocking the main door, I slip inside, and the bus pulls away. The light in front of me flickers and I look away from it as I climb the stairs. The doors are all closed and I'm glad I don't have to deal with the people who live in 21a and 25b. Whether from alcohol, drugs, or mental health issues, they tend to be unpredictable, and I've had enough of that today.

I get to my door, unlock it, and go inside my dingy apartment. There's a living room, a small kitchen, and a bedroom down a short, narrow hallway with a small bathroom right next to it.

I shuck my jacket and empty my backpack, putting my wet clothes from earlier out to dry. I turn on the shower and take off my uniform, throwing it directly into the hamper. I hate the smell that clings to me, like stale coffee and onions. I get in while the water's lukewarm because it never gets any hotter, scrubbing the stench of the diner from my skin and hair until I feel like some semblance of a human being again.

I was going to eat something, but as I get out of the shower, I realize how beat I am. I've been feeling more tired than usual for a couple of days now and I hope I'm not coming down with something. I still need another two hundred to make the rent this week and I know my landlady is going to come looking for me early. She wants me out because *someone* called the cops on the couple downstairs dealing Meth who, it turned out, were her son and his girlfriend. #itwastotallyme

Oops. How was I supposed to know that skeevy dude was her son?

I practically fall into bed, my body aching as I pull up the comforter and close my eyes, hoping that tomorrow will be a better day.

∼

Sie

THE CONTRACTED girl I fed from in the bar wasn't enough and I'm going to need more. Soon.

I'm getting worse. I should tell Vic, but, knowing him, he's probably already well aware. He isn't the boss for nothing.

I glance in the mirror and then away. Red-rimmed eyes, dark bags. Even the scars on my face are starting to show. Fuck, I feel strung out and I'm going to need another meal today, not just the little snacks that seem to sustain the others. A daily buffet of females is going to be required if I don't find a way to curb my appetite.

I wonder if that pretty little human will be back today. I groan aloud when I think of her, so different from the ones who usually come to the bar looking for us, for what we can do to their bodies and their minds. I don't love the contracted girls, but I don't hate them either. I rarely think of them at all to be honest. Sex with them is transactional. We get fed, they get high.

But that one from yesterday would taste so sweet going down. I know that much. She was trying not to appear innocent but compared with the other humans we have, I could smell it a mile off, her arousal too even though she was keeping those cards close to her chest. The things I'd make her feel ...

Stop torturing yourself.

There's a knock on my door.

'You up?' Paris asks from the hall.

'Yeah. What is it?'

'Dreyson didn't come back last night. Boss wants us to check it out.'

I frown as I look at my reflection again. I can't go out like this. If Vic saw me right now, he'd lock me up. I'm fucking starving, and that means I'm a danger.

'Get me a snack.'

There's a pause and I know what Paris is thinking; the same thing they're all thinking. How long will it be before I lose it? Before I go rogue and they have to put a bullet in my head? I snort. At this rate, I have a few weeks at best.

'Ok,' he says, and I can hear his resigned sigh through the door.

He leaves and I stare into the mirror again. I let my real self out, watching the scars that mar my face appear, not just as faint lines, but as the jagged, rough-edged, horrifying disfigurements that they actually are. My twisted horns are next, protruding like a dragon's as my skin turns to a mottled grey-purple. My long tail flicks and for a moment I feel free. Then that need coils within me, the madness always nipping at the fringes of my mind, getting stronger, threatening to engulf what's left of me.

There's a hesitant knock. That was quick. She must have already been nearby for one of the others.

I pull it all in, dipping into my reserves and everything recedes. My mind clears as my flesh turns a more human color again. The on-call girls who'll come at a moment's notice know what we are. Some of them even beg to see the real versions of us, but I never show them my other side.

'Come in.'

The door opens slowly and a human steps over the threshold. I can't remember which of the three this is, but as soon as I see her face, I smirk. She looks a little like the girl from yesterday. What was her name? Jane. That means one of the others asked for her specifically for that reason. I'm not the only one who's interested in that little human.

'Strip.'

Her eyes widen and I frown. She's not close enough for the lull.

'Come here.'

She walks towards me, her body tense. She doesn't really want me. No doubt she prefers Paris' gentle caresses or Theo's relaxed attitude when he isn't playing 'Doctor', but she signed a contract. She isn't allowed to say no to any of the Iron Incubi.

My eyes catch hers and the effect is immediate. Her body goes languid, her eyes falling closed.

'Strip,' I order again.

This time she does what she's told, drawing her short dress over her head. She's not wearing anything underneath.

I don't wait, practically springing forward. One hand to her breast and the other between her legs. She moans, already wet and I turn her, pushing her down onto my bed. Her legs open automatically, but as I line myself up, I pause. I feel a sudden need to be far away from this female. I don't want to fuck her. Confusion and hunger make me let out what, to my horror, sounds like a needy whine. My cock softens.

No! Not again!

This is the third time in a week. What the fuck is happening to me?

I'm so fucking hungry that I immediately start using my fingers instead, playing with her pussy until her legs shake and she comes with a loud cry. I close my eyes as the power of her climax fills me up. It won't last as long as a good, thorough fuck would, but it'll be enough to sustain me for a little while. At least it'll stop me from launching myself at some hapless human woman while I'm out in public.

I pull my fingers from her cunt and frown. Usually I'd be chomping at the bit to lick them clean, but the thought revolts me today. I wash my hands in my small bathroom instead and throw on my leathers, leaving her in a stupor on the bed. She'll come to later and feel euphoric for the next few hours, so I don't feel guilty for what happened. She's not new. She knows how it is here. It's literally *why* she's here.

I glance at the mirror. Healthy glow, no scars and no tired eyes. I feel much better, but, as I exit my room and make my way downstairs to the stupidly large foyer, I worry about what is going on with me. My dick isn't working right. It hasn't been for weeks and it's bad enough that I can't fuck the contracted girls anymore. How many times am I going to have to get them off a day to stay fed enough not to lose my mind?

Paris is leaning against the wall, playing on his phone. When he sees me, he gives me a once-over.

'Everything ok?' *I.e. are you going to go nuts while you're out with me tonight?*

'Fine. Let's go.'

CHAPTER
THREE
JANE

When I get into work the next day, I'm a little early. I haven't seen Dreyson at all. I snort softly as I go in the back door. So much for the Iron Incubi's help. Still, the deal was bound with magick, so they literally have to help me or they like die or something. I'm not really sure what happens to be honest. But I don't have anything to worry about when it comes to the bargain I've made. They already have my payment, so I've done my part. It's up to them to follow through. If they don't, well, it's their asses, but then I guess I'll be back to where I was yesterday just with nothing left to trade.

I walk through the hallway, and I see Chuck sitting on the phone in the office where there's a bank of four grey lockers for the staff. He ignores me as I take my backpack off and put it inside, securing it with the combination lock I carry around.

I'm already in my uniform under my jacket tonight so I wait in the corridor out of sight for the clock to read exactly seven before I start working. Sharlene comes to stand with me, and I give her a quick grin as we loiter, Chuck giving us the eye from the office.

But I'm not starting early.

He sure as hell won't pay us anything extra for it. I didn't used to care, but then he docked me for being five minutes late one night. I learned my lesson and now he doesn't get even a second more out of me than he pays for.

'Hey, did you hear about the body?'

My skin goes cold as soon as her words register, and I glance up at Sharlene.

'Body?'

She leans in closer, her creased face lighting up. Shar is a purveyor of gossip and there's nothing more entertaining to her than a juicy story.

'Yep! The cops were here earlier, Sarge said. He was taking out the trash and found some dead dude in the dumpster out back.'

'No way!'

I manage to look and sound shocked, I think mostly because I am, but my stomach bottoms out.

'That's crazy,' I say, knowing it'll spur her on. I don't actually need to ask her anything.

'I know! So, yeah, he opens the lid and there's just this dude in there and, you are not gonna believe this. It's so gross, but—'

His eyes are missing.

'His eyes? Gone!'

Not again. I swallow hard. *Don't throw up.*

'Gone?' I echo, hoping my voice sounds normal.

'Yep! Snatched out of his skull like...' she pauses, 'well, like someone took his fucking eyes!'

'That's so messed up,' I say on autopilot. 'Do they know who he was? Who did it?'

'Nope, but he was wearing biker leathers or something.' She purses her lips in disappointment. 'I wasn't here before they took the body and Sarge said there was too much blood to see the patch from what Club he was. Anyway, they think it's some gang-related thing, I heard. Cops are coming back later to talk to everyone who was here last night.'

I feel so sick. Guess I know where Dreyson went, which means that not only have they found me, but they were here last night. They know where I am. They know I tried to get help. They could be watching me right now.

My hands are shaking as the clock ticks. Seven o'clock. I keep my face neutral. I know how to do that. I look over at Sharlene on the other side of the diner already, picking up her tables as the servers on the last shift clock-off. I'll miss her when I move on. It's been a while since I had someone I could call a real friend. But, after tonight, I doubt I'll ever see her again. It's safer for her and her kids.

I go through the motions all night. I play the attentive waitress, getting all the tips I can. I'm going to need them. At least I won't have to pay that rent I owe if I can dodge my landlady until I sneak out tomorrow morning.

Two police officers arrive around eight-thirty and sit in my section. Male and female. They're supes. Shifters. Don't ask me how I'm sure. I have no clue and I don't know what they turn into, but they have predatory looks about them.

Why would the supe cops be investigating a human murder? Fuck. If I'm nervous, they might sense it.

I take a minute to push everything away. The dead body, the incubi, the fact that I'm going to have to skip town in the next few hours. I make sure my heart is beating relatively normally by the time I make my way over to their table.

'Hi there.' *Too chipper! Tone it down!* 'I'm Jane. I'll be your waitress this evening. Can I get you officers some drinks to start?'

Both of them glance up at me. The female looks like she's in her early thirties, dirty blond hair tied back in a bun. I try not to eye the gun at her belt. She gives me a friendly smile that comes across a tad condescending, but maybe I just have a little human chip on my shoulder. The male is a different story. He's a big guy, older than his partner, and his nostrils flare as he takes me in, suspicion in his eyes.

'Actually we're here to talk to you about the body that was found this afternoon.'

My mouth falls open. 'Me? Really?'

His eyes narrow a little and I'm kinda stoked I notice the cue. Better social skills, here I come!

'Your boss said you were working the late shift last night. You know anything about what happened?'

'Uh, just what I heard when I came in tonight. Sarge from the kitchen found some dude in the dumpster earlier.' I grimace. 'Heard his eyes were missing. *So* horrifying.'

At least I don't have to pretend the revulsion I feel at that *juicy* little detail.

'You see anything out of the ordinary last night? Around eight or nine?'

I make a show of thinking. 'No, not really. Had a group of college guys who like to come in sometimes and mess around, but they weren't here long. Other than that, some regulars. Oh!' I wrinkle my forehead. 'There was some biker guy.'

I point to the table where Dreyson was sitting last night. If they spoke to Chuck, they already know he was in here and that I served him. If I don't say anything, it'll look suspicious. Thankfully, there's nothing tying me to the Iron Incubi except that he sat in my section.

'He only got a soda and while I was dealing with the other tables, he slipped out without paying his check.'

'You didn't report it?'

I shrug. 'People do that once in awhile and it was just a drink, so ... I'm sorry I can't be more helpful. I didn't see anything when I left last night, didn't hear anything. It seemed like just a typical night to me.'

The female looks satisfied as they stand up, but the male towers over me, trying to intimidate me. Fuck, he's tall. I give the officer what I know from experience a supe like him wants, stepping away from him with fear in my eyes, not challenging him at all, and that's enough for him to relax a little.

'Knock it off, Lewski,' his partner says with a hint of amusement.

'Where do you live in case we need to talk to you again?' she asks me.

'Uh, just over on Bleaker.' *You know, the side of town for the dirt-poor human folk.* 'Complex 5343, Apartment 22a.'

They leave the table, the male pushing past me. 'Don't leave town.'

'Oh, I won't, Officer.' *'Til I'm done my shift and get what Chuck owes me anyway.*

I give him a friendly smile even though I'd love to kick him right in the nuts for being one of *those* supe cops, the kind who give the good ones a bad name.

'I'm almost always either there or here if you need to ask me anymore questions,' I reply cheerfully as they leave, and I can almost hear his annoyed growl.

After the officers go, everything returns to normal, and I spend the rest of the night planning how I'm leaving town and what I'm taking with me. It's almost midnight when the door opens and my least favorite group of dicks saunters in.

'Plain Jane!' one of them hollers in a stupidly deep tone and I frown as I glance at Chuck.

I was literally about to lock the doors and the fucker knows it, but he shrugs and slides the keys across the counter towards me. That's Chuck speak for, 'I'm leaving. Lock up when you're done licking the rich boys' boots for no extra pay.'

'I literally found a *body* earlier,' Sarge complains from the kitchen.

Chuck rolls his eyes. 'Ain't the first one you seen. Won't be the last. You don't like it? Good luck finding a new job with your record.'

Sarge mutters something I don't catch and then gives me a commiserating look from behind the grill in the kitchen as he fires it back up, flipping the boss the bird as Chuck turns his back.

'Gonna seat us, or what?' one of the frat dicks asks.

Another one chuckles. 'Careful, honey. You gotta earn your tip from Stacker tonight. No more freebies.'

They all snigger.

So Blondie has a name.

I could nope out of here now. Chuck will have slipped my money in the locker before he left, so there's no reason to stay. But I think about the clip full of cash that *Stacker* had yesterday. I sure could use that to set myself up in wherever I end up next … A half-assed plan starts to form.

I smile at them as I lock the door behind them and turn the sign to 'Closed'.

'Sure.'

I seat them in my section out of habit even though there's no one here but Sarge and me now.

Truth be told, I'm glad the diner's cook is here with me.

I mean, Sarge is pretty out of shape and I can hold my own when I need to, but Shar told me once that he used to be a 'deadly killing machine' (her words) when he was a SEAL back in the day.

He helped me out once when Chuck got handsy too. One night, I was at the diner late and Chuck cornered me, smelling of Bourbon. He didn't get the chance to put even one of his pudgy fingers on me though. Sarge came out of fucking nowhere, silent as snow. He knocked Chuck out cold *with the blade of his hand* like a freaking ninja and then he picked him up and put him back at his desk with the whiskey bottle in his hand.

All he said to me was, 'he won't remember,' and he never brought it up again. But he did make sure that I was never alone with Chuck at night after that.

Sarge is one of the good guys and while they clearly exist, they're about as frequently seen in Jane-land as fucking unicorns.

As soon as the guys sit down, I'm doubly thankful Sarge is still here with me. The guys have alcohol on their breaths and are acting more rowdy than usual, lunging across the table at each other and rough-housing like kids.

I wait for a minute while they look at the food options, hoping they'll just choose now so Sarge can cook whatever they want quickly, and we can get out of here ... but also grateful that they seem to have forgotten about yesterday's entertaining throw-the-menus-down-and-make-the-waitress-pick-them-up game.

They order drinks and food without much prompting, and I give Sarge their order. Nothing major, so I might actually be home by 1AM to get a few hours' sleep, pack up, and get to the bus station.

I bring their food out when the order's up and stand in the hallway watching them eat quickly. When they look done, I start clearing the plates. They seem to have sobered up from the food so they're a bit more subdued now too, I think as I take the dishes. They're balanced precariously, but I've been doing this awhile, so I know they won't fall ... at least until someone's foot shoots out from under the table, tripping me.

I go down hard with a cry, hearing the plates hitting the tiled floor and shattering around me. Groaning, I take stock of my body. My knees hurt from the impact, but nothing seems broken besides all the plates.

'Clumsy, clumsy. You should really be more careful, Jane.'

The guys at the table are laughing and I turn to look at them, not bothering to hide my fury.

'Think we've worn out our welcome, boys!' Stacker chuckles, throwing some money down on the table. They leave me on all-fours on the floor as they crunch past me, and I stand up carefully, so I don't cut myself on the broken China.

Then, I look at the table and see two things. One, that one of them has forgotten his jacket and, two, that they left just enough money to barely cover the bill.

Fuck. That.

I grab the jacket and run for the door, throwing it open and yelling, 'Wait!' into the parking lot. 'You forgot this!'

Stacker and the others are by a blue BMW, but I don't know my cars well enough to say what model.

'What is it, sweetheart? Can't get enough of us, huh?'

I trip on a rock as I get close to Stacker, falling into him with a cry.

'Whoa, dude, you treat 'em like shit and they still throw themselves at you.'

Cue more laughter.

Stacker pushes me back hard and I teeter on my heels before I regain my balance.

'You guys forgot this,' I say sweetly.

'Is this bitch for real?'

Someone at the back murmurs something about me being pathetic and thirsty, but I ignore all the comments as I hand the jacket over and go back into the diner to clean up without a backwards glance.

I lock the door behind me and see that Sarge is already taking care of the mess. I hear the car leave.

'What a bunch of assholes. Sorry, Janey-girl, I was in the can. You ok?'

'Yeah.' I stifle a grin as I pocket Stacker's thick money clip that I liberated when I 'tripped' into him. 'Let's just get done and go home.'

We finish cleaning up and I go into the office to grab my backpack out of the locker. I hope Chuck has paid me. I don't want to come back here tomorrow.

There's an envelope with two-hundred in it for the week at the diner. I shove half the bills from the money clip into it and put it in my bag, making sure it's zipped properly. I'm about to close the locker when a slip of paper catches my eye. I'm sure it wasn't in there earlier.

Frowning, I slide it out and hold it between my fingers. It's just a folded piece of regular printer paper, but my pulse begins to quicken as I take the edges and open it out.

You shouldn't have gone to the supes. Leave or your waitress friend is next.

Hands shaking, I crumple up the message and shove it in my jacket pocket. A part of me wants to cry, the rest just wants to curl up and go to sleep.

Instead, I take the other half of the money I stole and put it in Sharlene's locker in one of her work shoes. It's a risk, but she wasn't even here by the time Stacker was so she can't be blamed, and I'll be long gone.

I turn to go, but then hesitate. I grab the money back from her locker, take a wad from it and shove the rest back into the shoe. The other bills I put in the pocket of Sarge's clean apron that he keeps hanging behind the door. Like I said, he's one of the rare, good guys. He deserves something too.

Said unicorn is waiting for me outside and he locks up after me. He takes the keys too since he'll be here early tomorrow morning.

'You need a ride?'

I shake my head. 'No, thanks. There's a bus in ten so I'm good.'

I want to take him up on his offer. I'm so tired and it would be nice to be home sooner, but it's best if I'm not around anyone now. I'd hate for something to happen to him because of me.

'You sure, Janey-girl? It's late and ...' His eyes flick to the dumpster where he found the body.

'I'm sure, but thanks. See you tomorrow.'

I won't, but I want Sarge to have plausible deniability or whatever it's called.

We go our separate ways and I walk along the strip mall towards the bus stop.

It's quiet. Everything's closed and I try to stay within the glow of the streetlights. I've done this walk a hundred times at this time of night and never had one problem, but, whether it's from the note or Dreyson's death, I'm jumpy and I'll be glad to get on the bus. Hell, I'll even be happy to be on the move again tomorrow even though I don't want to leave. Maybe if I do some things differently next time, it'll take them longer to find me.

In my periphery, I see a car parked in one of the lots and something about it bothers me. I turn my head to look at it properly. It seems fam—

'Did you think I wouldn't know it was you?'

I stifle an involuntary shriek as Stacker materializes out of the shadows followed by his rich boy crew.

I turn to run, but it's already too late. Hands grab me and half-carry me into the nearby alleyway. My mouth is covered, and all my struggling does is tire me out.

I'm shoved hard against the wall and my bag is wrenched away.

I'm shaking and my knees feel weak. I'm regretting letting my anger get the best of me earlier, but I'm still glad I stole some of this smug fucker's cash.

The flashlight off a phone shines into my bag.

'It's here, but some of it's gone.'

'You little bitch,' Stacker snarls in the dark next to my ear, making me recoil. 'Where the fuck is the rest of my money? You think I'd let a gutter whore like you steal from *me*?'

The hand over my mouth loosens for me to answer, but I don't say anything.

He steps closer, one of his legs forcing itself between

mine. 'Well since I already paid her ... looks like we'll be having some fun with Plain Jane tonight,' he says, taking hold of the neck of my uniform and yanking it apart.

I hear the buttons ping off and the cold air hits my chest, but I still don't make a sound. His fingers curl around my neck as he keeps me where he wants me, his other hand brushing my thigh, travelling higher.

The lights appear on the others' phones, and I realize they're going to video whatever they're going to do to me. I'm not resigned to it, but I am completely frozen as he kisses my lips, grinding them into my teeth. I whimper at the pain, and he does it harder.

I feel something then, coming from him and into me. It *tastes* good, unlike any flavor I've ever experienced before. It's not like *food*. I doubt I could explain with words what it was, but I want more. It makes me feel so awake. Energized. I suck more in and let out a moan.

'Look how much she wants it!'

'These trailer trash girls love it rough, huh?'

'Pretty sure they just love to get paid.'

The answering chuckles are mortifying, but I can't stop—

Stacker draws back with a cry.

'What the fuck?'

He throws me away from him and I hit the ground, breathing hard. Then he laughs, the sound of it crueler than anything I've ever heard before – and that's saying something.

'I think we got us a baby supe here. Slummin' with the humans, Sweetheart?'

He steps forward, drawing back his foot to kick me and I curl into a ball instinctively.

'You shoulda stayed with your own, you dumb bitch.'

His shoe lands in the middle of my back and the agony is immediate. I scream. I can't help it even though I know he'll love the sound of it.

His friends have faded into the background now. I don't know if they're still documenting this. I want to tell him that he's wrong. I'm not a supe. But I can't talk now. I can barely think as I curl in on myself.

He's going to kill me.

∼

Paris

WE DRIVE AROUND A LITTLE. Sie, the morose fucker, doesn't have an iota of fun but I take advantage of the dark and the derelict streets in this part of town to pop some wheelies and run some red lights while we kill time.

Fuck! Going fast never gets old!

But Sie, the fun destroyer, puts a stop to my shenanigans, making us park in a dark lot while we wait for the human girl's shift to be over. He says she's going to come this way for the bus, but we've been sitting here for a half hour and I haven't seen a soul.

Then I do.

She's walking briskly and I take my eyes off her for a split second to tell Sie it's her. Then, she's just gone. I go towards the spot where she was. Probably saw us and hightailed it out of here.

A woman's scream has Sie and me both running. Maybe she wasn't trying to get away from us after all.

Sie's ahead of me, running into the shadows of an alleyway we couldn't see from where we were. I hear a shout and a scuffle, and I get ready for a fight. My eyes adjust to the darkness quickly and I can make out five humans. No, six. One's huddled on the ground. It's her. The girl we're here for.

She's curled up beside the wall and Sie is beating the shit out of the other four. He can handle himself, so I don't bother to help him. Instead I make for the fifth human, a big grin on my face because this is the shit that gets me up in the morning.

He's standing over the girl. His heart is beating fast, and I can feel the excitement pouring off him. He likes what he's doing to her. Like me, he enjoys the violence, but that's where our similarities end. My cheap thrills come from the challenge. This asshole's just a bully.

He raises his leg and I barrel into him a millisecond before he stomps on her, pushing him away.

Nasty fucker.

He turns, running at me with a yell. I clothesline him, putting him down hard, knocking him out cold on the asphalt. I turn around to see that the guy's friends are gone. Ran away like the little boys they are. I can't help my mocking laugh.

Looks like Sie grabbed their phones. Supe Fighting 101. Never leave the humans with any evidence. I'll get rid of the phones and wipe the Cloud when we get back to the house.

I turn to the girl who's still on the ground, but Sie's already there. I think he's going to pick her up and see if she's ok, but then I remember this is Sie.

He grabs her by her collar and hauls her up, pushing her into the wall. Even I wince at the crack of her head against the bricks.

'Where the fuck is Dreyson?' he says, his gravelly voice low and cold.

She doesn't answer at first, her head falling into the wall behind her as she looks up at him in a daze.

'Dead,' she croaks and goes limp, sliding down the wall as Sie lets her go.

Sie curses and leaves the alley.

'Wait,' I call in a loud whisper. 'We can't just leave her here.'

'Why not? We found out what we came here for. We even dealt with her stalkers. That's what we were paid to do. Got what Vic sent us out here for and the deal's done at the same time. Let's go.'

I roll my eyes and look down at her with a frown, my evening enjoyment evaporating. It doesn't feel right to leave her here in the dark, in the cold. She's not tiny for a human, but she is compared to us and, though I rarely feel anything towards anyone outside the Club, let alone a human, there's something about her. I knew it the moment I saw her come into the bar. She looked so uncertain and lost, but she didn't take any shit, not even from my rude ass. And when I'd touched her hand to seal the deal, her skin on mine had been like a brand. Never felt anything like it. Fuck. I'll bet she tastes like twenty-year old Scotch going down. Maybe we could contract her to the Club. I keep thinking we need some new girls ...

Not the right time, Paris.

'Vic'll want to know more about what happened to Drey. I'm bringing her to the house.'

Sie shrugs. 'She rides with you.'

'Fine.'

I pick her up and she doesn't make a sound. She's lighter than I thought she'd be, and she smells like human food.

My stomach rumbles as I carry her across the lot to

where we parked our bikes under a streetlight. Under the glow, I see that she's wearing a waitress uniform and my jaw tightens when I notice that her shirt is gaping open to the waist, giving me a good view of her breasts and fraying bra. Sex might be my reason for living, but I sure as shit don't hold with what those assholes were clearly planning.

I sit on my Indian, arranging her so she straddles me, and I can hold onto her while we ride. It's gonna be difficult to drive one-handed, but I've done it before and the house is just on the edge of town, not too far away. Guess there won't be any more messing around on my bike tonight though.

I pull the pieces of her shirt together, but the buttons have been ripped off, so I zip her jacket up to her chin instead, a part of me amused that I give a shit about her modesty. Korban would be laughing his ass off right now if he could see me.

She doesn't stir as we ride back to the house I share with the others. I wish I could say the same, but there's something about this girl that fires me up in a way I haven't felt in a long time, if ever.

I basically spend the journey trying to think about the least sexual things I can and even that doesn't work. I'm not hungry. I should be able to control myself around one human girl.

The wrought iron gates open automatically as we approach what Vic calls the 'Clubhouse' when we're around outsiders but is actually a mansion with grounds and a massive lake. We ride up the driveway which, no joke, is three and a half miles long. I checked once.

We pass the impressive entrance where a large front door opens into a mostly marble foyer and Vic's family's expensive tastes, instead heading for the underground garage around back. I stow my bike in my spot and climb off gingerly, keeping the girl in my arms.

Her head falls against my chest, and I frown, cocking my head. Having her this close feels oddly right and I'm not sure what to make of it. Don't get me wrong, I love the human ladies. I follow the rules though; only fucking the ones we have contracted to the Club and they can't get enough of me. I take my time with the on-call girls whenever I'm alone with them, and I fuck them fast with Korban when he needs to eat because that's the only way he can feed. But I always lull them and, when I'm done, they always have a blissed-out smile on their face.

But this girl feels different in my arms.

Sie stays in the garage, mumbling something about his bike making a noise he doesn't like. He'll stay in here for hours tinkering with his hog, so I leave him, taking the elevator up to the main house. I bypass the living areas completely, heading straight for the second-floor bedrooms and Theo, the only one of us with formal medical training.

I'm not much of a knocker, so when I throw open his door, Theo doesn't look surprised. At least, not at first. But then he notices what I'm carrying, and his eyebrows practically hit the ceiling.

'New contract? She doesn't look too good.'

I smirk. 'She's not one of the girls. This is the one from the bar yesterday.'

I lay her on top of Theo's bed, and she lets out a sound of pain, but doesn't wake.

Theo gets a good look at her and glances at me. 'Vic know she's here?'

'Not yet.'

'Better go tell him. You know how he is with humans who aren't the Club's.'

'Yeah,' I say, running a hand through my hair.

I'm not looking forward to that conversation and it's probably why Sie didn't come up with me. 'Look, she got the shit kicked out of her pretty good. I don't know how bad she's hurt.'

Theo's already checking her over. 'Supes?'

'Does it matter?'

He rolls his eyes. 'Wouldn't ask if it didn't.'

'Just some human fuckers preying on one of their own.'

Theo lets out a chuckle. 'You get just as many predators among the humans as you do the supes, bro. We just tend to forget that fact because we're near the top of the food chain. I'll take care of her. Go talk to Vic before he hears it from someone else.'

I nod and turn to leave, my eyes lingering on her for an extra second. What did she tell Vic her name was? Janet? Jane. That was it. Yeah, I'd definitely like a taste if I can get one.

I take the stairs down to the ground and start looking for Vic. He's usually in the games room or the gym, but both those are empty, and, in the end, I find him holed up in the study. Like I said, it's a freaking mansion.

This time I do knock, but it's on the door frame as I cross the threshold. Vic's sitting at the desk, looking deep in thought as he shuffles some papers around.

'We're back.'

He glances up and looks me over. 'Where's Drey?'

I don't bother sitting and I give it to Vic straight, drawing my thumb across my throat.

'Fuck,' Vic hisses, throwing his pen down on the polished desk. 'How?'

'Don't know yet. Found the girl. She's hurt so I brought her back. She might be able to tell us more.'

Vic frowns. 'You brought her *here*? To the Clubhouse?'

Mansion.

'Yeah.'

'What the fuck, Paris? You can't just bring outsiders here. What if she sees something she's not supposed to?'

I give him my best security guy WTF-that-ain't-gonna-happen look. 'She's unconscious, hurt pretty bad, so I took her up to Theo. He'll do his thing and then you can find out more about what happened to Drey. I'll keep her contained.'

'See that you do. Anything blows back on us, and this is on you. Let me know when Theo is done. I might as well talk to her since she's here.'

Vic goes back to his papers without another word, and I leave, heading to the kitchen to make myself a sandwich and wondering when the girl upstairs is going to be awake so Vic can interrogate her.

I wouldn't like to be in her shoes that's for sure. Vic's not gonna go easy on her even if she did pay us to get rid of those guys for her.

CHAPTER
FOUR
JANE

When I come to, I open my eyes with a gasp, my eyes flitting around, trying to figure out where I am. The dark alley has been replaced by a large bedroom, the cold ground by a comfy bed, and Stacker by an incubus. He's one of the ones from the bar, I think, but I can't be sure.

He's standing by a table, a First-Aid bag next to him. He's filling a needle with something clear, and I sit up, gritting my teeth against the pain in my chest and my back. He doesn't move, his eyes fixed on me.

Mine find the door.

'You're at the Iron Incubi Clubhouse and my name is Theo. I'm the medic. You're safe.'

The fuck I am!

He takes a step towards the bed, and I scramble out of it, keeping that needle in my sights.

He notices where my eyes linger.

'It's for the pain. You have a couple cracked ribs and some nasty bruises.'

Stacker really went to town on me with those kicks. What a prick.

If I was staying in town, I might be tempted to go find myself some revenge on that asshole somehow, but I'm leaving so I guess I'll have to turn the other cheek Amish-style.

The incubus takes another step forward and I turn and sprint to the door without hesitation, flinging it open and booking it down the corridor like the fires of Mordor are on my ass.

I chance a look back but he's not pursuing, and I realize why a second later as I hear someone coming up the steps in front of me. More than one. They're talking with each other in low voices.

Fuckity. Fuckity. Fuckity. Fuck!

I dart into the nearest room and shut the door quietly behind me. No one comes in and I breathe a sigh of relief as I turn. Another bedroom. Now I just need to find—

My mind and body freeze. I'm not alone.

There's a naked woman spread eagle on the bed. At first, I think she's dead and I get a shit ton of horror vibes; the token human girl stuck in a house with an MC of killer incubi. I'm sooooo gonna die!

Then I notice her breathing and my heartrate evens out. She's not a corpse. She's just breathing very slowly, staring at the ceiling with a funny little smile on her face. It's like she's in a stupor and has no idea that I'm there.

I cross the room to the windows and try one, but it won't budge. Painted shut. Outside, all I can see is black. No lights. No nothing. Where am I?

The handle of the door moves, and I hide in the first place I think of: behind the long curtain next to me.

Even as I move the curtain, I know this is a stupid plan.

But it's too late now. I'm committed. What is this? Scooby-Doo? You can probably see my feet and everything! Ugh!

Someone comes in.

'Still here, huh?'

My heart practically explodes in my chest ... but he's not speaking to me. He's talking to the woman on the bed. He hasn't noticed me at all.

Ha! Dumbass.

Emboldened by this guy's general lack of attention to detail, I chance a peek out into the room but there's no one there. Then I hear the muffled sound of a shower start.

I spring out of the curtain just in time for the biggest guy I've ever seen to come walking out of the bathroom. He's got like eight inches and two-hundred pounds of what appears to be pure muscle on me. We stare at each other for a split second, and I recognize him from the bar. He was sitting at the table, feeding off that blond.

His eyes move over me, and I run for it, but he's way faster than I'd have given him credit for considering his stature and he's barring the way out before I've gone two steps.

'If you wanted to fuck an incubus, all you had to do was ask nicely.' He smirks and I cock my head to the side as my heartbeat ratchets up.

'I don't want to fuck an incubus,' I say, avoiding his eyes.

He snorts like he doesn't believe me, and I shoot him an incredulous look.

'I don't!'

'Then why are you in my room, little girl?'

His voice is low and the way he says 'little girl' makes my knees go weak ... or maybe that's just the tremendous pain I'm in making it hard to suck in enough air ... or maybe it's just my back spasming where Stacker kicked the shit out of me.

I am little compared to him though, and my mind gets stuck on the thought. I'll bet most women are ... and men too. He's massive and it's ... hot as fuck. The muscles in my lower abdomen contract pleasantly and surprise makes me take another step back. I don't usually like – *he's using his tricks on me.*

'I don't want you,' I say because it's important to me that he knows, even though it won't mean anything to him. He won't care. He'll just use his supey powers to make me want him anyway and I'll end up like that girl in the bed, practically comatose and begging for more. Addicted to sex with him and his friends. I know how it works. I've heard the stories!

The horror of that scenario has me backing away from him some more, kinda wishing they *were* the murdering kind. Better dead than their mindless sex slave.

'Just trying to find my way out of your happy little fun house of sex, dude.'

He barks a laugh and then looks surprised at himself. To my own astonishment, he opens the door and moves as far away from it as he can get.

'Go, then.'

I do without a second thought, scampering back out into the hall ... and straight into another one, his hard chest practically hurling me to the floor.

I mean, what is this guy made of? Fucking diamonds?

He's fast, grabbing me before I can react, and I struggle in his tightening arms.

'Let me go!' I wheeze, feeling lightheaded.

'You got her, Kor? Good. Don't kill her yet. Vic wants to speak to her.'

Theo, the guy who was there when I woke up in the first bedroom with the short, dark hair and the tribal tats up one arm – that are framed nicely by the tight tee he's wearing – appears in my swimming vision.

'You got further than I thought you would. I'll give you that.'

'Where do you want princess bitch?' Kor, the one who caught me, grumbles.

'Back on the bed in my room.'

I'm scooped up unceremoniously, his fingers digging into my skin.

'You're lucky you just got out of Sie's room alive,' Kor says in my ear. 'You should know, humans don't make waves here if they know what's good for 'em.'

I narrow my eyes at him, try to keep hold of my anger, use it to keep me conscious.

But it's not enough.

~

Theo

I TAP THE ROUND, white chest piece of my stethoscope idly as Korban disappears down the hall carrying the limp girl. I watch him stomp away, and I wonder if he can be trusted not to break her neck while she's unconscious. Not many of us much like their kind in general. We all need them to survive and it's a bitch, but Kor … well, Kor fucking hates 'em and I can't say I blame him.

I glance at Sie's closed door and drop the end of the stethoscope, taking it off and putting it in my pocket. Sie doesn't like the medical stuff. Puts him on edge.

I need to make sure he's good. Poor bastard's trying to

hide it, but things aren't right with him. He won't appreciate my concern. He'll almost certainly bite my head off, but I'm the Club doctor so, with a resigned sigh, I knock twice.

The door opens quickly and Sie's looming on the other side of the threshold, almost like he was just standing there waiting for me. Maybe I am that predictable.

He glares. 'What?'

'Nothin'. Just wanted to make sure you're ...' I peer past him and make out a figure lying unmoving on the bed. That's not like Sie. He usually feeds in one of the common rooms or at the bar, not in his own bed.

'Who's that?' I ask, straining through the shadows of his dimly-lit room.

'What do you care?' Sie glances back and shrugs. 'I don't know her name. One of the contracted.'

'Monique?'

He shrugs again. 'Who gives a shit? She's one of ours and she's alive, just blissed out of her mind.'

I try to gauge his expression without being obvious, my fingers playing with my stethoscope in my pocket absently. It's definitely Monique. I can't see much, but I recognize the dress. She was wearing it earlier when I called for her. I sucked a lot out of her this evening, and I know she was already tired. How much of her did Sie take? And, now that I'm thinking about it, why Monique? He usually sticks with Carrie. Did he seek her out for the same reason I did? Because she resembles the other, *uncontracted* female? The one that's right now being put back in my bed, but that the rules say I'm not allowed to touch? Fuck. Just thinking about the rules makes me want to break them.

'You sure she's ok?' I ask, not letting him know my concerns.

Sie snorts. 'Even if she's not, she signed on the dotted line. Vic makes sure they know the risks they take to get their fixes.'

I can't help my frown. 'We have the girls contracted to the Club around for our own convenience, not so we can take too much from them and endanger their lives.'

'No, you sanctimonious fuck, we have girls contracted to the Club because of the Council's bullshit laws against taking from unwilling humans.'

I don't let my concern show, but this isn't like Sie. He's always been fine with the rules before, more than fine. He's usually the sanctimonious one when it comes to the underdog.

He's worse than I thought he'd be and I'm afraid I know what the problem is. I need to talk to Vic.

'You want me to take her with me?'

He glances back at the prone woman on the bed. 'No need,' he says, coming out into the hall.

I'm forced back a step.

He leaves his door ajar and walks purposefully towards the stairs, ignoring me now. I guess we're done talking.

'She's a big girl,' he calls back. 'She'll find her way back to her bunk when she comes to. You might wanna see to yourself instead of worrying about me. I can hear you messing around with that 'scope in your pocket. Maybe go see one of the girls or something. Get rid of some of that nervous energy...'

I watch him go, taking my hand out of my pocket so I stop playing. Fuck Sie's great hearing.

My friend is definitely on a downward spiral though. I guess I've known it for a while, but I hoped I was imagining at least some of it. He's been antsy and pissed off for weeks, but this was a whole other level. The look in his eyes has me worried. He should be sated after Monique; well fed and sex-drunk. Hell, I still am, and I fed from her hours ago.

But Sie doesn't look like he's eaten at all, though he clearly has if Monique's state is anything to go by, and that's not a good sign. It's taking more to satisfy him and he's trying to hide it, but he won't be able to for long. If the beast inside gets too hungry, my brother will go feral. I've seen it before. The madness is rare, and no one knows why it happens to some of us and not others, but if Sie doesn't get himself together, he won't be able to control his hunger. He'll feed from *uncontracted* humans. He'll *kill* uncontracted humans. And if he goes rogue, even Vic won't be able to save us from the ton of bricks the rest of the supes will bury us under.

Hurting humans is no big deal because it can be swept under the carpet pretty easily with cash, but the supe authorities shut down murder real fast; makes the humans nervous and they might be weak, but there are a hell of a lot more of them than there are us. No one wants anymore bad press. Not after the shitshow last year with those girls' bodies found in that club in Houston.

I stare down the hall though Sie is long gone. We've been brothers a long time. Could I kill him if I need to? I already know the answer. To save the MC? Yes, but let's hope it doesn't come to that.

I make my way back up to my own room and find the girl still unconscious. Vic will want to talk to her soon.

I take out a pair of cuffs and attach her right wrist to my headboard, telling myself all the while that it's for her own safety first and foremost and not because I find immobilizing her hot AF.

Truthfully, I don't need her running off again as soon as she feels able and not just because she was knocked around pretty hard tonight and shouldn't be *running* at all. There's also the fact that, though I'd swear up and down that the Club follows the rules with humans to an outsider, the truth is that if I hadn't been there when Kor caught her or if Sie had found her first, Vic would probably have had to try to get answers from a dead girl. Not impossible to do, sure, but not optimal either.

I leave her in the bed and grab the syringe off the table that I'd been filling before she rabbitted. Taking in the pale skin and blue veins of her arm, I inject her carefully, so she won't bruise.

'It's just a painkiller,' I murmur even though she's not awake to hear me.

I feel a presence at my back.

'She's not awake right now,' I say without turning around.

'So I see.'

Vic comes into my periphery, looking down at her with a detached expression. He eyes the restraints speculatively.

'She ran as soon as she woke up last time, so I've had to take precautions.'

'Uh huh.'

He doesn't sound convinced and I cringe a little while my back is to him, a tad embarrassed that my motivations are so easy to read.

'Wake her up. I want to know who killed Dreyson. He was an asshole, but he was almost a full member. We can't let that go unpunished.'

I nod and go to the locked cabinet in the corner of my room where I keep my medical supplies to grab the ammonia salts.

'Any idea who did it?'

Vic shakes his head. 'It could be any of the other supe factions. Tensions are high.'

'Tensions are always high,' I scoff.

'Higher than usual then. At least the deal we made with her for that orc stone is done. Once she tells us what she knows about Drey, we can cut her loose.'

'Yeah,' I say absently, not telling the boss what I'd rather we did with her. He won't go for it anyway. He only takes the ones who want in, and I already know she won't.

I crush the packet of salts between my fingers and put it under her nose. She starts, her eyes opening wide as she coughs and groans, curling her free arm around her middle and realizing at the same time that her other one is stuck above her head.

Her nostrils flare as she starts to panic.

CHAPTER
FIVE
JANE

'Relax. Vic just wants to talk to you.'

I rattle the metal of the cuffs. I'm in pain and pissed as fuck. 'Why?'

'Because Drey is dead and I want to know what you know,' Vic answers, but that wasn't what I meant.

'No, I mean why am I chained to the bed?'

'Because you're a human girl in a house of hungry incubi,' Vic answers readily. 'You don't get to wander around.'

I scowl at him. 'Let me leave then.'

'You can go when you've answered my questions.'

I flex my other hand, reminding myself that only one is cuffed so I don't start hyperventilating. Full-blown panic is just around the corner, popping it's head out to look at me every few seconds and that will get me nowhere I need to be. These assholes will just put me out and sedate me and then try again when I'm calm. I want this done. I want to get out of here, grab my stuff, and leave town before anyone else gets hurt *or killed* because of me.

I can live with Drey's death and maybe that makes me a

horrible person. But I couldn't deal with something happening to Shar or her kids.

'Ask,' I say, relaxing into the bed, trying to stay as calm as possible.

If I don't try to move my arm, I can pretend it's free.

'What happened after you and Drey left the bar the other day?' Vic asks.

'I went to the diner to start my shift. Your boy came in a little while later and ordered a soda. Then I noticed he was gone. I finished my shift and went home around midnight.'

'And Drey was found yesterday morning?'

'Yes. Sarge, the cook, went to take out the trash and he was in the dumpster. That's what I heard anyway.'

'You didn't see him?' Vic's piercing eyes are unwavering, and I try not to get lost in their inky depths.

I shake my head. 'I didn't hear about it until I got to work …' I look out the window and notice it's still dark outside. 'Tonight, I guess. The supe cops came to Gail's to talk to me about it.'

'What did you tell them?' His tone doesn't change, but I flinch anyway as I feel an invisible weight pressing on me. It's like extra gravity, pushing me into the mattress.

'Tone it down. She's just a human,' Theo murmurs and the pressure I feel eases.

'I didn't tell them anything.'

He looks me up and down with an unimpressed expression. 'Did they believe you?'

I nod even as I frown at his insinuation that I'm not a good liar. I'm an awesome liar, but maybe it's better if he doesn't know that in case I need to tell him some fibs at some point.

Vic turns to the doc. 'Looks like it was a rival gang.

Maybe from the city,' he says in a low tone, forgetting me for the moment.

'Maybe,' Theo agrees. 'The mutilations were pretty specific though. Haven't heard of anyone around these parts cutting out the eyes before.'

'Could be a new player in Metro. That might explain the missing shipments.'

I frown at them both. I'd assumed they'd know I was the reason their friend died. I thought that's why they brought me here. But they think this has something to do with their world, not mine.

I wonder if I should tell them. If I do, will they blame me? Will they still let me go? But if I don't say anything, they won't realize the danger. Do I care? I don't know, but if I want them to have the best chance of helping me, maybe I should make sure they know as much as I do.

'Take her back to her shitty apartment in the morning.' Vic turns to me. 'We fulfilled our end of the bargain. Your stalkers won't bother you again. Sie and Paris saw to that.'

I stare at him in confusion as he starts to leave. What is he talking about?

'Wait.'

He swings back around, not bothering to hide his annoyance and leveling me with a look that says, 'My time is worth more than you. Why are you wasting it?'

'What exactly did 'Sie and Paris' do last night?'

'They beat the shit out of your stalkers.' He says it slowly, as if I'm the idiot here.

So I speak the same way back to him. 'Those guys last night weren't my stalkers, they're just some asshole customers from the diner who like to fuck with me.'

Theo's eyes narrow and his eyes flick down to the jacket

I'm still wearing. I follow his gaze, but ... it's just a zipped-up jacket. What is he looking at?

'Paris said they were assaulting you.'

I shrug, making the handcuffs clank and my panic rachet up a notch.

'I might have pissed them off,' I say, looking away because what happened was my fault. I've gotten cocky lately, figured Stacker wouldn't even notice the money was gone, or that he wouldn't care. I should have known he was smart enough to figure out who took it and get retribution.

'What did you do?' Theo asks, though I can see that Vic is impatient to leave and getting annoyed with his friend's questions.

'Doesn't matter,' I say, mostly to placate Vic because I need him to listen to what I'm saying. 'What matters is that those guys weren't the ones I'm afraid of.'

I flinch a little because that's not quite true after tonight. They've gone from a group of annoying rich boys to a mob of men who were going to rape and kill me. The thought of them all crowding around me with their phones up while Stacker started touching me makes me break out in a cold sweat and I swallow hard, burying it.

'You're not clear of our deal yet,' I say and I'm just a little bit satisfied by the crease that appears between Vic's eyes as he mulls over what I'm telling him.

'You said you've never seen them,' he says. 'How do you know it wasn't those guys?'

'Those little frat pricks?' I scoff. 'No way.'

I sit up, grabbing the headboard with my bound hand. I need to make them understand that I didn't go to them with some dumb problem that the cops could have handled. This is a real thing and they'll be earning their fee.

'The ones I need help with have been dogging my steps

for years. I run and they always find me. Wherever I settle, whatever new life I make. It's always the same. Sometimes it's only a matter of weeks. Once I had eighteen months. But, sooner or later, a note will appear. Always in different handwriting, or a text from a random number. It tells me to move on or someone I know will die.' I heave a sigh. 'So I go.'

Both of them look unconvinced.

'What happens if you don't do what they say? You *have* tried that, right?' Theo asks with a smirk. 'How do you know this isn't some joke?'

'Well, even if I could get past the idea that someone would actually spend years doing that to someone for no reason ...'

I look down at the bedspread and I try not to remember the first time. I did think it was a weird joke that I didn't get. I tore up the note and ignored the warning. *Never again.*

'They killed someone I cared about ... and they did the same to her as they did to Dreyson.' I say slowly, emotionlessly, and I see them glance at each other.

Pushing away the grief and guilt, I chance looking at them both in the eyes for a second. 'Did you think I didn't know what I had? That I'd give up an orc stone just for the Iron Incubi to mete out a beating to a few local assholes who like to mess with me?' I give Vic a smirk of my own because that probably *was* what he thought. 'I might be a human, but I'm not that fucking stupid.'

His eyes bore into mine and I know he's mad, not because I notice anything specific in his posture or expression, but because I would be if I was him. I've made him look like a fool and when I see Theo's quick, wary glance at his president, I know I'm right. I look back at Vic, trying to see the signs for myself because unless I'm looking, specifically trying to find them, I would never notice and I'm trying to practice. I want to get better at it.

At first, I don't see anything. He looks the same as before, but then I realize he's clenching his jaw ... and one of his fists actually. Then I feel that pressure again and Theo flinches away from him with a small hiss. I don't move, but I'm second-guessing riling him up. Vic is angrier than I thought if he can't control his creepy power and even his buddy is scared.

'Give me back the orc stone and we'll break the deal,' I offer because he clearly wants me out of here. 'I was going to leave town in the morning anyway.'

Vic says nothing, just stares at me as if he's having some kind of war with himself. I decide to give him a moment because internal struggles I understand.

'Did Drey die because you ignored a note?' Theo asks quietly from the other side of the bed away from Vic.

I get the distinct impression that if I give the wrong answer, I'm not going to live very long here.

I swing my head around to look up at him. 'No. I only got the note tonight. They knew I went to you for help. I'm sorry. I didn't know they'd ... I didn't even know they'd found me again.'

'Why did you come to us in the first place?'

'I mentioned something to my friend Sharlene. She works at Gail's with me. She told me about you.'

'And where did you get the orc stone?' Vic asks out of nowhere and I glance at him. The pressure is gone again so I guess that means he's back in control of himself.

'I didn't steal it, if that's what you mean. It was my mom's.'

'And where is she now?'

Vic steps closer to the bed, forcing me to crane my neck to look at him properly.

I meet his gaze. 'She died a long time ago.'

'Whoever these assholes are, they killed one of the Iron I's. We're bound to make them pay,' he says, ignoring my reply.

'I still need to leave,' I insist. 'I won't put people I care about at risk.'

'Odds are they don't know she's here,' Theo says to Vic like I'm not even in the room. 'Sie and Paris would have noticed if someone else was there watching her tonight or followed them here and we have border protection in place to stop outsiders from surveilling us. They can't even set foot on the property unless we let them.'

My mouth falls open. 'I'm not going to pin my hopes for my friends' lives on your opinion of the *odds*.'

Vic shrugs. 'You don't have a choice. You're not leaving the Clubhouse grounds, sweetheart. If you try, we'll just find you and drag you back. Then your stalkers will *definitely* figure out you're here and your little friend Sharlene will be down two eyes and her flimsy, mortal life because of you.'

'She has kids,' I say faintly.

He steps closer and gets in my face. I cower back in the bed, not liking how close he is, not liking that I *like* how he's towering over me ...

'I'm a demon, baby girl. Do you think I give a fuck?'

I shake my head and he backs off, giving me a cold smile before turning back to Theo. 'Keep her here until I have chance to talk to the others about our *uncontracted* house guest.'

Vic leaves without another word and I'm left reeling in the bed.

'That go the way you thought it would?' Theo asks me lazily from the other side of the room.

I blink at him. 'I'm ... not sure. I didn't really have a plan.'

He gets a look on his face that I'm used to seeing, like he doesn't get me at all, and I look away from him. I don't like that look. It makes me remember how alone I am.

'Can you at least take the cuff off?' I ask.

'Sorry, roomie. Can't trust you not to run and I don't have time to babysit you. Vic wants you here so he can try to ensure your safety.'

He goes back to packing a bag with bandages and other medical things. 'Welcome to the lion's den, princess,' he mutters.

'Please.' I pull at my arm. 'I don't like it.'

He turns with a sigh and brandishes the key, stepping forward and taking the cuff in his hands. His fingers brush against mine and I feel an awareness that's similar to when the one at the bar touched me and the other grabbed me in the hall. Theo doesn't seem to feel whatever it is though.

'I don't give a shit if you don't like it.' He drops my wrist and chuckles.

My heart sinks. I can't keep my panic at bay forever. 'Then sedate me.'

That gives him pause. 'You'd actually rather I drug you here in a house of hungry incubi than have one wrist tied to the bed?'

'I don't like it,' I say again.

For a second, I think that maybe he's going to help, but then he levels me with a stare and his lips turn up into a nasty-looking grin. He raises his hands in mock apology as he backs away. 'Like I said, I don't give a shit, princess, and no one here is going to give a flying fuck about you or your comfort, so you better get used to it.'

He turns around and leaves, locking the door behind him.

I'm rapidly beginning to dislike their nicknames for me I think as I look around the room.

I'm alone.

I pull hard at the cuff, and it hurts, but I don't care. An irrational part of me is afraid they'll never come back and set me free. I know that's dumb – I'm literally in Theo's bedroom, I'm pretty sure – but logic is fading away, leaving whatever's left. I mean I probably won't gnaw off my own hand like a fox caught in a trap, but the more upset I get, the less pain I'll feel until later.

I try to claw back my calm with varying levels of success, tears sliding down my cheeks. I'm stuck here in more ways than one. I should have just moved on. Trying to get help has made everything so much worse.

∽

Korban

'Why the fuck is she still here?' I growl, pushing myself off the wall where I've been waiting in the corridor, trying to keep bad memories at bay and hating that another human is in the house. One's too many and now there are four!

Vic gives me a look. 'What do you care?'

Vic doesn't stop walking so I follow him. 'I don't. We just have shit to focus on. We don't need another human female in the house. The ones we have contracted are bad enough.'

At the top of the wide, sweeping staircase, Vic stops and

turns to face me. 'Don't give me that. You avail yourself of the on-call girls often enough.'

'Only so I don't starve,' I hiss.

Vic shrugs. 'What's one more? You won't even notice her.'

'I won't be responsible for anything that happens to her here,' I mutter and Vic's penetrating eyes land on mine.

'Whoever killed Drey is linked to her. She's staying here until we get justice; 'til we make them regret fucking with us.'

'You didn't even like Drey,' I scoff. 'Fucking affirmative action. He was only here to make up the numbers and keep the supe authorities off our backs.'

'My personal feelings don't matter. He was basically one of the Iron I's. An attack on one of us is an attack on us all. You know that. Besides, we lost a human, we gain one. Consider her *making up the numbers*.'

Vic starts descending the stairs.

'Alex!'

My use of his real name makes him turn back with a sigh.

'What? I got shit to do.'

'Why does she need to stay *here*?'

He turns back around and starts walking again. 'Because I say so. Deal with it.'

Our asshole leader leaves me there at the top of the stairs clenching my jaw so hard I feel like my teeth will crack.

Fuck!

My hands still tingle from when my skin brushed against hers in the hall when I caught her. I don't know what that means, but I don't like it. I feel antsy, my body buzzing unpleasantly.

I have a fight tomorrow night, but I don't know if I can wait that long and I know I won't be able to sleep, so I make my way downstairs to the gym.

The lights are low and when I catch my reflection in the mirrors, I make a face. I look like shit. I'm going to have to feed properly before tomorrow night or there's no way I'll beat Callaghan. The thought of having to fuck one of the girls turns my stomach like it always does though.

I don't bother to warm up, just start hitting the bag that's hanging in the center of the room with everything I have, losing myself in the sound and the feel of my fists hitting the black leather.

Thud. Thud. Thud. Over and over and over.

I don't know how long I'm there, but by the time I come out of the zone, I'm practically standing in a puddle of my own sweat and my arms feel like limp noodles. I'm dead on my feet, which was the point. At least I'll be able to sleep now.

I grab a quick shower in the adjacent bathroom, letting my mind quiet as the hot water sprays over my aching muscles.

But thoughts of the human upstairs intrude before I can stop them. The fruity smell of her brown hair when I grabbed her in the hall, the feel of her body against mine. I look down and, to my shock, I'm hard. When was the last time thoughts of a human female did that to me?

I already know the answer. Not since I was in that house. This time I don't let the thoughts in. I lock them down tight before I find myself taking a late-night stroll down a very dark memory lane and wondering how the fuck I got there. Instead, I take myself in hand.

Literally.

I don't think about Paris. I think about *her*.

I imagine her lips around my cock, my fist in her ponytail, taking her mouth. I'd fuck her throat hard, making her take all of me. She'd whimper and gag around me. She'd squirm under my hands, her gorgeous brown eyes watering, mascara making tracks down her cheeks.

I come hard, bracing myself against the white tiles as I shudder in the steam and then I frown as I turn off the water.

What the fuck was that? I never – and I mean NEVER – want humans. Not the females, not the males. None of them. Paris literally has to get me hard with his mouth or his hand so I can feed properly from the contracted females.

What is it about this girl? I need to figure this out. I need to see her again.

I throw on some clothes and I make my way up to the second floor where Theo's room is. The girl is staying in his bed. I guess he's on a couch somewhere.

I stifle a yawn. Pummeling the pads did the trick. I'm beat and looking forward to my own bed now, but one last thing before I hit the hay.

I find Theo's door locked, but it's easy enough to pick it and I enter the dim room.

She's still in the bed where I put her earlier tonight, but she's asleep, curled up on her side facing away from me.

I watch her for a few minutes, taking in her oversized jacket and black leggings with her bare feet, trying to figure out what it is about this human girl that draws me in when none of the others ever have before.

I go closer, around the bed, carefully avoiding the parts of the floor that I know creak, so I can get a better look at her.

Her brown hair is in a messy ponytail. Wisps of hair have escaped the elastic, curling around a face that looks so serene in sleep. Her eyelashes are long, fanning over her pale skin. I cock my head to the side. She's pretty, I guess, but there's nothing about her that's *extraordinary*.

I've seen human females before who were beautiful – I mean silver-screen gorgeous – the kind of women who made me wish I wasn't broken so that I could want them because I knew that it would be amazing with them even for a night.

But my dick never got hard in the shower because I thought about their bodies or their hair or their lips.

While I was carrying her, her body had felt good against me, but it was a fleeting thought. I wasn't really paying attention to her in my rush to get her contained so I wouldn't have to deal with her. Now I'm wishing I'd slowed down a little and been more present in the moment.

And I can't even tell much more about what her body looks like even though she's right in front of me because of that massive jacket she's wearing zipped up to her fucking chin ...

Glancing at the door that I left open, I listen for a minute. There are no sounds in the house. I'd bet good money that everyone's asleep ... the same as she is. I look back at her slumbering there like she doesn't have a care in the world.

Could I?

I shouldn't, but could I? Without waking her?

The challenge is almost irresistible, and I edge closer. She hardly moves, but I can tell by her eyes that she's in REM.

From this angle, I can see that her wrist is cuffed to the bed, and I roll my eyes in amusement. Theo loves tying up the on-call girls too. I admit I've done it a time or two. It makes me feel more in control when I'm feeding. But, unlike me, he gets off on making them even weaker than they already are to us. I grin. He probably gave her some bullshit about not wanting her to escape. As if she could.

Oh, Theo, you perverted bastard.

Standing over her, I'm struck by how innocent she looks *and how I'd love to corrupt her*.

She's blissfully unaware of how much danger she's in or she'd never sleep in this house.

The way I didn't sleep. For months.

Memories of expensive perfume, breathy moans, and the feel of chains around me make my body tense. I force them back and realize I've taken out my butterfly knife and I've opened it. The razor-sharp blade is already resting lightly against her cheek. Slowly, I trace it down to her throat.

I could slit it right now. From ear to ear. It would be so fucking easy. Vic would be pissed because he thinks that she'll be useful, but I won't get any flak from the others. Sie'll probably give me a high five. It'll just be a case of cleaning up the blood, getting Theo a new mattress, and burying the body on the grounds somewhere.

But as the twisted images recede to the back of my mind, I don't really want to do it. There was a time not long ago that I wouldn't have even hesitated. Maybe I'm getting better.

I put the knife away with a hard swallow, my hands shaking a little.

She moves onto her back suddenly and I freeze, but she's not awake. In fact, she's just made what I came over here to do that much easier.

My eyes take her in again and, now that I'm so near, I see that her cuffed wrist is raw and bruised. She's hurt herself trying to get free. Dumb bitch must have been pulling with all her strength for hours, I think as I watch her face for signs of waking, but she doesn't stir again.

I take hold of the jacket zipper and very slowly pull it from her neck all the way down to her thighs. Another quick glance up to her face and I gently pull the jacket apart. The first thing I see is a thin, gold chain around her neck with a matching infinity symbol looped through it. My eyes move down and I'm surprised by the sight of her tits, cupped in a grey bra. Why isn't she wearing a ... I belatedly notice a blue, button-up shirt with a nametag that says 'Jane' on it, but most of the buttons have been torn off, making it gape to her waist. I make out faint bruises on her throat, chest, and ribs and trace one of them lightly. *Fingermarks.*

I don't know the particulars of why Paris and Sie brought her here tonight. I'd assumed it was just because of Drey, but it looks like something else happened too.

Was it Sie? I discount that idea as soon as I think it. Sie isn't far enough gone to attack a human *yet* and Paris would have said something as soon as they got back if he had.

Whoever it was ripped her shirt apart and grabbed her hard, maybe started giving her a beating too. The force of my anger shocks me. I'll lull the on-call girls when I need to and I'll fuck them when necessary, but they all know what they're getting into when they show up here for their interview. Vic makes sure of it. He makes 'em watch informative videos on incubi and everything. They consent when they sign-up and they can leave after their time here is done. This girl didn't have a choice.

Like I didn't.

I let out a breath and turn away, annoyed that I now feel some sort of kinship with this *human,* and I don't know anything more about why the fuck I'm interested in her than I did before.

I leave the room, not bothering to lock it. Theo will know I've been there anyway. I chuckle a little when I imagine his reaction when he finds the door open in a couple hours. Knowing my penchants, he'll think the worst. Then he'll watch the video and see what I did.

I go down the hall to my own room and I sink into my bed. Closing my eyes, I see her face in my mind again. Now, thanks to my dumb escapades tonight, I see her tits too. Again, my dick starts getting hard and I grit my teeth.

She needs to go.

CHAPTER
SIX
JANE

The next morning, I'm woken by the door banging open and Theo barging into the room. I try to sit up, startled, but get pulled back by my wrist that hurts like a bitch now since I spent a good hour and a half trying to get out of it last night.

His gaze lands on me as he lurches forward, his eyes moving over me frantically. His hands come up to rub at his temples as he closes his eyes and lets out a breath.

'Fuck,' he mutters. 'That asshole.'

He walks across the room towards me, and I notice his eyes lingering on my chest.

I look down and gasp. My jacket is unzipped and giving him a great view of my old, used-to-be-white bra aaaaaaaannnnnnnd my boobs.

How did that happen? I sleepwalk sometimes, but I've never sleep undressed myself before.

I fumble to yank the edges of the jacket together as quick as I can with one hand, wincing as my cuffed wrist pulls again. I'm in such a panic that I can't grab it and I can feel my cheeks getting hot.

Fucking get it together, Jane!

Mortified, I'm finally able to pull it closed and take myself off display, wrapping my arm around my middle to keep it secured. I don't look at him until I'm certain my face is blank.

'What the fuck did you do?' he demands, and I see that he's staring at my wrist.

I look up and grimace at the sight. The skin around the cuff is mottled purple, and the skin is broken in places. I guess it does look pretty bad.

I look away. I didn't realize I'd done so much damage to myself and it's making me feel queasy. I move it around gingerly, testing that nothing's broken or pulled out of joint. Everything works though. The injury is only skin deep although my wrist does feel a little stiff now that I'm thinking about it.

I'm starting to panic again, and I know that if he leaves, it won't matter how much it hurts, I'll start trying to get free again.

'I promise I won't go anywhere,' I plead.

He looks angry with me, and I wonder why. If anything, I should be angry with him. He's the one that left me here all night even after I told him I don't like my hands being immobilized.

Asshole.

I see him take the key from his jeans pocket, but I don't even bother to look at him in case this is another trick. I'm not giving him the satisfaction.

But then my arm comes free, and I cradle my cold, aching hand. I blink back tears of relief.

'Thanks,' I mutter through clenched teeth, but only because it's polite.

'Vic spoke to the others. You can move around the

house for now, but you don't go outside. Understand?'

He looms over me, and I only just stop myself from shrinking away.

'Follow the rules or you'll be back here,' he taps the headboard, 'with every one of your limbs tied to my bed. I promise you that.'

I give a jerky nod. I'll agree to anything right now if it keeps me free. But there's something I notice. I *think*. His expression is almost likes he *wants* me to put a foot wrong so he can do what he threatens. But maybe I'm wrong.

'And stay away from the Iron I's, especially Sie and Korban. They like humans even less than the rest of us.'

I frown at him. I don't know all that much about incubi, but I thought they loved humans to be honest.

'Sie's the big one and Korban has the shaggy hair, right?'

He nods. 'Oh, and the house girls. Stay away from them too.'

'House girls?'

'The contracted humans.'

At my blank look, he lets out a sound of impatience. 'The ones who live here.'

I frown at him. 'Wait. So you hate humans, but you have a bunch of them living here?'

His eyes gleam dangerously. 'Well, we're incubi. We need to eat.'

My eyes widen. 'So, what, like they're slave girls you guys keep and use for …'

Ew.

My stomach drops a little. I'm stuck here. What if they—

'No!' He takes a step back, giving me some space.

I feel my brow pucker. 'Have I offended you?'

'Yeah, you kinda have. The girls who contract with us *want* to be here. They literally sign up.'

'So they get paid?'

He snorts and his gaze moves over me. 'Looking for a job?'

I make a point of not looking into his eyes. 'Not even a little bit.'

He barks a laugh. 'They get paid when they've done their time, but they have a roof over their heads, food, a clothing allowance while they're here.'

'Where is here anyway? How did I get here?' I ask, changing the subject so abruptly that he blinks a couple of times and there's a bit of a pause before he answers.

'What's the last thing you remember?' he finally asks.

I swallow hard, thinking about last night in the alleyway. 'I was on the ground, I think. Stacker was kicking me. No, wait, it was after that. The big guy. He threw me up against the wall and asked me about Drey. Then, I guess I passed out.'

'Paris brought you back on his bike. You have some cracked ribs and some bumps and bruises.'

I let out a slow breath. 'And now I get to stay. Goodie.' I pull my hair tie out. 'How long are you going to keep me here for?'

Theo shrugs. 'Vic will speak to you about that later,' he says cryptically and my eyes narrow.

'I can't help you find them,' I say. 'I don't know who they are. I've never seen them.'

Again, Theo shrugs. 'Vic thinks you can. Anyway, it's not me you have to convince. I have nothing to do with the decision. You want a shower?'

He gestures with his head to the door across the room.

'You should take one,' he says. 'You smell like coffee and ...' he sniffs. 'Something else.'

'Onions?'

'Yeah, that's it.'

'Soup special was French onion last night.'

Again.

Guess I don't have to worry about coming out of the diner reeking of food anymore.

Theo goes into his closet and comes out with a nondescript sweatshirt. He puts it on the bed with some grey sweatpants that look massive. He surveys me and then looks at his clothes.

'Actually, I'll see if one of the girls has something you can borrow,' he says.

He leaves the room, closing and locking the door behind him.

I don't wait, sliding my legs over the side of the bed and putting them on the plush, beige carpet. I stand up slowly, testing my weight on my legs. I feel a little sick, but I'm probably just hungry.

I take small steps to the bathroom, holding my side as if that'll make it feel better. I gape as I turn on the light. It's huge. There's a shower and ... is that a jacuzzi tub? I thought this was an MC clubhouse and I don't know what I expected, but I think it was more stained floors and liquor bottles, maybe a nasty, stained commode behind a rickety door. This is so fancy!

Who are these guys?

I turn on the walk-in shower. It's one of those kind where the water drips down from a massive, flat showerhead like rain. There are even jets that spray water at you from the sides for, like, if you forget to wash a crevice or something.

While the water heats up, I undress, taking off my jacket and my ruined uniform. I toss it in the trash. Won't be needing that again.

There are different bottles lined up on a shelf, so I choose one and smell it, wrinkling my nose. Too sickly sweet. I pick up another, which is neroli and something I've never heard of, and I find it's subtle enough not to mess with my nose. It's one of those manly, everything-in-one soaps since wasting time getting clean with multiple products is apparently not a masculine thing to do.

I lather my hair and body as I read the other labels, hoping for conditioner because otherwise my hair won't feel right and will be hard to brush.

I find one and am stupidly relieved. I know it's a small thing to care about, especially considering the circumstances. I know it's dumb too, but I can't turn it off. I used to think that everyone was this way, and it took a long time to realize that they aren't, that tiny things like this don't bother everyone to the extent they upset me. Well, time and someone caring enough about me to take me to a doctor who referred me to a psychiatrist, who referred me to a child psychologist who diagnosed me as autistic.

I smile a little at the memory as I wash away the soap and massage the conditioner into my hair. Angie was the last in a long line of fosters I was placed with. All the others pegged me as too difficult from the outset, but not Angie. She was pretty much the only one who ever cared after dad disappeared. She paid out of her own pocket to make sure she found someone who could help me. She'd talked about adopting me, even started the process. That was the dream of so many kids in foster care, so I knew it was a big deal even though I hoped my dad would come back.

Then, the first note came, telling me to leave if I knew

what was good for me. I thought it was one of the asshole kids at school messing with me because they did that, so I ignored it.

And Angie, the only mother I'd ever known, was ... taken away from me.

I wash the conditioner out of my hair, my mood circling the drain like the water that has just sluiced down my skin with thoughts of her. I was fourteen when that had happened. Over ten years of running, a decade of never settling anywhere, of trying not to let myself make friends to keep people around me safe. No wonder I'm exhausted.

I turn off the water and grab one of the plush, fluffy towels that match the bathroom exactly *of course*. It's like a fucking hotel here. Well, except for my demonic roommates.

I put my long hair in a small towel and wrap what I think is called 'a bath sheet' loosely around my body.

When I leave the bathroom, Theo's room is still empty, but there's a small pile of clothes on the bed. Some leggings that aren't dissimilar to the ones I was wearing, a thong which I wrinkle my nose at (yes, I prefer cotton granny panties, but I have worn a thong before and I know I *can* without it making me crazy so long as it isn't too lacy), and a thigh-length shift dress that feels like rayon. It'll do. At least it's not polyester or wool. I'll end up scratching my skin raw and I've hurt myself enough since I've been here.

I throw on the ass-floss underwear and the leggings before I grab my old bra from the bathroom floor and put on the dress. I noticed a full-length mirror on the back of the bathroom door earlier and I finally get a good look at the bruises mottling my breasts and torso as I hold the dress up just under my bra.

'Fucking Stacker,' I mumble as I stare at myself.

'There's a painkiller by the bed if you need it,' Theo says from just behind me and I gasp, whirling around and dropping the hem of the dress.

When did he come in?

'Who's Stacker?'

'Just one of the guys from last night.' I reply a little breathlessly.

'He was the one that did that to you?'

I nod.

'You said he and his buddies were customers at the diner. You pour them a shitty cup of coffee or something?' he asks, taking my injured wrist and turning it this way and that before dabbing some Neosporin on the places where the skin's broken.

I give him a lopsided grin that I think surprises him. 'I was sick of their bullshit, and I was gonna leave town anyway, so I stole Stacker's money clip out of his pocket.'

He chuckles. 'What kind of a chump carries a money clip?' he asks, producing a bandage and wrapping my wrist up neatly.

'I know, right?'

I look at Theo's handywork. I don't usually like people I don't know touching me. I always shy away from it. But his hands felt ... kinda nice.

Incubus voodoo. I need out of here!

'Thanks,' I say, hoping he hasn't noticed that I'm onto him. 'Anyway, Stacker noticed quicker than I thought he would.' I shrug. 'He got most of it back.'

Plus the last money I'd gotten from the diner this week so I'm flat broke.

At least I was able to give some of it to Sharlene. Something good came out of last night.

Theo gestures to the painkiller in front of me. 'The pill

should last a while but let me know if you need any more.'

He backs away and I slide the little blue tablet off the table, swallowing it down with a gulp from the glass of water next to it. Maybe I should be more suspicious, but there was plenty they could have done to me last night and they didn't. I'd rather just feel better so I can start planning my escape.

'You can stay in this room while you're here. We don't have any others free right now.'

'Where will you go?' I ask.

'I'll bunk with one of the guys.'

'Thanks, I guess.'

He snorts. 'You're probably hungry … I know I am,' he mutters as he turns away. 'I'll get you something to eat … Unless you're feeling up to coming down to the kitchen yourself?'

I should do a little recon of this house while I can.

'I'll come down with you,' I say because there's no fucking way I'm staying here for any longer than I need to. If I see an out, I'm going to take it.

~

Theo

I LEAD the girl to the kitchen, taking her past the other guys' rooms and down the back stairs instead of via the grand staircase that leads to the foyer.

I glance back at her once in a while to mark her progress since she was hurt pretty badly last night, but she doesn't look at me at all, instead surveying everything she passes from the original wood paneling of the hall to the plush, cream carpet runner we follow.

Although she seems to be taking everything in, her face remains mostly blank, giving nothing away although she's a human locked in a house of incubi. She must be nervous at least, but I can't see any real evidence of it. I do notice that the painkiller must be taking effect, however, because she's not holding her ribs anymore.

The stairs lead us directly to the kitchens, which, despite this house being old as fuck, is a contemporary masterpiece fit for a Michelin Starred chef. The abrupt change in décor makes her stop and she blinks, looking around unhurriedly at the marble countertops and modern appliances. She steps further into the room and does a slow 360, stopping at the wide fridge.

'Thought you guys didn't eat …' she trails off as she opens it and finds it well-stocked.

Stan, the guy we pay to bring our groceries every week, just made his delivery yesterday so it's full of fresh produce.

'Food?' I snort. 'Yeah, we eat food just like humans do. We just need a little extra for our demon sides.'

For the first time, I see her twitch and I know she's suppressing a shudder. She *is* scared, I realize. She's just better at hiding it than most humans I've come across.

She closes the fridge and turns away, looking out the bi-fold doors to the patio that leads to the lush, green lawn and then to the forest beyond. She's back to giving me no inkling of her emotions.

What would it take to make that wall she's hiding behind crumble I wonder … Maybe I should show her my other form. That'd probably do it! Hiding a grin, I open the fridge she just closed.

'Hungry?'

She nods, not looking at me still, and I frown. Why doesn't she …

Then I roll my eyes. I know why. I'll bet she got told that we need eye contact to exert our power over her kind. I almost laugh out loud. *Humans.* They'll believe anything.

'Silly, silly girl,' I mutter to myself as she wanders aimlessly around the room. 'Want some cereal?' I ask louder.

'Ok.'

She abruptly sits down at the breakfast bar, looking at me expectantly and I frown. What is this broad's deal?

But I grab the carton of milk from the door of the fridge and get a bowl and a spoon out. I rummage around in the pantry for my cereal, and I set everything out in front of me. But as I open the box, she stands.

'I can do that,' she says, giving a flinch when I look over my shoulder at her.

'It's no problem.'

'No. Of course,' she acquiesces, but her body remains tense.

With another roll of my eyes, I grab everything and put it down hard in front of her.

'Think I'm going to poison you, or something?' I ask, a little insulted that she'd think I'd try to off her in such a dumb way. I'm a fucking incubus. I could literally kill her a thousand much cooler ways than poison.

But as she looks at me, I see a little surprise in her expression. That wasn't what she was afraid of at all.

She looks away as I stare down at her, filling the bowl. I watch as she puts the spoon next to it, sitting down as she drenches the cereal in milk. As soon as there's enough to just cover the flakes, she picks up the spoon and begins to eat quickly, not looking up from her food.

It's a minute or two before she does glance up and finds me still watching her. Instead of looking at all self-conscious as I'd expect, though, she tilts her head to the side a little as she swallows what's in her mouth.

'I don't like it when it gets soggy.'

Sure. Because that explains everything.

She takes another spoonful immediately, wiping her chin with the back of her hand when a drop of milk trickles down from her mouth.

I nod slowly. 'Right. Look, I have to go ... see to some things. Don't leave the house. Understand?'

She nods with her mouth full and gives me an absent finger wave as she gets back to her breakfast and continues to stuff her face.

I back away from her slowly, trying to make out what about her is so *off*. Why does she interest me? Maybe it's because she's different. Yeah, that must be it, I decide. She's ... *interesting*. The contracted girls aren't like this one. They seem more like *normal* humans. This one not so much. That's all it is.

I step into Vic's study and I'm glad to find him already at his desk. Though I see as I catch sight of the clock on the wall behind him that it's almost eleven; later than I thought. I glance out into the hall before I shut the door quietly, making sure none of the others are lurking.

'We need to talk about Sie,' I say, not beating around the bush.

He looks up and leans back, his chair creaking. 'What is it?'

'He's on the edge,' I say. 'I went to see him last night before he and Paris headed out and Monique was blissed out in his bed.'

'Good. At least he's feeding.'

'Not good,' I tell him. 'He looked like shit. Like he hadn't had anywhere near enough. When I spoke to him, he played it off like he was fine, but ...' I run a hand through my short hair, 'he didn't sound like himself.'

'What's your medical opinion?'

I sit down hard, but when I talk, I practically whisper. 'I think that if he's not getting enough food, it won't be long before he loses it and, when he does finally explode, he'll take this whole MC down with him.'

Vic's eyes are steady as he watches me; for what, I can't say. Melodramatics, maybe?

Then he sighs. 'What can we do?'

I raise my hands up in front of me. 'I don't know. Vitamins? Supplements? New on-call girls? Maybe I take a trip to the fae markets to see if they have anything.'

'Fuck. That.' Vic growls. 'I'd rather cut off my left nut than go begging those sly pricks for help.'

I stand up. 'We can always pay.'

'They'll only want the things we least want to give,' Vic sneers and I shrug.

He's not wrong. Those fae assholes want all the things. First-borns of the humans; their very souls if they can get 'em. But with supes it's usually a favor. You won't know what they'll demand, but it'll be at a time and place of their choosing and you have to pay it. No matter what.

'I'll look into options,' I say.

Vic gives me a nod. 'Where's the girl?'

'Eating breakfast in the kitchen.'

'Alone?'

I shrug. 'Where's she gonna go? As soon as she sets foot outside, we'll know. Besides, we're at least four hours' walk from civilization.'

Vic lets out a sound of disgust and goes back to his laptop. Guess I'm dismissed.

I return to the kitchen, half-expecting her to be gone,

but she's still there and it looks like she's on her second or even third bowl of cereal too.

Is this bitch going to eat the whole damn box of my favorite cereal?

I checked the pantry earlier. There aren't any more, only some wheat bran shit. Stan isn't bringing more of the *good* cereal for six whole days. My eyes narrow at Jane before I see that she's not alone. Carrie is lurking in the doorway that leads to their room in the basement.

Ok, that sounds bad, but, seriously, they've got their own little apartment down there with skylights and a nice bathroom and everything. It's not like we keep them in a dungeon or something.

When Carrie sees me, she blinks, her eyes widening just a little as she comes closer. I know what she wants, what they always want, and I can smell her arousal from all the way on the other side of the kitchen.

'Do you need me?' she asks breathily.

I shake my head. 'Sorry, sugarplum, I don't have time right now. Maybe later, hmm?'

She pouts at me and glances at Jane. 'New girl?'

I shake my head. 'Not exactly.'

Carrie leaves as silently as she arrived, floating away like a feather on the breeze.

'Are you done?' *Eating all my cereal, you fucking monster?*

She nods, thank fuck, and I put the box away, high in the pantry and behind the nasty cereal. This bitch is not getting any more of the good stuff if I can help it!

I don't speak to her again, leaving her in the kitchen alone now that I've protected the last of my multigrain goodness as I go to the library to begin researching what we can do to help Sie with his issue before he goes starving-incubus-psycho (technical term) on us all.

CHAPTER
SEVEN
JANE

As soon as Theo and his 'sugarplum' – who I'm pretty sure was the same blond girl from the bar the other day – are both gone, I'm on my feet and striding to the doors at the back of the kitchen that lead out into the massive, manicured lawn that sits at the edge of what, even in the daytime, looks to be a deep, dark forest of twisted trees and probably secret pools where you aren't allowed to touch the water on pain of death and shit like that.

Seriously?

Like why couldn't they live in a normal rancher or even a duplex? No, it had to be an actual *mansion* with what I can only assume is geometric parquet flooring from the Roaring Twenties and original oak paneling from the days of Yore.

Yeah, I know enough to know it's old, but not much else.

Fucking supes though.

I don't try the door. Not yet. I need to explore the house first, maybe learn what I can from 'Sugarplum' and her other human-food buddies to maximize my chances of escape.

I leave the room, going down a wide hall with more pretty flooring and what must be an actual crystal chandelier hanging down from a twenty-foot molded ceiling.

I thought these guys were just an MC like their human counterparts seem to be – street thugs who do a ton of shady shit that's about as far from my daily life as you can get – but I'm getting the feeling they might be a little *more* than Shar led me to believe.

The front door opens, and a massive guy walks into the foyer I'm standing right in the middle of. As soon as I see him, I turn tail and run back into the kitchen before he notices me.

I'm not scared! It's just, I recognized that one. That's Sie. I was in his room and, after the things he said to me last night, and that girl half-comatose on his bed, I think I'm well within my rights to not want to be near him *at all*.

Back in the kitchen, I look around as I hear heavy footsteps coming down the hall behind me. There's nowhere to hide.

My eyes dart around and settle on the alcove 'Sugarplum' disappeared through. I lunge for it, finding a door that's open. I close it quietly behind me and find a set of stairs going down.

This must be where they keep the human foodstuffs, I think as I descend slowly, listening intently for the door above to open.

But it doesn't.

Maybe he didn't see me.

I make my way down to a small and minimalist, but comfortable-looking living room. Natural light comes through skylights, but the glow is muted, and the glass is frosted so I can't see where they come out upstairs.

There's a small kitchenette which, although not as grand as the main one upstairs, has the usual necessities plus a fancy coffeemaker I'd have no idea how to even turn on.

There are two doors that lead off the main area and they're both open, so I peek into one and find three matching twin beds in a row that reminds me of Goldilocks and the Three Bears, and I wonder if one's hard, one's soft and the other's just right.

Two are occupied by girls that don't look like Sugarplum; the brunette I saw in Sie's bed last night and a redhead. Maybe it *is* like Goldilocks but it's girls and their looks instead of mattress hardness.

Creepy.

Realizing that I'm watching people sleep and that's really creepy too, (I hope these assholes aren't rubbing off on me) I go to the next door. It's a bathroom, not as large as the one upstairs that I used this morning, but it has a nice-sized tub and a shower. There are makeup brushes and beauty products all over the surfaces, colorful eye palettes by the mirror and—

'Who the fuck are you?'

I jump a little and see the reflection of the redhead behind me, thankful she didn't wake up to me ogling her while she slept.

'Hi, I'm Jane,' I say as I turn around.

She nods. 'What's up?'

She comes into the bathroom and stands in front of me.

'Do you mind?' she says.

'Sorry, no! Of course...,' I stutter as I leave her to it.

The door closes behind me and I look around, searching

for another door out, but there isn't one. That's gotta be a building code violation, right? Doesn't there need to be another exit for like safety?

These are supes, I remind myself. If there was a fire or something, it would be their people who showed up, and they sure as hell wouldn't give a shit about a few humans trapped in the basement.

The bathroom door opens, and the woman steps out into the living room, her red hair now in a messy ponytail. She's dressed in some booty shorts and a tank top, and her eyes are smudged with yesterday's makeup.

She barely glances at me, going directly to the coffeemaker and pushing a button. She grabs a couple mugs from the cabinet and rifles through a drawer for a spoon as I hear the machine start grinding the beans. Only then does she look up at me.

'Put your stuff in the bedroom,' she says. 'You're new so they'll probably call for you this afternoon. A bed'll be delivered sometime this week. It usually is. Until then, you can take the couch when you're not with one of the Iron I's.'

I'm confused, but I don't have time to say anything before she starts speaking again, looking me over with what I've come to realize from my time at the diner is a critical eye.

'Too many clothes,' she mutters. 'They won't like that either.'

It takes me a minute to realize that she thinks I'm contracted.

'Oh!' I say. 'No, I'm not ...'

She glances at me again and looks me over even more thoroughly.

'You're not one of us?' she asks.

I shake my head and she looks like she wants to ask the question, but she doesn't.

'What's the deal with you?'

I jump and turn around to find Sugarplum sitting on the couch just behind me. Where did she come from?

'I'm just staying here,' I say.

She snorts. 'Humans don't just stay here unless they've signed the papers. Not even the human members of the MC get to bunk in the *House of Vicious*.'

'House of Vicious?' I ask.

She snorts. 'That's what 'Vic' stands for. Vicious.'

At my blank look, she looks at the girl making the coffee and raises a brow.

'You know. The Iron I President.' She puts her feet up on the coffee table. 'It's not really his name, I heard. It's sorta a family thing. His dad is a big deal with the supes or something.' She looks me over like the other girl did. 'What's your name?'

'Jane,' I say.

'I'm Carrie,' Sugarplum says, slowly plaiting her long blond hair into a single braid. She gestures to the other girl. 'That's Julie.'

Carrie's wearing a short, shift dress like the one Theo gave me and, as she stands up and it rises, I see that she's not wearing anything under it. She doesn't say anything about knowing me from the other day when I went to the bar to hire the Iron I's, but then she was indisposed, I guess, and I don't think she ever looked my way actually.

'Sorry if I'm not supposed to be down here,' I say. 'I was trying to get away from the big one.'

'Sie,' both women say together, glancing at the room behind me where the third one's still sleeping.

'How is Monique?' Carrie asks her friend.

The redhead shrugs. 'She made her way back here sometime early this morning. She's ok. Groggy, but no bruises.'

'That's a plus, I guess,' Carrie says. 'Weird that he called for Monique though.'

'You think so? Really? First, Theo and then Sie within a few hours?'

Carrie looks at me and must see whatever it is that Julie's talking about because she snorts, a look passing between her and her friend. 'Guess not.'

'What do you mean?' I ask, trying to figure it out in case it's important.

'Don't worry about it,' Carrie mutters with a shake of her head.

Julie brings her a cup of coffee that she accepts with a nod of thanks.

'You want one?'

I shake my head, still trying to figure out what I have to do with Sie's choice of female company. 'No, thanks. I was actually gonna take a look around.'

'Have fun,' Julie says, taking her coffee and going back to the bedroom.

Carrie sits back down on the couch. 'I'm guessing you already know to be careful of Sie.'

I nod.

'Don't turn your back on the shaggy-haired one either. That's Korban.' She starts messing with her phone, sighs, and makes eye contact again. 'Look, I don't know how well you know these guys, but I should probably tell you, human code and all, don't trust any of 'em. They might need us to stay alive, but we're just the food. Remember that. They don't like us.'

My forehead creases at her words. 'Why not?'

She shrugs. 'I don't know, and I don't really give a shit. I'm under contract so it doesn't matter anyway.'

'So, like, you can't leave?'

'Nope, but most of the girls who come here don't have anywhere else to go anyway, so it works out. They make it worth our while. I'll have fifty grand in my pocket when my three years are up.'

I know what she's talking about, I suppose. I have nowhere to go either. I could easily be one of these girls ... if it wasn't for, you know, the way I am.

A funny little pang hits me in the chest. It's not that I wish I was one of the contracted girls, but it would be nice to have the easy friendship that these two at least seem to enjoy with each other. Sometimes it's hard being all alone, always looking in at the party that everyone else seems to instinctively know all the rules to and knowing I don't understand the first thing about how to join it.

Silence pervades the space. Carrie's attention is now fully on her phone and coffee, and I feel like I'm intruding.

My chatting skills aren't the best and, after obligatory subjects like the weather, conversations easily fizzle out if the other person isn't making the effort. Plus, I get bored.

'Well, thanks,' I say, 'I better ... mosey on.'

Mosey on? Ugh.

I turn and head up the stairs, thankful to escape what's quickly turning the kind of awkward I don't know how to deal with. I peek out into the kitchen and find it nice and empty. I don't know what I'd do if I had to go back down there.

I find the foyer and the pretty chandelier and start snooping around the front of the house. The first door I find leads into a study with shelves of old, leatherbound books that look like they're purely decorative behind an imposing and messy desk that clearly isn't. The haphazard papers on said desk are written in a language that isn't English and it doesn't take me long to designate the room as relatively uninteresting.

I find a black pool table in the next room with a black leather couch, massive flat screen TV on the wall, and a shit ton of different gaming consoles.

I used to love video games as a kid and I decide I like it in here, but as I look at them more closely, I realize it's been a long time since I played. I don't recognize any of them. I doubt I'm any good these days anyway.

I am good at pool though. Very good. You wouldn't know it and that's my secret weapon. When times are hard, I've been known to hustle a game or two. No one ever expects the girl who just tripped over her own feet to kick their ass, but, at the end of the day, it's just geometry.

I like this room better, but I don't stay. I'm on a quest to get out of this place, after all, not to make myself comfy.

Walking across the other side of the foyer, a long hallway leads to the other end of the house. More steps take me to—

Holy shit! It's a gigantic, motherfucking pool!

Like, there's just a pool in the middle of the house and set into the bottom are the skylights I could see from the basement.

I look around me. Same as in the kitchen, one whole side of the room seems able to open completely onto another manicured lawn with yet more forest beyond.

'Are we literally in the middle of a State Park?' I mutter.

There's no one here, so I dip my bare toe in the water. It's heated, of course, and feels stupidly, fucking divine.

'Pretty much.'

I stifle a shriek and whip around, finding one of the

other incubi, luckily not Korban or Sie.

I recognize him instantly. 'You're the bartender from the other day.'

'Paris.' He smirks.

'Paris,' I say quietly, and he stares at me for a minute in absolute silence.

I'm not sure what his problem is so I stare right back *at the plant behind him.*

He doesn't move and I give him a noncommittal, half smile as I walk around the pool away from him.

Is he broken? Supes are so weird and it's me saying that so ...

I hear him chuckle low as I make my escape.

'You're welcome by the way,' he calls.

I turn back.

'For what?' I say a little too aggressively, my voice echoing around the pool, making me flinch.

'For saving your ass last night.'

I'm taken aback, but I'm obligated. 'Thanks for bringing me here ... I guess.'

'Well, if we hadn't stopped those guys, you'd probably be dead right now.'

That's fair.

'Thanks,' I say softly, but I do mean it this time.

'Don't mention it,' he says.

'But you mentioned it,' I say with a frown.

It doesn't look like he heard me as he walks across the pool room away from me, out another door I hadn't even noticed.

This place is a fucking maze.

I walk through yet another door off the pool and find a gym complete with mirrors everywhere, mats, punching bags, cardio equipment, and some kind of combat circle. This is their space. I can tell that right off as I back out slowly, the stench of sweat hanging in the air making me cringe, but, at the same time, it's weirdly soothing.

I start from the front door again, right underneath the chandelier and decide to take a look at the next floor. I climb the main stairs. They're carpeted in red over the marble. I feel so out of place here. Even without my demonic roommates, I'd still feel the need to leave asap.

At the top, there's a mammoth landing and a wide hall that leads to the left and the right. I take the left. I can remember this from last night. There are two wings. Are they called wings? I have no idea, but that's what I'm going to call them.

At the end of the left wing is Theo's room where I spent the night, which means that this – I walk past a closed door – *this* is Sie's room.

Just as I pass it, the damned thing opens and, before I know what's happening, a hand pulls me inside.

∼

Sie

I SLAM her up against the wall a little harder than I intended, and she lets out a small cry. Not much more than a whimper really.

My first impulse is to throw her on the bed and fuck her, feed from her now while I can ... just because she's here. But I pull the darkness back, not giving into its desires.

I wonder if she's already getting lulled just by my close proximity, but she doesn't seem like she is. Her head is turned to the side. She isn't looking at me. She doesn't need to be for me to get inside her head, but it amuses me that she thinks that makes any difference at all.

'Get. The. Fuck. Off. Me,' she says quietly, her voice like steel.

She's terrified, but I only know that because I can feel her body shaking. Her fear doesn't come across in her tone and it's not on her face.

'What the fuck are you still doing here?' I growl, wondering what Vic is thinking.

She should be gone by now. I'm starting to panic with her in the house. She can't stay here while I can't do anything with her ... unless ... maybe she's under contract.

I pull her away from the wall and look down at her. She doesn't answer and still won't meet my eyes.

'Look at me,' I say and her jaw sets as she slowly lifts her eyes from the floor. They travel up my chest and land on the tattoo that's poking out of my shirt near my collarbone.

'My face,' I say, gripping her tighter.

She winces and slowly lifts her head the remaining inches. The eyes that look up at me are like a doe's. She's trying so hard to pretend she isn't prey.

Cute.

But she is.

'Have you signed a contract?' I say like I'm asking her how her day was.

'No,' she grinds out. 'I'm not yours, so get your damn hands off me.'

Fuck! Her choice of words. *You might not be mine yet, little human, but you will be.*

I pull her flush against me before I realize what I'm doing. I can't help it, her body fitting so nicely with mine even though she's tiny. She goes even more rigid and there's a very specific part of my anatomy that, surprisingly, starts going rigid as well. It's been so long since it just *worked right.*

'Why you?' I wonder aloud.

'I don't want this,' she says, trying to pull away. 'Whatever tricks you play with my mind with your supey mojo ...'

Supey mojo? I almost smile. She's funny.

'...I don't want this. I didn't want it last night and I don't want it now, so unless you want me to start screaming this fucking place down, let me go.'

I do because she *is* out of bounds and right now all I'm doing is torturing myself. I'm not so far gone that I'll make her do anything against her will. At least I hope I'm not. But I know it won't be long before I am. She's not safe here.

'Get out,' I say.

She takes a step back, but that's all. Even though she could escape me, she doesn't, and I'm a hair's breadth away from losing control. I need her out of my sight. On a whim, I let her see the real me, the demon behind the human facade. The scars are the first to appear, then the horns grow out of my skull. My muscles become even more defined as my skin turns from thin and human to the thick, greyish sandpaper hide of an incubus in his prime. My long tail flicks out behind me.

Her eyes widen as she takes in the changes happening so quickly before her. Still, she doesn't run. She's staring at my face, but not in the abhorrence that I've come to expect. That in itself gives me pause. Her hand comes up and a finger touches my bicep innocuously. There's nothing seductive about it. *At all.* And yet I ache. For the first time in months, my dick is hard at the right time and it's for a girl I can't have.

Her whole hand is stroking my arm now. Where I find the will not to throw her on the bed and rut her senseless, I'll never know. I breathe out slowly and I step towards her again. She's frozen, her face blank, but she's still stroking me.

I lean close, whispering in her ear, 'If you don't leave right now, I'm going to lull you and then fuck you on that bed over there. I'm going to feed from you, bliss you out of your mind and leave you there like I did that girl you found here last night. And then I'll tell the other Iron I's. Vic will make you sign the contract and then you'll be ours to do what we like with.'

My words get through to her. I hear her blood pumping faster, her heart rate increasing sharply at my threats. Her mouth opens but no sound comes out.

I force myself to put some distance between us. 'Get. Out.'

The spell is broken. She turns and runs, knocking into the door jamb hard as she scrambles out of my room. I hear the creaks of her racing down the hall and Theo's door slams a moment later.

I catch my monstrous reflection in the mirror. *Fuck.* I look worse than I thought. Why didn't she scream? Why did I have to *make* her run?

Maybe I was using my power on her a little. It's hard to tell these days to be honest.

I make the demon recede as I watch.

My phone vibrates and I draw it out of my pocket. It's Vic.

I answer it.

'We need to talk.'

I don't say anything, walking into the corridor as I end the call and glancing at Theo's room. There's a two-inch thick oak door between me and the girl, but it might as well be an ocean. Let's hope for the MC's sake that it stays that way.

CHAPTER
EIGHT
JANE

I slam the door behind me, making the wall shake. I sit on the bed and put my head in my hands and then I stand up again a moment later, pacing around the room. My mind is in overdrive, everything all in a jumble. I keep going through everything that just happened over and over and over from the moment he pulled me into his room; how he touched me, the things he said, the things I *saw*. There's a rational part of my brain that's telling me to calm down. But I can barely hear it above the roar of everything else.

I sit down on the bed again, and then stand straight back up. I'm too wired. Upset. I realize that my cheeks are wet. I need to go somewhere where I can be alone for a while, and no one will find me. There's nowhere to hide in this room, but the bathroom has a lock on the inside. I go in and push the button in the center of the handle after I close myself in, sinking to the floor by the door and staring at nothing.

I don't know how long I stay like that, but my legs are cramping and I'm uncomfortable. I know water will help, so I get rid of my clothes and turn on the shower. I step under the hot spray, sitting down on the tiles and focusing on the water hitting my shoulders, streaming down my body, dripping off the end of my nose as I stare at the dark tiles beneath me.

I start trying to detangle the mess in my head. Sie. I shouldn't have even gone near his room. He's so big, so mean, so threatening, so *intense*. I'm rattled. I should be terrified of him. Maybe I am. But there was something ... I put my head in my hands, my mind going in circles until it exhausts itself. I don't move and it's a long time before I stand up and turn off the water.

The bathroom's really steamy and I grab one of the towels and wrap myself in it. I don't want to leave my sanctuary, so I sit on the closed toilet seat. I feel myself swaying. I've probably been rocking just a little bit this whole time because it makes me feel better.

My head throbs, my ribs ache, and my shoulder ... I look down and find a fresh bruise. I remember hitting something while I was trying to get away.

I hear Theo's bedroom door open, and I stand up, trying to compose myself. My time is up, and no one needs to know about this.

Theo calls my name and I take a deep breath as I open the door, making sure the towel is secure. The coldness of the air outside the bathroom makes me shiver. The lights are on in the room. It's dark out.

How long was I in there?

The clock by the nightstand says eight-thirty. It's been hours.

Theo's talking and I haven't been listening to a word he's been saying. I look at him slowly blinking away the grogginess.

'Did you hear me?' he asks.

He looks annoyed.

'No,' I say. 'Sorry.'

'Where were you? I've been looking for you. You can't just disappear like that when the security system is down.'

'Well, I didn't know it was down.' I glance back down at my hands. 'I was just in the bathroom.'

'For six hours?' He doesn't believe me.

'I fell asleep in the tub,' I lie and his eyes narrow.

'Fine,' he says. 'Get dressed. Vic wants to see you.'

I nod and he leaves the room. I sink down on the bed when I'm alone again. All I want to do is curl up and go to sleep. I feel exhausted.

I go over what happened again with a clearer head. Did I give Sie the wrong impression somehow? I look down at myself. I was dressed like a contracted girl.

Is this my fault? Maybe he thought I was one of them. But, no, he asked me if I was contracted. I told him I wasn't.

An angry part of me pipes up. *No matter what he thought, it didn't give him the right to pull you into his room, touch you up, and threaten you!*

But I touched him too. His skin when he changed was so ... impossible not to reach out and caress. I'm like that with things I like the look of ... I get bitten, pricked, and stung a lot.

I dry myself off slowly, remembering the things he said to me about keeping me here. I shudder. Is that what they're planning to do to me? Use their power on me? Turn me into one of their possessions? Make me sign a contract for three years?

Would it be so bad? I think about that seriously. How would it work considering that my experience of sex can be summed up in one shitty night with some random guy I didn't know because I never *want* anyone? At least ... I never did previously.

Before I walked into that bar, I'd kind of come to the conclusion that all that stuff wasn't for me; that the only significant romance I was ever going to have in my life was with my vibrator. After all, I'll never be disappointed with it unless I forget to charge the damn thing.

Feeling a little better, I get dressed again, putting on the clothes I had on before. I find a comb in a drawer, which I use to detangle my hair. I put it up in a wet bun on top of my head.

My hands are still shuddering, and I shake them out, trying to get rid of the extra stress.

When the door opens again, Theo's back in the doorway.

'Come on,' he says like he's taking me to my death.

What does Vic want with me? Maybe he's decided to give me my orc stone back and let me leave town.

'I know where the study is. I can get there by myself,' I mutter.

He shrugs. 'Vic told me to bring you, so that's what I'm going to do.'

'You do everything he tells you?' I can't help but goad.

He snorts but doesn't rise to my bait.

I shuffle along behind him slowly, glancing at Sie's closed door with trepidation as I skirt around it. Thankfully, it doesn't open again, and we go down the windy staircase.

Theo takes me directly into the study that I peeked into earlier, but now Vic is sitting in there behind the desk. His gaze finds me briefly and then his attention is back on his laptop, his fingers tapping away on the keys. He's got glasses on, and an errant thought runs through my head. I didn't know incubi ever needed glasses. Maybe they don't in their demon forms.

Without warning, my mind gives me a picture of Sie when he changed in front of me, his black horns coming up from his head winding just a little, smooth and black, his piercing eyes that stared practically into my soul, his skin that felt so warm and silky but thick and calloused in places. The tattoos had disappeared, and, in their places, he had scars I remember, crisscrossed and jagged all over his neck and chest and a single long one across his cheek from his ear to the side of his mouth.

'Sit,' Vic commands as if I'm already their pet, and I'm brought back into what's happening here and now, a little annoyed. I do as he says though because I don't have it in me to fight him after everything else today.

The leader of the Iron I's looks a little ... surprised maybe? .... when I take a seat in front of him without argument. His eyes narrow a little bit. I don't think it's in anger, but right now I'm definitely not going to be able to figure out his or anyone else's nuances of emotion, so I just stare at the wall behind him, and I watch from my periphery.

He frowns and glances past me with a look at Theo, I guess.

'I don't know,' Theo says.

Vic gets up and they stand together at the edge of the room, talking behind me in hushed whispers. I can still hear most of what they're saying, but I can't seem to find it in me to care. I just want to go to sleep.

'The hell's wrong with her?' Vic whispers.

'How the fuck should I know? I left her in the kitchen, and she vanished for five hours. Finally found her in my room.'

Vic growls. 'How did she disappear when we have more than one security system keeping tabs on her?'

'Paris had some trouble during the tech upgrade and the perimeter magick is still on the fritz. It's messing with the other spells we have in place.'

'Is it back up now?'

Theo nods. 'It's all online as of ten minutes ago.'

'Where was she while all of this was happening?'

'She says she was in the bathroom.'

They both stop and look at me. I ignore them.

'Where was Korban?' Vic asks finally.

'You know him when he's got a fight. He's been in the gym most of that time.'

'And Sie?'

'He hasn't left his room.'

At the mention of Sie, my arms curl around myself. There are too many feelings and they're too intense for me to understand today. It's going to take me a long time to figure out everything that happened and everything I felt and although I'm scared, I don't think it's of *him*. It's of *my reaction* to him. Almost all of these men... demons ... have touched me now and I haven't shied away from their hands like I do everyone else.

I wipe my own hands over my eyes. I don't know what to think and I sure as hell don't know what to say.

Vic comes back to his desk and sits down.

'Where were you?' he asks me sharply.

'In the bathroom,' I say.

'For four hours?'

'Five hours,' I correct him with a mutter. 'I fell asleep in the bath.'

I repeat the lie easily, but Vic isn't fooled.

'Where were you really?'

I don't answer him. I'm sure as hell not going to tell him that I had a run in with his buddy and had to spend hours getting over it. That's fucking ridiculous.

So my jaw sets mulishly, and I just stare at the books on the shelves behind him.

'Get Sie in here,' he orders Theo, but his eyes don't leave me.

He's looking for my reaction, I realize, so I don't give him one. I just sit in front of him and it's not until a few minutes later, when I hear footsteps coming to the door, that I'm out of my seat without even realizing it and backing away to the far wall.

As Sie enters the study, he doesn't see me at first, giving Vic a small incline of his head.

'Time for the fight?' he asks.

'Not quite yet,' Vic says, glancing at me.

When Sie follows his eyes, his fists close at his sides, and I look away from him, my arms hugging my middle tighter.

'She can't fucking stay here,' he snarls, spitting the words at me.

I'm tired and I can't hide everything when I'm tired. Before I know it, I'm backed into the corner trying to make myself small on the floor, not looking at any of them. I'm trying not to rock, but I'm not sure how successfully.

'Get out,' says Vic.

At first, I hope he's talking to me, but the massive presence that was Sie disappears instead.

There's a shadow over me and I glance up to see Vic. Dread courses through me. What's he going to do?

'Get up,' he says.

I don't obey, just curl my knees closer into myself. I

know he and Theo share another look, and the silence is palpable. I wish they'd all just leave me alone.

'Get her back in the chair,' Vic says, going to sit behind his desk again.

Theo picks me up and I don't fight him. He sits me where I was before. I'm still watching the floor.

'Look at me,' says Vic.

Why do all these guys keep telling me to do that like I'm going to just give them power over me? I'm not stupid! I grit my teeth and stare at the books behind his head again.

'No, not fucking behind me,' he commands. 'At my face.'

I shake my head.

'If I wanted to use my power on you, I don't need your eyes to do it,' he says. 'That's a human myth.'

My eyes focus on his face, snapping me out of my haze, and I gape at him. 'Is that true?'

'Yes,' Theo says from behind me. 'Some incubus started it to fuck with you.'

'Me?'

'Humans,' he clarifies.

'I don't give a shit who started it,' Vic says. 'When I tell you to look at me, fucking look at me. Now, what did he *do*?'

He means Sie.

'Nothing,' I say too quickly.

He stands up and leans over the desk, but I meet his eyes this time. I don't say a word.

'It doesn't actually matter what he did,' Theo mutters. 'What matters is what she will say once she leaves.'

'I won't say anything,' I vow. 'There's nothing *to* say.'

Vic ignores me. 'Take her back to your room.' He looks at his watch. 'The fight starts at ten. Get her some food, make sure she's settled, and then join us at the warehouse.

Maddox is supposed to be there tonight to watch Callaghan and Kor, so we all need to be there for this one.'

Theo nods and goes to pick me up. I get out of the chair with a scowl in his general direction, wondering who Maddox is and what these guys are into besides kidnapping and imprisoning humans.

'I can walk,' I say, and he throws up his hands in supplication with a dumb little smile on his face.

He takes me back upstairs in silence and, again, I skirt past Sie's room.

'*Something* happened,' Theo insists. 'I know you're not telling the truth and so does Vic.'

I shake my head, saying nothing.

'Sie isn't himself,' Theo continues. 'If he's done something, I need to know what.'

We enter his room, and he shuts the door, closing us in.

I sit on the bed, hoping he's not about to begin another inquisition.

'I'm tired,' I say. My stomach rumbles.

'And hungry,' he observes. 'Stay here. I'll be back.'

He leaves me to myself, and the silence is just what I need. Although I'm hungry, I sink down into the bed, cover myself with the blanket, and close my eyes.

I'll be stronger tomorrow, I promise myself. I won't let Sie do what he did today ever again. I just hope it's not too late. I don't like everyone knowing what happens when I can't mask anymore. I've learned to hide it because I don't like the way people look at me; like I'm a freak. I don't like the way they talk to me; like I'm dumb. I don't like the way they treat me; like I'm less than them. But I guess the supes are already going to since I'm human and all, so maybe nothing will change if they find out. Theo and Vic suspect something, though, and I don't know why that upsets me. But it does.

∼

Vic

I watch Theo escort her out and my mouth morphs into a thin line. I call Sie.

'Get the fuck back in here,' I growl into the phone and end the call without waiting for his answer. He comes striding in a minute later, looking like he just doesn't give a shit about anything. Maybe he doesn't anymore.

'What did you do to that girl?'

My fist comes down hard on the desk to punctuate my question. The asshole doesn't even flinch.

Fuck it.

I let my power out and I watch him tense, then grimace.

'Sit the hell down.'

He sits, folding himself into the chair that looks too small for him.

'I'm going to ask you again,' I say. 'What did you do to the *uncontracted human female* that has been in our house for less than 24 hours?'

'She shouldn't be here,' he snarls low. 'You told me she would be gone by today.' He gestures at the door. 'Why the fuck haven't you thrown her out on her ass?'

'She's here because I want her here. It's my decision, Sie, not yours! You want to be in charge? You know what to do!'

Sie scoffs. 'I don't and if you want her here, you deal with the consequences of having a sheep amongst the wolves.'

'Well, I sure as fuck can't let her go now, can I?' I mutter, sitting back down in my seat hard. 'We have the contracted girls so that we aren't tempted to feed off humans that haven't consented. That's the way it is now. You don't like it? You can thank the fae. I'm just trying to stick to the laws they actually care about.' I rub my temples. 'She'll leave here and go straight to those supe cops she spoke to in the diner with stories of assaults taking place in this house by members of the Iron I's. Those assholes have been just waiting for a reason. They'll come down on us faster than you can say 'Twenty girls found dead in club'. Fuck,' I mutter, throwing my pen down on the desk.

'I'll fix it,' Sie says, almost looking contrite.

'You can't fucking fix it! You saw her. The damage is done. There is no way she's gonna leave this house and not take us down.'

Sie puts his head in his hands. 'I didn't mean...'

'I know,' I murmur. 'Fuck. I know. If it hadn't been you, it would have been Korban. At least we aren't looking for a place to stash her body tonight.'

'What are you going to do?' Sie asks.

'The only thing I can do now. Get her under contract.'

Sie looks surprised. 'I don't think she's the type.'

I let out a mirthless chuckle. 'Oh, I know she's not the type, but it's either that or kill her and that's just a fucking waste. Lucky for you there's a reason besides who my father is that I'm the president of this MC. I'll speak to Paris later tonight and have him contact his guy,' I say. 'By tomorrow, I'll have a file on her. And, who knows? Maybe having a new girl will help you.'

Sie doesn't give anything away and I roll my eyes. 'I know how close you are. You're probably a couple weeks away from losing yourself. Maybe this girl will take the edge off until we can figure something out.'

Sie stands up. 'If she doesn't help ... if I get worse, I want you to do it.'

I nod. 'Don't worry. It'll be me,' I say grimly.

The thought of shooting my first lieutenant and best friend in the head after he's gone insane makes my stomach roil. 'We've been through a lot together, huh?'

'Yeah.'

I come around the desk. There's not much difference between us in height. He's just broad as fuck. We hug each other tight, and I hope that the interest that I've seen Sie give this girl means something.

'It's different with her,' he mutters as if he can read my thoughts.

'Good,' I say, 'but wait until she's under contract before you go near her again.'

Sie's lips fold into a thin line and I know he'll try his damndest not to go near her again at all.

He leaves my study without another word, and I sit back behind my desk with a sigh. I put on the glasses that Theo made me start wearing last year for screen work and I think about how I'm gonna get that weird human girl to sign a contract, giving her body to the Iron I's for three years. Maybe the money will sway her, but I don't think it will. And there are other things to consider too. There's no way she was in the bathroom for however many hours today. I mean Theo will check the feed from the camera in his room, so I'll know for sure, but there's something about her that's *off* anyway. I feel like she's hiding something big. We need to know what it is in case it blows up in our faces.

But once she's under contract, not much is going to matter. The rules are murky and if she reads the fine print, she'll know that she's basically signing all her rights as a human away. Neither the supe courts nor the human ones will touch a contract like that with a ten-foot pole. She becomes ours. Our plaything for three years.

I reach down and adjust myself. Ever since I saw her in the bar, I've wanted her. I just didn't think I'd get the chance, so I didn't seriously consider having her. But this time tomorrow, she'll be ours and I can't fucking wait.

I work for a while and when it's time, I suit up and grab my bike. It'll take an hour to get to the warehouse a couple towns over. Kor and the others probably left a while ago. Even Theo is probably gone by now even though I made him take care of the girl. I heard him in the kitchen making something for her to eat a while ago, but it's been quiet ever since then.

I start my bike up. For the first time in a while, things are looking up for Sie. If this girl can help him even a little, then I'm going to do everything I can to make sure she gets the chance to. I go slow until I get to the main street three miles down, and then I punch it, taking the long, straight roads as fast as I can and letting my full power out just because no one's here to know it for what it is. I never feel so relaxed and free as I do when I'm riding like this at night, the light isn't even on because my eyes can see. I let the demon in me out, stretching my neck and I go faster still, breathing everything in.

When I get to the first traffic light, the beginning of civilization, I switch on the headlight, and I put the demon back in the box. Life is good, I concede, but there's something in the back of my mind, a nagging feeling that everything's about to change and I don't like it. I don't know what or how. I just hope we can survive it.

CHAPTER NINE

PARIS

The mob's already wild and it's not even time for the main event yet. I crane my neck to see what's happening, but it's only some shifter supe getting his ass kicked by another one. Already bored, I scan the warehouse floor as I assess the numbers. It's massive, so it doesn't look that busy until closer to the ring itself. There, the crowd's about ten bodies deep and, counting the rest in the bleachers that are set out like an ancient amphitheater, I'd guess there's at least three-hundred people here. Decent turn-out. We'll make some good money tonight so long as Kor wins, which he shouldn't have a problem doing. He hates Callaghan and that'll make him fight extra dirty.

I can't fucking wait to watch that shifter fucker get his ass handed to him either.

I see a mix of shifters here tonight, a few rich-looking and very shady fae, and even one or two humans. Finding Sie in the bar that's been set up for us to view from, I get a beer and sit with him.

Kor isn't even here yet and he probably won't arrive until

the last second. He doesn't like being near this many people and I don't blame him, but I love the atmosphere. It makes me want to jump in the ring myself and throw some punches.

I glance down at my watch. Vic will get here soon too. He always makes an appearance well in advance. Thinks it looks bad on us if he misses anything. As I glance at the other supe leaders around the bar, I suppose he's probably right.

My gaze doesn't linger at any of the other tables though. I don't need to inadvertently issue some kind of challenge. Korban is meant to be the one fighting tonight, not me. I watch Sie while not making it obvious that that's what I'm doing.

He looks like hell. I heard Vic and him talking in the study this afternoon. I wasn't trying to listen, of course. It's not my business. But I got the gist.

'Looks like it's gonna be a good fight,' I comment.

Sie nods and gives a non-committal grunt, taking a long gulp of his beer.

'You ever think of getting back into it?' I ask him. I heard he used to fight in the ring once, but it was before the Iron I's and well before my time.

He gives a tiny shake of his head that I'd have missed if I'd blinked, and he doesn't say anything else.

'So you and the new girl, huh?' I side-eye him and watch his jaw tighten.

Oooh, what did he do?

'Nope,' he says, 'I can't stand that little human bitch.'

I give a short chuckle. 'My mistake.'

'Riding with her on your hog the other night give you a taste?' he prods, but I don't rise to the bait.

'Yep,' I say. 'Had that tight little ass rubbin' all over my lap the entire way back. I can't wait to take her for another test drive.'

'Well, you'll get your chance,' Sie mutters and my ears perk up.

'What?'

'Vic's going to lock her into a contract.'

'No fuckin' way! How's he gonna get her to sign?'

Sie shrugs. 'How does Vic do anything? I don't fucking know. I don't fucking care either. Don't want anything to do with her. She's trouble through and through.'

I smirk. 'I like a little trouble.'

Sie gives me an amused snort. 'Yeah, you do.'

Theo comes through the door and saunters across the warehouse floor to sit at our table.

'Vic with you?' I ask.

He shakes his head.

'Done babysitting for the night?'

'Shut the fuck up, Paris,' he says, but he's grinning. 'You're just jealous she's staying in my room. You wouldn't believe what's she's done in front of my cameras so far.'

Sie shakes his head. 'You're a sick fuck.'

He laughs, but his eyes are hard when they meet Sie's. 'At least I didn't assault the girl and almost put the whole MC in a shit ton of hot water. At least I'm not making Vic clean up my mess. *Again!*'

Sie slams his fist down on the table. 'Fuck you, Theo.'

He grunts as he stands and leaves the table, his chair toppling over. He makes his way to the edge of the crowd around the ring and melts into it.

The shifter supe is still getting his ass beat. Stupid fuck keeps getting back up, staggering around like a marionette on a string. Fight's already done. Dumb asshole needs to realize it.

'Why do you rile him up like that?' I ask Theo and he shrugs.

'I'm sick of his shit is all. He's Vic's lieutenant. Just because they've known each other a long time, he thinks he can do whatever the fuck he wants and there won't be consequences.'

'He's suffering,' I mutter from behind my bottle.

Theo scoffs at my words. 'We're demons. Maybe we're meant to suffer.'

I roll my eyes. 'Don't give me that theological bullshit. You're going to start sounding like a member of the Order and I don't think they let supes join.'

'Maybe they have a point.'

'Even if they do, we're going to have to deal with them sooner or later. It's been, what, almost ten years since the world found out about supes. The Order have to realize by now that we're not just going to go away.'

Theo looks nostalgic. 'Ten years. It was easier when they didn't know anything about us, that's for sure. Remember when we fucked around at bars, picking up chicks? We could feed from anyone, anywhere, anyhow as long as we cleaned up after ourselves. No one gave a shit.'

'It's probably for the best,' I say.

'Yeah, it probably is,' he grants.

'So what has she been doing in your room that you've caught on camera?' I ask, unable to resist.

Theo smirks a little. 'Besides practically pulling off her own arm trying to get out of the cuffs, not much actually,' he hedges. 'The only time she's really been in there is when she's sleeping and when she disappeared yesterday, she actually was in the bathroom for all of that time. I don't have cameras in there though. I do have *some* standards.'

Giving him a grin, I glance at my watch again. 'It's almost ten.'

Theo inclines his head, gesturing at the screen behind me.

I turn and see that Kor is already in the ring.

Huh.

I turn my chair around to watch and I check my phone. Usually he lets me know when he arrives, but there's nothing from him. I frown, but from what I can see of the ring, Korban looks normal. He's dressed in just some black shorts, letting everyone see his rippling muscles, the tats that cover his back and his chest. His knuckles are wrapped in gauze and as he rips off the bandages, underneath the skin is raw and bloody.

'He should have healed from his last fight. It was over two weeks ago,' I say quietly.

'He's been pounding the pads in the gym all day,' Theo says.

That's not like him. He usually relaxes in the sauna after a little pad work. He definitely doesn't tear up his hands like that. But I don't say anything out loud, instead watching him and Callaghan begin to circle each other. Callaghan's saying something as usual.

Smartass fuck.

I see Kor's eyes darken with rage for a second, but he gets himself under control so fast that no one in the crowd sees he's pissed off. I only do because I know him so well.

Their clash is sudden and brutal, fists flying, fingers gouging, legs kicking anywhere they can. This fight has no rules, but I'm not worried. Kor is an awesome fighter, and he rarely loses. After the first round though, I turn my chair back around. I know he's going to win, but tonight I don't like the journey of him getting there. No matter how much he loves the fight, he's been through a lot.

I know that every time an opponent lands a punch, he feels it deep. He hasn't told me everything that happened to him, but he's said enough, and that little human girl better watch her fucking back. Once she's contracted, she'll be a little safer. She'll be on the books and there'll be a record of her being in the house.

That's not to say it wouldn't be easy enough to hide a body and say that we didn't know anything about her if the authorities came snooping. They might suspect, but they wouldn't be able to prove anything. It makes me wonder why Vic didn't choose that route. Sure, contracting another human female to the Club isn't a big deal, but getting rid of a body would be a whole lot easier.

I hear the crowd cheer and glance back. Callaghan is on the floor, Kor standing over him, his eyes expressionless.

I feel a moment of pride for my best friend, my lover's victory. He truly is magnificent, and I'll be showing him just how proud I am of him later when we get back to the house and he needs me to sate his battle lust.

I'm just about to get up when I see Vic walk out of the crowd. He comes and sits down with us.

'You late?' I asked with a raised eyebrow.

'I got caught by Maddox on the way in. He wanted to talk about the missing shipments. That, and he heard one of our guys was found in a dumpster.' Vic's lips curl up into a small snarl. 'Good news travels fast. Bad news, faster.'

'What did you tell them?' Theo asks.

'That we have it handled in-house. He's invited us to his nearest club next week to discuss protecting the shipments though.'

I can't help my grin. I love *The Second Circle* and it's been awhile since we partied.

Vic gives me a warning look. 'We're going to *The Circle* for business, not pleasure.'

'For you,' I mutter, vowing that I'm going to party like it's 1999.

The club is perfect for Kor too. No humans, and it's by invitation only. Maddox, the leader of the only other incubi clan around here rarely lets outsiders enter his domain.

'Can't it be both?' I ask louder.

Vic looks me up and down. 'Not usually for you.'

I laugh sheepishly. That's fair. Last time I went out with the crew, I was drunk for three days straight and can't remember a thing.

'But at least if we're at *The Circle*, we can take a look around. We'll just need a distraction for Maddox.'

'I'm guessing you already have a plan for that.'

Vic nods. 'I just might.'

The crowd is going wild, and I look back at the screen. The fight's over. Korban, of course, is the winner. The referee has Kor's arm held up high, and Kor's just standing there in the middle of the ring. He doesn't look happy, but he doesn't look upset or angry either.

As he ignores the crowd, looking directly at the camera, I stand up. I know what that look means and it was directed at me.

'He wants to leave,' I say.

Vic nods. 'Victory party tomorrow night with the whole club at the house. Make sure everybody knows. Any luck with your guy?'

I nod. 'He got back to me. He'll have everything he can find want on her delivered tomorrow. In the morning probably, he said.'

'Good.'

I leave the table without another word, eager to go find Kor, but on the way out, I get waylaid by one of Callaghan's crew.

He smacks into me as he passes and turns back. 'Your boy better watch himself,' he sneers.

I shrug and he pushes me again.

It's just half a breath before I move in and have a knife pressed to his right kidney.

'Maybe you better watch *yourself*, friend.'

Giving him a wink, I leave him standing there, an astonished look on his face. They all think I'm the weak link and that suits me and the Club just fine. Few know the truth. I'm Vic's wildcard. I could kill a third of this room in my fucking sleep and not break a sweat, so we pretend that all I do is fuck around and get drunk. I rarely show anyone the reality, but I'm not going to stand by as Korban is threatened and not do something about it.

Outside, the silence is welcome, but it's sudden and almost eerie. There's a noise-cancelling spell on the building so once the door to the warehouse is closed, no sound escapes at all.

A trashcan falls to the ground in the darkness down the alley and my eyes narrow as I peer into the shadows. Is someone—

The door opens, and Kor strides out into the street.

The noise forgotten, we mount up without a word to each other and ride through the town side by side. It's only midnight, but we don't stop anywhere until we get out into the sticks about halfway between the warehouse and the Clubhouse.

Korban turns down a dirt track, and I follow him closely, taking it slow.

He parks his bike by the side of the wide trail and walks out into the dark woods.

Taking off my helmet, I grin and follow him.

He's disappeared as I get into the woods though and my heart beats faster as I look for him. I chuckle low when I feel him pressing against me. He doesn't say a word, unzipping his pants as I turn and fall to my knees.

I know what he wants.

I take him in my mouth, licking at the underside of the head, tickling his balls gently with my short nails. He groans and I fight a smile.

Yeah, I know what he likes, especially after one of his fights. I pull on him gently, sucking hard. Taking him down my throat, I gag as he fists my hair pushing himself deeper so that my nose touches his abdomen. I fight for breath, but he holds me there, his shaft seeming to grow even larger. I look up into his eyes that glitter in the dark as he watches me.

There's a strange glint in them that I haven't seen before. He doesn't move and my breath is running out. I tap his thigh and his expression turns cruel for a millisecond before he pulls himself out of me and gives me a second to breath and my vision to return to normal before he thrusts right back into my mouth, forcing me to swallow him down and taking me hard.

Gagging hard, tears stream down my cheeks. He comes down my throat, throwing back his head with a roar and I swallow every single drop of cum he gives me. He pulls away too abruptly and zips up his pants, drawing me to standing. His lips find mine, and I kiss him back hard, moaning as he bites my lip.

'Do you need to feed?' I ask.

'Not tonight,' he growls, his voice full of promise and I feel almost giddy with anticipation.

No one has the stamina that Kor does, and I have a feeling we're going to be up all night.

∼

Jane

I OPEN MY EYES. It's still dark. I glance at the green, neon numbers glowing next to me. 2:30. I shiver, but it's not from cold. Why do I feel like there's someone watching me? I pull the covers up to my chin, gazing out fearfully into the darkness. An irrational part of me doesn't even want to put my hand out over the side of the bed, which is ridiculous. I'm a grown woman!

I don't hear anything; the house is completely still except for the random creaks that I guess all old buildings have. I huff, finding my courage. My hand shoots out for where I think the lamp is. My fingers smack into the brass hard and I stifle a curse as I fumble for the switch. Finding it, I turn it on, and a warm glow floods the room. I'm alone but as my eyes find the door, I see that it's ajar. I know Theo closed it after he brought up my dinner around eight. Someone's been in here while I've been sleeping. I shouldn't be surprised. I mean this isn't even really *my room*, but the idea of them watching me at my most vulnerable leaves a nasty taste in my mouth.

I leave the bed and grab the bottle of water that I left on the tray Theo brought, taking a few swigs. Dinner was nice and I think he even cooked it himself; steak with a baked potato and some greens.

It was better than the unpalatable food Sarge made for

me at the diner most nights. I send a silent apology to my friend. I know it was just a job to earn a living for him, it wasn't like he was trying to be a chef or something.

I sigh. I miss Sharlene. I can't even call her because my phone is dead, and my charger is in my apartment. I wish I could just go see her, but even when I get out of here, I can't risk it. It's bad enough that I didn't move on like they told me. Technically I left town, I guess, but ... what if they find Shar in the dumpster next? What will her kids do? The youngest one is barely eight and she doesn't have any family to take them. All three would be forced into the system. I can't let that happen. Having had a taste of foster care after Dad disappeared, I don't want that for them. Granted, I wasn't in it for all that long before Angie took me in and reminded me what it was like for someone to really care again ... and then I found her after school in the kitchen, beaten, two black pits where her eyes had been, a note laying on her chest telling me to leave and never look back.

I put my head back on the pillow and stare at the ceiling, turning off the light and laying there in the dark, but once I've started on these memories, I know that I'm not going to sleep anytime soon, so I turn the light back on and sit up again.

I should talk to Vic tomorrow, tell him again that I need to leave and, if he won't let me, I need to find a way to escape. I can't stay here any longer and it's not just because of Sharlene and her kids. The Iron I's scare me. It's different than I feel when I get one of those notes though. I can't put my finger on why, but I'm jumpy. I can't relax here. I always feel like I'm looking over my shoulder, that things are happening around me that I just don't understand.

I roll my eyes at myself. I mean, that's normal for me.

I'm pretty oblivious at the best of times. I don't mean to be, it's just the way my brain's wired. I'm usually inside myself somewhere, thinking about other things while events go on just outside my orbit.

Trying to distract myself, I stand up and look around Theo's room. He's taken his medical supplies elsewhere since I've moved into his room, so the table that was cluttered with interesting doctory things before is spotless and dull now. I find a small drawer in the side of it, and I pull it open, finding the Med school diploma of one Theodore Aramaus Wright. I don't know what I expected, but Theo's an *actual* doctor.

Huh.

I close it up and go into his closet for the first time, finding it's the massive, walk-in kind. I catalogue the space. Despite the fact that it's bigger than my apartment's kitchen, this might be a good, quiet corner to curl up in when I need some alone time, and don't want anyone to see me.

Next, I meander to the bathroom and decide to start the Jacuzzi bath. I haven't actually been in it yet. I know it's a weird time to be getting into the tub, but I can't think of anything else to do. There's no TV in here and the last thing I want to do is go tiptoeing around the Iron I's house in the middle of the night.

I peel off the clothes I'm wearing, the same ones I wore all day yesterday and the day before ... and in bed at night too. They're starting to smell ripe. I need to go to my apartment— No! I *need* to escape from this fucking house. *Then* I'll go get my stuff before the landlady throws everything out on the curb.

I could use some of my clothes ... and that's what I'll say tomorrow. If I can get one of them to take me to my place and let me pack my up shit, I might be able to make a run for it. That's going to be Plan A.

I step into the bath and sigh as the hot water seeps into my bones. I'm so tense. I pick one of the bodywashes off the side and smell it. I like it. Inhaling deeply, I realize it must be the soap Theo uses. I like the way he smells. I like the way they all smell, all different ... all sexy.

I sit up sharply, the water sloshing over the side a little. Where did *that* thought come from? *Sexy?* I mean, they're all good-looking. Of course they are. They're incubi; a species literally made for dumb humans like me to find irresistible when they turn on the supey charm. I'm just so surprised at myself. I don't usually think about anyone in that way no matter how pleasing they are to the eye.

Mulling that over and not really coming up with a reason for why I might be interested in five demons and not one male of my own species, – well except the horrifying idea that they're somehow *making* me want them; using their voodoo on me without me even feeling it, which chills me to my very soul – I wash my body with Theo's soap, finding that the scent calms me down and lulls me into a very relaxed state.

When I've had a nice, long soak, I let the water out and leave the bathroom with my towel around me. I can't face the clothes I've been wearing now that I'm clean, so I don't bother putting them on, sinking into the bed with a long, slow breath out. Turning off the light, I close my eyes and wonder if I'm even going to be able to fall asl—

IN THE MORNING, the door swings open and I'm groggy as I open my eyes, but it's not Theo who comes sauntering in like a runway model, it's Paris.

I sit up in the bed, pulling the covers over me as I remember that I didn't get dressed after my bath last night. He doesn't seem to notice I'm naked under the blanket though.

'Where's Theo?' I ask.

'Club business,' he answers. 'Looks like you get me this morning, princess. Up and at 'em.'

He stands at the foot of the bed impatiently and clicks his fingers. 'Come on.'

I look down at my body that's still well covered by the comforter. 'I can't with you standing there,' I say.

'Why?'

I gesture to the clothes on the floor. 'Because that's the only outfit I have ...'

He stares at me like I'm an idiot.

Yep, he's definitely all beauty, no brains.

Pity.

'This is ridiculous,' I say, deciding there's no time like the present to put Plan A into action. 'I need to go get my stuff from my apartment if you guys are really going to make me stay here any longer. I have no clothes, no deodorant. I need to brush my hair. My teeth!'

He casts his gaze over the leggings and shirt on the floor.

'The only outfit?' His eyes seem to glow for a second as they move over me, like he has x-ray vision or something.

Oh, shit! What if that's one of his supey powers?

I shift under the cover, trying to hide myself somehow in case he can.

'You ever think maybe Theo's keeping you like that on purpose?'

'Clotheless?' I angle my head to the side, not really understanding what he's getting at.

'Oh! So I don't escape. I guess that would work; gets too cold at night right now to be running around without clothes.'

He shakes his head a little bit, as if he isn't sure what he just heard, but it wasn't what he expected, and I know there's something I missed. My stomach sinks, but luckily, he doesn't dwell on whatever weird thing I just said. He doesn't try to make me feel stupid like some people do and it endears him to me.

Oh no! Stockholm alert!

'I'll take you a little later,' he says. 'Throw on some clothes from Theo's closet for now and come down to the kitchen. I'll get you something to eat.'

I nod and he leaves the room, closing the door securely behind him. I get out of the bed and put on the outfit that I had on yesterday. Theo's sweats are massive on me. I'll end up losing my pants on the way down the stairs or something.

I wrinkle my nose, but they're not actually too bad. A night on the floor probably aired them out a little.

I make my way down to the kitchen, using the stairs that Theo showed me the first day, so I don't have to go past Sie's door.

When I step into the room, I see Paris with his head in the refrigerator, moving stuff around and humming absently.

'What do you want?' he asks when he notices me behind him.

'Cereal,' I say without missing a beat.

He shuts the fridge and heads into the pantry, coming out with a box of something I've never seen before. It doesn't look nice and the acute disgust I'm feeling must be written all over my face because he looks at it in question.

'You don't like this one?'

I shake my head.

'That's the only one that was in there.'

My eyes narrow. He's lying. Either that or ...

'I had a different one before,' I say. 'Do you mind if I take a look?'

He gestures with his arm. 'Knock yourself out, sweet thing.'

Sweet thing?

I decide to ignore the endearment, going into the pantry, trying to figure out which one of them doesn't want me to have the nice cereal. I find the empty space where the good stuff was before. There's nothing there and I frown. There was too much cereal in that box for it to already be gone unless more than one person in this house eats it. But if that's the case, why only buy one box?

I reach up onto the shelf where I can't see and my fingers brush against something. *Ha!*

I get up on my tippy toes and pull myself up a little bit, grasping the glossy cardboard I can feel and pulling it down.

Yes!

Theo must have hid it from me. Now that I'm thinking back, maybe he did look a little bit off when I helped myself to that second bowl ...

Well, it's mine now!

I clutch the box to my chest and turn only to find Paris behind me, the morning sun shining through the windows and silhouetting him in the doorway.

I can't see his face, but he doesn't move as I step forward to leave. He's boxing me in.

He doesn't say a word, but I see his head turn as he

looks behind him, his Adam's apple bouncing as he swallows hard and closes the door, plunging us into darkness.

He surges forward and cuts off my startled cry, his mouth taking mine hard. I rear back, dropping the box of cereal, but he moves with me until my back scrapes against the shelf at the back.

His lips are moving against mine and, without letting thoughts intrude for once, I mimic the motion on pure instinct. He lets out a guttural sound, one hand cupping the back of my neck and drawing me closer. His other hand holds me under my chin, angling my face up to his.

As if finally realizing that I'm not fighting, he lets go of my neck, his hand trailing down my spine to grab my ass, and I give a muffled squeak as I'm forced closer to him.

His whole body is hard and I do mean his *whole body*. He pushes me into the shelf again, his hand grabbing my thigh and pulling my leg up, opening me. He winds my leg around his waist and rubs himself against me. Fingers graze the apex of my thighs through my clothes and I gasp into his mouth, my knees going weak. I know that what I'm feeling isn't real, but it's so so good that I don't care.

He pulls away a tiny bit. 'Fuck,' he breathes, 'I knew you'd taste sweet.'

'But I haven't brushed my teeth,' I mutter, my mind having caught up to my actions and shattering the moment.

He retreats with an abrupt laugh before he seems to come back to himself and lets me go, pushing himself away from me.

The door opens and he starts to leave. I follow. I sort of don't want him to stop. I've never been kissed like that before. The other stuff neither. I want more.

'Shit!' he hisses and turns back. 'I'm sorry I—'

He closes the distance between us and I'm excited for him to kiss me again, but instead, he pushes me into the shelf hard, making me swallow a cry of pain as it presses my bruised back.

'If you tell anyone about this, I'll make your time here so much worse than it needs to be!'

And then he's gone, leaving me breathing hard in the pantry.

Frowning and trying to get control of myself. I can practically hear my heart beating in my chest and the roaring in my ears is like a summer downpour on a steel roof.

I pick up the cereal box with a shaky hand and take it out of the pantry, pushing everything away practically involuntarily. There's a bowl and a spoon on the breakfast bar already and I pour out a generous amount of cereal. I add the milk, eating it quickly while it still has its crunch.

Belatedly, I see that Paris isn't gone. He's by the window, surveying their stupidly massive lawn with a look on his face that I don't understand.

'What time can we go?' I ask between mouthfuls.

'As soon as you're done,' he says. 'It's already past ten. Best get it done this morning before the party later.'

'Party?'

'Yeah. Korban won his fight last night.'

'Oh.' I chase the final piece of cereal around the milk with my spoon. 'Does he win a lot of fights?'

Paris nods. 'Kor is a force of nature,' he says with a proud grin that makes me think he and Korban are pretty close.

'We always have a party after,' he continues, 'but Vic usually uses the celebration as an excuse to get the full club together along with our business associates. We usually make some pretty good deals while everyone's drinking and having a good time.'

Finally capturing my quarry, I find to my disappointment that it's soggy. I sigh. What a shitty end to my breakfast. I put the bowl in the sink and turn to find him watching me.

'What?' I ask.

'Dunno. I just ... I don't usually talk so much.'

To your food, you mean?

'Don't blame me,' I say, shrugging. 'I don't usually have people talking to me so much.'

He frowns. 'Meet you in the garage in five,' he says, walking past me slowly.

His fingers brush through the hair of my ponytail and I frown at him, but he's already gone. Maybe there was a bug, I decide as I run up to my room to grab my jacket. If everything works out with Plan A, I won't be coming back here.

I go down to the main foyer using the back stairs and going through the kitchen and the hallway past the study again to stay away from Sie's room. I hear Vic in his office, the keys of his laptop clicking, and I skirt around the open door, making sure he doesn't see me.

As I stand in the middle of the high-ceilinged entrance hall, I realize I haven't actually been in the garage yet. If there's a way into it from the house, I don't know it, so I try getting there via the front door.

Outside, rain is threatening, and I consider the murky sky with a long look. Maybe my next move should be to Hawaii. Bet it doesn't rain all the time *there*, I think as I make my way to the side of the house.

Turns out, the garage is very easy to find. It's freaking huge! Three massive doors lead into a cavernous annex; the kind with the black, button rubber flooring you see on TV and in car showrooms. There are a bunch of different kinds of bikes in here.

But not one car.

I frown.

'How are we getting there?' I ask Paris who's fastening a helmet onto his head.

'On my bike,' he says slowly like I'm the most moronic human ever.

'I don't know how,' I say, hoping that'll be the end of it.

He chuckles, giving me a once over. 'Not by yourself, babe. You'll ride with me.'

I try not to bristle, ignoring his condescending, alpha-hole words because I *know* women ride these things *by themselves.*

'No,' I say, 'I mean I can't—' I swallow hard. 'I can't go on one of those.'

How do I explain to him without sounding like a fruitcake?

'How do you think you got here, sweetheart?' he smirks.

'Stop calling me names,' I order him. 'That was different.'

'Names? How was it different?'

'Yes, names. I wasn't awake.'

'I'll call you whatever I feel like, doll face. I could knock you out for it. Put you between my legs like I did the other night.'

'Doll face?' I erupt into a peel of laughter. 'Who are you? Al Capone?'

I think about the other part for a second. 'I really don't want to be knocked out,' I say finally.

He turns his face away and I think he's hiding a smile. 'Well, this is the only way we're getting there, so if you want to get your stuff, hop on.'

'What if I have too much to bring? How will we get it back here?' I persist.

I don't, but he doesn't know that.

'You can pack it up and I'll get one of the prospects to pick it up later.'

Not waiting for me to reply, he pushes the bike out onto the driveway and straddles it.

I follow slowly, making my feet move after him. My heart sinks and my legs feel like jelly, but if I want to escape, I'm really going to have to do this. Pulling out my earbuds from my pocket, I push them into my ears firmly, hoping they stay put and that they'll be good enough.

'You won't go too fast?' I mutter.

He chokes back a chuckle, and hands me a helmet.

'Depends.'

I decide I don't want to know what it depends on. I've already given him too much power by showing him my fear … and how much I wanted him in the pantry … so I get on the back of the bike gingerly and buckle the uncomfortable helmet onto my head.

'Put your legs up like that,' he says, moving them into the position for me, 'and keep them away from the exhaust. It gets hot. Hold on to my waist. Just like that, baby. Tighter.'

I roll my eyes as he glances back.

He smirks. 'Don't want you falling off the back, bunny.'

Ugh, the names are getting dumber.

I snort, but as the bike starts moving, I do grip onto him as tightly as I can, and he shudders. I assume he's laughing at me as I press the side of my helmet into his back and I hold on for dear life … and I tell myself I don't care that he's amused at my expense.

He revs the engine, and my senses are stunned by the

roar for a moment, my body locking up. Everything in me tenses and I realize too late that the earbuds don't do nearly enough to block out the sound. I hate these fucking things and I'm not going on one again. Plan A needs to work.

We take a long, winding driveway, that I only notice because I periodically make myself open my eyes, until we get to a main road. He turns left and I force myself to keep an eye out, so I know where we are.

He begins to speed up and I try not to scream as we go down the road for a few minutes. He turns again at a crossroads. Left this time. I see signs to Welford. Fifteen miles away. I could walk that. It would take three or four hours, but it could be done. Just in case Plan A doesn't work, if I can get off the grounds, I can get to civilization. From there, I can follow my original idea and get a bus far away from here. I'm still seriously considering Hawaii. Plan B is born as we roll into town.

'Where do you live?' he yells over his shoulder.

I point down the main road, put up three fingers and then point to the side. Miraculously, he gets it, passing the next three blocks before taking a right. I tap his arm and point to my building. He nods and turns in, parking in a space close to the door.

He turns the ignition, and the bike finally stops. I breathe a sigh of relief as I get off the back clumsily, my arms and legs shaking a little from working so hard to stay on.

I don't understand the lure of a bike. I'd rather take a car ... hell I'd rather take my slow legs any day of the week.

'There, now. That wasn't so bad, was it?' he asks.

I don't answer him. 'Are you waiting down here?'

'Nope.'

'Come on then.'

I walk up to the broken door and tear it open because it sticks. Practically bounding up the two flights of stairs, I try to ignore the stench of urine in the stairwell and the used needles in the corners.

'You live here?' he mutters from behind me.

Something crawls up into my chest and I think it might be embarrassment.

'Yeah,' I say, rubbing the back of my neck.

I get my key out of my pocket and unlock the three deadbolts, opening the door and going in as I hear movement down the hall at 21A.

Not now.

When I look back, Paris is standing at the threshold, taking it all in. 21A is suddenly blissfully silent. I leave him to his judgements as I move around the room, picking up my favorite blanket, a hairband, a pair of shoes I like.

'Didn't you ever want anything better for yourself?' he asks, like it's all so simple.

'Yeah,' I say simply, rolling my eyes at Judgy McJudgerson.

Is this guy for real?

He closes the door and I almost laugh at how out of place he looks. I glance at the pre-furnished, moth-eaten sofa that looks like Mary Poppins' carpetbag threw up on it.

'Make yourself at home,' I say, knowing that he won't. Even I can see he hates it here.

He stares down at the couch like it's going to give him VD, making no move to get any closer to it, and I shrug, going into my bedroom and starting to pack.

I don't bother with the sheets off my bed, nor the touch lamp on my bedside table. I'm only taking the things that I came here with that fit into the two small duffel bags I found at army surplus. All the stuff I've bought since I've been here can stay. I only care about my clothes and the couple things I have to remember my past by anyway.

I grab the bags from under my bed and pull out the few outfits I have hanging in the closet, throwing them in. I go into the bathroom, snatching my toothbrush, and some of the other necessary toiletries I'll need on the road from the shelf by the mirror. I hesitate, but then open my bedside drawer and grab my dildo too, stuffing it in my backpack underneath a couple changes of clothes, and some basic toiletries. (What? A girl has needs even on the run.)

I throw everything in, taking stuff out of my drawers and my hamper until everything in this room that I brought with me is in the bags.

I hear Paris rustling around in the living room and glance out as I go into the bathroom again to make sure I haven't forgotten anything. He's looking at some books on the small coffee table that were also here when I moved in. I have never actually even looked at them myself, so I have no idea what they're about.

I'm confident that he's suitably engrossed though, so I tiptoe across my bedroom to the window. I spray it with WD-40 frequently, so I know it'll be silent as I pull it open. I also know it's big enough for me to fit through. I dump the bags first, letting them fall to the ground behind the bushes and hoping one of the dogs that mills around the area hasn't shit down there recently.

I tiptoe back across the room.

'I'm just gonna go to the bathroom,' I call and close the bathroom door as I watch him. He doesn't even look up.

What are those books about?

I climb out after my stuff. I made sure that I could do this as well – as soon as I moved in. I always have an escape plan.

Holding onto the windowsill, I lower myself down, dropping the last few feet onto my bags that cushion my landing a little behind the bushes. I'm on my feet immediately, grabbing them and hauling ass around the corner of the duplex. Once I know I'm out of sight of my apartment, I slow to a walk. Don't want to attract attention. Two streets down, there's an old line of garages. The last one has a broken window, but the old door is locked, or at least rusted shut. I've had my eye on it for weeks. No one ever comes here. I've even been inside, and everything was dusty and covered in dirty cobwebs.

I give a furtive glance behind me. No one's following and I can't be seen from the road now. I pull myself inside, trying not to disturb the layers of dust as I push my bags out of sight into the flatbed of an old, rusted 1950's truck that looks like it was abandoned to time years ago.

Making sure no one sees me, I leave the same way I came in, taking only the backpack that contains all necessities for the road in case I can't come back for a while.

I walk down the back alleys quickly, trying to stay out of sight of the main road. Paris will know I'm gone by now. He'll be looking for me.

I head towards the parts of town where there are more people, feeling better amongst others for once. Supes can get away with a lot, but even they can't just kidnap a human in broad daylight with other humans looking on in horror.

It takes ten minutes to get to the coffee shop I'm making for. It's not far from the bus station and has WIFI so I can figure out my next move in my own time.

For a moment or two, I toy with the idea of going to the diner just to make sure Shar is ok, but I know that would be a mistake. I say a silent goodbye. At least I was able to help her out with the money a little. I'll text her once from the road later.

I walk into the cafe with my earbuds in, so no one tries to talk to me. I guess I have one of those faces because people do.

All. The. Freaking. Time.

Grabbing a latte, I sink into a corner at the back. I plug in my dead phone and wait for it to turn back on as it charges. I know I need to get rid of it, but I also need internet to figure out where I'm going next. I'm too broke for Hawaii, but maybe I can start making my way south slowly ...

It loads up and I see multiple texts from Shar. I grimace. She'll be so worried. I send her a quick one back just to say that I had to skip town and that I'm sorry for not saying goodbye, half-hoping that whoever's on my trail will somehow see it too and leave her alone.

I bring up the bus station schedules, taking a look at what's going where today. I'll have to leave the phone. I know it can be tracked, but I'll be loath to do it. I won't be able to buy another one for some time. I mean I guess it doesn't matter. It's not like I'll have anyone trying to get in touch with me.

A pang of sadness, loneliness maybe, takes me by surprise. I'm so sick of living this way. Tears come to my eyes and I sniffle as I close them, willing the waterworks away. This is no time to fall apart.

I wipe my eyes and open them, catching sight of something that has me gasping loudly and throwing myself back in my seat, my heart instantly beginning to thud hard in my chest. Paris is looming over me and even I can tell he is furious with me.

'Get your ass up,' he says in a quiet, steely tone that makes me shiver.

I glance around, hoping for a little help from my own kind, but no one's looking. In fact, they're going out of their way *not* to look.

Traitors.

'Don't you dare.' He leans in close. 'The Iron I's own this town. Cause a scene now and when the supe cops get here, they won't be taking me in, baby girl, they'll be taking you and I can guarantee supe county lock-up will be a lot worse than whatever you think I'm going to do to you.'

I nod. As threats go, it's a good one. Humans taken to supe jails don't usually come out again; and if they do, they aren't *right*. Everyone knows that.

I slowly put my phone and charger in my bag and stand up.

'You're dumb even for a human,' he tells me. 'Now, your shit can rot wherever you left it. You ain't getting it back and you only have yourself to blame.'

When I don't move fast enough, he grabs me, taking hold of my forearm and I wince as he pulls me along.

'Get your fucking hands off me,' I growl.

He actually listens to what I say, turning back and gesturing with his thumb out to the street. 'Then get your ass out that door and onto that bike.'

I follow the order, making sure my earbuds are in properly and my bag is secure on my back in preparation for another fun trip on the loud machine of death.

'How did you find me?' I ask, wondering if it was the phone.

He doesn't answer, and I flinch as he starts the bike. He peels out onto the road without warning, making a car honk it's horn. My senses scream and I do too, grabbing hold of him as tightly as I can, my fingers digging in hard, but he doesn't seem to care.

His speed doesn't let up the whole way back, taking corners like he's drifting in a freaking car, skidding all over the place. He even does a wheelie. The journey terrifies me to the point of tears. My whole body's shaking in anger and upset by the time we pull into their pretentious fucking driveway. If he thinks he can scare me into doing whatever it is that they want though, he's in for a nasty surprise.

Plan B it is.

CHAPTER
TEN
KORBAN

I'm in her room, smelling her sheets like the pervert I accused Theo of being. Why I'm in here again, I have no idea. I was here last night too, watching her sleep. I wish it wasn't as creepy as it sounds, but it definitely is.

Still feeling the buzz from the fight last night, I walk around the room. I can smell her in the air but it's not enough. I go back to the bed and grab her pillow, inhaling deeply. Theo's scent is mixed in and it's fresh, but I don't think he's been rubbing his body all over her sheets. That's not really his style. She's probably using his soap.

Interesting.

An idea comes to me, and I run down the hall to my room, taking my own bodywash out of my shower. Making sure no one sees me, I dart back to Theo's room and place it in the bathroom next to his.

I don't know what I hope to get from this ... is this *jealousy*? No, I scoff to myself. I don't know what this is, but I'm probably just bored. Maybe I need Vic to get me some more fights.

Last night's was a good one. I gotta hand it to

Callaghan. I hate that fucking asshole, but he gives me a good run for my money. I still won despite him trying to rile me up though, trying to get me angry so I'd make a mistake. Told me he heard one of our guys had died like a pussy. It's been, what three days, maybe four, so him knowing that wasn't a surprise. Everyone does by now. But then he said he couldn't wait to have a chance with our new girl the next time he was at the house. How the fuck could he know about her? I made sure I didn't have her scent on me, so it wasn't that he could smell her and was guessing.

It's a problem because it means that we either have a break in our magickal borders that's letting in surveillance, or, worse, we have a mole.

I walk around the room again and see the hamper lid askew. I open it and feel inside. There's something at the bottom. Small, silky. No way! I draw out a little red thong slowly, hardly able to believe my luck. I smell it.

Fucking heaven.

There's a part of my brain that's saying this is way past weird, and that I'm definitely as depraved as Theo, perhaps worse, but I don't care.

I hear a door slam downstairs and stuff the panties in my pocket for later, leaving the room and flipping off the camera hidden in the light on the wall because I know Theo's going to watch the tape later ... if he isn't right now.

I go downstairs to speak to Vic. For once, he's not behind his desk, but playing pool by himself in the games room. I grab a cue and take a shot.

'We have a problem,' I say.

Vic looks up at me in question.

'Callaghan knew we have a new girl last night. Told me he heard she's pretty, but she's not all there. Said he's going to play with her next time he's here. We pimping out the on-call girls now?'

Saying it out loud pisses me off and I don't bother to hide it. I'm not in the fight now and I don't give a shit what Vic has in place with the other three girls, but we aren't sharing this one.

I take my shot too hard and my ball flies off the table.

I have Vic's attention. 'No. We've never loaned out our contracted girls. He was fucking with you. How did he know about her?'

I shrug. 'A hole or a mole.'

Vic lets out a breath. He looks tired. 'Get Paris to do a full security diagnostic. Magick and tech. If someone's spying on us, I want to know how.'

'And if it's a spy?' I ask.

'It won't be one of the Iron I's. Probably one of the human prospects; maybe Young or Andreas. They've gotten a little mouthy lately and they're buddies, right?'

'Yeah,' I confirm. 'Paris said they knew each other before. Met on the inside.'

We shoot some balls for a few minutes, not really playing a game just killing time.

'You've been in her room again.'

I stifle a grin, not even bothering to hide it.

'Can't get anything past you, Columbo,' I say, taking another shot. 'Is that a problem?'

Vic levels me with a look. 'Depends on if you want to fuck her or kill her.'

'Fuck, marry, kill?' I laugh. 'I haven't decided yet,' I say in all honesty.

'I'm contracting her to the Club today.'

That's a bombshell that gives me pause. A few days ago

I would have raised hell over this, but now ... 'But Sie wants her gon—'

'Sie will deal with it,' Vic interrupts, 'and it seems like everyone's a little bit interested in this girl, Sie included, so try not to kill her just yet.'

'I'll do what I can,' I say with a frown because if the darkness takes me, I won't be in control, 'but maybe make sure she's never alone with me.'

Vic nods. 'She's already been told.'

'How are you going to get her to sign?'

Vic just about hides a dark smile. 'Taking a leaf out of our friendly fae's book; trickery and leverage.'

I snort. 'Sounds about right. How much did we make last night?'

Vic looks me in the eye. 'Few hundred grand. Enough to keep them off our backs for a couple months. Plus that orc stone gives us a little wiggle room if we can sell it soon.'

'Nice.'

'Next one's in three weeks,' he says.

I nod. 'With who?'

'Mad Dog. Will you be ready?'

I grin, already anticipating it. 'I'll be ready.'

The last ball rolls into the corner pocket and Vic puts his cue down on the table.

'Be out of the common rooms later,' he advises. 'Bunch of humans will be here setting up for the party tonight.'

I sigh. *Great.*

Vic goes back into his study, closing the door and I turn on the TV, flicking through the channels for a while but nothing holds my attention for more than a few minutes. I turn it off and wander into the kitchen. Two of the on-call girls are in there talking. They go quiet when they see me.

'The fuck you doing up here?' I growl.

'We're sorry,' the redhead murmurs, backing away towards their apartment downstairs. 'We didn't know you were here.'

I let out a snarl and laugh as they scurry back to the basement. They make sure they're never alone with me either. Paris is always there when I need to feed, making sure I don't accidentally go too far. Even now, I'm overcome with the desire to follow them and wring their little necks. I grab a water from the fridge, and head down to the gym instead, closing myself in. Turning the volume on the sound system all the way up, I put on something loud with a good bass to drown out the anger and the fury that I feel anytime I'm around humans ... mostly human females.

They always look so fucking vulnerable. Like butter wouldn't melt. The truth is they're the vilest monsters of them all; worse than dryads, sirens, and witches combined. They're just easier to kill.

I start hitting the pads, the only way I can work out my anger that doesn't involve killing. Murder is still murder if they find a body, even when it's human scum. I punch the bags until it's time to get ready for the party and I'm sure the humans who were here setting up are gone.

We're about to spend the next few hours being congratulated by everyone who made money last night. The entire Club will be here plus business associates and friends. There'll be wagers made for the next fight already.

I stare at myself in the mirror. I'm not looking forward to it one bit. Odds are that I'll last an hour before I go out looking for the potential border break that's letting outsiders catch a glimpse of what goes on up here. Maybe Paris has even found it already, and we can go close it together. My dick hardens at that thought. His mouth felt so good last night, I'm aching for a repeat performance of my lover pleasuring me on his knees in the woods.

Vic

I'M SITTING in my office, a contract in front of me, when I hear the front door slam hard.

'Get. The fuck. Upstairs,' Paris says loudly and then I hear a whimper and the telltale creaks of someone running up them.

Paris enters the study a second later.

'What happened?' I ask, wondering what's got the usually happy-go-lucky Paris so pissed off.

'Took her to her apartment to get her stuff. She tried to give me the slip. Found her an hour later in a café a mile or so down the road. Dumb human was charging her phone. Pinged me as soon as it came on. If you're going to contract her to us, do it today. She'll keep trying. Lock her in. Make sure she knows she can't get away.'

Shit, I don't think I've ever seen Paris so worked up, but I nod. 'That's the plan. Where is she now?'

'Sent her to her room in tears like a naughty little girl.'

Fuck ... when he calls her that ... I was going to try and resist her until after Sie had taken her for himself, but now I can't get the image of her on her knees in front of me, looking up at me with those beautiful brown eyes out of my head.

I see Paris smirking in front of me and I know he chose his words on purpose. I shake my head, but I give him a grin. 'Sit the fuck down. I have a job for you to do asap.'

Still looking amused, he takes a seat.

'Korban thinks we have a hole.'

Paris puts his game face on immediately, his relaxed demeanor melting away like it was never there. He's all business now.

'What happened?'

'Callaghan knew about the new girl last night at the fight. Thankfully, he thinks she's already contracted to the club, so anyone else who knows she's here will probably assume the same. There's no way anyone could know about this already. We've either got a break in the perimeter or a spy. Shore up the border spells and check the tech security before the party starts.'

Paris nods, but then looks at his watch. 'Shit. I can do the tech stuff no problem, but the spells will have to wait until the next full moon, which isn't for a couple days. I can get Korban to go look for a breach along the properly line though. He's good at finding stuff like that.

'Good. I don't want any surprises tonight. There will be a lot of people here who'd love to see us go under and I'm not about to make it easy for 'em.'

'I'll get it done, boss. Oh,' he reaches into his jacket pocket and pulls out a manila envelope. 'This was in the P.O. Box.'

'This is our girl?'

He nods.

'Have you looked at it?'

'Haven't had a chance.'

I take the envelope from Paris and put it on the desk.

'I'll look at it later,' I say, but I doubt Paris has bought my lie. As soon as he leaves, he knows I won't be able to resist tearing it open and finding out everything I need to know about our little on-call girl prospect.

'Be careful with Kor where the new girl's concerned,' I warn.

He scoffs as soon as my words register. 'He doesn't want anything to do with one of those human bitches. Trust me. Getting him to stay properly fed is a fucking nightmare.'

'Be that as it may,' I say, thinking about that look in Kor's eye while he was talking about her earlier, the fact that he's been watching her, 'just keep an eye on him.'

'Will do, boss,' he says, but I already know he won't. He'll start doing what I've told him to do and focus completely on his task, forgetting about everything else.

I take out my phone and call Theo who I heard come in the door a few minutes ago. 'She's in her room. Bring her down, would you?'

'You're gonna do it now?' Paris looks excited.

'I just want to test the waters,' I say. 'Plant the seed.'

I tap the envelope. 'I'll get everything I need from here to make it happen.'

Paris chuckles. 'She's not gonna know what hit her.'

She comes in a minute later looking petulantly at Paris, and I have an urge to bend her over the desk and give her a good, hard spanking.

'Sit down,' I say sternly and find myself tickled when her eyes cut to me at the tone of my voice and she sits, looking *chastened*.

'You weren't completely straight with us when we made the deal at the bar last week. You didn't tell us they've been following you around the country for the past ten years killing people. You know, the *additional* things you mentioned the night Paris brought you in.'

She raises her chin in defiance and my palm twitches. 'I answered your questions at the time. It's your fault if you didn't ask the right ones. You still have to help me,' she says quickly. 'I paid you and the agreement was magickly binding.'

I sit back in my chair, looking like I don't give a shit. 'Actually, we don't.'

'What?'

'Well, the exact words that you agreed to were 'we will keep you safe', which we are. We said we'd take care of the guys who were stalking you, and Paris and Sie technically did. Those frat boys *were* stalking you. We held up our end. It's over.'

Her jaw tightens. Oh, she's angry. 'You can't just—'

'Yes, I can. I already have,' I say, 'but I'll tell you what.' I hand her the documents I've been looking at along with a pen. 'You contract with us as a human female belonging to the Club ...'

Her eyes widen as she opens her mouth, but no words come out.

'Yes,' I say, 'as one of the contracted girls. In return, you can live in a house known for its security.' *Once we take care of the potential breach anyway.*

For a few moments, she says nothing, taking a look at the contract, at me, and at Paris still standing behind her.

'You want me to be a walking snack?' She blinks. 'But you already have lots,' she says faintly.

I ignore her. 'Full room and board and, at the end of the three years, you get fifty grand.'

I've stumped her. She wasn't expecting this, I realize, not at all.

'Yeah, sure,' she says. 'That sounds great.'

She sounds like she normally does, no inflection in her tone. Is she serious? I actually can't tell, but my eyes narrow. Is she really going to make it this easy?

She scrawls on the contract with a pen and hands it back, getting up and leaving the room.

Neither of us make a move to stop her. Wondering what that was, I glance down at the line she signed on and let out a laugh at what it says:

Fuck. You.

Paris snatches it from me and looks surprised. 'She's got more backbone than I gave her credit for.'

I stare at the spot she just vacated. She doesn't know it yet, but she's sealed her own fate with her little challenge because there's no way she's walking away from this house. We'll get her before the week is out, I just need to find the right leverage.

'Make sure she goes back to her room,' I say to Paris.

My palm is tingling again. I can't wait to redden that delectable little ass. Paris closes the door behind him, and I don't wait, taking my dick out of my pants and moving my hand along the length of it, imagining I'm slipping into her tight, wet cunt even as I wonder why I'm so fired up over this little human.

Soon, I promise myself, my hand moving even faster as I think about how she'll feel, the noises she'll make as she's pleasured thoroughly by a demon. I come hard, shooting straight into the waste basket under my desk.

I tuck myself away. Hopefully I'll last longer when I'm with her, I think sardonically, although it doesn't really matter, the lull will make sure she's pleasured with every single touch I give her and then she'll crave more. By next week, she'll be our willing little whore.

My eyes fall on the drawer where I stashed the envelope. *No time like the present.*

I take it out and rip it open. A thin folder falls onto the desk, and I freeze as I notice the photos clipped to the front. One is of a little girl smiling in a school picture, but it's the other I'm interested in. It's of the same girl in the lap of a man who must be her father. A glance at the description on the back confirms it. I zero in on the man's face. It's a little blurred but I'm not wrong.

No fucking way!

A slow smiles spreads over my face. I wanted her in case she could help Sie, but this ... I don't know how this is possible, but she might be exactly what I've been waiting for.

If I believed in coincidences, this would be a fucking doozy, but I don't. She's got to be the mole we're looking for. It all makes sense. Her disappearance the other day while the system was down, how difficult it is to read her, the way she just showed up in the bar dangling that irresistible carrot in front of us ... But I can turn this to our advantage and there's no way I'm letting her escape us now. We can get some payback and more besides. I just have to do this right.

I slide the photo off the front of the folder and, hold it up in the air in front of me. I flick open my lighter and put the flame to the corner of the glossy paper, watching the flames lick the face of our enemy, and promising silently that he won't be a thorn in our sides for much longer.

CHAPTER
ELEVEN
JANE

I'm pacing around the room, my nails digging into my palms. How did I not see this coming? They're demons. Can't fucking trust demons! What do they want me for? I'm not like those girls downstairs. I'm not trying to be an asshole but, really, I'm not like them. Sometimes I wish I was, but I *can't* be. Anxiety claws at my chest, the same question going round and round in my head. Why me?

Why did Paris do those things in the kitchen? Why did Sie corner me in his room? Why not just let me leave or even kill me? They must just be messing with the human because, as far as I can tell, ever since I came here my presence has only brought out feelings of mild annoyance to intense hatred of my kind in these men. Maybe it has to do with dead Drey. It can't really be about me, after all. I mean what would they possibly want me for? Yeah, I know they're sex demons but c'mon. It can't be *that*.

I glance out the window. It's dark. I can't stay here. Not another night. Because if I know anything, it's that someone like Vic is a leader for a reason. He won't take no for an answer.

I can hear noises, music pumping, and other sounds of fun times. I've been up here all afternoon worrying while the doors have been opening and closing downstairs. I make sure I have all my stuff in my backpack, and I'm just about to leave the room when my phone rings.

I frown as I glance at it. It's Shar. For a second, I contemplate not answering but she probably just wants to know that I'm safe, so I take the call.

'Jane?' Her voice is panicked.

'Are you okay?' I ask.

There's a nervous laugh. 'Are *you*?'

'Yeah,' I say. 'I'm sorry. I had to disappear, and my phone was dead. I couldn't contact y ...'

The line crackles. 'Did you hear about Sarge?'

My stomach does a nasty flip. 'What? No.'

'He's dead, Jane. They found him in the kitchen this morning with his eyes gone just like that other guy from the dumpster. Diner's closed until further notice. No one's even seen Chuck in days. I don't know what to do. They're saying it's a serial killer. Those supe cops have been asking about you.'

She's silent on the other end for a few seconds and when she talks again, she sounds scared. 'I don't know what's happening. I feel like someone's watching me. I've felt it for a couple days and ... I don't know ... I thought maybe I was just rattled, but then Steph came home from school this afternoon and said she thought she saw a car following her ... I ... I think I'm next. What am I going to do, Jane? What about my kids? The supe cops aren't going to do shit to keep us safe.'

'Do you still have that cash I left you?' I ask, guilt and sadness washing over me.

I've put another person I care about in danger; kids who might lose their mom or worse because of me. And poor Sarge ... Another friend taken because I didn't leave like I was told.

'Yeah.'

'Use it. Take your kids and go to a motel outside of town under a different name. Stay there. I'll call you soon.'

I end the call before my voice breaks. I feel like I'm going to throw up. I can't let them get anyone else. I have to go. If I go back to the diner and then leave from there, maybe they'll see that I'm doing what they want, and they'll leave Shar and the kids alone.

Instilled with new purpose, I open the window and do a Jane, throwing my backpack down to the ground, but it's too high for me to climb out this way like I did at my apartment, so I close it again and head for the door.

I peek out into the hallway. There's no one around and I slink down the back steps to the kitchen, going slowly so no one notices me. But I realize pretty quick that there's a giant issue with my plan. There are people everywhere. There's Champagne, wine, beers, *canapes*. It's a full on, rich supe soiree. Maybe every party for the supes is like this but the point is, everyone's dressed up and I ... I look down at my jeans and oversized jacket that's ripped down the pocket from the daring apartment escape this afternoon. I look like a hobo so I can't even pretend I belong here.

All the doors are open and, conscious of curious glances I'm garnering, I make for the open doors that lead onto the deck. If I can get out into the darkness, head to the woods, I have a chance.

I get outside, and there's practically no one out here. I

think it's a good thing, staying in the shadows as I move towards the steps that lead to the path that goes around the house, but there's a group of guys standing almost in my way. I don't look at them, moving with purpose. Maybe they won't even notice me.

'Is that the new girl I heard about?'

I freeze in the dark, knowing he's talking about me.

'Where are you going, sweetheart?'

I move a little faster, and I'm so fucking close, but one of them bars my way. I duck under his arm, but he grabs my jacket, and I try to shrug it off, but can't get my arms out of it before I'm surrounded.

I'm drawn by my hair into the light coming from the house, but not so close that anyone can see me. I shake free, slapping the hand away and I hear chuckles.

'Relax, girl. We just want to get a look at you.'

Someone takes my chin and forces my head up. I pull away, and I get a slap across the cheek that makes me cry out.

'Behave, whore,' says a cold voice.

I lock my jaw and stare at the ground, wracking my brain for a plan to get away while at the same time wondering what's going on lately. Why is everyone so fucking interested in little old me all of a sudden? It's bullshit is what it is!

'Take off her jacket. I want to see if she's got bigger tits than the other three.'

My jacket is ripped off me, leaving me gasping in just my tank top, trying to make myself as small as possible while still staying on my feet. My head is in a whirl. Someone's fingers skirt along my collarbone and I jerk away.

'Don't fucking touch me,' I hiss.

Someone grabs me again and I don't think, letting my

lizard brain take over. My teeth come down hard and I hear a yowl.

'Bitch bit me!'

I'm shaking as I'm taken in a punishing grip by two of them, my arms twisted around behind me.

'You need a lesson on where you stand, human.'

A third one, a lean dude with a crew cut, makes sure I see him pull his fist back.

'Right at the bottom,' he says with a nasty smile, grabbing my face hard. 'If we want to touch you, we will. If we want you on your knees swallowing our dicks, you beg for them. If we want you to take them somewhere else, you bend over, hold yourself open for us, and say 'thank you'.'

I look away from this colossal asshole, tensing my stomach muscles but I know it's not going to matter. These guys are big. Shifter big. I'll be on the ground, coughing up blood in about two seconds.

But before his fist lands, he's hauled away and the hands holding my arms go slack. I rip myself the rest of the way from their grasps and I run, tripping down the stairs of the deck as I try to get away from the monsters. I don't hear anything, but I'm suddenly restrained and held tight against someone. I scream, wondering which of them has me now.

∽

Sie

I'VE BEEN WATCHING from the shadows ever since I saw her come outside, pretending she wasn't sneaking around. I didn't do anything to stop her, wondering what she was going to do now that she had found herself a very small chance of getting out of here. Was she just trying to escape? Or was she going to make off with Vic's family's silver too?

My crazy head tells me she needs to be punished for running, but the 'punishment' it supplies is an image of her hanging by her wrists in the cells with my head buried between her spread legs.

I drag myself out of what's quickly becoming a full-fledged hallucination.

Out on the deck, Callaghan and the pricks he brought with him notice her and what I see in their eyes, I don't like. He and his buddies are permanent fixtures at our parties, like a lot of the other fighters are even though none of them are part of the Club itself.

I've told Vic more than once that I don't like him here. But we do a lot of business with his boss, so they get an invite. I'm sick and tired of him and his asshole friends coming to our house and acting like it's theirs.

I watch for a little while longer, lost in that punishment I want to give her again, and, when I come back, I see they've surrounded her. She's in the midst of them. I hear them goading, laughing, telling her she's there to serve them.

No, fuckers, she's here to serve me and my clan, not your pack. Fucking mongrels. She doesn't want you.

Unable to help the possessive growl that comes from deep inside of me, I stride forward, and I grab Callaghan's arm before it causes damage to our newest girl's face. He might be a good fighter in the ring, but out here I throw him back easily. I have 50lbs on this asshole. If I still let loose in the ring these days, I'd beat him easily.

'Get your own human!' I snarl, practically throwing him over the guardrail of the deck. I hear him hit the ground with a low thud and he groans. I glare back at the two others who are already backing away from her and me. They've let her go, and, before I know it, she's diving into the dark.

'We're sorry, man. We didn't know she was yours.'

I sneer at the blatant lie. 'Maybe make sure everyone knows who she is because the next time someone outside the Iron I's touches what's ours, an army of spellcasters will be needed to find whatever pieces are left of 'em.'

They take a couple more steps back, both of them paling. I think the one on the left might have even pissed his pants a little.

Pathetic.

I leap after the girl, following her easily. She hasn't even made it to the trees yet. I grab her and she screams, her body rigid as I pull her back-first into me.

With a roll of my eyes, I pick her up, throwing her over my shoulder and carrying her into the house. I take her back up to Theo's room, avoiding the party as best I can, and put her down. My brain is screaming at me to take her to the cells, do what I want with her. But I resist.

She stares at me, her eyes wide, and as soon as my hands leave her body, she runs.

I dart back to the door, prepared to stop her from trying to escape again, but that's not where she goes. Instead, she practically throws herself into Theo's closet, not even turning on the light and closing the door hard behind her.

What the fuck?

I give it a minute and she doesn't come back out. My crazy seems to have quieted in the face of hers, so I open the door and turn on the light, not sure what to expect.

'What are you doing in there?'

She doesn't answer, and, at first, I can't see her. I scan the small space and catch sight of her face. It's like that closet scene out of E.T., but instead of stuffed animals, it's Theo's clothes. I push some of them aside so I can get a better look at her.

She's backed into the corner like an animal, her knees drawn up and she's struggling to get something out of her pocket. Pulling out a little case with some wireless earbuds in it that she fumbles with, she tries to put them in her ears with shaking hands. She's rocking a little, breathing hard.

What is wrong with this human?

'Please leave me alone,' she whispers, but she doesn't make any eye contact with me.

This is way, way out of my comfort zone. I don't have the first idea of what to do for this girl besides lulling her and I'm not allowed to do that. I know she hasn't signed.

'I'm gonna go get Theo,' I mumble.

I go back down to the party, mentioning Callaghan and his friends to a couple of the prospects. I want them out of here. Finding Theo in a quiet conversation with Vic in the study, I poke my head through the door, catch his eye and jerk with my head. He comes out a second later.

'What is it?'

'Just come with me,' I say, and he looks a little worried, but he follows me back up the main stairs and along the hall to his room.

'Where is she?' he asks when we get inside.

'In your closet. Be careful. I think she's gone a little loco.' I move my forefinger around my ear in a circle to punctuate my words.

Theo gives me a look and I shrug.

Yeah, I know. Pot. Kettle.

'Look for yourself.'

Theo goes into his closet, and I follow.

'What happened to her?'

'Callaghan and his buddies scared her a little, but I ran them off before they could do much. I have some prospects taking care of them now.'

Both of us watch her. She doesn't stop her little rocking motion, but she does glance up.

'I can hear you, you know.' She taps the earbud. 'They don't work.'

'Then why are you wearing them?' Theo asks.

'I just am,' she whispers.

'Okay, princess,' Theo says in a calm voice.

He sounds almost *kind,* and it throws me a little. I've never heard him talk to the on-call girls like this. Maybe this is just how he talks to *uncontracted* human girls.

'I need to find out her medical history,' Theo mutters. 'She's not right.'

'Great,' I mutter. 'Vic's making us keep a defective one.'

Theo gives me another look as he closes the door and I shrug again.

'You think I give a shit what she hears me say about her?'

He ignores my question. 'Did Vic get a file from Paris' guy yet?'

'No idea. I know he's going to have a conversation with us tomorrow about her though.'

Theo waves me out of his room. 'I'll stay up here now, see if she wants anything in a little while.'

I nod, glad someone will be with her while I go check on the prospects' progress.

'Anything I should know about what happened to her?'

'Not really. Like I said, Callaghan and the other two were giving her a hard time, but I broke it up pretty fast. I've been warning Vic about him for months.'

'You and me both,' Theo sighs. 'Are you feeling okay?'

'Why?' I growl, feeling defensive.

He puts his hands up. 'Just wondered. You seem a little better tonight than you have lately.'

I snort and leave him with the crazy girl, but I wonder if he isn't right in his assessment. Maybe I don't feel so on the edge.

Going back downstairs, it looks like Callaghan and the others have been rounded up and I smile darkly. The two prospects I chose for that particular mission are big guys known for not pulling their punches. Both of them have sisters too. Callaghan and his cronies are going to regret trying to take what's ours before they're kicked off the property for good. I'll talk to Vic about them tomorrow. I've been letting things slip, I realize. I'm Vic's lieutenant and somewhere along the line I stopped acting like it. It's time to remedy that.

The house girls aren't at the party. They tend to stay away from the other supes if they know what's good for them.

I go down to their rooms. Their basement apartment is always open for us. I find all three of them there and though they're relaxed at first glance, as soon as they notice me, they all tense up, looking wary.

What I heard Callaghan say upstairs about our girls has me wondering if he and others have been making free with them too. I want to know the truth.

'I'm not here to feed,' I say.

The blond one, I think her name is Carrie, stands up while the other two stay behind her, cuddling together on the couch and looking at me in equal parts fear and eagerness.

Carrie raises a brow at me.

'I need to know something,' I say, staying where I am. I

was serious when I said I don't want to feed right now, not from them anyway.

'What is it?' Carrie asks, thinly veiled suspicion in her voice.

'Just had a problem upstairs with some of our guests thinking it's ok to touch our contracted humans. Anything like that ever happen to you girls?'

They look at each other, incredulity written on all their faces.

'Do they think it's ok to *touch* us?' She laughs, and it's a brittle sound. 'We're the house whores, incubus. What the fuck do you think?'

She looks away and so do the others.

'That stops now,' I mutter. 'From now on, anyone not me, Theo, Paris, Korban, or Vic even *looks* at you with anything but the deepest respect, and you tell us.' I swear under my breath. 'If you'd bothered to read your contracts properly, it says your favors are strictly ours. No one else has a claim to you outside the Club.'

Carrie sneers, looking back at me with hatred in her eyes. 'Like contracts with humans matter to the supes,' she snaps and then thinks twice and takes a step back as if she's afraid I'm going to retaliate.

'It stops now,' I say again, and turn around, not bothering to say anything more.

I return to the party and grab a beer. I think about going back up to Theo, but I can't stomach it. I don't want to be around the female anymore, so I'll go back out onto the deck and drink alone in the dark, hoping that my actions tonight have done *something* good for this Club.

CHAPTER
TWELVE
JANE

I sit in the closet for a long time with my earbuds in, trying to block out the errant sounds of the party downstairs. I'm not shaking on the outside anymore, but I'm sure as shit shaking on the inside.

All the awful places I've lived, all the times I've walked home in the dark and in the span of a week, it happens twice. Two times I've been attacked and there hasn't been a damn thing I could do to save myself. I'm a fucking damsel in distress.

Move over Sleeping Beauty. Ugh!

Theo's left me alone, I think to go get me a drink or some meds or something. I stopped listening after I heard what Sie said about me. I don't know why it hurt. Maybe if they think there's something wrong with me, Vic won't want me for their little MC anymore. They'll let me go and I can save Shar and the kids and all will be right with the world again ... at least until my stalkers catch up with me.

I stand up, shaking off the last of the fear. I need to get out of here and there's no time like the present. I sneak out of the room and down the back stairs again. The party's quieter now, and the kitchen's deserted. The doors to the deck are still wide open and I make my way quickly over to them. Freedom is so close, but I freeze in the middle of the kitchen. What if they're still out there? What if they catch me again and there's nobody to stop them?

I've decided to forget for the moment that the incubus who saved me is the one I'm most afraid of here, that he took me back to my room and was practically a gentleman. I didn't get that vibe off him in his room the other day, that's for sure. I mean I was rocking in the corner like a crazy woman though. Maybe that shit doesn't get his supey dick hard.

I can't stay out in the open like this, I remind myself. I push through the fear and go out onto the deck.

I can hear the sounds of a fight in the woods, and I wonder if that's where everyone's gone. Works for me if it gives me a window of opportunity.

I scuttle down the wooden steps of the deck and around the side of the house, grabbing my backpack and throwing it over my shoulder. I don't take the driveway cuz I'm not a fucking idiot.

I go off into the woods in the direction of the road, but halfway there I veer off to the right. I don't know why, but it's a feeling in my gut that I've learned not to second guess, a part of me knows something that the rest doesn't and it's usually right.

Making my way through the trees slowly because it's dark and I'm travelling by the light of the moon, I wonder if there are ravines out here and if I'd see one in time to stop myself from falling to my death. There's nothing to do but keep going now though. I'm committed to Plan B.

I'm heading for something, but I don't know what. I can feel a buzz, but it's not electricity, it's something I'd never felt before until I got to this house and there's less of it – whatever it is – close by, so that's the direction I'm headed.

I see the road before I leave the tree line. It's deserted, but I won't be traveling along the side of it anyway. I just want to cross it to get off the MC's property. There's a path in front of me, like a little animal trail, and I follow it, but as I move down it, someone grabs me, covering my mouth.

Not again!

This is fucking ridiculous.

I try to scream, but it's way too late for that. Is it one of the guys from the deck? My body goes rigid as I'm hauled off my feet and into a hard chest.

'What's this?' says a harsh whisper in my ear. 'A little human girl lost in the forest?'

The grip tightens painfully. 'I'm not going to overlook the fact that you came *right to this spot,*' he growls, and it's not the sound of his voice that I recognize, it's his scent; like leather, and a flower I can't name.

Korban.

His hand is still around my mouth, so I can't say a word as he squeezes me. I let out a whimper as his arms constrict me like a snake. How long before my bones begin to break?

'Please,' I cry, the sound muffled by his hand, and he moves it away as he breathes me in deep, making me shiver.

'No screams, little human?' he asks.

'Who am I going to scream for?' I wonder aloud and I hear a low sound escape from him.

'Who, indeed?' he purrs, and I get the feeling I've misunderstood something.

'What are you doing out here?' he asks.

I tell the truth. 'Trying to escape. Obviously.'

He lets me go and I turn around to face him. Even in the dim light, he looks remarkably unscathed for a man who was in a fight just last night, but I guess he did win so ...

I glance up. The moon is obscured by cloud, and I can't see anything. I take a step towards the boundary, and he takes two.

'You're not getting out,' he says, and he sounds so fucking happy about that.

My lip curls into a sneer.

'Fuck you,' I mutter.

'What did you just say to me?'

'I said, fuck you. Fuck you and the Iron I's and your supey dicks and your dumb, massive house. Just let me go so I can leave town and my friends will be safe!'

Close to tears, I lunge for the boundary, but of course he catches me. I find myself on my back, the wind knocked out of me as he throws himself on top of me, making my ribs twinge for the first time since I took that clearly *magickally* strong painkiller Theo gave me the other day.

∼

Korban

I CATCH HER EASILY, throwing her on the ground and straddling her. She struggles under me until my hand wraps around her throat and I cut off her oxygen.

She freezes.

'Yes,' I coo, 'you're going to tell me who you're working for, aren't you, you human bitch?'

She can't breathe and she's beginning to struggle again, but I want her to know how serious I am. I *could* kill her out here and there wouldn't be even one fucking repercussion if I did. I won't even get in that much trouble with Vic since she's probably a spy anyway. I mean, she came right here to the breach in the perimeter. She knew exactly where it was.

I let her go just a little bit and she pulls in air, wheezing hard.

'I don't work for anyone,' she gasps.

'Wrong answer.'

I put pressure on her windpipe again, and her pretty, pleading eyes widen.

'Don't play dumb with me. You know where the hole in the border spell is. How, if you didn't put it there?'

She claws at my hand, and I let her answer.

'I don't know, I promise I don't,' she squeals in panic. 'It was just luck. I was trying to get to the road and—'

'Bullshit! I was only looking for the breach but maybe we do have a spy as well. After all, it was you who came to us with that pretty little bauble that those fae fucks have made sure Vic is just desperate enough to not be able to resist. So where'd you get it, huh?'

'It was my mom's. She left it to me.'

'Please!' I say with a laugh. 'Do people in your human world actually believe this shit?'

'It's true!' She looks indignant rather than terrified and I give her a bemused look.

'I'm going to ask you one more time,' I say, 'and then I'm going to choke the life out of you. Do you understand?'

She nods, looking uncertain.

'What are you doing out here?'

'Trying to escape.' She looks at me like I'm an idiot.

'Why now? You got what you came for?'

'I didn't come for anything,' she says. 'You guys brought me here, not the other way around. I never asked to come. You guys took my payment, the only thing I had of value, and then told me the deal was done because you handed a few college kids their asses, instead of taking care of my actual problem. I just want to go so I can leave town, and no one kills my last friend and her little kids because of me!'

She shakes her head. 'Fuck this,' she says under her breath. 'I can't do it anymore. Maybe if I was gone, they'd be safe.'

She sounds defeated, and I wonder if she's going to tell me the truth now. Her arms fall to the ground at her sides, and she closes her eyes, breathing deeply and relaxing under me.

'Just do it,' she whispers. 'I'm tired.'

Her head falls to the side, and she breathes in slow. I squeeze, calling her on her bluff, but she doesn't fight me. She just lays under me while I choke her, and I frown. It's not fun anymore and I can tell she's the type who doesn't go back on what she says, come hell or high water ... But there are other ways I can get her to talk. She doesn't need to sign a contract if I suspect her of activities against the Club. I have carte blanche to do whatever I need to if it means obtaining the information I need.

I slowly shift, letting her breathe again and very gently opening the top button of her jeans, pulling the zip down ever so slowly and watching her face while I do it.

I see her frown as she feels me.

'What are you doing?' she asks. 'Still trying to get truths out of me even though you think I'm a liar?'

My hand delves into her jeans over her underwear, and she tenses, her eyes flying open to find mine.

I keep her locked to the ground by her neck, as I move

my legs in order to spread hers a little bit. Not too much, just enough so I can—

My finger slides down her crease and she gasps a little, her eyes not leaving mine, and something hits me, powerful and delicious.

The taste of her is like an expensive dinner and I haven't even lulled her yet. I look down at her face, expecting pleasure. Passion. But it's blank. Expressionless. She feels it, just doesn't show it.

I dig my knuckles into her just shy of painful and watch her mouth open on a whimper. I want to go further. Right now. Damned if I can stop myself.

I make sure she can take in air because for once I don't want to kill the bitch I'm going to fuck. This one's special somehow, at least for right now, and I wonder if this was what I've been feeling every time I've watched her, smelled her, since she got here.

I move her underwear to the side, noting with amusement that her panties are massive as I slip a finger into her. The sound that comes from her is something between a whine, a moan, and a whimper, and I fucking love it. There's fear in her eyes, but she wants it too. I can feel how much as I thumb her clit, as I move my lone finger in and out. She's tight and I'm filled with the urge to bury my face between those thighs.

She comes fast and suddenly, fingers clawing at the dirt beside her as a cry is ripped from her throat.

It echoes through the trees.

'That's right, human, let Korban make you feel good,' I murmur, glad that Paris isn't here for this one.

I don't need him tonight, I realize in surprise. I've never actually been with a woman without Paris, not since I got out of that place.

I frown, pulling my finger from her and, unable to stop myself, I suck it clean, holding back a deep, possessive growl of pleasure.

'Fuck,' I breathe, glancing down at her.

She's panting, eyes staring at the sky. She's not moving though I've let her throat go and she could if she wanted. That delicious lust that was coming from her before is completely gone now, as if it was never there at all.

She's blinking hurriedly and sniffling. I stand up and tower over her.

'Get up,' I say.

She gets to her feet slowly, her clothes in disarray, avoiding looking at me altogether.

'Fix your clothes,' I growl, and she flinches as she does what I say, pulling at them, rebuttoning and zipping her jeans.

I push her in front of me.

'Move,' I say, taking her back to the house and inside through the pool door.

I pull her straight into the gym, wanting somewhere that I can contain her and that's one of the only rooms in the house without a window.

I push her down to sit on the mats in the middle of the room where I can keep an eye on her while I empty her backpack out on the table. Rifling through the contents, I find nothing that's from the house, nothing about who she really is. There are some clothes and other necessities and that's about it. My eyes widen at what I find hidden at the bottom of the bag. Is that a dildo? It's so pink ... *and sparkly*.

I glance at her, wondering if she's playing with me, but she gives nothing away. She's just sitting cross-legged, staring at the floor. I throw everything back in including her little toy.

'Who are you working for?' I ask again.

Nothing. She doesn't show that she's heard anything I've said. I stand over her and her eyes don't move from a single spot on the mats in front of her.

'Look at me,' I order, and she slowly lifts her head.

Her expression is as blank as it was out in the woods. She's wrapped her arms around herself like she's cold.

'Get up,' I order her again, pulling her to her feet.

I take her through the hidden passage behind the mirror that comes out in the pantry, and we go through the kitchen and up the back stairs back to Theo's room.

Thankfully, it looks like the party is over and there doesn't seem to be anyone in the house. They probably went to the bar or something, but I check my phone just in case. I have messages on the group chat asking if I've seen the new girl and I let everyone know I just saw her wandering the house and brought her back to her room. I don't want them knowing anything else just yet.

As we go into Theo's room, my guiding hand comes off her. Not looking back, she kicks off her shoes and goes straight into Theo's closet, not even turning on the light.

I stare after her, wondering what the fuck she's doing.

Weird human.

She doesn't act like a spy. She doesn't even act like an on-call girl, always brushing up against the guys, always wanting the high. I can't fucking stand being around them most days.

But not the new girl. She hasn't even looked at me since the forest unless I've made her. I scratch my head, wondering if I should stay in the room but decide against it. She has nothing left in her now. She won't be running again. Not tonight.

I go back to my room and lay on my bed sated in a way I haven't been before. It's like eating a turkey dinner with all the trimmings but stopping before you make yourself feel sick, knowing that you've eaten something that tastes delicious and is made with only the finest ingredients. That's what she's like; the finest Swiss chocolates or vintage wine. Quality.

I take out the little red thong that's still in my pocket and then my dick out of my pants. I wrap it around the base of my hard shaft tightly as I jack off to thoughts of her underneath me in those woods, the sounds she made, the feel of her. I jerk myself fast and rough. I make it hurt and come hard thinking of her swallowing it down.

I lie back and put her underwear back in my pocket. That little scrap of satin comes with me everywhere now like a perverted little talisman.

I wonder if I should tell Vic what went on tonight, but I decide not to just yet. He'll only worry that she's not contracted officially. Even though I can theoretically do whatever I like with her now that I suspect her of crimes against the Club, the supe authorities and those fucking fae assholes have us by the nuts. They'll make us jump through all kinds of hoops to prove it just so it looks to the humans like they give a shit, so I'm gonna keep her to myself for the moment.

Maybe I'll tell Sie. I know he could use a pick-me-up. Maybe we'll take her together.

I like that idea. It would be fun to play with her, watch her and Sie, maybe the others too. I bet they can make her scream just as well as I can.

I lay back in my bed with a sigh, wondering how my interrogation of her is gonna go tomorrow because that's what it'll be even though I'm going to lull her so good she's not going to know what she's saying while I ask her what I want to know. I'll get the information I need out of her one way or the other and then we'll see how Vic wants to punish the little human infiltrator.

CHAPTER
THIRTEEN
JANE

I spend the rest of the night huddled in Theo's closet, feeling numb and overwhelmed, my ribs throbbing from Korban's tackle. I can't believe what happened out in the woods. I can't believe I *let* that happen. Logically, I know I couldn't do anything to stop it. Korban is huge and strong and … But the scariest thing is that I didn't *want* him to stop.

When I finally venture out, the room is deserted and the door to the hall is closed.

I take a hot shower to help with my bodily aches and scrub my hair with my own shampoo and conditioner that I brought from my apartment while I'm at it, as Korban was so generous as to leave my backpack by my door after he rifled through it and accused me of spying.

For who? *Why?*

I notice a new bodywash next to Theo's and I smell it tentatively. It smells like heaven and I breath it into my nose as deep as I can get it, washing my body with it and then, because I hate feeling prickly, shaving with what I'm guessing is Theo's razor.

When I can tear myself away from the amazing aroma of the new soap, I come out of the bathroom and get dressed in some clean jeans and another black tank.

Eyeing the clothes from last night that are soiled and dirty, I put them in the hamper, not sure what I'm feeling as I look at the reminders of being on the damp ground, Korban's hands on me, around my throat. I wouldn't ever have dreamed I'd like something like that. Usually any kind of discomfort makes my brain go crazy, but ... I touch my neck gently and it feels a little bruised, but I didn't notice any marks in the mirror. My lower muscles contract and I frown. How can my body know what it wants when the rest of me hasn't got a clue?

I put it out of my mind for now. It'll take time to mull over everything and figure it out and there are more important things to worry about than Korban's fingers in my pussy. After last night, and my third unsuccessful escape attempt, it's looking like I'm going to have to go with Plan C. Every time I try to get out of this house, things seem to go worse for me.

I need to help Shar and her kids, and I think I know what will provide the best outcome. When I haven't been reliving what Korban did to me in the woods, I've been thinking about Plan C, and I think I've covered every angle, but there's only one real way to find out.

I leave the room, going downstairs via the main stairs this time because I'm not about to hide when I need to be strong for my new plan. Putting on my big girl panties, but still second guessing myself the entire way, I finally make it to Vic's study door.

I take a deep breath. As long as Shar and the kids are safe, what happens to me doesn't really matter. My hand still shakes as I raise it to the door though and I hesitate one final time.

I steel myself against the uncertainty. I don't want those kids to lose their mom, and I sure as hell don't want Shar to lose her life because she decided, one fateful shift, to talk to the odd new girl at the diner.

I'm frozen like an unexalted statue, a piece of very shit modern art, standing in the grand foyer while I go through it again in my head, wondering if I've missed something, if something else will work, but I don't think so. These men and my situation are a rock and a hard place. There's no getting out of it. At least, not anytime soon.

It's true that I still have no idea what Vic's true motivations for wanting me as a fixture in his house are, but it doesn't matter anymore. A part of me is just glad he'll take me because the truth is if I can make this work, at least Shar and the kids will be ok.

Hopefully I can undo some of the damage I've caused to their lives, and my actions won't weigh as heavily on me as they do now. I'm drowning in guilt, and I hate it.

Another deep breath and I'm bringing my knuckles up to rap on the door, but it opens right at that moment before I even touch it. I fall back a step in surprise, staring into the golden-brown eyes of Paris.

At least he doesn't seem mad at me still, going by his hands which are not in fists, and the fact that his teeth aren't still grinding together.

'What are you doing out here?' he asks.

Is that suspicion I hear? Has he been talking to Korban? I need to get this done before Vic changes his mind and won't have me.

'I need to speak with your boss,' I say, strolling into the study without waiting for an invitation.

Vic's there alone with Paris, and I sit down in the chair.

'Do you still want me to sign your contract?' I ask, getting right to the point.

Vic sits back, steepling his fingers like a much hotter and not-quite-so-yellow Mr. Burns as he looks at me, not giving anything away. He shrugs like he doesn't care either way, but I know this is just a ploy.

I roll my eyes at his games. Shar and the kids don't have time for this. 'I'll sign it,' I say, 'but I want you to do something for me.'

'Demands, huh? What is it?' Vic asks, seeming more curious than anything else.

'My friend from the diner, Sharlene ... she needs help. Whoever got your boy, Dreyson, killed Sarge, Gail's cook, the other night too. She's afraid.'

'We heard about the cook,' Paris says from behind me, and I wonder what else they've kept from me.

'You didn't think I should know that Sarge was murdered?' I ask.

Vic shakes his head. 'Nope.'

'But he was my friend,' I say and Vic snorts.

'Someone like you doesn't have friends.'

I don't let him see how close that comment hits to the mark, but inside I flinch hard.

Fuck. How true that is. *He hit the nail right on the head, Jane.*

'Sharlene and her kids are in hiding. She's afraid she'll be next. She thinks they're watching her.'

'She's probably just being paranoid,' Vic says condescendingly, and I narrow my eyes at him.

'It actually doesn't matter whether you believe she's in danger, or not,' I reply. 'I'll sign your contract, but I want Shar and her children taken care of. Right now they're at the Lucky Eight Motel. I want you to send her and her kids somewhere where they'll be safe ... like Hawaii,' I say. 'Yes, Hawaii! I want you to set them up in a nice house ... in a good neighborhood with great schools ... by a beach.'

'Anything else?' Vic asks, and I can't work out from his tone whether or not he's entertaining this crazy plan of mine.

'Money for her to live on until she can get a job,' I say, 'and I want weekly calls with her. Video calls. I want to know she and the kids are really okay.'

'Done.'

The sound from Paris behind me indicates that I'm not the only one who's shocked that the leader of the Iron I's just agreed to all this.

But I stand up, and I don't show the fact that I'm 100% floored and exuberant as hell. I can't believe he just said yes!

'Good,' I say. 'I'm not signing anything until it's done. I want it written into the contract that if you don't hold up your end this time, I get to rip the damn thing up and you have to let me go.'

He laughs in my face, and I can't help but wince for real.

'Do you really think that would matter? Why would we even care?'

I shrug. 'I have no idea to be honest, but you want me here for something and I'm telling you I'll stay without a fuss if you keep my friend and her kids safe. It's a small price because, trust me, I can be such a *pain in the ass* that you will either have to let me leave your happy little motorcycle funhouse, or fucking kill me.'

Vic stares at me for a few seconds looking for something, but I don't know what. Then he nods.

'As soon as everything's ready, I'll have the contract for

you, but you sign your name in blood this time and if you even think about trying to escape again, your stalkers will be the least of 'Shar and her kids' problems.'

I make an effort to look him right in the eye. I'm not going to show fear. I need this too much.

'I won't,' I say, standing up and leaving his office without another word.

Neither of them tries to stop me and I wander around the house a little, wondering if I'll be allowed to come up here to use the pool or the gym if I feel like it.

Do they let the other girls leave their little underground bunker, or do they have to wait until their incubi masters are hungry?

My heart starts to beat faster as I think about what they might ask of me physically. I've never done anything like this before. Prior to coming here, my experience amounted to a disappointing one-night stand when I was just trying to get rid of my virginity and countless times alone trying to wring whatever pleasure I can out of myself with a vibrator on my clit.

Are they going to expect that I know all the things? Because I definitely don't know all the things. I mean I know *some* of the things. I've seen porn, but theory and practice are totally different. I stifle a laugh. Maybe I don't need to worry about the contract. Maybe they'll rip it up as soon as my almost complete inexperience becomes apparent, when they see what a shit show my emotions are, the social ineptitude, the nonverbal overloads.

I don't see anyone as I amble around. Paris and Vic are still in the office. The other three, I have no idea. Sie spends a lot of time in his room I've noticed, and I've seen Theo leave in the mornings only to return at the end of the day looking exhausted. Korban I hardly ever see at all. Guess he's a night owl.

I find myself walking up to the second floor past his room. What am I doing? Hoping to see him again? I think about last night when he caught me trying to escape. I swallow hard because although at the time I was scared, I know it wasn't about him. My gut tells me that none of these guys are really going to hurt me. My fear is of the intense reactions I'm having to them, that I don't understand or know what to do with.

Of course my gut can be a fucking liar that has got me into trouble more times than I remember, so maybe it's best not to trust any part of my body except my head.

I run my hands over my face, and I go back to my room. Sitting down on the bed, I put my head in my hands.

I don't feel like I'm going to lose it or anything, but I'm anxious. I wonder if I should tell Vic about my problems. At best he won't care, but at worst, he'll find a way to use them against me. I guess they'll probably just lull them away with their magickal mojo anyway.

That thought makes me pause. Can they do that? Maybe that'd be best and then I can spend the next three years being their malleable, little, sex doll. I wrinkle my nose, but maybe it won't be so bad. I'm not the only human girl here, after all. They can't want it ALL THE TIME!

I frown, following a train of thought that makes me even more nervous only because I don't know the answers yet. Will I be able to say no sometimes? I guess the contract will explain it all ... but then I remind myself that none of it matters anyway. I don't care what I have to sacrifice to make sure the people I care about don't die, don't care if I have to give up this one last thing, my freedom. It's a small price for Shar and the kids' lives and, really, how much freedom have I actually enjoyed this past decade anyway?

Darkness comes and I realize I haven't eaten all day. I'm not hungry though. My stomach is tied up in knots. I haven't moved all afternoon, so I stand up to stretch my legs, going into the bathroom to splash my face with cold water, taking a moment to brush my hair into some semblance of order and put it up in a ponytail.

When I come back out, Korban is standing in the middle of my room. He's between me and the exit.

In front of him again, I take a step back with the realization that my dumb gut *was* wrong. This guy is scary and scowly and almost as big as Sie ... and he closes the distance between us before I have time to do anything.

He grabs me by the back of the neck and draws me closer to him. He takes a deep breath in through his nose, smelling me.

'Fuck,' he groans, 'I'm in the lead.'

I have no idea what he's talking about. I'm frozen, my heart humming in my chest, my blood pumping hard. Fight or flight doesn't work on me I guess because I'm not doing either. I'm just standing there short circuiting.

My eyes lock onto his face. He doesn't seem to notice my panic as he begins to unbutton my shirt. Outraged, I finally find my wits enough to slap his hand away.

'I know you want more after last night,' he says in an arrogant way that makes my lip curl. 'I'll give it to you, human, give you that high you're chasing. Do you want it? Do you want me to let my power flow out? Do you want me to make your body relax for me? When I'm done, you'll be in bliss. I hear it's like an orgasm that lasts for hours.'

I don't say anything.

'Yes,' he says, his grip on me tightening the longer he talks. 'Your kind always want it, don't you?'

'No,' I say, looking up into his face and I'm happy to find I'm not lying.

Fuck this guy.

The way he's looking at me makes me want to get away from him. Even I can tell this is just business. He's cold. Last night felt different. I couldn't see him, but I know he wasn't like this. He's using me for something.

'I haven't signed your fucking contract yet,' I say, shaking off his hand and turning away from him.

Wrong move.

He grabs me by my hair and pushes me over the bed, holding me there easily.

I thrash, getting a lucky kick into his knee and he grunts in pain, the pressure pushing me down easing enough for me to slip out and roll away to the other side of the bed.

'No!' I say in a forceful voice even though I'm close to angry, scared tears. 'You can't just come in here and do this!'

He looks at me like I'm a puzzle he just can't quite figure out.

'You're a human female,' he says like that explains everything. He rolls his eyes when I just stare at him. 'Human females are always up for it whether ... whether we want them or not. It's the way you're made.'

'Well, I'm *not* made that way!' I snap.

He doesn't seem to understand what I'm saying, so I say it again slower.

'I don't want your *bliss*,' I say out loud.

He snorts like he doesn't believe me. 'Stop playing hard to get. It doesn't suit you.'

'You don't know me.' I scowl, taking a step towards the door. 'I'm not like other girls.'

I cringe because I sound like one of those girls who think they're so cool and edgy and different and *better* than the other girls somehow. Except that I *am* different. It's just not the cool and edgy kind at all. And I'm not better. I'm worse.

'What I mean is,' I tap my temple and I give him a look. Am I really going to have to spell it out?

'C'mon. You must be able to tell,' I say, suddenly feeling close to tears again and it's not from anger or fear this time ... I don't know what it's from.

'You can see I'm not the same.' I look away, my voice feeling like it's going to break if I talk again and give me away. I don't want him to see me crying.

'I can make you want it,' he threatens.

I sigh heavily and cast my eyes back to him, forcing my words to be even and strong. 'After I've signed your contract, do whatever the hell you want. Until then, don't fucking touch me.'

He looks surprised, and then a grin spreads across his face. 'Alright,' he says, 'I can play by your rules, little spy.'

The door is flung open at that precise moment and Theo's standing in the doorway. He looks me over first. His eyes taking in my clothes, perhaps the fact that I'm still dressed.

He sneers at Korban. 'What the fuck are you doing in here?'

Korban shrugs. 'Check your cameras and find out.'

My eyes widen and dart around the room. 'Cameras?'

Theo's eyes narrow at Korban. 'Get the fuck out!'

Korban chuckles as he saunters into the hallway. 'See you after you've signed, girl. You better be ready for me.'

'Do your job right, sex demon, and I will be,' I return with way more bravado than I actually feel, and I hear him laugh from down the corridor.

∽

Theo

Kor leaves the room, a shit-eating grin on his face that I'd love to smack off it.

He has me nervous. Though I'd never admit it out loud, my fingers are tapping a mile a minute on the pad of the stethoscope in my pocket. I look over at the new girl. She's not meeting my eyes but this time it's not because she's afraid of my power. She looks even more on-edge than she was before. She seems ok, but my eyes cut to the door Kor just disappeared through.

'Did he hurt you?' I ask.

She looks surprised by the question but gives a little shake of her head.

I don't believe her. 'You have to tell me if he has.'

She shakes her head again and goes into the bathroom, closing the door. Guess our conversation is over.

My phone buzzes and I look down at it. Vic wants us in the study for a meeting. This can only be about her.

I smother a grin at my childish excitement as I make my way downstairs. The other guys are already there, the room looking tiny as all five of us crowd inside. Usually we do this in the games room where there's more space.

Vic throws the bolt, locking us in, and no one says anything, eyeing our president expectantly as he walks around the room to sit behind the desk.

'The new girl has agreed to contract with the Club,' he says, not making us wait.

I know my own eyes are lighting up in anticipation and I see the same look in Paris'.

Sie just looks annoyed by the whole thing, and Korban, the one I expected to crow the loudest as we have three humans living in the house already, stays silent. Considering where I just caught him, it's telling that he's not saying anything.

'How'd you get her to do that?' I chuckle, and Vic shrugs, not giving anything away as usual.

'Should have everything in place in a few hours. I called you here because Maddox invited us to *The Circle* tonight.' He pauses. 'We're going to take the new girl.'

'Why?' Sie growls. 'We never bring any of the others.'

'A distraction, so we can take a look around. You know how he covets what's ours and he's already interested in her. Kor found the hole in the perimeter last night, but Paris can't plug it until the full moon. If Maddox is making a move, I want to know what it is, and what it has to do with some human.' He leans back. 'And, anyway, she should see what supes are really like when the humans aren't watching. Maybe then she'll be a little bit more grateful that we've allowed her into the Club.'

Sie walks to the window and looks out. 'I don't like it. Something's off about this whole thing.'

He looks at Korban for back up, but Kor just shrugs.

'She's just a pretty human. Dime a dozen. Bring her if Maddox wants to see our new house whore. I don't give a shit.'

I frown. Korban has his own agenda, but I'm fucked if I can see what it is.

'She'll need some clothes. Can't show up there representing the Iron I's dressed like we picked her up in a shelter.'

Vic waves a hand at Paris. 'Make sure she has something expensive to wear.'

He and Kor turn towards the door.

'Wait,' I say. 'Did you get the info on her yet?'

Vic nods. 'I skimmed it. Jane Mercy. Twenty-five. Parents gone. Other than the stalkers thing, there's not much out of the ordinary about her.'

'Can I see it?' I ask.

Vic takes an envelope out of a drawer and frisbees it over to me. I open it and slide out the folder of documents. It's thin.

'Not much on her,' I comment.

'There's not much to know. Her mother died when she was young, father disappeared when she was ten. She was in foster until she was fourteen and she's been moving around ever since.'

I start perusing the documents. 'Unmarried. No children and no relatives. Couldn't find a more perfect girl if we tried,' I mutter.

And then I get to the last page and find a medical report on there from a child psychologist.

I scan the title. 'Signs of Autism or Asperger's Syndrome.' I take a look at the date. It's from over ten years ago, which explains the outdated terminology because Asperger's as a diagnosis has been mostly phased out these days.

'She's autistic!' I facepalm, so much clicking into place. 'How did I miss it?'

'She's what?' Vic and the others are frowning at me.

'Autistic,' I say again.

They all look at me with blank expressions on their faces.

'She was diagnosed as neurodivergent when she was a teenager.'

Paris grimaces. 'What the hell does that mean? She's a retar—'

I cast such an angry look at Paris that he shuts his mouth before he says the rest of *that* word, but it's only a second before he continues.

'Wait! Like Rain Man? If we throw a box of matches over the floor, would she be able to count them at a glance? Should we take her to Vegas?'

I stare at him in disgust until he notices, and the grin disappears.

'Fucking educate yourself,' I say, but I look over at Vic. 'Do you still want her?'

Vic doesn't seem overly bothered. 'What does it mean?'

'In her case?' I look through the rest of the report quickly. 'This is a decade out of date, but at the time ... looks like sensory issues, some problems communicating, being overwhelmed in school, nonverbal episodes.'

'What do you mean by sensory issues?'

'No two people with the condition are the same. Could be bright lights, loud noises ...'

'Earbuds,' Paris says. 'She put earbuds in when we rode into town. She was pretty upset when we got back. I was angry, revving the bike a lot, taking the turns hard ...'

I nod, remembering her putting them in last night too. 'Yeah, sounds about right.'

'Told you she's defective,' Sie mutters and I roll my eyes.

I turn back to Vic. 'She seems to get along just fine mostly, but if you're still serious about contracting her, I'm going to send you and the others some websites to read up about the condition.'

'What's the point?' Kor growls. 'She'll be no different from any of the others once she's lulled anyway. There's no point talking about this anymore.' He changes the subject. 'The hole I found is down by the stream. It's barely wide enough for a child to crawl through, but easy to fly some drones in. I could do a sweep, make sure no one's watching still.'

Vic nods and stands up. 'Do it.'

Kor opens his mouth like he has something to add but hesitates.

'Is there more?'

Korban grits his teeth. 'Yes. The girl tried to escape again last night.'

'You told us you found her in the house.'

'Well, I didn't. She was in the woods heading directly for the hole.'

Vic eyes Korban, not bothering to hide his flash of anger. 'You're telling us this now?'

'I didn't know we were going to keep her, but I'd bet she's here for a reason. How else could she have known exactly where it was? Do you still want to contract her?'

'Yes.' Vic's chair creaks as he leans back in it. He doesn't look surprised by Korban's suspicions at all. 'Once she's signed the papers, betraying the Club comes with its own set of punishments. If she truly is working with someone against us, we can find out easier if she's here and then we'll make this work to *our* advantage.'

I wonder if she truly is a spy. I can't say I get that vibe off her at all, but dammit, Jim, I'm a doctor, not a Machiavellian mastermind! What I am wondering is why Vic is so adamant that he wants her though.

'I need to do some research,' I say, leaving them to it and going into the games room.

Sitting on the couch, I open my laptop and I start looking into adult autism. The more I read, the more I'm certain that the psychologist was correct in Jane's original assessment. She seems to be able to get through life ok, but I've definitely noticed some behaviors that fit; sensory overload, lack of emotional response in some situations, not understanding some of the more intricate social cues ...

Part of me is excited, kind of like I have a new pet project, but Kor was right. We probably won't even notice it much. Once she's in the lull, she'll act like every other girl. Once she has a taste of what we can give her, she'll willingly spread her legs for the high and beg for the pleasure we provide. She won't be able to help it.

CHAPTER
FOURTEEN
JANE

There's a sunbeam coming in through the window and I'm staring at it, lost in a scenario where I tell Vic where to stick it and somehow find a way to escape with Shar to Hawaii, never to be found.

'Well?'

Vic's voice draws me back to my actual reality. I'm sitting in his office again, just him and me. I look down at the contract. I've been in here for an hour at least, reading fine print and there's like twenty pages of it. I guess it's all pretty standard stuff for taking on a human, not that I'd know personally. They have to provide me with clothes, food, and a roof over my head, basic necessities like soap, and, in return, I feed them whenever they call, *however* they want. Anxiety turns my stomach as I read, finding an addendum at the end that lays out exactly what they're obligated to do for Shar and her kids. I read it over slowly at least a dozen times, trying to make sure it's as airtight as possible. It's not like I can consult a lawyer on this shit.

I finally look up at Vic, and I give him a single nod. He picks up the pen from his desk, his eyes not leaving mine.

He hands it over and, as I take it, my fingers brush his and I can't help the small gasp as my skin seems to come alive under his. I can't tell if he feels the same thing, this electricity that makes my body feel so warm. Maybe he's doing it on purpose. I've felt it before with the others. Maybe it's one of their incubus tricks.

I suppose I'll be learning all about those now. Resigned, I don't fuck around this time. I just date and sign. I hand it back to him and the finality of all of this settles over me. My head swims a little and I have to remind myself of why I've done this.

Shar is safe now, already in Hawaii. She spoke to me on a video call, told me everything was legit, and that the human guys who had come to take her from the hotel and put her on a private jet with the kids had been polite – and hot! She was practically speechless for her though, despite the fact that I'd texted her to let her know what was happening. She thanked me over and over and then asked me how I'd done it. I smiled like I hadn't heard her and ended the call because I didn't know what to say.

Vic immediately turns to the final page to make sure I actually signed the document with my name this time.

I stand up and he pins me with a look.

'Aren't you forgetting something?' he drawls.

I don't say anything, wondering what he's talking about.

He takes a letter opener from his desk and hands it to me. It's sharp; sharper than a letter opener has any right to be in my opinion. I cock my head in question.

'I told you, you sign in blood.'

'Oh, right.'

Swallowing hard, I slice the pad of my finger and I push

it into the paper by the side of my signature, making a crude, crimson fingerprint.

The look he gives me is predatory and I resist the urge to run. It's way too late for that I think as he circles the desk and grabs my hand. I can do nothing but stand there as he brings my bleeding finger up to his mouth and licks it, his eyes never leaving mine. Something coils low in my belly, and I'm shocked that it's desire.

I pull away from him. He can use his power on me now, lull me, do whatever without repercussions, but surely they won't start everything *right now*, will they?

He lets me go, surveying me. 'You know what you just signed away, don't you? You did actually read the contract, right?'

'Yeah,' I breath, 'it's just ...' I shake my head. 'So what happens now? Do I move down to the dungeon?'

'Dungeon?' He gives a small chuckle. 'Not quite yet. For now, you'll stay in Theo's room. There really isn't enough space down there for another girl.'

'Well, ok then.' I incline my head and we just stare at each other for a few moments longer.

I feel like he's wondering what to do with me.

'Go back to your room,' he commands, and I resist the urge to disobey his words even though I want to.

I turn around without a backwards glance, leaving Vic's office and climbing the stairs.

I stop short as I enter my bedroom, seeing Paris is in there. It's late and there's a tray on the desk with a sandwich on it.

Paris has put something on the bed, and I can't pretend I'm not curious as I approach him slowly and peer over his arm. There's a dress laid out on the comforter. A very short dress.

'The others' clothes are virginal compared to this,' I say under my breath.

He laughs.

'They don't usually come out with us except to the bar sometimes,' he replies.

'What?'

He regards me with what I think is amusement. 'Vic didn't fill you in, princess? You're coming with us tonight.'

'Where to?' I ask faintly.

'A club.'

'A club?'

'Yeah! You a good dancer, human girl?'

'No.' I say plainly.

He laughs. 'We'll see.'

I'm a little confused, but I don't say anything else, just nod like I know exactly what's going on.

'We leave in an hour. Eat your food. Take a shower. Be downstairs by eight.'

One-hundred and ten percent business all of a sudden, he's gone before I can ask him anything else. So, I eat the sandwich, turning my nose up at the brown bread but gobbling it up anyway because I'm hungry and I have no idea when I'll get to eat next. These guys don't exactly keep to normal hours as far as I can tell.

I take a quick shower, using what is fast becoming one of my new favorite shower soaps. I leave my hair down, but I bring an elastic with me in case it gets to be too much. It curls around my face a little and I brush it away as it dries. The dress is ridiculous. Bodycon and spandexy. There's even a black bra and matching thong.

How do they know all my sizes?

The glittery shoes are a problem. They're pretty. But strappy, four-inch stilettos? I try them on, and plod around the room like a toddler, almost turning my ankle in the process. I don't wear heels for a reason. Can't work 'em. I kick them off and carry them as I make my way down the stairs to the foyer at exactly eight o'clock.

All five of them are waiting and none of them are dressed the way I thought they'd be; the way other guys dress when they go out around here. Long shorts and button down, short sleeved shirts are the height of sophistication for the guys who go to the college. These guys are in another league. Each is dressed in a black suit, black shirt, black tie, black shoes. The Iron I insignia is embroidered into the left lapel of their jackets subtly in black, so it only just shows up to shine a little in the light.

I realize I haven't been in the presence of all five of them since that day at the bar when I first met them, and I'm surprised to find that I feel a little more comfortable with them than I did before. It usually takes me a lot longer to get that familiarity that so many people seem to just *have* with others.

I feel their eyes roving over me as I guess mine were over them, and I flinch away from their stares, belatedly wondering how I can ride on the back of a bike to wherever we're going dressed like this.

'Put on your shoes,' Vic practically snaps. 'It's time to go.'

I look down at them in my hand. 'I can't,' I mutter.

'What?'

I think he sounds impatient, but I know it when I feel that pressure on me. I take a step back.

'I can't walk in them,' I say. 'I don't wear shoes like these.'

'Just put them on,' Sie growls from where he's leaning against the wall.

Suitably cowed by his tone, I do what he says, sitting down carefully on the stairs and trying not to let them see my fifi trixibelle in this short as fuck dress.

When I stand up and start to walk, I get to the bottom of the stairs before my heel goes to the side and I fall into Sie. He grabs me, stops me from hurting myself, and I find myself staring up into his stony eyes. My cheeks burning, I murmur a thank you and get my balance. His hands fall to his sides, clenched into fists and I wonder if he wants to hit me. I try again, stepping away from him extra carefully.

I can feel them all watching me, and I look past them at the front door, putting as much effort as possible into not falling over.

This is so humiliating. *Clumsy Jane can't even walk in some dumb high heels.*

I see Theo whisper something to Paris, who hisses a curse and leaves the foyer. He comes back a minute later while I'm still trying to get to the door and throws my black ballerina flats at my feet.

'Just wear those,' he says.

He murmurs something else just outside my hearing and I look up sharply because I'm pretty sure I know what word he just said and I don't like it one bit, but he's already walking out the door. I gratefully take off the strappy sandals and leave them by the wall as I slip on the other much more comfortable and easier to walk in shoes.

I can't help the smile that takes over my face, and I look up to see Sie staring, looking taken aback. But then he just walks past me. They all go outside, and I'm left to follow awkwardly. Guess that's the evening's theme. I worry again about riding a bike, but, when we get outside, there's a long, black limousine parked in the driveway. The relief I feel is palpable. No trying to stay on the back of one of their hogs while internally freaking out at the sounds. I had to leave my earbuds because I have nowhere to put them except in my ears for the whole night and I feel like that might be frowned upon.

I shiver a little in the cold night air as I walk quickly over to the limo and wait as the others get in first, leaving me out in the darkness for a stolen moment. I stare up at the stars, wishing I was somewhere else – like with Shar in Hawaii – and let out a sigh as I slide into the car ... right onto someone's lap!

I yelp as one of them palms my ass, throwing myself away and hitting the carpeted interior hard.

I stare up and I'm surprised to find that it's Vic.

'Sit,' he commands, and I look around to obey, but the only seat free seems to be in the middle of him and Theo.

I plant myself between them, trying to take up as little space as possible, trying not to accidentally brush up against them even a tiny bit.

I feel Theo watching me and I glance at him.

'What?' I ask softly, aware that the others can hear everything.

'If you need anything tonight ... I mean if you ... *become distressed* at all, just tell me, ok?'

A little puzzled by his caring attitude considering it wasn't all that long ago that he refused to untie my wrist from his bed and told me he couldn't give a shit if I was in discomfort, I frown at him and I notice his eyes flick to the yellowing bruises there as if he's remembering the same thing.

'Ok,' I murmur, and he nods.

No one talks as we drive. The privacy screen between us and the driver is up the whole time, but no one says another word.

I shift uncomfortably, trying to pull down my dress that I'm a thousand percent sure I can feel rising up to my waist with every movement I make. I know they're looking at me too, but I stare down at the floor, not letting my eyes drift higher than their calves as they all take up as much space as they possibly can. I thought limos were meant to be huge, but with five guys all over six foot and broad as hell packed in here, this might as well be a hot box.

I feel the pressure that comes from Vic when he's angry and I must flinch or something because Theo says something to him above my head that I don't catch, and the pressure goes away. I curl my arms around myself and draw myself in closer. I'm not brave right now; not in the presence of all five of them at once.

I can't believe I've signed my life away to them for three years. Holy shit! What I've done is finally sinking in and my stomach is rolling. I stare out the tinted windows. I'm only just able to see the shadows of the trees that line the road if I strain past the glare from the little strips of light that decorate the panels around the limo's interior.

I swallow hard, feeling hot and light-headed. Sweat beads at the small of my back and I take a shallow breath. My stomach pitches and I glance at Theo.

'Stop the car.' It comes out too low.

'What did you say?' Theo asks.

'Stop the car!'

One of them knocks on the glass and the car slows. I'm scrambling over Theo and throwing the door open before the car stops, just in time to throw up all over the asphalt.

I heave a couple of times, but the sandwich was the only thing I ate and that's all over the road now. There's nothing else in my stomach. I wipe my mouth with the back of my hand. Shit. At least I didn't vomit all over myself or one of the guys.

I slide back over Theo and into my seat, wondering if I should feel more humiliated that I threw up in front of them all or because they probably all just saw my bare ass as I was hurling.

'Are you done?' he asks, and I nod.

'Yeah. Sorry.'

Theo closes the door. I take a shaky breath and Vic is holding a glass in front of me.

'It's water.'

I take it from his hand gratefully, being extra careful not to touch him at all.

'Are you okay?' murmurs Theo as the car starts to move again and it's on the tip of my tongue to ask him why he gives a flying fuck if I'm okay or not. But then I guess I'm their property now. They have a vested interest in my wellbeing. Can't feed from me if I'm too sick. Or maybe they can. I have no idea. Maybe he just doesn't want me to vom all over his pretty suit.

'I'm fine,' I say.

I sip the water. It's nice and cold and it takes the sour, stomach acid taste out of my mouth.

The rest of the car journey goes by in silence. None of them are looking at me now, probably disgusted at my human display, I think, and I have to force my lips not to twitch when I think about how they definitely weren't expecting *their food* to upchuck *her food*.

My stomach has settled now that it's empty, and I can hear Theo and Vic's phones alternately vibrating. They're having a text conversation with each other beside me. I try not to be paranoid, but ...

We start going past buildings and other cars and a

glance out the window confirms that we've re-entered civilization. It's a busy street with bright lights and neon signs and lively music coming from more than one bar.

The limo stops and Vic opens his door. The sounds of the street flood in, but the noises are pleasant, not grating. I give Theo a questioning look.

'Am I supposed to go too?'

He gestures with his head towards the open door, and I see Vic's hand venturing back inside to help me out. I hesitate just for a second before I take it and he eases me from the car. I take great care not to flash anyone, pulling my dress down as he places my hand on his arm like we're in *Bridgerton* or some shit.

Well-dressed bystanders on the street are watching who gets out of the car, and I don't feel out of place for once even in my flat shoes. It's almost like I fit in somehow. Just a little. My eyes widen at the bright, glitzy clothes of the people milling around, drinking, laughing, having a good time.

The others are all out of the car now too and Vic's already striding towards an impressive-looking club. The sign above the door has a golden circle with a number two in it and there's a very long line trailing down the street and all the way around the block.

Looks like we'll be waiting awhile.

I glance over my shoulder to see the other four trailing behind us, two abreast, but when we get to the line, Vic makes no attempt to try to find the end of it. Instead, we go right up to the front doors. No one says a word as the bouncers just let us through, but more than one pair of jealous eyes in the line tracks our progress as we move past the red velvet ropes and into a dim corridor.

Vic ushers me straight through some double doors and I can hear bass reverberating through the wall. Next to me, there's a set of stairs going down, but we go past it and through more doors towards the music. It's dark inside the club ... and crowded. There's a bar on one end of the room, crystal chandeliers and carpeted areas with comfy chairs. The dance floor is massive, spanning almost the entire room.

There are women dancing on podiums in short dresses like the one I'm wearing, and a horrible thought crosses my mind. What if they want me to go up there and do that? I have zero rhythm. I've been known to dance on the rare occasions that I've been clubbing, don't get me wrong, but I look like a fucking idiot. My trick is to be drunk enough not to care.

I'm led along the edge of the dance floor, through an alcove, and up some steps. A guard comes off the wall at the threshold of another room and stops us, but a British (I think) voice from inside says, 'Let them through.'

We go into an elegant room overlooking the club. You can see the whole place from up here. There are a couple of empty tables by the windows that are level with the podiums ... for viewing the dancers, I guess.

'Welcome.'

I notice a group of five men sitting in a round booth to the side. I glance back, glad to see that the other four guys are still behind us. I take in everything I can about these new guys as I survey the room, trying not to make it obvious that that's what I'm doing, and I know without a doubt that they are incubi as well. I'm guessing they aren't part of the Iron I's though. I didn't know there was another clan so close by. I thought incubi clans stayed away from each other for the most part so I'm a little surprised when the one who said 'welcome' gets out of his seat and he and Vic embrace quickly.

'Are you okay?'

I jump as I feel Theo's breath next to my ear.

'Fine,' I say again.

His gaze falls on the strobe lights that are lasering around the club. 'Is the music too much?'

Surprised, I look up at him and shake my head even as I scowl. 'Why would it be?'

The bass is loud and pulsing, but these aren't the kinds of sounds that bother me. I can lose myself in the right kind of music, but it's been a while since I've been able to. I miss having earbuds that work.

'You didn't seem all that well earlier. Just doing my job as the club medic,' he says.

He puts a hand at the small of my back and my breath catches as he propels me forward towards Vic who takes my arm in a gentle grip that tightens as I try to pull out of it.

Resigned, I stop attempting to get away. The other incubus in front of Vic seems to suddenly notice me.

'And who have you brought with you tonight?'

Definitely British.

Vic doesn't spare me a look. 'Just a new girl.'

I try to ignore his slighting words, adamant that I'm not going to let him make me feel bad. The other incubus' eyes move over me.

'A pleasure.'

He offers his hand and I take it without bothering to even look at Vic for any kind of permission. I'm just a new girl, right?

'I'm Maddox,' the man in front of me says and *he kisses the back of my hand like he thinks he's Prince Charming.*

Ew.

I resist the urge to wipe my hand off on my tiny dress. I wish I hadn't taken this pompous dude's hand to spite Vic now. I notice the other guys at the table watching me with interest and I boldly meet their eyes. These assholes might be as hot as the Iron I's, – yeah, they definitely are! – but I don't like the vibes they're giving off. It makes me realize how much I'm drawn to Vic and the other Iron I's, and I don't know what to make of that at all.

Maddox eases me forward and I go with him, glancing back at the Iron I's who are all stony-faced as they watch the other guys make room for me in their already crowded booth. Maddox seats me and then takes the place at the end, closing me in. It's only the fact that the Iron I's are here that stops me from freaking and climbing over the damn table to get out.

'So,' he turns to me, speaking loudly enough for the room to hear, 'you're contracted to the Iron I's, eh?'

'That's right,' I say quietly.

He snorts. 'You should have come to us first. We would have given you more money, darling.'

I'm not sure what to say to that so I don't say anything.

'Get her a drink,' he orders no one in particular.

I make sure the others are still here, not putting it past them to abandon me to the mercies of these *other* incubi. Oddly, the thought terrifies me. I'd much rather be with the Iron I's for some reason. Maybe it's just a 'better the devils you know' type of deal.

Literally.

Vic is sitting in a chair by the table and is speaking with Maddox again, ignoring me completely. Kor and Sie are by the door that leads to the club, standing watch, I guess. Paris is gone and so is Theo.

A drink appears in front of me, and I glance at Vic. It's

just a cocktail, but even I know you don't take a drink from some stranger in a club. However, the magnanimous leader of the Iron I's deigns to give me a brief moment of his precious time, looking over for a second to give me a nod.

I'm also not one to turn down free booze, so I take a sip. Coconut Rum is the pervading taste and it's good! I take a longer gulp.

Vic's phone rings and he looks at it. 'Excuse me,' he says to Maddox. 'I need to take this.'

He leaves the room, Sie following and leaving me with just Korban and the rest of these new guys, and I'm suddenly uncomfortable although I'm not fully sure why. Everything seems fine, but none of the Iron I's are here with me now except Korban and he's staring at his phone, not paying any attention to what's going on at the table.

I tense as I feel Maddox's hand graze the outside of my bare thigh and I think it's a mistake until his hand moves up and inwards towards—

My head whips around towards his and I practically snarl at him. 'Get your hand off me!'

He looks surprised and then his eyes narrow. I shudder as I feel *something*. Rearing back and inadvertently colliding with the other one I'm sitting next to, I grab my drink and throw it in Maddox's face.

He hisses and something passes over his features. Surprise maybe? No. Shock.

His hand, which had been gripping my thigh, disappears. He's deadly silent and so are all the others. They're all watching me, and I can feel them trying to use their creepy voodoo on me.

I shudder at the power as it crawls over my skin, leaving trails of prickles. They're all trying to lull me. Each one is different. It's not a smell or a taste. It's not a thing I can describe with one of my regular senses. This is something else, but *similar*. Like a sixth sense.

Ugh I hope I don't start seeing ghosts or something now.

'Stop it!'

The feeling peters out and I know they've stopped trying, but I'm seething, my entire body locked up in rage and I'm afraid that I'm going to meltdown or shutdown very soon. There's nowhere to hide.

'What the hell's going on here?'

It's Vic and even though I hate him too, I'm so relieved he's back that tears – of righteous anger, not damsel-in-distress-ness! – come to my eyes.

He's staring at Maddox's still dripping face and he looks as pissed off as I am. But this is Maddox's territory. I don't understand their relationship, and while I'd love to see Maddox get a broken jaw, I don't want to find myself in the middle of an incubus brawl.

'An accident. I'm so clumsy,' I force out with a chuckle. 'Sorry about that.'

'No need to apologize,' Maddox says, using the silk pocket square from his suit jacket to wipe himself. His eyes don't leave mine. 'It was my fault entirely.'

Vic's phone rings again and he curses. 'Busy night, I'm afraid. Give me five and then we'll talk,' he says to Maddox and before I can say a word, he's gone again.

I eye Maddox and his clan warily, but they don't try anything else. Instead, they talk to each other in a language I don't understand but I know they're talking about me. I can usually tell when people are, and incubi are no different it seems.

Another drink appears in front of me, but I don't touch it.

'Where did you say you're from?' Maddox asks, and I practically see all the others' ears perk up.

'I didn't.'

Maddox sighs. 'Look, I'm sorry if I had the wrong idea.'

'For assuming that every human wants to be fed from by a gang of incubi?'

'For assuming you could be lured away from your clan by us,' he clarifies.

My lip curls. Why would they want to? Surely they have girls chomping at the bit to be one of their on-call girls.

'How did you know we were trying to lull you? I've never met a human who could fight it before.'

I shrug. I don't know, but I'm not about to tell him that. 'I need to go clean up,' I say instead.

Maddox lets me out of the booth, and I stumble from it, flinching when his hand comes up to steady me just as Vic comes back into the room.

The Iron I President is suddenly the one holding me, somehow crossing the room in an instant, and snarling at Maddox.

'She's not yours. Don't overstep, *friend*.'

Maddox raises his hands. 'Wouldn't dream of it, mate. Come, let's talk.'

As soon as Vic lets me go, he turns away from me. I walk a bit shakily towards the entrance, passing Sie, who's reappeared and is staring out the window towards the dancefloor, and Korban. He's still staring at his phone. I slip out of the VIP area, and no one follows me. I don't even think they register my departure. I probably shouldn't be wandering around alone, but I just want to go somewhere quiet for a minute.

I find the Ladies' room down by the side of the bar and I go inside. There are some other girls tidying up their makeup at the vanities, but no one really looks at me. I go into one of the stalls and sit down, heaving a sigh.

What was all that about? What is this whole night about? *Why did they make me come with them?*

I sit for a while, hearing most of the girls leave before I come back out. The music is muffled in here and it's nice to be away from all the prying eyes. I glance at myself in the mirror in front of me. I look so out of place, I think now. The feeling that I had before of belonging is gone again. A girl comes and stands next to me, reapplying her lip gloss. She meets my eyes in the mirror.

Shifter of some kind.

'Cute dress, human girl,' she says.

'Thanks.'

'Are you okay?' she asks. She looks a little bit drunk, and her cheeks are red from dancing. 'You're not here by yourself, are you?'

'Oh, um, I just left my friends for a little while.'

'Ok, well …' She gives me a funny look. 'Just don't walk around here for too long by yourself, huh? There's a bunch of vamps in the basement club and the shiftiest fae lord I've ever fucking seen by the bar. No joke. It's not safe for you here tonight without some serious backup, babe.'

I give her a genuine smile. 'I'll be careful,' I promise.

She looks dubious, but shrugs and then practically skips out the door and I grin after her.

Tipsy girls in club bathrooms, am I right?

I run my hands through my hair, putting it back in order before I head out into the main club again. I'm making for the VIP area, when I'm pulled through a door and slammed up against a wall.

'I knew I'd get another chance with you.'

I freeze in fear because I know that voice. It's the guy

from the other night; the one who caught me out on the deck with his friends. My breathing stutters. His fist is already pulled back to finish what he started before.

'I can't believe they're loaning you out already,' he mutters.

Instead of hitting me though, his knee forces itself between my legs and I'm suddenly so sick of all these supe assholes just thinking they can touch me whenever they want. I level him with the vilest look I can muster.

'I'd rather you beat me to fucking death!' I say, pushing myself hard off the wall and spitting in his face.

But my bravado is forced out of me as he grabs my wrists and pulls them above my head, his grip hard and bruising.

Restrained, I start to panic. He says something, shouting at me, but I can't even hear the words above the roaring in my head. I can't get out of this. Claustrophobia grabs me as I struggle, and a cry is ripped from my throat.

∼

Theo

WHERE THE HELL IS SHE? I'm scanning the crowds, looking at the bar, noticing how many supes there are here tonight who I wouldn't want near my worst enemy let alone Jane. I catch sight of Paris dancing with a girl whose presence I barely register. I jerk him around towards me.

'What is it?' he asks.

'Have you seen Jane?' I yell into his ear.

He shakes his head and I see his irritation at being interrupted morph to a flash of concern. I knew he was more interested in her than he let on. He's probably just being careful because of Kor's jealous streak.

'Go tell Vic,' I shout, and he nods, making for the VIP room.

'I was only gone for fucking ten minutes,' I say to myself.

I went back to the others after completing my little mission to find Maddox and his clan just sitting at their table, looking like they were in a daze. Vic and Sie were nowhere to be seen, Paris was already on the dance floor pretending to be the brainless playboy Vic wants him to seem, Korban was playing on his phone with a scowl on his face, and no one was keeping an eye on the new girl in a club full of supes that could – and would – kill her as soon as look at her.

I stomp down the corridor behind the bar where the bathrooms are, jerking open the ladies' room door. I can smell her in here. Or, rather, I can smell Kor's bodywash. I noticed that in the limo earlier when she was sitting so close. Kor, that sly bastard, must have put it in her bathroom hoping she'd use it, but I haven't figured out why.

'Jane!' I call inside.

'There's nobody in here except me,' a girl calls back, 'and my name ain't Jane.'

Fuck!

I change direction, walking back up the corridor. I see a door that says 'Private', and it's only half closed. With a bad feeling as I smell the lingering scent of Kor, I approach it just in time to hear a cry.

I burst through, vaguely aware that at least one of the Iron I's is behind me, and I find *fucking Callaghan* with his hands on what's ours.

I tear him away from her and push him towards ...

Maddox? Maddox is here? He doesn't usually get his hands dirty.

'How did you get in? I told you you're not welcome here anymore, dog,' he growls low.

Callaghan is taken by two of Maddox's crew and hauled away and Maddox just stares at Jane with a look on his face that I can't discern ... and I don't like.

Before I can say something to him, Vic appears, flanked by the others. I tell them what happened in as few words as possible, and glance behind me at Jane.

She's in the corner clutching her arms, her clothes in disarray and looking down at the floor. I suppress a curse at the dress that Paris found her to wear. It hugs her body like a second skin and I fucking love the sight of it, but so does every other male here. I concede that it wasn't the dress that made Callaghan drag her in here though. He was just waiting for his chance after he failed at the party, and we gave it to him.

I hope bringing her here tonight was fucking worth it.

Vic blocks Maddox's line of sight and we're on exactly the same page. I don't want anyone seeing her like this either. No one except me and my brothers.

I walk over to her. She doesn't move and I notice she's shaking a little.

'I'm going to fix your dress,' I tell her, easing it down to cover what little modesty she has left in this thing.

Her eyes flicker with recognition just for a second.

'Let's go,' Vic says but I shake my head.

I've been glued to the monitors almost obsessively when she's in my room and, while it's been awesome to watch her when she doesn't know it, I'm starting to work out her tells as well.

'I think she's headed for an *episode* that will cause a

scene and the limo will take forever to get back here at this time of night. It's too busy still.'

'What do you suggest we do?' he hisses. 'We're in the middle of the fucking club. There are supes all over the place just looking for weakness to exploit.'

'Finish your discussion with Maddox,' I say. 'I'll make sure she doesn't lose it here.'

Vic swears loudly but concedes. 'Find us when she's feeling better.'

I give him a nod and he shuts the door to the supply closet we're standing in.

'Jane, are you ok?'

She looks at me, nodding her head faintly and it's not reassuring at all. I need to hold her. I don't examine that thought too carefully as I pick her up, wondering if she's going to fight me. But she doesn't. She just curls into me, burying her face in my neck, inhaling my scent, and something in me gives way.

She's nothing like any of the other humans I've known.

Remembering that I read online how music might help, I carry her out into the hallway and towards the dance floor. I roll my eyes as I see Paris back in his spot, moving between two shifter girls like he doesn't have a care in the fucking world. Ignoring everyone else, I let her down in the middle of everything, close to the speakers to drown out any other noise. I catch Paris' eye and he makes his way over to me. At least with him here too, we can keep the crush of bodies away from her.

Her eyes are closed and she's standing in front of me. I take hold of her hips and get her to start swaying with the music. Paris is behind her, looking at her warily and I find myself hoping that she didn't hear what he called her earlier. We're definitely going to be having a reckoning about that.

I see the moment she starts to relax, to feel better, and I know the music is helping.

Maybe the movements are as well. I sway with her in time with the beat, Paris at her back doing the same. And then Paris' hands settle around her waist, but she doesn't startle. If anything, she stretches into his touch and he steps closer, crowding her against me.

When I next look down at her, her chest is pressed against mine and we move in unison with her sandwiched between us.

It feels like the rightest thing in the world and it's as if her body was made for this. I notice Vic, Sie, and Korban watching from the sidelines, staring at us, their eyes hungry. I'll have to make sure they know that she'll need respite when we get home. There'll be no playing with our newest on-call girl tonight.

I glance up at the VIP room window. Maddox and his clan are all staring down as well, their expressions the same as my brothers. They want her, I realize. Vic brought her as a distraction, but it looks to me like it's worked too well. What does Maddox want with her? They have their own house girls and while Maddox is always interested in what we have, he's never so blatant about it.

Vic sees where I'm looking and nods. He's seen it too. There's something weird going on. I'm only hoping that something in the many documents I photographed in Maddox's office while he was playing host will be enough to figure out what the hell it is, if they're moving against us. I find myself kind of hoping it's not Maddox and his guys. If any incubi clans could truly be called friends, it would be us and them, but we'll still fucking gut them if they turn on us and they'd do the same. That's just the way the supe world works. There's no room for weakness.

But as I look down at the woman in front of me, I think that maybe now I have one ... maybe our whole clan does, they just don't know it yet.

CHAPTER
FIFTEEN
PARIS

When we leave the club it's the early hours of the morning and even I'm ready to hit the hay. The limo is waiting for us out front and the busy street from earlier is practically deserted now except for a few late-night stragglers swaying along with their buddies.

Theo's walking with the new girl and I smirk. She looks tired now, but she'll know what exhaustion really is once Vic's done with her tonight. I look at our Pres pretending not to notice her, but I know he's itching to be first. Looks like Theo might already have dibs though. I get into the car. I don't care if I don't get her tonight. I won't need to feed for a couple more days anyway and there's always one of the other girls. I'm not picky. Food is food where the humans are concerned. That's what I've always said anyway, but as my eyes find Jane again, I wonder if that's still the truth.

The way she moved between me and Theo ... my dick is still hard. I could have fucked her there and then on the dance floor, and I would have if I thought Theo'd have let me.

I sit closest to the privacy screen, tapping on it when everyone's in and the door closes. We start to move. Jane is between Theo and Vic again, and I notice she leans heavily on Theo. I shake my head. He's already got her wrapped around his finger. She has no idea. But she will. Within about thirty seconds she's asleep and I let out a laugh.

'I guess she should get the nap in now, huh?'

Theo looks at Vic and sits up straighter, opening his mouth to speak, but Vic gets there first.

'No one's to touch her tonight.'

My mouth falls open. Vic doesn't have a reputation for being patient and he's certainly not known for his mercy. I mean the males in his family are literally all nicknamed 'Vicious' for fuck's sake.

Theo relaxes back into the dark leather of the car, and I realize that that was what he was about to say too.

'Did you get what we needed?' I ask Theo.

What I really want to say is 'what the fuck is going on with you guys?', but I don't.

'I was able to get into the office. I photographed a bunch of files, but you know Maddox. He's old school. There weren't any hard drives or anything like that, just paper and cryptographs,' Theo snorts. 'I half-expected a microfilm. Fucking English bastard.'

But then he looks thoughtful. 'I don't know about you,' he looks at Vic, 'but I didn't get a vibe off them like they're planning something against us.'

Vic shakes his head. 'I've known Maddox a long time. He's a slippery motherfucker, but I can usually tell when he's about to pull a play out of his back pocket.'

He glances down at the woman beside them. 'She played her part to perfection even if she doesn't know it,' he comments casually, but I notice his fist tightening.

'What *was* that about?' Korban asks. 'I've never seen him take such an overt interest in one of our girls before, not even when he's at the Clubhouse.'

Even Kor sounds a little jealous, and my jaw clenches.

'Neither do you,' I retort and then wish I'd kept my mouth closed when he looks at me with his eyes narrowed.

I shut up and look at Vic, hoping he'll fill the silence. He does, still watching the girl asleep beside him.

'Perhaps you were right about her, Kor. Maybe she does have something to do with him. They seemed friendly.'

This is news to me, but Korban shakes his head. 'If she's a spy, it's not for Maddox. She didn't want to sit at their table. She just didn't know how to say 'no'. Plus,' he looks out the window, 'that spilled drink was no accident. She threw it in his face. He said something or, more likely, did something she didn't like.'

The growl from Vic is audible. 'Why didn't you say something while we were there?'

Korban turns his head very slowly to stare at him, not backing down although I know he can feel Vic's power directed at him because I can see the cords in his neck straining. Even I shiver at their exchange, wondering if Kor is about to launch himself across the limo at our President.

'Because we don't have the manpower to deal with a full-blown war right now,' he growls back. 'Not over some *human* spy.'

Vic leans back in his seat and stares out the window, quietly seething just as Korban is.

I have a feeling that I won't be sleeping in Kor's bed tonight and see I'm right when we pull up to the house a few minutes later and he practically leaps out of the car and stalks off into the woods.

My own cold bed it is.

The rest of us begin to go our separate ways too, but when Theo goes to grab the girl, Vic beats him to it, picking her up easily, and cradling her as he stalks into the house.

Theo follows. 'She's too tired. You know she's not like the other—'

Vic whirls around, jaw clenched, but then he makes an effort to relax when Theo stops short, looking wary.

'I'm not going to feed tonight,' he promises, 'but she's coming with me.'

Theo backs off at his warning tone. Vic clearly isn't in the mood for anymore arguments.

But then Vic beckons me by flicking his head up towards the stairs. I follow him, wondering what the hell's going on as he leads me to his bedroom.

He goes inside and dim lights come on automatically. He stops at the bed and looks back at me. What am I doing here? I pull the black comforter down and Vic lays her in the middle of the mattress, covering her with the blanket.

She doesn't stir.

'Keep this on the DL, but I want you to ask Korban if he felt Maddox or any of the others calling on their power,' he says low.

I look down at the sleeping girl in front of me. 'You mean with her?'

Vic nods.

'Why?'

'Because there's no way that Maddox didn't try to lull her. I might consider him a friend, but we've always had a rivalry like that. We brought her out with us, signifying she's more important than the other girls. He would have tried to steal her from us, contract or no, just to fuck with me, and then paid us for her later. I had a plan in case he tried, but it's not normal for him not to make an effort.'

'Okay,' I say slowly, not really getting where Vic's going with this.

He rolls his eyes. 'If she was lulled, how could she throw a drink in his face?'

His eyes widen meaningfully as he stares at me, and I suddenly understand. 'Have any of us used our power on her?'

Vic shrugs. 'I haven't tried to lull her, but if the others have, I don't think they'll admit it, especially if it happened before she was under contract.'

'You think she's what? Immune to us?' I whisper it because ... Fuck. What would that even mean? I've never heard of it not working on a human before. I give an incredulous chuckle. 'If we can't lull her, how would we even feed from her?'

'Never taken a human without your magick, huh?' Vic lets out a dry laugh. 'You might have to learn how to make a girl like you without it,' he says, turning away and waving me out.

I leave the room, deep in thought, wondering if it's possible. I've never even heard of a human who could withstand the lull, who could fight our power.

I lean against the wall in the hallway and sigh. The on-call girls don't love us, but once they're under our power, the lull makes them feel so good that it's worth it to them ... that and the money they'll receive when their time is done, of course.

How would I even go about ... I shake my head. I wouldn't even know where to start. Going down the corridor to Kor's room, I give it a knock. He's still walking around the woods or he's ignoring me. Either way, there's no answer.

I stomp back down the hall and lay in my own bed

trying to sleep, but as I close my eyes my thoughts keep drifting back to being on the dance floor. I danced with probably a dozen different girls and guys while Korban watched, but I don't remember even one of them except for her. Maybe she's getting under my skin like she's under Vic's and Theo's. Fuck, even Sie can't take his eyes off her. The way he looked at her when she came down those stairs in that little black dress I picked out ... She did look sexy as hell, just like I knew she would, gauging from the feel of her that first night I brought her here.

I wonder if I need to be careful where Kor is concerned. I thought he'd hate her like he does all the others, but after what he said in the car, I'm second-guessing myself. I've never been jealous of one of the on-call girls before, but Kor has never shown any human even one ounce of interest. I don't blame him with how he started life when his incubus power came in, but do I need to consider the human girl a threat to my relationship?

I close my eyes, wondering if Vic is following his own rules about not touching her tonight. I grin in the darkness. No way.

∽

Jane

When I wake up, the first thing I notice is that the bed feels different. The sheets aren't the high thread count Egyptian cotton that I've become used to on Theo's bed. They're satin and although my fingers move around, feeling the slick texture, I decide they're much too slippery for my tastes. Give me cotton any day.

I crack an eye. I'm on my belly. The sheets are black.

Where the hell am I?

The last I remember, I was trying not to fall asleep in the limo after dancing with Theo and Paris for hours.

My heart rate ratchets up a notch. I've never danced like that before. I didn't even know I could! The way they had my body moving, undulating with the beats, pressing against them ... I felt like they *wanted me*. I know it's a trick, logically. It's what they do, but it felt nice to be on the inside for once even if it was just pretend.

I frown. It's weird that I didn't wake up when we got back. I didn't drink anything except for a few sips of that first drink so unless the drink was spiked ...

I sit up, taking stock of my clothes. Yes, the tiny dress is still on me although it's bunched up to my waist. Did they feed from me while I was out? Do other things? Would I even know?

Feeling a little bit sick, I glance around the room, and I'm startled to see Vic sitting in a plush chair close to the bed, watching me. His tie is loose, and his jacket gone. His black shirt is undone, showing his thick neck and the tops of his pecks. I swallow hard. How can rumpled Vic be even hotter than buttoned-up Vic?

He doesn't say a word as he stands up and seems to stalk across the room towards the bed. I pull the covers around me like that's going to make any kind of difference. My head tips back so that I can follow his eyes with mine as he gets closer and closer and closer.

It makes me want to jump out of the bed and run. It takes everything in me to stay still and that's only because I know that he'll chase me. I'd never outrun him.

Stopping right next to me, he stands there for a moment, his eyes all tortured or something. He's giving me serious Edward Cullen vibes regardless of the fact he's not a vampire.

He reaches out slowly and takes the black satin from my grasp. I'm tense. This is going to happen whether I want it or not. I close my eyes and, with a resigned sigh, I flop back on the bed, my arms coming down to my sides as I try to relax. When nothing happens, I look up at him.

'Well?' I say.

He stares down at me. 'Well, what?' he asks. He sounds amused. 'What are you doing?'

I frown at him. 'My job,' I mutter. 'Isn't that why I'm here?'

I come up on my elbows and they slip on the satin uncomfortably. Maybe I'll get some answers now that it's clear he didn't want me for *this*. 'Or was there a different reason you wanted me to sign that contract?'

He looks like he can't quite understand what I'm talking about, but then he changes the subject.

'You have done this before, right.'

I feel like this is a game, but, as usual, I don't understand the rules.

'Yes,' I say.

His eyebrows rise.

'I have!' I say, just a little bit defensive.

He sits at the edge of the bed and his eyes look into mine. 'How many times?'

I give him a look. 'How many times have *you*?'

'Four thousand, six hundred and three.'

My mouth drops open. 'You kept count?'

'No, I'm fucking with you.'

'Oh,' I chuckle.

'Are you going to tell me?'

I wince a little. 'Once.'

I can feel his power rise up, flitting over my skin. It's the same as I felt on those guys last night, but his is *different* and I feel myself leaning in towards him even though my mind feels clear. He doesn't move. It's as if he's waiting for something.

'Do you *have* to lull me?' I ask, unable to keep the trepidation out of my voice. 'To feed, I mean?'

The power disappears and he answers me readily. 'I don't *need* to, no,' he says, taking a piece of my hair and putting it behind my ear. 'We do it that way because it's faster when we're hungry and because it's meant to be more pleasurable for the human. It takes the fear away as well.'

'I'm all for that in theory,' I mutter, 'but I don't think I want—'

My voice leaves me as he sits on the bed and climbs over me slowly.

'Then I won't,' he murmurs.

He's still on top of the blanket that's half covering me and he's not even touching me, but I freeze because I don't really know what I'm supposed to do now.

I thought I would be in the middle of the lull. I thought I'd be oblivious to everything except pleasure. That's what it said on the box, but I'm completely in the here and now, awkward as usual. I mean I'm not looking a gift horse in the mouth. I don't want to be brainwashed to have sex no matter how pleasurable it's supposed to be, but also ...

'Can we just get it over with?' I ask, trying to make my body soften, but it won't. Every muscle is locked up tight.

He frowns and I stare down at the comforter, wishing I could sink into the mattress.

'Did something ... happen before?' he asks carefully, and

I try to figure out what he means, realizing all at once what he's asking.

'Oh, no,' I say. 'He didn't rape me or anything.'

'He?' Vic doesn't move, his hands on the bed on either side of me, still not touching me at all.

'Yeah, he was a guy. I haven't tried it with another girl.'

I see his Adam's apple bob.

'Do you want to talk about it?' His voice sounds strained.

I shrug. 'If you want. I'm not adverse to being with another girl I don't think, but it'd have to be the right …' I look at him and see his lips are turning upwards. He's struggling not to smile. He's amused by me.

Oh.

'You mean talk about the guy I was with.'

He nods his head, looking like he's trying not to laugh.

I sigh. I wasn't going to go into this. 'We only did it the one time. It's just … I was trying to get it done.'

'It?'

'Well, I'd never had sex before. I was 19 and, well, everyone seemed to have done it and I thought … I was working at a bar in Phoenix and there was a guy there and he kept looking at me. He bought me a drink. My coworkers said that meant he was interested so I took him back to my place and …' I shrug. 'I didn't like it. It hurt and he smelled like he'd rolled in aftershave.' I wrinkle my nose at the thought. 'I never knew his name. I don't think that's odd for one night stands though. He left when he was done and I never saw him again.'

Vic doesn't say a word but there's something in his face and I try to work out what it is, hoping it's not pity.

'It's ok,' I say. 'I—'

'Close your eyes,' he interrupts softly.

I shut up and do as he says, hoping that this is when we get this over with because the waiting is what's killing me. Once the first time is done and I know what to expect, I hope it won't be so bad, but no one's really explained what it's like with an incubus. Maybe I should have talked to the girls downstairs. It's probably too late to do that now ...

I crack an eye open and Vic's still over me.

'What are you doing?' I ask.

He chuckles a curse. 'It doesn't matter what I'm doing. I'm not going to hurt you. Do as you're told.'

I close my eyes again with a snort and then his lips are on mine. Gentle. Just a light, feathering caress. My eyes snap open and I rear back because this was completely unexpected, but he doesn't do anything else. He moves back a little bit, giving me space.

'Sorry,' I mutter, feeling like a broken doll.

He doesn't say anything, but he gets off the bed.

'Are you hungry?' he asks.

I nod, glad he doesn't seem upset, even gladder he's not making me do anything right now.

'Come on.'

He turns around and pads to the other side of the room and I see he's barefoot. Something about that makes me wish he'd come back to the bed and kiss me again now that I'm expecting it. I like Bedroom Vic more than Office Vic, but I still jump out of bed while his back is turned and pull last night's dress down over my ass.

Vic takes my hand and I let him pull me slowly through the hall and down the stairs to the deserted kitchen, all the while not being able to stop thinking about how weirdly right his hand feels in mine.

I errantly wonder if it's still considered 'the walk of shame' if you didn't actually *do* anything.

'What do you want?' he asks.

'I'll get it,' I say going into the pantry and rising on my tippy toes to find the cereal box that I hid from Theo on the top shelf at the back. It's still there and there's a little bit left. As I shake it, I can't help my grin.

'What's that look about?' he asks.

'I love this cereal, but Theo keeps trying to make me eat that other stuff.'

'Yeah,' Vic says, 'he's weird about it. Anyone else has a bowl and he gets pissed. The store Stan shops at hardly ever has it in stock or something.'

'Well, I don't like the other one you have, and he got upset that I was eating his one, so now I hide the box so I can eat it first.'

Vic, who's just taken a sip of coffee, makes a noise and chokes, bending over the sink. Coffee splutters out of his mouth as he coughs, and I realize he's laughing.

I smile and his eyes lock on mine for a second before they look away. I don't usually look into other people's eyes much as a matter of course. It always feels weird; too personal maybe, but I kind of like doing it with him.

'Are you going to be okay in here for a minute by yourself?'

'Uh huh,' I answer absently, getting the milk from the fridge.

When I next look up, I'm by myself. At least I think I am until Carrie enters my periphery.

'You contracted with them?' She's shaking her head. 'Are you fucking retarded?'

I recoil a little bit at that word, a word that all too often was used by the other kids at school to describe me. It left a mark that's still there even all these years later.

'Are you one of those supe groupies who thinks *demons*

are going to catch feelings for you because I'll tell you right now, they don't have it in 'em to love anyone or anything but themselves, their brothers and their Club.'

'No,' I say, matching her cold tone. 'This is business, that's all.'

She snorts and disappears back down the steps and I wonder for a second if I should call her back so I can get some more information about what exactly to expect from the lull and all of this other shit when these guys finally decide to use their power on me, but she's already gone.

I take my bowl to the table by the window and sit down before I pour the milk, so I can eat while I look out over the immaculate lawn. The day is overcast and drizzly, the deck looking sodden and slick.

Vic appears in the kitchen again just as I'm finishing up.

'Are you finished?'

'Yeah,' I say, picking up my bowl and watching him.

His demeanor has changed somehow, and I cant my head, trying to figure out what it is that's different. I think I'm starting to understand these guys a little better now that I'm getting to know them.

When Vic left a minute ago, he was bedroom Vic. Now he's all business and the friendliness I've been receiving from him all morning seems to have been replaced by anger or something close.

The food I just ate churns in my stomach. What's happening now?

CHAPTER
SIXTEEN
VIC

I watch as she gets up from the table and puts her dish in the sink. She turns on the water.

'Leave it,' I order.

She looks over her shoulder at me, a lot more tense than she was earlier. Maybe she's picking up on my mood because I can tell she's a little afraid.

Good.

This morning she did two things no other human ever has. First, she got under my skin. Fuck knows how, but she did it. Perhaps it was her artlessness that intrigued me when she woke up in my bed, trying to keep herself covered by the sheet even though I saw everything while she tossed and turned through the night as I watched from the chair. Second, despite what I told her up there, I did try to lull her and she resisted it. No, that's not the right word. She didn't need to resist it. It simply didn't work on her. At all. I want to know who this girl is.

She's scared of me, but she doesn't fall to her knees begging, whimpering, crying like other humans have done when faced with my wrath.

'Follow me.'

Her face is blank as she does what she's told, all emotion disappeared from it as soon as I came back into the kitchen.

I can't let her get to me like this again. I thought I could keep complete control around her, but I was a fool and if I'm not careful it'll cost us everything. I have to remember where she comes from, *who her father is.*

There's more to this than I thought. It was the orc stone that threw me, made me assume she was a just spy for one of the supe factions, or even for the fae themselves. It wouldn't be the first time they'd used a human to do their dirty work. Even when I saw that picture of her with *him*, I didn't think he could have sent her. Why would he send his own daughter into a house of sex demons?

But maybe this the result of an alliance between humans and a few opportunistic supes who want to get rid of the competition.

I look back at her and try to see her as a dangerous entity, but it's difficult. She's just a human girl to my eyes.

But I failed to lull her this morning. I wonder if it's because of her condition. Maybe her brain is different, so our power doesn't work right. Was that why she was chosen?

I tried it the old-fashioned way too; just a little tip-toe of seduction to see what she would do, but even then she didn't react the way I thought she would. I'd expected either hysterics or fear, not the resignation bordering on anticipation. She wanted me even though she was scared. Maybe she's going native. Wouldn't that be a trick? Send her back to her father a willing little incubi whore ...

I look back at her again and my eyes narrow with the way the shadows bounce off her in the corridor. She looks so much like him in that moment that I wonder how I could possibly have missed it at first. I have to grit my teeth, so I don't let the anger out. I know she can feel it when I lose control of it.

Is she as wily as he is, I wonder? How did he orchestrate this so well? How did he make Paris bring her here? Did it start when she dangled herself in front of us like a prime piece of meat that day in the bar, pretending she had no idea that her covered body was even more of a temptation to us than what she's wearing now?

She's not an open book like the other females I've come across, but I'll crack her and then I'll make her tell me the whole plan.

I decide to keep my knowledge to myself for now. I want her alive and if the others know she's a plant for the Tertiary Order ... Fuck. A supe spy would be bad enough, but a spy for the Order? There wouldn't be any saving her from Kor. I might as well tear out her throat here in the corridor where it'll make less of a mess.

I take her down the hallway to the games room. I've already made sure the others are in there waiting.

She stops at the threshold, and I jerk my head towards the room. I see her swallow visibly. She looks like she's going to her execution.

Not yet, little mole.

But I'm sick of her drawing this out. I roll my eyes, grab her by her forearm, and thrust her inside.

Theo and Paris are playing some first-person combat game I don't remember the name of, but at my grim look, Paris pauses it.

'We need to talk,' I say.

I put her in front of the TV before all of us, knowing that this will be intimidating for her and hope she doesn't crack too soon. A minute part of me feels guilty when I see her hands shake as she hides them behind her back, but I don't look too closely at why that might be. She must have known the risks before she walked into the bar with that fucking orc stone and started this whole thing.

'I just heard that there was a bombing in the city last night.'

That gets their attentions, even Sie who's reading in the corner looks up.

'That's the fifth one this month,' Theo mutters, chucking his controller down next to him, the game forgotten. 'Where?'

'A shifter club. Twenty dead, thirty more injured.'

'The Order?'

I watch the girl closely, but she doesn't give anything away at the mention of her people.

'They claimed responsibility online, yes.' I confirm.

Now, to see if Maddox *did* have anything to do with this. I can't really see him betraying his own kind, but he might know more about her than he let on last night. Even if she is working for the Order, though, we have a legitimate claim on her no matter what. Stupid girl signed the papers.

'What happened in the club while you were at the table with Maddox?' I ask her.

She blinks at me, staying silent for a long moment. She looks confused as if she thought she was being brought in here for another reason and I almost laugh. Did she think we're about to have an orgy right here and now?

I mean, the idea does have merit.

I look at her standing there in that short little dress because I haven't let her change and I see her pull it down surreptitiously, but of course everyone notices. She fidgets under everyone's eyes.

'What do you mean?' she asks in a small voice.

Oh, she's good. She's a credit to him. I'll make sure to tell him before I gut the fucker in front of her.

'Why did you throw your drink in his face?'

'It was an accident.'

'Don't give me that!' I snarl at her lie.

When she flinches, stepping back, I follow, taking her chin in a light grip between my fingers.

'There's something you should know about me, princess,' I say. 'If you lie to me, I will put you over my knee and I will spank that deceitful little ass of yours until you tell the truth.'

Her eyes widen and her mouth opens, but no sound comes out. She's scared but the unmistakable lust that comes off her almost brings me to my knees.

She's got the predilections of a much more experienced female and the energy she gives off is potent as hell. I sigh almost inaudibly as tendrils of power top me up like a tiny, delicious amuse-bouche.

'Are you going to answer my questions honestly?' I ask, clearing my throat and glancing at the others who are looking at her in various stages of surprise ... and much more hunger than before. This might be a problem.

Her eyes don't leave mine and she nods mutely.

'Why did you throw your drink at Maddox?' I ask again.

'Because you left me at that table by myself and he touched me.'

She sounds accusing, but I can't very well tell her that we left her there on purpose, knowing she'd distract him and his clan like a glittering ring to a magpie, so we could take a look around his club.

'He touched you?'

She nods.

'Where?' I struggle to keep my voice level and my power in check, resolving to go back to *The Circle* later and pay Maddox back with a broken jaw.

'He put his hand on my thigh and then he moved it up ...' She looks away, her cheeks reddening. 'So I threw my drink in his face.'

My jaw tightens again, starting to ache with all this tension.

'Go on.'

She shrinks down a little bit, and I hear Theo murmur behind me. I'm pushing at her with my power, something only I can do as leader of this clan. I drive it back and she breathes a sigh of relief.

'Did he use his power on you?' I ask, wondering if she's going to lie herself into a corner so soon.

'They all did,' she whispers.

My eyes narrow. 'How could you tell it was all of them?'

'I ... don't know.'

My palm twitches. 'Why didn't you tell us then and there?'

'I don't know,' she says again. 'I was sitting at the table and Korban was there, but he was on the other side of the room and he wasn't—'

She breaks off and I look over at Kor who's staring like he wants to cross the room and snap her pretty little neck.

'Korban wasn't paying attention?' I say.

She looks down, not saying anything.

'Answer!' I command.

'He wasn't paying attention,' she whispers, recoiling.

I watch her for a few seconds. She doesn't wilt anymore, just stands there. She's gone back to what she was doing when she first came here, staring past us not at us.

Anger courses through me. How dare she come here to

take us down and not even stare at us in the face while she does it?

'Which one of us will feed from you first?' I wonder aloud, and I see her body tense.

It's the fear of the unknown that's going to get to her, I realize. She's more scared of that than anything else. I'm only just able to keep the self-satisfied grin off my face. I know exactly how to torment the little human who finds herself locked in the den of monsters and it's not with force.

'How about a game?' I say and practically see the guys perk up. 'How about we give you five days to choose?'

Her eyes find mine. 'What do you mean?'

'You have five days to decide which one of us you want to be the first.'

I smirk at her gob-smacked expression. She wasn't expecting that.

'F-five days?' she asks. 'But—'

'You have five,' I repeat, 'Five to choose which one of us you want to pop your incubus cherry. Do you want Paris' gentle touch? My rough one? Theo's games? Kor's fury? Sie's madness? You pick. But once it's done,' I step closer and whisper in her ear, 'you come whenever any of us call for you, and you do everything you're told just like the other girls. Now, leave us.'

She turns and scurries away like a little mouse and I grin at her retreating form. The guys are silent, but Paris and Theo both have competitive gleams in their eyes.

'Which one of us will it be?' I ask, already knowing she will never choose Kor or Sie because they scare her, so that leaves Paris, Theo, and me.

'She'll choose me,' Paris says, folding his arms and leaning back.

'You sound real fucking sure for a guy who doesn't

know the first thing about seducing a human without the lull,' Theo laughs.

Paris starts to get defensive. 'That's only because I've never bothered trying! She wants what every human girl wants. Clothes and shoes. Pretty little trinkets. She'll choose me well before the five days are up.'

'You think so?'

'Think she'll choose you? The guy who watches her from his cameras and jerks off to the monitors?'

Theo snorts and gets up. 'Never know. She was very aroused by Vic's spanking threat. Maybe she's a little freak in the sheets. Speaking of the cameras, I'm gonna go see what she's up to.'

He gives me a wink and I frown at him, deciding to check my room for recording devices before I next have her sleeping in my bed.

I head to the study to get some work done before I start getting calls from the other supes about the bombings, but before I can do anything, Sie comes in and sits down.

'You can last five days, right?'

'I don't need to.'

I look up sharply, wondering if Sie's going to play the game with Paris and Theo, but he just gives me a look. 'I told you, I don't want her. Anyway, I spoke to some of Maddox's clan in the club last night, but they didn't give me anything.'

'Did you expect them to?' I ask.

He shrugs. 'If they drink enough, sometimes things slip out.'

'Meanwhile, another of our shipments has disappeared. I've got the fae on my back because their shit is going missing on our watch. Twelve coordinated attacks by the

Order this year alone ... They're getting bolder and there are a lot more humans on their side than there were before.'

'They've got a pretty good propaganda campaign going on,' Sie says, stretching his neck, 'especially after what happened in that club last year.'

'Fuck,' I mutter. 'The turning of the tide. What a shit show that was.'

'Have you considered that it's the Order that's fucking with our operation?'

'Yeah,' I say, not telling him that I suspect Jane to be one of them, 'but to be sure we're going to have to go into Metro and find out for ourselves.'

Sie nods. 'When do you want to go?'

'Next few days. Will you be well enough?'

'If I'm not you can put a bullet in my brain.'

I make a show of chuckling but, when he leaves the room, I sober pretty fast. The last thing I want to do is put a bullet in my best friend's head. I thought he was feeling better, but he looks like shit again today.

I pour myself a whiskey and down it in one. We'll have to take the new girl with us. Not only to continue our little game, but because I'm sure as shit not leaving the little Trojan Horse here alone to snoop around or let our enemies in when they storm the gates. Plus, despite what Sie says, I know he's interested in her. It would be a good idea to have her on hand in case he loses it. She can be useful in more ways than one and I still think she might be the one to give him what he needs even if he is fighting it.

∼

Jane

I'm still reeling from the little meeting Vic made me attend, though it's been hours. Why would he let me decide which one of them gets to feed off me? Is it really just a game? If I've learned anything about Vic since I met him, it's that he doesn't do things for no reason. He's always got a plan.

I'm sitting in what I now call *my room* because all of Theo's stuff has disappeared. The table is gone too and in its place is a comfy chair.

My mind is racing and there's something else going on. I can't relax. The place between my legs is pulsing. I wipe sweat off my brow. It's not even hot out. Feeling this way isn't usual for me. I mean yeah sometimes I feel like I want …. But it's never been like this before. Maybe I'm ovulating. That can affect a girl's sex drive, right? I'm pretty sure that's a thing.

I go into the bathroom and start the water running. Maybe a relaxing soak will chill me out. I take off my clothes and slide into the bath, leaning my head back and closing my eyes. The tub fills up quickly and I turn off the water with my toes with a sigh. But that niggling need, that feeling, won't go away. If anything, it's stronger now.

I bite my lip and look towards the door. It's closed. I have an uneasy feeling but I'm going to need to do something before I combust. There's no way I'm choosing one of those assholes!

My hand goes to my breast, touching the nipple lightly and I gasp as a zing goes directly to my pussy.

What was that!?

I do it again and can't help my low moan. I've done this before. Of course I have. But I don't think it's ever felt like this.

I can't seem to help myself now, teasing my nipples

until they're hard and swollen before my hand slides down my slippery skin to my mound. The first flitter of my fingertips has me throwing back my head and my mouth opening wide on a breath. Nope! It's never felt like this before. I feel like I'm going to explode if I don't touch myself again and my legs shake in the water as I do, but the sensation isn't enough. My vibrator is in my bag, which is in the bedroom. I lurch from the bath and grab a towel, not even bothering to dry myself properly as I throw open the door and practically sprint across the room.

'What the fuck is going on?' I mutter to myself as I frantically look through my backpack.

My one and only toy is fucking florescent fuchsia and resembles a disco ball. Can't miss it, but I still have to dump the whole contents of the bag on the floor before I find it!

I pick it up, get on the bed and spread my legs in anticipation as I go straight for the sweet spot with no preliminaries, my heart beating fast, my breath rapid but when I flick the button, nothing happens.

No.No.No.No.NO!

I sit up, disappointment making me want to burst into tears. I'm not one of those people who's very good at doing it manually because I get *there*, and my fingers stop doing what they're supposed to do, and I end up losing *it*.

I lean back with a miserable sigh, my eyes actually tearing up, and my door opens without warning; no knock or anything. I shriek, scrambling up the bed and covering myself with the towel. Theo's in the doorway. He strides into the room like it's still his and I'm too vulnerable for uninvited guests.

'Get out!' I cry, throwing the nearest thing at him instinctively. The pink, sparkly dildo flies past him, thudding into the wall like an ominous ... pink, sparkly dildo.

My eyes widen as he slowly looks over his shoulder at the wall and then the floor where my 'weapon' lies still and probably broken now.

'Did you just throw *a sex toy* at me?'

'Why are you in here?' I ask, deflecting like an expert. 'Aren't you supposed to give me notice or something?'

'Nope.' He comes closer, a look in his eyes that I don't understand.

I'm starting to panic. 'But Vic said I have—'

'Relax, sweetheart. I'm not going to feed. I just noticed that you need a helping hand, that's all.'

I straighten, my eyes wide. 'What?'

His hand points up to the ceiling and I see a tiny divot in the corner of the room by the light.

My hand covers my mouth. 'You've been watching me.'

Korban literally said in the plainest terms that there were cameras in here. How had I forgotten? Even in my needy haze, that's a pretty fucking important thing to remember!

'You knew they were there, princess,' he says, a smile alighting his face as he looks me up and down.

I can feel the color leaching out of my skin and I grasp the towel tighter.

'Are they in the bathroom too?'

He keeps up his perusal of my body. 'No, but maybe I should put some in there, huh?'

'No and turn that one off.'

'No can do. Security.'

'You can't just watch—'

'Actually I can. Like I said. Security. Says it in the contract that you signed. You *did* read it, right?'

I open and close my mouth. I read it a few times, but I don't remember that.

He comes towards me, and I retreat, finding the headboard at my back. He looms over me.

'What are you going to do?' I ask, hating the waiver in my voice.

He doesn't seem to like it either and he stays where he is.

'You haven't done this much, huh?'

I shake my head.

He takes off his shirt and I roll my eyes at him. 'Is this your idea of seduction? I don't think it's working. I mean, I'm no expert here but I don't think—'

'*I think* you think too much, Jane,' he says very quietly. 'Why don't you let Dr. Wright take a look?'

I almost laugh at the Doctor Wright thing because, you know, Doctor Wright, Doctor *RIGHT (get it?)*, but I don't. Instead, I swallow hard as I stare at him. I don't know why I find what he just said so hot but my heart actually skips a beat and, by his slow smile, he knows what he's doing to me.

'Miss Mercy,' he tuts, 'I'm afraid that if you want me to find the source of the problem, you're going to need to submit to an *examination*. Lay back on the bed and try to relax.'

Holy shit ... new kink unlocked!

I wonder if he's using his power on me right now because my heart is humming in my chest and all I want to do is lay back, close my eyes, open my legs, and see what *Doctor Wright* does next. That's not like me at all. It's got to be his incubus mojo but at the moment with the way I'm feeling, I don't even care.

I lean back, the towel still wrapped around me, and he seems surprised he's gotten this far.

He spreads my knees apart slowly and I shiver as he stares down at me.

I'm hairless *down there*, not because I was planning for anything to happen but because I prefer it from a sensory perspective.

All at once, his head's between my thighs and his tongue licks from my ass to the top of my pussy, making my hips jump and drawing a cry from me. I prop myself up on my elbows looking down at him, curious as to what he's doing that feels so good.

He doesn't look at me, just spreads my legs apart more, but the towel gets in his way. With a hiss of impatience, he pulls it away and I yelp as my body is displayed for him.

He looks his fill, and my eyes dart to the camera in the corner. Is someone watching the feed right now? He turns his head and when he sees where I'm looking, he gives me a dark smile.

'Oh yeah, at least one of the others is definitely watching this. Maybe all of them.'

Instead of feeling repulsed, something in me revels at the thought. I want to be ... watched? This is new too.

'Get out of your head, Miss Mercy,' he growls into my core, the hum on my clit making my entire body flex.

He pulls me apart and draws back, looking down, a deep sound coming from his chest that I think means he likes what he sees. Holding me open, he takes the middle finger of his other hand and plays with my hole, but he doesn't enter me. One finger then two fingers stretch just the entrance and I lie back with a groan as he settles into a rhythm of sorts.

His head descends again, taking me in his mouth and whirling his tongue over me. I come hard with a cry, my whole body going rigid. I try to close my legs, but he holds my knees wide and, somehow, he draws out the waves of pleasure as they break over me, making this last far longer than any orgasm I've given myself.

When his hands finally leave me, I stare up at the ceiling trying to catch my breath. I realize that I'm still naked, just lying on the bed ... just like the girl with the dark hair I saw my first night here on Sie's bed.

I'm her.

I pull the towel around me, closing my legs and curling into a ball on the bed. What was I thinking? I wasn't thinking. I wasn't in my right mind.

He's sitting on the bed looking at me and I take a shaky breath.

'Did you ... I can't believe you just did that,' I say.

Except that I can believe it. I should have expected it. He's a demon after all. Joke's on me.

'What are you talking about?' he asks.

'You used your power on me. You made me ...'

His lip curls into a sneer. 'I didn't make you do shit.'

Shaking his head, he stalks out of the room, slamming the door behind him, and I'm left wondering what the hell just happened. He didn't feed from me, I'm sure of that, but what was the point? Why did he come here? Why did he do *that*?

I glare at the camera as I wrap the towel around me tightly and go back into the bathroom, shutting the door and getting back into my bath that's now lukewarm. I curl my knees into my chest. It doesn't feel like he forced me. It doesn't feel like I didn't want it. My body is still humming from what he did, but it's sated too.

And I want more.

I put my head in my hands. Is this how it starts, the need for them like a drug?

Is it like what I've heard about heroin? One time and you're hooked on a high you can never forget about? Is sex with these men going to be the first thing I think about when I wake up and the last thing I think about before I fall asleep at night? A traitor's voice in my head asks if that would be so bad.

An hour ago I would have had an answer, but now ... I don't know.

CHAPTER
SEVENTEEN
SIE

It's almost sick watching Paris with the new girl. I sit in the corner of the games room with a book, watching her glance tentatively at me every once in a while as she sits next to him on the black leather couch. He's teaching her to play video games.

I snort. He's putting a lot of effort into this game and it stinks of desperation. I side-eye Kor. He's staring at them too, a hungry look in his eye - for Paris or for the new girl I can't say.

I swear under my breath. She's going to end up dead for one reason or another I think as I stand up and leave the room. My body is humming. Things have been a little bit better recently but I'm still on borrowed time. I crack my neck and head up towards my room, but halfway up I change my mind to go back down through the kitchen to the basement door. It's open as usual. I could just text Carrie or one of the other ones. Hell, there's even a bell in my room to call them like sex maids or something, but for some reason, I feel like I need to go down. The steps don't make a sound as I descend which is a feat considering my size. When I get to the bottom, all three of them are watching TV, sitting practically on top of each other. Two of them are just staring at the screen and a third one is crying quietly between them. I clear my throat and Carrie gets up. The others don't even turn around. She looks a little worse for wear.

'What's going on?' I ask.

'You tell us,' she says, folding her arms.

I shake my head, not understanding the reason for her attitude.

'You get a new girl and suddenly none of us are worth our salt?'

'Are you fucking jealous?' I sneer. 'Is that what you're moping around down here for?'

'What the hell are you talking about?' she growls at me in a pretty good imitation of a wolf shifter. She points to the other two. 'We don't give a shit who you assholes are feeding off, but incubus withdrawal is a real fucking thing and all our contracts said you can't just stop feeding from us cold turkey.'

'You haven't been called,' I guess.

'None of us have,' Carrie murmurs. 'It's been days and we're all feeling it.'

She clutches her belly and a look of pain comes over her face.

I'd come down here thinking I might feed, but now that I'm here the thought makes me feel sick.

Fuck!

I'm hit by the realization that the only female I want is upstairs and I'll be fucking damned if I start pussyfooting around, trying to curry her favor so she chooses me.

I can't help myself but maybe I can help them even if I can't feed from them.

'I'll bring you something to ease the symptoms,' I say.

'You didn't come down here to feed?' she asks, and tears are actually coming to her eyes.

'I'm sorry,' I say. 'I'm a danger to all of you.'

'Bullshit,' she says. 'Now the new girl's here none of you want anything to do with us? What the fuck?'

'I don't have an answer for you,' I say, 'but I can get you something that will help.'

'Fucking do it then,' Monique hisses from the couch, and I raise my eyebrows.

She must be very out of sorts if she's talking to one of the Iron I's like that. She's usually the one who's the meekest.

I go back upstairs, thinking that I'll need to make a call to Stan to have him take a special trip to one of the fae markets. I wasn't lying. There are ways for them to get over this that don't involve us feeding from them, but I hadn't actually realized that they hadn't been called lately. That's something I should know being the Club lieutenant. I've dropped the ball again.

I get back to the games room. Jane's laughing next to Paris and it's the first time I've heard her having fun. I inadvertently think that she's got a nice laugh. It sounds *real*. My gaze falls to her and, from my periphery I see the others in the room doing the same.

I turn, stalking out of the room to Vic's office. I knock and don't bother to wait for an answer as I walk inside.

'The on-call girls are going through withdrawal,' I say.

Vic looks surprised. 'None of us have been feeding from them? I thought it was just me.'

'So did I,' I say. 'I should have realized.'

'Are they okay?'

'Not really, but I'll call Stan to pick up some of those fae potions asap. They'll be right as rain in a day or two and it should keep them going until they're needed again.'

Vic nods absently, not saying anything else. He goes back to whatever he's doing, waving me out.

I decide to go back up to my room, and I pass the games room on the way up. I can't help but glance in at her. She's still sitting with Paris, but she looks lost in thought. She's not smiling or laughing anymore. Her eyes find mine. Guileless. I wonder again how long she's going to last here as I tear my eyes away and make myself leave, refusing to be a puppy following on her heels.

I go back up to my dark room. I let my glamour down and stretch, staring at myself in the mirror. I look like shit.

I look starved.

My physique is thinner, and I feel weaker. Maybe I should have fed from the girls downstairs, but I know who I'd rather have bouncing on my cock while I taste her lust and even thinking of her makes my dick lengthen.

I tear off my clothes and get in the shower, blasting the cold water, afraid of what I might do in this state if I come across her in the house without one of the others around to stop me.

What the hell was Vic thinking contracting her in the first place?

The frigid water does nothing, and when I step out of the shower, I still have a problem that I need to take care of if I want to sleep.

∼

Jane

DEMONS AND DEBTS

IT'S SURREAL. That's the only way I can put it. Since Vic's little ultimatum, giving me five days to choose the weapon of my fate, Paris, Theo and even Vic have been nicer to me. They smile at me when they pass me in the hallway, teach me to play videogames ... *eat me out in my bedroom.* I mean that was only the one time ... But even though Theo left angry, when I saw him later, he pretended nothing had happened, like he'd never been mad, like he'd never even had his head between my legs.

I still don't know what to think about what happened. I don't feel violated, but maybe that's because of how my brain works. But they shouldn't get away with taking advantage of me just because I don't have the same reactions that another human might. But maybe it wasn't like that. I'm so confused.

When I came downstairs for breakfast this morning, Theo was already in the kitchen. He told me he'd gotten three boxes of the good cereal delivered just for me. I had two bowls and he didn't bat an eye.

Then he invited me to the games room. I'm currently standing in the hall like a little bitch, plucking up the courage to go in. Fuck this!

Digging my fingernails into my palms, I walk inside. Three of them are there. Only Vic and Sie are missing. I've noticed they all tend to hang out here when they're not in the gym or off doing whatever it is they do. Other than yesterday, I haven't really been in here.

I feel a little bit shy as all three of them turn to stare. Theo beckons me to the couch, and I go, flinching a little as he pulls me down to sit between him and Paris.

They turn on a game.

'Have you played this one before?' Theo asks.

I shake my head.

Paris hands me a controller. 'It's really easy,' he says, and he shows me what buttons do what.

At first, I'm sitting between them rigid, wondering what their game is, wondering if they're going to turn on me.

But as the minutes pass and I get into the game, I find I'm actually not bad at it and my two companions are pretty easy-going, even funny, when they're just being friendly. I begin to relax, sitting cross legged on the couch and getting into the game. I don't win, but I'm close.

Paris says something funny and I laugh, just as Sie comes into the room. He immediately turns and walks out again.

'Don't worry about him,' Theo says. 'He's just jealous.'

'Jealous of what?'

Paris is observing me with a weird expression on his face and Theo's hand slowly moves to my knee.

I instantly know that Paris was one of the guys watching on the camera while Theo ... I look down at his hand and my stomach rolls a little. I'm such a fucking moron because, in all the fun, I forgot what this was, just as they had probably intended. They're trying to butter me up, make me lower my guard so I'll choose one of them. They probably have a bet on who I'm going to pick. That's something they'd do. Demons. *Guys*.

I excuse myself and go back up to my room, hoping no one follows me. I head straight for the closet but when I get inside, I find all Theo's clothes gone. In their place are women's outfits. Hanger after hanger. Designer. Expensive. Coarse fabrics like gauze, beads, and *wool*. Textures I'd never want against my skin. Eyes widening, I step inside. All of them are in my size. They're for me. I finger the fabrics.

It doesn't smell right in here. It had Theo's scent before, but now it smells like dyes and chemicals from new clothes. It smells like a department store.

'How do you like them?'

I whirl around to the sound of Paris' voice. He's leaning up against the door jam.

'I—'

'You don't need to thank me, princess.' He shrugs, looking me up and down. 'I told them to choose things that would look good on you.'

'Who?'

He shrugs. 'The personal shopper. Sent them your measurements, some photos and they did the rest.'

'Oh,' I say, faintly feeling a little sick from the smell of the new clothes and also the GROSS INVASION OF PRIVACY I've been subjected to *again*. I look up at the camera.

'You were watching, weren't you?'

He lets out a little groan. 'I have to say you were hot as fuck taking Theo's mouth, his fingers spreading you so wide like that. The camera was a little far away to get a good look at you though ...'

He takes a step towards me.

Nope!

'Well, thanks a lot for the clothes. They're *super-duper*!'

I dart past him as I move through the door and, thankfully, he doesn't try to stop me.

In case he does decide to follow, I go down the back steps quickly, in through the kitchen, and out the back door, breathing in the fresh air.

I don't stop. I walk quickly across the deck and down the steps. I head for the woods. I'm not trying to escape this time. If I had balls, they've got me by them now that Shar is involved. But I need to be away for a little while to get my head together.

The weird tingle I felt before when I was trying to leave the grounds isn't there now, but I can still feel the hum of the perimeter. I guess it's magicked or something. I follow the trails, trying to keep my mind off the bullshit, but failing.

I feel ... sad and it's so dumb.

Fuck those guys because even though I knew their friendliness wasn't real, two hours was all it took for them to start drawing me in, messing with my head, making me feel like I could belong even for a little while.

Tears burn the backs of my eyelids, and I wonder if Vic knew what he was doing. Of course he did. These five days weren't meant as a respite, they were supposed to be a punishment, a suffering purgatory with an inevitable outcome.

I keep heading further into the trees. It looks different out here in the daylight. I slow my pace, not wanting to go too far, but also not in the mood to return to the house yet.

Maybe I should try to beat Vic at his own game and just get this over with. It's only day one and it already feels like it's been an eternity. If I choose now, then the waiting is over.

I turn back towards the house, making my mind up in a split second. I have to decide and then get it over with. But which one? Paris I discount immediately because of the clothes incident and his entire demeanor. He's acting like such a dick, like all he has to do is whip it out and I'll fall on it with pleasure. Theo's out too. He seems to think me choosing him is a foregone conclusion just because of what happened in the bedroom. Vic? No. He's far too intimidating and he was so cold and mean after that night at the club that I don't really want to be around him. Korban is a no as well. He's angry and he stares. I get the feeling he'd enjoy hurting me. That leaves Sie. He hasn't been more or less friendly and he hasn't changed anything in his interactions with me. He hasn't tried to buy me either. I mean I haven't really even spoken to him since that first day in his room. He doesn't know I exist, I'm pretty sure. Perfect. Well, not perfect at all, but under the circumstances, he's probably my best bet to get it over and done with quickly.

At least I was able to save Shar and her kids, I tell myself again. I say this multiple times a day like a mantra. It makes me feel better.

I go back inside and to Sie's room. No point in delaying the inevitable any longer. I knock and my heart beats faster. My legs twitch as I think about running away before he opens it, but I don't move. No one answers after a minute, and I look tentatively behind me. There's no one around to see as I open the door and slip inside, but he's not there. Should I wait?

No.

My courage is already failing me, drying up like a dammed river and I slowly back out of the room, sort of afraid he's going to simply appear now that I've chickened out.

I go back to my room. Paris is gone thankfully. The closet door is still open and the whole place smells of the new clothes. I look at them again, draped on their hangers like smelly specters, some of them wrapped in plastic, and am suddenly filled with anger. Did Paris think that this would make me fall to the floor in front of him and spread my legs? He definitely did. Fuck him and fuck all these expensive things that reek and feel awful.

I bundle up all the clothes, tearing them from the rail.

Then I notice the shoes in neat rows on the floor beneath. Each pair of heels is at least four inches high. He *knows* I can't walk in shoes like that.

Even more incensed, I stomp across the room, and I throw the clothes into the hallway. Then I grab all the shoes I can fit in my arms, and I throw them out too.

I look up at the camera.

'I hope you're watching right now, asshole.' I don't know if it even has audio, so I stick up both my middle fingers for good measure, staring into the tiny lens as I go back into the closet and close the door.

I sit in the dark, letting my mind go blank. It's quiet and my mind stops running at a hundred miles a minute. I draw my knees to my chest and hug them tightly, resting my head on them. I'm aware of a pulsing between my thighs, the same feeling I had before. Is this Vic or all of them fucking with me too, making me want them? Or are they trying to make me decide sooner?

My fingers move into my pants and between my legs. My breath stutters as I touch myself, but all it does is fan the flames. It's not enough. With a cry, I pull my hand away, standing and pacing the tiny room. I have so much energy and I don't know what to do with it.

Maybe I should go down to the pool ... nope don't have a suit and the mere idea of going back into the hallway to pick through the clothes Paris bought makes my blood boil. I'll be fucking damned if I'm going to do that. But I can wear what I have on now in the gym. I can just pedal on a bike until I have no energy left.

Maybe then I'll be able to sleep tonight without writhing around and wishing one of them would come to relieve the ache.

I leave the closet, flinging the door open and wading

through the pile of clothes in the corridor as if they aren't even there. I run down the stairs, trying to escape this arousal that's inside of me, this need my body has all of a sudden.

'Fucking incubi,' I mutter.

Fuck them and their games. I'm not going to let them win.

CHAPTER
EIGHTEEN
SIE

I've been in my room for hours. I can't relax, just keep tossing and turning on my bed. I throw on some clothes and head down to the gym. Maybe I can work out the tension that way.

I start pummeling the pads as soon as I get in there. Korban was in here recently, but he's not now. Maybe he's been doing the same thing I am.

A half an hour in, I hear the door open. I assume it's Kor, but I don't bother to make sure. When I don't hear any movement, I stop working over the pad and turn to look.

She's standing there, her eyes locked on me, shifting nervously from foot to foot.

'What the fuck do you want?' I snarl at her.

She swallows visibly but doesn't run. 'I just wanted to work out.'

I scoff at her. 'You shouldn't play games, little girl.'

She mutters something to herself that I don't catch before she goes over to the bike and gets on. She starts to pedal hard, ignoring me as I turn away and start hitting the bag that hangs from the beam in the center of the room.

I try not to notice that she's there, but I keep seeing her in the mirror. She's going for the bike hard, pedaling as fast as she can. I see her increasing the tension making it harder for herself until she can hardly pedal, but still she keeps trying.

I turn around and growl at her. 'What the fuck are you even doing?'

'What the fuck do you care?' she retorts, almost unable to speak because she's so out of breath.

I abandon the bag and stalk towards her. She stops pedaling, eyeing me.

'What?' she pants, clearly furious for some reason. Then she closes her eyes and sets her jaw. 'Never fucking mind.'

She dismounts and walks past me, smacking into me with her shoulder hard enough to push me back a step. I wouldn't take that from one of my own brothers let alone a human.

I grab her forearm and pull her back, staring into her eyes, just like she's staring into mine. 'What did you come down here for?' I growl at her.

'I told you,' she snarls back. 'I just wanted to work out. I can't sleep.' She says the last in a pleading tone, but then her pupils dilate.

'And I told you to stop fucking playing.'

I want to throw her away from me but I don't.

'I'm not playing!' She struggles in my grasp. 'Fuck all of you and your awful magick. Fuck Vic's nasty little game. Fuck Paris' bribes. Fuck Theo's cameras. Fuck Korban's staring at me like he wants me dead and fuck you for ... being so indifferent all the time!'

There are tears in her eyes and my arms fall away.

'I went to your room earlier, but you weren't there,' she confesses.

'Why did you go to my room?' I growl.

I know why, but I want to hear her say it. I need to hear her say it.

But then her nostrils flare and she lets out a tiny whimper as she turns away.

'Because I wanted— What the fuck is wrong with me?' She whispers to herself.

I was going to let her leave, but her words ... the scent of her that pervades my nose, sweet and seductive. For some inexplicable reason, she's chosen me.

Something in me gives up. I can't fight it anymore. The darkness wins.

I grab her as she leaves, pulling her back inside, throwing the door closed and thrusting her hard against it. I thread my fingers into her hair and use my new grip on her to keep her where I want her as I push my body against her back, sandwiching her between me and the hard wood.

'You're not going anywhere,' a voice says, and I barely recognize it as my own.

The madness is finally taking over and there's nothing I can do. I'm trying to make myself let her go and shout at her to run, but as I turn her around and throw her against the wall, taking her throat in a firm grip – as my hands begin to rip at her clothes – I know it's too fucking late. I can only look on and hope that I don't kill her.

~

Jane

HE RIPS my shirt down the middle with one swift move and I see his hands aren't hands anymore. They're claws.

Big.

Calloused.

Purple and grey.

I'm shaking as he takes my throat in his massive fingers, but he doesn't squeeze. He's not trying to kill me. He lets out a satisfied growl as he looks down at his handiwork very slowly. He traces his claws up my stomach to my bra, tickling my skin and making me shiver. He puts one of those sharp talons under the bridge between the cups and, with a flick, slices it like paper, baring my breasts.

My eyes don't leave his.

He doesn't look like Sie anymore, and it's not because he's showing me his true form. I've seen that before. It's as if the Sie that was here a few moments ago is gone, like he's not in control of himself. His motions are jerky like he's trying to stop but can't.

The thing is, I don't want him to stop. This is insane. I know it is. I know I shouldn't want this, but with the way I'm feeling ... My skin is so sensitive, the muscles in my abdomen are contracting, between my legs is soaking. I'm practically moaning, wanting to submit to him. I need his hands on me.

This is all kinds of wrong because I know that he wouldn't stop even if I wanted him to. It's just luck that I want this too.

Anticipation and need war with the abhorrence I feel that I'm letting him do this, that I'm not fighting him at all. I'm a fucking feminist! But this is what I need. It's like my body's not my own right now just as his doesn't seem to be.

I give into the sensations because I have to. I can't not.

'Stay there,' he growls, and the command makes me feel weak in the knees.

His hands come down and shred my leggings, pulling them and my underwear off me completely. My shirt, hanging off me like a rag, is the only piece of clothing still on me and it covers nothing.

He looks me up and down, his eyes practically glowing, and then he backs off.

No! Don't stop now!

But I guess he's just trying to get a better look at me because he points a finger up and moves it in a little circle, wanting me to turn for him.

I push myself off the wall and do it, reveling in his attention, knowing that this isn't me but still unable to stop myself.

'Very nice,' he mutters almost to himself and then he beckons me. I take a step forward and then another and I'm suddenly on my back on the mat. He's between my legs, fumbling with his pants. His body is bigger now, his skin has a mauve hue that I only saw a little bit of in the darkness of his bedroom before. I love looking at him. He's beautiful.

His clawed fingers play with my pussy and I tense, but his touch doesn't hurt. In fact I moan, opening my legs wider for him as he worries my clit, pinching it gently, rolling it and eliciting sounds from me that I've never made before.

One of his clawed fingers thrusts into me and I jerk, stifling a cry at the intrusion and sure for a split second that he's cut me, but there's no pain. He's being careful, this monster; far more gentle than the human boy I shared my first time with.

If that's not irony, I don't know what is.

Our eyes are locked, and he's holding me down by the throat, keeping me where he wants me while his other hand leaves my cunt and explores my body. He pinches my nipples, watching me closely as I squirm under him, writhing, wanting more and yet terrified that he won't deliver what he's promising, that I'll be left disappointed.

Every nerve ending in me is screaming for something and he's making the sensations build. I'm ravenous but not for food and I don't understand this hollow feeling in my abdomen. But it hurts, tendrils of pain radiating out and making my eyes tear.

He leans over me and licks my breast, swirling his long tongue around it before nipping it hard enough for me to squeal.

I open my mouth to beg him for more than his thick finger, but before I can utter a word, he seizes it with his own, his tongue mingling with mine. He's as desperate as I am for this.

Almost of their own accord, my legs wrap around his waist pulling myself closer to him, and he lets out a small gasp of his own as if he's surprised.

He draws back a little, looking into my face as he grinds against me. 'You want this, human?'

I nod, not even trying to pretend that I don't.

'I want you bound before me, spread and waiting, your pussy tied open for me to look at whenever I like. I want you on a table on a platter for me to devour at my leisure. I'd pour fine wine down your body and lick it from your tits, from your hot pussy, and from your ass while the other Iron I's watched and wished they could have you too. I'd hold you over my cock and make you beg to be allowed to take it. I'd make you plead with me to fuck you and scream my name at the top of your lungs when I make you come. I'd make sure that all of them knew that you chose me to pleasure you.'

His words make me whimper and I feel him nudge

against my core. Hot. Hard. He pushes into me and he's so big it feels like he's splitting me open.

I cry out. It hurts *so good* ...

I arch under him as he takes hold of my hips, impaling me completely. It seems to lessen the other pain I'm feeling as he pulls out and pushes back in, hauls me up to sit on his lap. He doesn't let me choose the pace though, just picks me up and slams me back down on his length.

I scream in pleasure, burying my face in his chest, taking in the scent of him like smoke and leather. He sets a punishing rhythm, my thighs clenching around him tighter with the sounds he makes.

I have a sudden realization in the middle of all of this that I've never been so turned on in my life before.

I'm climbing higher and higher, my body feeling like I just can't get enough. Something in me takes over and it feels like I'm working purely on instinct. I want ... to bite him? That can't be right. But his hand takes my throat again, stopping me as I lunge forward, and he roars, but I know – don't ask me how – that he's pleased by what I just tried to do.

He fucks me even harder, pulling my hips up and slamming them down, plunging himself into me over and over and over until I can't take anymore, my legs shaking as my entire body goes rigid and I scream his name in release.

He follows immediately, letting out a long, low, powerful groan as I feel him pulsing inside me.

He finally lets me go and I fall back against the mat, my body still locked with his. I'm breathing heavily, confused but satisfied in a way that I have never been before. The pain I felt is gone. It's like I was starving before and didn't know it. My skin feels warm and my body is so comfortable, relaxed, and alive. I can hardly even open my eyes and it's not because I'm tired, it's because I feel so good.

I crack my eyes open so I can watch him. He's still in front of me and he moves back a little, his body slipping from mine. He's back in his human form and there's nothing on his face to suggest that he's upset, but I know he is. It's weird, but I feel like I'm somehow tuned into him on some level.

He looks down at me and his eyes become tortured.

'I'm so sorry,' he whispers, and the anguish in his voice makes tears come to my eyes.

I want to tell him it's okay, but my eyes close and I float away like a leaf on the breeze.

CHAPTER
NINETEEN
VIC

I'm sitting in my study when Sie throws open the door and barges in. That's not unusual, but it's the look on his face that has me getting to my feet, heart beginning to hammer in my chest.

'What is it?'

My second paces the room, his hand over his mouth.

'I've done something,' he says.

'What?' I ask.

He can't even look me in the eye.

'What have you done?' I ask more forcefully.

'I didn't mean to. I didn't know ... I just ... I couldn't stop.'

'What – *Who* are you talking about?' I ask, afraid that he's killed one of the on-call girls downstairs.

'The new girl. Jane,' he murmurs as if only just remembering she has a name.

'Where?' I'm already heading for the door.

'I put her back in her room.'

'Is she alive?' My heart is pounding in my chest so hard I can barely breathe.

Sie nods and my relief is profound.

'Is she injured?'

'I don't think so.'

I let out a sound of frustration. 'Then what the fuck's the problem?'

'You don't understand! I ... I wasn't myself. I lost control. I ... she struggled ...'

I take a deep breath. It's bad, but if she's alive, then this could have been much worse.

'Did she say she wanted you?'

'Yes, but—'

'But nothing. She knew what she was getting into. She signed the contract. That means she consent—'

'Fuck, Alex! I know what it means,' he hisses at me and I flinch at his use of my actual name.

He buries his face in his palms and I take pity on him, putting my hand on his shoulder.

'How was she when you left her?'

'Unconscious.'

'Did you hurt her?'

'I don't know. I was in my demon form. I wasn't gentle. Nowhere near. And she wasn't lulled. I guess I was too far gone to use it ....'

I take stock of my second-in-command. He seems more himself than I've seen him in probably months. Whatever he did seems to have helped. That *was* the original reason for contracting her before I knew who she was, I remind myself as I leave the study and head up to Theo's old room. My heart is in my throat, not knowing what I'll find there.

I go in and she's laying on the bed. Still. My brow furrows as I step into the room, but she's just breathing slowly, stretched out like a cat in the sun.

'Jane,' I murmur.

Her eyes flutter open and her smile is slow and languid. I find myself being drawn closer.

I hear Sie behind me and I'm still not sure what the problem is. She doesn't seem like she's in any distress.

I give Sie a look and he seems as confused as I am.

'Are you sure you made her do something she didn't want to do?'

'I don't know. I thought at first ... but then she...' He doesn't say anything more.

Jane seems fine, but Sie is pacing the room.

'I'll take care of this,' I say. 'Let her sleep. Maybe it's best if you go up to Metro with Paris tonight. Set up some meetings and we'll join you tomorrow. That'll give you time to take stock and Jane can recover her strength before you feed from her again.'

'Again?' Sie asks, his voice barely above a whisper.

'Yes, 'again',' I say with an edge to my voice. 'Whatever you did with her has sated you. You're yourself again in ways you haven't been in a long time. You'll take from her whenever you need to and that's an order.'

Sie doesn't look happy with my edict, but he nods his head and backs out of the room.

I look down at Jane. She's asleep now, a small smile playing on her lips.

She looks so pure, but soon she'll be ours in every way. I can't wait to show her father how we've despoiled his daughter. His fault for sending her to us in the first place.

I text the group and let them know that Sie has won the game as I leave the room. I doubt Sie will tell anyone anything about it and the thought of having to watch any more of Paris and Theo's saccharine sweet behavior around her makes me want to dig out my eyes with my own claws.

I couldn't have done even an hour longer let alone the whole five days.

Now for the next part of my plan.

I go down to my study and open my top drawer. Inside is a mass of papers detailing a shipment coming into the port at Metro in two nights full of magickal weapons and fae artifacts. It's bullshit, of course, there's no such delivery, and even if there was, there'd be no physical documentation like this, but I'm going to have an ambush waiting for whomever is stealing our merchandise. And our little human is going to give whoever she's working for all the information they need to be exactly where we want them to be. If we're lucky, we can take them all down in one fell swoop.

I take out the dummy paperwork for this irresistible shipment that's meant to take place in a couple of nights and place it haphazardly on the table, leaving the drawer open with the key in the lock as if I was in a hurry and forgot to put it away.

Closing the door behind me, I head to the games room to shoot a little pool, thinking about how Jane is going to play right into my hands.

Now that the game is over, I did tell her that things would be working as normal, and I find myself anticipating traveling with her on this trip. The others will take their bikes, leaving just her and me by ourselves in the limo.

I pour myself a double and knock it back. It's going to be one interesting, and, if I have my way, very enjoyable, *ride.*

~

Jane

I wake up slowly, stretching my body and moaning because it feels so amazing. My eyes open and I see that I'm in my room. It's dark outside and the clock says it's almost midnight. I've kicked the covers off and I notice I'm not wearing any clothes.

I sit up.

Right. Because Sie ripped them all off me.

My hand covers my mouth as I remember what happened in the gym. I swallow hard as the muscles of my core clench at the thought of what Sie did ... *what I wanted him to do.*

I take the sheet from the bed and wrap it around myself when I can't see my backpack with my clothes in it anywhere. I'm sure it was by the table. I snort. Korban probably took it to rummage through it again since I'm such a fucking *danger* to the Iron I's.

I fan myself with my hand. The room is stifling. My skin feels like it's burning up but it's not hot to the touch. Going to the window, I try to open it, but it won't budge. After a few moments of investigation in the low light, I see that two nails have been driven in through the top of the frame. I frown. That makes no sense. It's too high for me to escape this way. I peer down into the darkness. Maybe they thought I'd jump.

I sit back down on the bed but I'm still too hot. I need some fresh air. I feel closed in now and the need to be outside takes over.

Leaving the room, I pad down the main stairs as quietly as I can, but when I get to the front door, I need a key even to unlock it from the inside, which I don't have.

Heaving a sigh, I'm rolling my eyes as I go to the kitchen one. I mean, seriously, we're in the middle of an estate with magickal boundaries. Do they really need to lock this place up like a fortress? No one's getting anywhere near the house.

I have the same problem in the kitchen. Fuck!

I get myself a glass of water, hoping it'll do the trick, but it doesn't and then I remember the pool. I don't have a suit, my brain helpfully supplies, but at this point does it matter? There are probably cameras in every room and I'm pretty sure all of the guys have seen me with nothing on. And they should be asleep by now anyway, right?

I make my way to the other side of the house, the scent of chlorine hitting my nose as I open the door that leads to the pool. It's warm in here, warmer than the other rooms, and it feels even more uncomfortable. I want to leave, but I know the water will feel good so I lose the sheet, tossing it on one of the loungers close by.

There's just enough light to see by as I descend to the first step, breathing a sigh of relief as the water cools my toes. I take two more steps down quickly and sigh heavily.

I don't do laps. It's not really my thing. Instead, I just sit on the lowest step I can, submerged up to my neck, playing with the water. I feel it swirling between my fingers, the ebb and flow putting me into a very relaxed state. I don't think I've been in a pool since my school days. Probably when Angie used to take me. I push away the bittersweet memories of my almost-adoptive mom. I wonder what she'd think of me now.

Outside, I hear the muffled sound of the garage opening and a bike goes by the window that looks out on the driveway a minute later. It sails down the winding private road. It's too dark to see who's on it, but I stay where I am until it's long gone.

I stand up, making my way out to where the towels are stacked, taking one and drying myself vigorously. A creak sounds from out in the hallway, and I grab my sheet, crossing the room and peering out the cracked door. There's no one there though so I slip out into the corridor and tip-toe back to the foyer.

I'm about to go back up to my room when I notice that the study door is ajar and the desk light is on. There's no one in there and usually when that's the case, the door is locked. I know because I've seen the guys try the handle a couple of times when they're looking for their president and he's been elsewhere. It's his space and he doesn't like anyone in there when he's not.

I step into the room, taking a look around. He's definitely not here and I shouldn't be either. I move around the desk to turn off the desk lamp simply because it's a waste of electricity when I notice some documents on the desk.

I try not to look. Really! I actually don't give a shit what they're into. But I see my name poking out of a folder underneath the pile and I can't help it.

I move the sheets of paper aside that have nothing to do with me until I see it. My picture clipped to a folder.

Heart beating faster, I open it, scanning the sheets with all my personal information. My Social, a list of most of the places I've lived and when. My whole life on four pages.

Then I get to the last one and I can't breathe. It's the medical report the doctors gave Angie, detailing the 'Asperger's Syndrome' that's overshadowed my entire life. It says everything. My sensory issues and overloads, the shutdowns. Everything.

They know about me.

I stifle a sob. I don't know why I'm so upset, and I know it'll take me awhile to unpick the mess in my head, but for now I let myself feel it. I start questioning all my interactions with the Iron I's. When did they know? Was this why

Theo was actually kind to me the other night at the club? Was this why they wanted me to sign their contract? Did they want me here because I'm different? A novelty? A freak? I just wanted to belong ... even if it was pretend, but they knew all along.

Keeping my sobs as quiet as I can, I take the folder and put it in the drawer along with the rest of the papers, almost trapping my fingers in it as I close it because I can't see from my tears. I turn off the light and leave the room, but as I turn the corner into the kitchen, I bump into Paris.

Shit.

I try to will the tears away, but at the same time I know I can't hide how upset I am, so I try to avert my face away from his, slinking past him.

I think I've made it until I feel his hand on my shoulder turning me back to face him.

'Hey, sweetheart. Are you ok? What's wrong?'

Is he genuinely worried? No, he's probably just trying to avoid another *episode* with the crazy girl. The thought of how he danced with me the other night and probably laughed about it later with the others sends me into an emotional tailspin and I let out a cry that mortifies me.

'Hey, hey. It's ok. Tell me what's wrong.'

His arms are around me and I try to push him away, but I can't. I want his succor, comfort from a guy who called me a retard before we left that same night. I cry harder. I'm so lonely I'll take scraps from demons who can't stand me, who think I'm literally less than them, less than the other human slave girls they literally have no respect for.

I'm so pathetic.

I vaguely hear Paris on the phone as I'm crying into his chest and I feel him pick me up, carrying me upstairs.

Probably wants to fuck the freak, see how weird I am in the sack.

My tears are drying up now and a cold fury is quickly taking the place of my desperate sadness.

We get to my room, and I struggle to be let down. The moment his hands leave me, I'm sprinting to the closet, throwing it open and then slamming the door. As soon as I'm alone, I grab my hair on either side of my head, pulling it hard, my mouth opening on a silent scream of anguish.

The pain grounds me, punishes me, makes me feel good on some fucked up level. But it's not enough and even though there's a voice in my head screaming at me that I'm making this a thousand times worse, I silence it maliciously. I want it to be worse. I deserve it.

I hit myself in the forehead like I'm banging on a door as hard as I can. The knowledge that I'm hurting myself, the thudding of my knuckles on my skull – One. Two. Three times, then four – is enough for all of it to disappear and I'm left in the silence.

In the dark.

I fall to my knees, my actions over the past few minutes rushing at me with clarity I didn't have a few moments ago.

I sink down on my heels.

Fuck. Fuck. Fuck. What have I done?

There's a tentative knock at the door and, even though I don't say anything, it opens.

Theo peers inside. 'Can I do anything?'

I shake my head. 'No.'

He leaves me by myself and, although I'm glad he does, I wish I could fall into a 'meltdown exhaustion sleep' in someone's arms tonight instead of all alone.

But I don't call him back. Fuck him. Fuck all of them. I just need to do my time and not forget that despite their incubus wiles, they don't and won't care about me for real. I can't care about them either.

But I think it might already be too late.

AT SOME POINT in the night I leave the closet in search of my bed. I curl up under the blankets, my heart heavy and my stomach leaden.

At least I didn't throw up.

THE MORNING IS MET with a breakfast tray on the table with Theo's cereal on it; dry in the bowl with a jug of milk so I can pour it in myself. Even though I'm still reeling from last night, my dumb heart thaws toward Theo just a tiny, tiny bit as I eat it.

My door opens and Vic strides in.

'Get up,' he says. 'We leave in two hours.'

'Where are we going?' I ask.

'Metro City.'

My eyes widen. 'What's in Metro City?'

'Iron I business. Pack for at least four days.'

He's gone before I can tell him that I have no clothes since my backpack hasn't reappeared and Paris' bribes are long gone.

I get up and take a shower, wrapping myself in a towel. I take a look through the closet, but I was thorough. All that's left from my blitz yesterday is one, errant, four-inch Jimmy Choo.

I sit on the bed, cooling my heels for the time being, and my eyes land on a white paper bag that's on the bedside table; the kind with little twisted paper handles that you get at boutiques.

I sigh. Something else to throw out into the hall.

I turn it upside down on the bed and a white box falls out along with a folded note.

> *Sorry you didn't like the clothes. I got these for you. ~P.*
>
> *P.S. After you chose Sie.*

I open the magnetic box, expecting some flashy, heavy jewelry made out of something horribly uncomfortable like live scarab beetles or something. (Yeah, that was a thing like a hundred years ago. Totally read about it. At the end of the night, rich ladies would put their moving scarab beetle necklaces in dishes with wet sponges to keep the damn thing alive for as long as possible. I know! Fucked up, right?)

But instead, I gasp at the sight of a pair of *very* high-end noise-cancelling headphones nestled in fucking satin. I know what these are and they're worth like ten grand because of the magick they're infused with! If I had wet dreams, they would be about these headphones.

I shouldn't accept them. I should throw them outside just like the other stuff, I say in my head even as my fingertips are reverently stroking the finely crafted steel with filigree flowers etched into the metal. They're beautiful and the conjure worked over them will block out everything, literally someone could shoot a gun right in front of me and I wouldn't hear it go off with these on.

I lift them out of the box and try them on. I can't even try to stop myself. They connect to my phone automatically and, for the first time in months, I hear a song from my favorite playlist coming through quality sound speakers instead of the tinny phone ones. I close my eyes and listen for a minute before I take them off and put them in their special satin bag.

Nope. I'm not giving these up. Integrity? What integrity. Guess everyone really does have their price.

There's a knock at my door and I stare at it for a second because no one ever does that, they just come right in.

'Enter,' I say in my best hoity toity voice and the door opens.

'Forty minutes,' Theo says as he steps inside. 'You're not dressed yet?'

'I don't have any clothes.'

'Sure you do.' He opens the closet, steps inside, and freezes. 'I thought Paris—'

'I couldn't wear them,' I interrupt in a mumble. 'They were scratchy and itchy fabrics and smelled funny and they were only so I'd choose him.'

'But you chose Sie.'

I glance up, wondering if he's mad that I didn't choose him. 'Yeah.'

'Do you mind if I ask why?'

'I wanted it over and done with and I know that you guys were only being nice to me so I'd pick you. You don't even like me. I know that. But he didn't pretend. I guess I know where I stand with him.'

'So he didn't make you do anything you didn't want to do?'

'No,' I say, surprised. 'Not at all. I picked him fair and square, and he didn't do anything I didn't want.'

'Ok,' he says, seeming placated. 'Come on.'

He pulls me up to standing.

'Is this an on-call girl thing?' I ask, not meeting his eyes.

'No, Miss Mercy. Not unless you want it to be,' he says, his tone turning all *official*.

I swallow hard at the doctor voice, and he winks at me.

I can't help my chuckle and the little roleplay from the other day goes through my mind. I want to ask him about it, but I'm not sure where to start.

He leads me out of my room and down the hall in just my towel and I pull it closer around me.

He brings me to the room he's sharing with Paris.

'Where's Paris?' I ask.

'He went to Metro ahead of us earlier this morning. Sie left late last night. We'll meet up with them there today.'

Sie's gone? He must have been the one who was leaving last night while I was in the pool. Right after we … I frown. What did I expect? Cuddles? Love? What happened may have been a big deal to me, but it was probably just another encounter with an on-call girl to him.

Theo opens a drawer in his bureau, taking out a set of clothes and I recognize my leggings, the ones that I was wearing at the diner that night when I first came here.

'I kept them just in case,' he says, handing them to me and turning around.

'Thanks,' I say, wondering why he's acting like a gentleman when a few minutes ago he was talking like he wanted to get me into bed.

I get dressed quickly though, finding my comfy undies in the little pile and a grey tank top that isn't mine but fits me well enough.

'You'll need the right outfits in Metro. I'll make sure Paris gets you some more clothes when we get there,' he promises as he looks me over.

He must see something in my face because he gives me a smile.

'He'll go through what kinds of things you like with you, ok? I'll make sure he knows what he did wrong last time, but I have a feeling he already knows.'

I nod, relieved that I'm not going to have to throw out another whole closet full of clothes.

'I know you don't like some fabrics and stuff,' he says, 'but you can't just wear jeans and sneakers. The Iron I's have a reputation to uphold so you do need to dress the part. We'll make sure it's nothing you can't handle.'

At the reminder that he knows about my medical history now, I look down. 'When did you find out about ...' I swallow hard.

'When did I know you're autistic?' His tone is gentle. 'Only a couple days ago. I'm sorry I didn't realize sooner.'

'I hide it,' I whisper.

'You don't have to do that here.'

I give a disbelieving scoff. He has no idea and the last thing I want is all of them looking at me like I'm crazy ... *crazier*.

'Was that what last night was about?' he asks.

I nod. 'Partly. I — Did you guys make me sign because I'm ...'

'Different?'

'A freak.'

He's in my face as soon as I say the word, making me back up a step. 'No and don't you ever say that about yourself again. No one here thinks that, so don't think it yourself or I swear I'll tie you down to my exam table and edge you for so many hours that every time you hear that word in general conversation afterwards, you'll break out in a cold sweat.'

Edge me for *hours*? I mean I know what edging is, but for *HOURS*? My eyes widen and I swear my underwear is instantly damp even as I worry about his threat. But I also can't not ask the question that pops into my head.

'You have an exam table for ...?'

He shrugs. 'You know a little about what I'm into, Miss Mercy. What do you think?' He smirks. 'How do you feel about PVC?'

An incredulous giggle explodes from me before I stifle it, my self-effacing thoughts forgotten. 'You want me to wear a rubber nurse's uniform, or something?' I laugh.

Theo's eyes seem to glow for a split second. 'Fuck that'd be hot,' he breathes.

'Do you always do it like that?' I blurt, wanting to know more.

'What? Medical play? Not always, but I like it. I think you do too, Miss Mercy.' His eyes move over me. 'Maybe we'll try something on my exam table next time?'

I feel like my eyes are going to bug out of my head any second.

'Where is it?' I whisper.

'Maybe I'll show you when we get back,' he teases.

I can feel my blush and he chuckles.

'But, unfortunately, there's no time now, princess.'

'Why are you being so nice to me?' I ask. 'The game is over ... right?'

He doesn't answer right away, grabbing a black jacket and handing it to me.

'The game was over as soon as you chose Sie,' he confirms.

'Then why? What's in it for you?'

'I like you.'

I frown. He likes me? Even though he knows about everything? I want to believe him, but is he messing with my head again?

The jacket he's given me is a little bit too big, but I like the way it swamps me, and I know I won't get too cold on the motorcycle later.

'Go grab your stuff and meet us downstairs in five.'

I run back to my room and find a small backpack on the top shelf of Theo's closet to replace my missing one. I pack up my toiletries from the bathroom, grab my phone and charger and my new headphones too, not able to stop myself from looking inside the bag at them before I pack them in a separate pocket so they're extra safe.

When I get downstairs, Vic is waiting for me in the foyer, looking at his watch. He's dressed immaculately in another black suit, but his tie isn't knotted. It hangs loose down his black lapels. Only half Bedroom Vic, I muse. I wonder what that means.

He looks up, sees me, and frowns. As he opens his mouth, I know what he's about to say, and I put up a hand to stay his words, but Theo swoops in and takes over.

'She couldn't wear the stuff Paris bought. We'll buy her some things when we get there. Plenty of time.'

He winks at me, and I can't help the small smile that plays on my lips. Except for Shar, I can't remember the last time anyone treated me like I matter. I'm trying not to let Theo and Paris get to me, but it's hard.

'Let's go,' Vic says, and Theo ushers me out.

I go into my bag to grab my new headphones, but then I see the limo. At first, I think we're all riding in it together, but Theo doesn't follow us.

'Kor and I will be a half hour behind you,' he says.

Vic lets me get in first and I clamber to the far side as he lowers himself into the seat after me. The door closes and the car immediately starts to move. The privacy screen is up and now that it's just me and Vic, I'm feeling very nervous, so I just stare out the window in complete silence as the minutes tic by.

Bored out of my mind, I finally chance a look up at him and see he's regarding me with a curious look on his face.

'Will it help if I lose the suit?' he asks me in that low baritone voice.

I nod jerkily. Bedroom Vic was much easier to be around.

He takes off his jacket, folds it in half lengthways, and lays it on the seat next to him. Next, he unbuttons his top two buttons and slides off the tie.

I swallow hard and try not to show it. Will he stop there or is he literally taking off the *entire suit*?

'The shoes,' I mutter, remembering his bare feet in his bedroom.

'The shoes?' he asks.

I give him another nod, so he kicks them off and then he stops and I'm forced to level him with a stern look.

'Socks too.'

He gives me a grin that makes him look like the world is lifting off his shoulders and I find myself smiling back.

'Bedroom Vic,' I say to myself, and he gives a low laugh.

'I've done what you asked,' he says, his eyes gleaming, 'but now you pay a forfeit.'

My eyes narrow. I didn't know this was a game, but in hindsight I should have.

Demons.

He pats the seat next to him and, after a moment's hesitation, I half-crawl across the car. I sit beside him.

'That wasn't so hard, was it?'

I shake my head, not looking at him, my anxiety ratcheting up to DEFCON 1.

His fingers graze my cheek, and he moves my head up to look into my eyes.

'How much longer until we reach Metro,' I ask, hoping to delay the inevitable but also hoping we have time to do what he wants.

'More than enough time for what I have planned,' he murmurs into my ear and his words terrify and thrill me in equal parts.

He licks my neck and I shudder.

'You're mine for this entire car ride,' he whispers, 'and you're going to be a very good girl, aren't you?'

Heat pools between my legs and he chuckles low. 'I knew you'd be submissive from the moment I saw you. Take off your jacket and put it next to mine.'

I do what he says with shaking hands, my comfortable clothes feeling suddenly restrictive.

'Now, come here and sit on my lap.'

I shudder as I shuffle forward.

'Look at me.'

My eyes dart up and back down again. That's all I can manage.

He chuckles again. 'I know you're nervous, but I can tell you're enjoying it too. I smell how turned on you are.'

My cheeks heat as he draws me forward to sit on him, my legs straddling the top of his. He wastes no time, his hands running up the inside of my thighs and brushing against my pussy through my clothes. I gasp at the sensation.

'Good girl,' he coos, and I feel so elated that I let out a small whimper.

'You like it when I praise you?'

I nod slowly, mortified that he can see so much of me.

'If you please me, baby girl, I promise I'll—'

There's a sudden screech of wheels in front of us and we're thrown forward and then to the side, hitting the window hard.

I scream as the world spins and in the back of my mind I'm realizing it's the car rolling. Vic has me in his arms, like he's trying to protect me and then everything goes black.

∼

Theo

I HEAR the sirens long before they pull up to the driveway. The house is on fire, the whole back caved in.

'It had to have been a bomb,' Kor mutters as I stand, staring at the smoke pouring from the windows from the upper floors.

My ears are ringing, and I can barely hear him.

'Blew just after *she* left.'

'You think it was Jane?' I say, swiveling my neck to look at him.

'I don't believe in coincidences. I've been on to her from the start. So has Vic.'

'What the hell are you talking about?'

'He thinks she's working for someone.'

'Who?'

Kor shrugs. 'Whoever's been fucking with our shipments.'

I look at the ground. 'I don't believe that.'

Kor laughs and the sound is ugly. 'Look around you, brother, and get your head out of your ass. She drew you in and you fell for it. Hell, she even started doing it to me. She's good. I'll give the treacherous little bitch that.'

The house is an inferno and I'm on my knees. I start

coughing again. I tried to get back in to save Carrie and the other girls while Korban attempted to find a way down via the old steps from the gym, but we couldn't get to them. There was too much smoke and the upper floor had collapsed into the kitchen, trapping them if they even survived the initial blast.

Kor is still shaking his head in anger as the fire crews pull up. They start fighting the flames, using a combination of old-fashioned water and even older-fashioned magick.

It doesn't take long before the blaze is mostly out, but the house is basically a smoking, blackened skeleton of protruding beams.

When I feel well enough to stand up, I see that Korban has at least saved our bikes.

'How could this happen? The wards were in place. Paris made sure everything was working after he patched the hole in the perimeter. Have you called Vic?' I ask Korban.

'He's not picking up.'

He sounds worried. Kor doesn't *get* worried.

What the fuck is happening?

My phone rings. I turn up the volume and put it on speaker.

'Is this Theodore Wright?'

'Yes. Who is this?'

There's a pause. 'Do you know an Alexsandre Makenzie? You're on his phone as the emergency contact.'

My stomach twists. 'Yeah. Is everything ok?'

'I'm sorry to be the one to tell you this, but your friend and a human woman with him have been in a car accident.'

'Are they ... are they ok?'

'The human suffered some cuts and abrasions, but your friend was hurt pretty badly. They're both being transferred to Metro Gen as we speak.'

'Thank you,' I say. 'I'll be there as soon as I can.'

The call ends and I see Kor on the phone as well. He's listening intently, mumbling the right things before he hangs up and I give him a questioning look.

'There was a random drive-by on the Boulevard. Paris is ok, but Sie was shot. He's in the ICU in Metro General.'

I'm silent for a minute. 'The house, Sie, and Vic.'

'Someone just declared war on the Iron I's and Jane's working for 'em,' Korban snarls.

'She was in the car with Vic,' I protest, but Kor's already on his bike and I scramble to my own.

I need to keep up with him because if he gets to Metro General first, Jane is a fucking dead woman.

Thanks for reading and I'm sorry for the cliff! I couldn't help it - it's just how the story unfolded!
BUT this series is complete and you can read Book 2 now!

Continue reading for Chapter One of Debts and Darkness; Desire Aforethought Book Two.

**LET'S TALK SPOILERS!
Join My Discord!
https://geni.us/KyraSpoilers**

EXCLUSIVE EARLY ACCESS TO THE FORBIDDEN?

The whispers in the dark are true – **a six-book spin-off of the tantalizing Dark Brothers series** is coming.

Which means... **I need you...** to reach into the shadows of temptation and be the first to feel every pulse-pounding moment.

My ARC Team is OPEN...

Yes, I need YOU to join my ravenous, Addicted Readers of Carnality.

If your heart races for brooding antiheroes and the fiery heroines who tame them, if your soul yearns for love stories laced with the sweet poison of passion, then *whisper your consent.*

PART ONE
SNEAK PEEKS

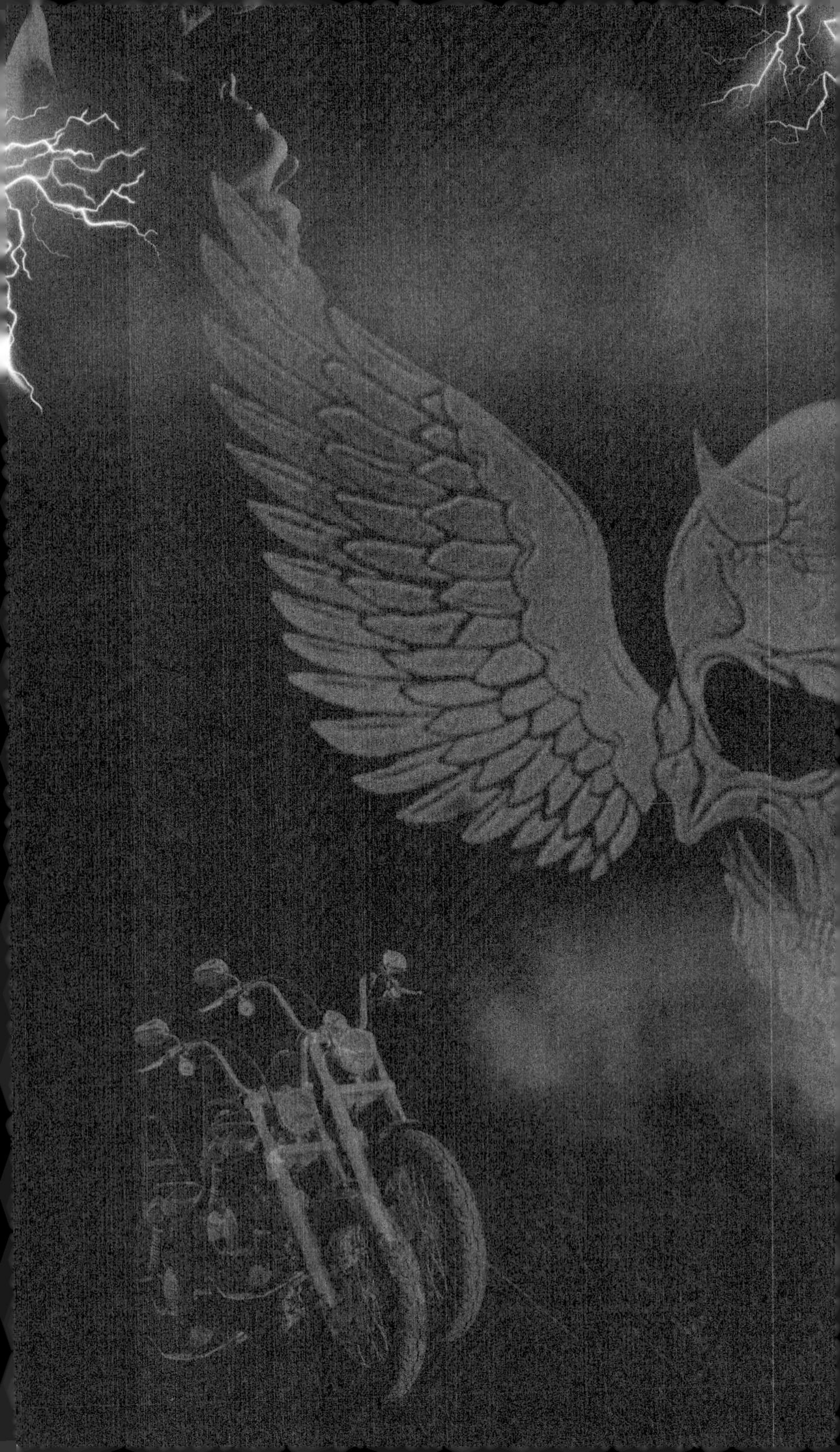

CHAPTER 1
DEBTS AND DARKNESS
CHAPTER ONE

The house is gone. Sure, there are other places we can go, other properties we own. But that was *our* Clubhouse. My mind is reeling as I follow Korban, keeping up with him even though he's trying hard to leave me in the dust.

Could this really have been Jane? I can't imagine her trying to kill us. But why not? How well do we actually know her? Maybe I've been unconsciously assuming things about her based on the way her brain is meant to work. Maybe it's blinded me. I mean was that medical document even real, or a plant for us to find and make us underestimate her? Is everything we know about her fake?

I try to treat humans and supes equally but, in that same vein, a human can be just as cunning as any supe or fae. I forgot that where Jane was concerned.

I take the next turn as tightly as I can, using my advantage to overtake our enforcer. He gives me a look, a dark smirk that says he's not going to let me win.

It's on, motherfucker.

Even if Jane is guilty, I have to get to her before Korban

does. I have a duty of care. I have no idea what he'll do but if he's even half as angry as I am, he'll take it out on her if I give him the chance and he's very ... *creative*. There are reasons he's feared almost more than Vic and, as far as he's concerned, she tried to take us down. He thinks it was her who planted the bomb that has destroyed the mansion, somehow had a hand in Vic's accident, and Sie getting shot in the street. She'll get no mercy from him.

The truth is, I don't care whether or not she had something to do with the attack on the Iron I's right now. I just can't let Korban torture her for information or kill her in some human-hating rage. My brothers might not agree with me, but I'm a doctor before I'm a member of the Club. When Vic wakes up, we'll decide what happens to Jane, but, until then, I'm keeping her safe, even from my own brothers if I have to.

I throw caution to the wind as I step on it, going as fast as I possibly can down the backroads towards Metro. It's not long before I reach the suburbs. I lost Korban a while back, but he's probably taking the highway. I'm hoping that I know these roads just a little bit better than him since I come through them almost every day on the way to the clinic, which is only a block away from Metro Gen, the main hospital where Vic and Sie will be taken ... if they aren't already there.

Parking my bike outside the side entrance, I leap off and practically sprint through the doors. I know where I'm going, so I don't stop especially when I see Korban in my periphery. He came in via the main door and he's only about five seconds behind me. I hear the elevator ding open, and I run for it, sliding into it and pressing the number three hard.

'Come on. Come on. Come on!' I mutter, rapidly tapping

on the button to make the doors close faster, my other hand playing with the stethoscope in my jacket pocket.

It finally shuts and starts to move. I'm pacing the tiny space like an insane animal at the zoo.

Should have taken the stairs.

Should have taken the fucking stairs.

When the elevator opens, I dart out onto the third floor and make it to the nurse's station just before Kor bursts through the heavy fire doors from the stairwell.

'I'm looking for Alexandre Makenzie,' I say to the nearest nurse, a petite healing sprite whose eyes widen in alarm as Korban barrels up behind me.

'Room 306, Doctor,' she says, staring at Kor and then at me. She lowers her voice. 'Are you okay? Do you need me to call security, Doctor Wright?'

I'm surprised she recognizes me, but I guess she's seen my face around the hospital from time to time. I turn my head, snorting in Korban's direction.

'No need, but thank you …' I glance at her nametag. 'Harriet.'

She nods. 'I'll take you to him.'

The sprite walks down the hall, looking back once or twice as if she's afraid Korban is going to attack.

'Relax,' I hiss at him. 'We're in a fucking hospital, not the ring. You can't do anything to her here anyway.'

He grunts and falls into step next to me as she leads us to Vic's room.

Vic is laying in the bed, a monitor beeping at regular intervals.

'He's unconscious at the moment,' she says, 'but that's just the drugs we gave him. He's got two cracked ribs and a deep laceration to his,' she checks the notes, 'left leg. Looks like he was experiencing breathing problems when they brought him in.' She tapers off, going silent as she reads. 'He had a collapsed lung, which is why he's still up here, but he's well fed so his healing will be fast. An incubus like him will be okay in a couple of days. We're just waiting on the paperwork to send him downstairs.'

'Where's the girl who was with him in the car?' Korban growls.

'The human? They have their own hospital a few blocks away. I don't know why they didn't get an ambulance to take her there straight from the scene. Anyway, we don't allow humans up here since all the troubles lately.' She says the last part quieter like she's afraid of being overheard. 'I think she asked one of the other nurses where she could get a coffee, so she might be downstairs.'

I frown. I mean I know about the new rules since the Order has stepped up their attacks in the area, but last I heard there were still a few rooms for human patients who ended up here for whatever reason because this is still a hospital.

'Is she okay?' I ask, wondering if anyone has even checked her over.

It doesn't sound like it.

When I turn, Korban is already racing to the elevator.

Fuck that.

I don't wait for the nurse's response.

This time, I book it to the stairs, basically throwing myself down to the second floor. I run through the long hallway, dodging medical personnel and patients alike, to the small coffee shop at the end. The elevator doors open just in front of me and I hear Kor growl a curse as he sees I'm just ahead of him again.

I win, asshole.

I scan the tables for Jane and see her sitting in a corner

facing away from everyone. She has a coffee in front of her, but it doesn't look like she's even had a sip. She's just staring down at it.

I make my way over to her, giving Kor a glance, letting him know that I will start some shit if he tries to force her out of here with him. He might be a better fighter, but this is my arena and 'a doctor being attacked in a hospital' will not go well for him.

She looks up as I get closer and I notice that faint bruises have already come up on her face. Looks like she was bumped around pretty good in the crash.

I bend down to her.

'Are you okay?'

Her gaze is unfocused, but she shrinks back into the chair a little bit as Korban approaches, towering over her. I give him a look and he rolls his eyes, but he takes a step back.

'Jane.'

She looks at me.

'Are you okay?'

She gives a tiny nod of her head.

'Come on.' I get her up carefully and lead her with small steps back to the elevator.

'Why are you being so gentle with her? Half of us are in the fucking hospital because of this bitch,' Kor hisses low in my ear.

'I'm a fucking doctor first,' I whisper back.

We take the elevator back upstairs in silence, and when the doors open and Jane steps onto the floor, all the sprites at the nurse's station look up at her like hungry birds at a handful of seed.

One of them shakes her head and comes over, her white shoes thudding on the floor as she mumbles something.

'I'm so sorry, Doctor. I'll call security right away.'

She turns to Jane, looking angry. 'I told you earlier, you aren't welcome in this hospital. I'm calling security right now. I suggest you leave before they get here. They aren't paid to be courteous to *your kind.*'

Jane steps backward, bumping into Korban and seeming to wither under the angry sprite's stare.

That's not like her. She's not herself, not at all.

I open my mouth, angry beyond words. Whatever the Human Policy is right now, this is still a hospital. No matter the species of patient, they're obligated to heal everyone, but Korban gets there first.

'She's with us,' he snarls, putting a hand on Jane's shoulder and urging her past the nurse.

I stay back for a moment, confident that Korban isn't going to do anything to Jane, at least not right now.

'She was in a car accident. Has a doctor even checked her over?'

The nurse looks surprised. 'The humans have their own hospital in Metro, Doctor,' she says, her tone turning disdainful.

'Did you get her an ambulance to that hospital?' I ask, clenching my jaw.

'That's not in my job description.'

'You're a fucking nurse!'

She jumps at my outburst. 'Yes, *Doctor*, I am a nurse *and an employee of this hospital*. Do I need to call security to have *all* of you escorted from the premises?'

Any pretense of respect she was giving me is long gone and I know she'll make good on her threat, so I make a mental note of her name because I WILL be filing a formal complaint about this.

Jen Prifty.

'That won't be necessary, nurse.'

I move past the angry sprite, ignoring her in favor of seeing how Vic is doing properly and finding Sie, who should be in the ICU somewhere too since he was only just brought in.

But I don't want to spend too much time here. In addition to getting Jane away from these nurses who are now speaking in hushed, snippy tones to each other while side-eyeing us over the counter of their station, I want to get back to our townhouse and check her over myself.

I want – no, I need – to make sure her head's okay and that she doesn't have any internal bleeding.

I keep my eye on her, watching her movements like a hawk as we enter Vic's room. She rushes over to the bed and peers at Vic who's still unconscious.

'Is he okay? They wouldn't tell me anything, just made me leave as soon as the paramedics brought me up here with him.'

'He'll be okay,' I tell her, and she looks ... *relieved*.

I'll think on why that might be later, but she certainly isn't acting like a saboteur. She could have run when they made her leave the ICU earlier, but she didn't. Was that because she's not guilty or because her knock on the head has left her confused?

'They're letting him sleep it off. What happened?'

'I don't know. We were in the car. There was a screech, maybe the brakes, and I don't know if we hit something ... but then we were rolling over and over.'

'We need to get the police report,' Korban mutters, looking suspiciously at Jane again while he takes out his phone.

'What happened next?'

'When I came to, there were supe cops everywhere and

they were taking Vic away in the ambulance. He was awake and they weren't going to let me go with him. They were going to take me somewhere else, but he made them bring me too, so that I was in the ambulance with him and they brought us here, but when they took us to the ICU, they told me to leave so I went down to the coffee shop because I didn't know what else to do and my phone was in the car ...'

She's rambling and I can tell she's getting distraught. I put my hand on her shoulder and draw her backwards towards me, not really thinking about what I'm doing. I just don't like seeing her upset. She goes along with it, but her body is stiff. I guess without some heavy bass, we're not quite there yet.

Just then, Paris pokes his head in through the door.

'I got your message,' he says to Kor. 'I spoke to my guy in the Metro PD. He's sending me the report on the crash as soon as it's on the system.'

'Good,' Korban says. 'How is Sie?'

'He's in a room a couple floors down. He's a little beat up, but he's healing pretty fast. You know how he hates hospitals though. He's acting like a caged bear. He already told the nurses he's leaving as soon as his shoulder stops bleeding no matter what so he'll be out later today.'

Kor looks Jane up and down with an expression I can't decipher, but it's definitely not suspicion.

'Helps that he fed recently.'

'What the fuck happened out there?' I ask.

Paris shrugs at us. 'We'd just set up the meeting for later today and were heading to the Metro house when a truck pulled out in front of us. They fired on us from the cab. Sie got hit in the shoulder. It could have been worse, but his bike's totaled. I skidded onto the sidewalk and got a little scraped up, but by the time I could get myself together, the fuckers were long gone and Sie was just layin' in the street. I thought he was dead ...'

Korban puts an arm around Paris' shoulder. 'Are *you* okay?'

'Yeah, nothing I can't handle,' Paris replies flippantly.

'There's nothing more we can do here until Vic's awake,' I say, keeping a grip on Jane who tries to move away from me. 'Let's get to the house and figure out our next move from there.'

'And if they try again?' Korban asks, looking at Vic's vulnerable state.

'Even if they do, you've seen how security is here with all the attacks recently. They have this place locked up tighter than an alpha's asshole. Nobody is getting in here.'

'Try again?' Paris asks, his confusion evident.

'Sie, Vic, the house? Are we going to pretend this is anything other than a coordinated attack?' Korban growls.

'No,' I concede.

Paris' neck rolls in Korban's direction. 'What happened to the house?'

'We'll talk about this later,' I say to Korban, and he shuts up, his eyes narrowing on Jane again.

But she doesn't notice, not that that surprises me. She is pretty oblivious most of the time, but I'm worried she's got a concussion, or worse.

'Come on,' I murmur, taking a last look at Vic's strong vitals. 'Let's get out of here.'

The four of us leave, going down to the front entrance where I hand a very spaced-out Jane to Paris since he doesn't have his bike. It's only a short ride from here to the house, but I still have to make myself let go of her.

As I watch Paris help Jane into a cab, I wonder how I'm going to navigate the protective feelings that seem to be emerging for a human who might be out to get us. I can pretend to the others that this is because I'm a doctor, but it's bull and they know it.

Paris will side with Korban on principle, going along with whatever he wants to do with her. I need to keep her safe somehow, but without Vic at my back, that just got a whole lot harder.

∼

Jane

I'm feeling pretty out of it as Paris pushes me into the cab and I slide over. He gives the driver an address and we pull away from the hospital. I don't know how long it's been since the accident. I'm a little fuzzy, but everyone seemed to get here really fast and they said something about Vic upstairs.

'Is Vic okay?' I ask.

'Yeah ... he's going to be fine.'

'And Sie?'

'And Sie.'

Paris looks at me weirdly. I let my head fall back to the headrest, closing my eyes.

'Hey.'

I look at him.

'I don't think you should fall asleep until after Theo takes a look at you. Did they check you out at the hospital?'

'I don't think so,' I say, but I honestly don't remember.

He slides closer to me, peering into my eyes.

I rub my hairline, trying to think, but other thoughts keep intruding. How hot Paris looks right now, how he moved on the dance floor with me the other night, how he kissed me in the pantry that time ... did those other things.

'You're a really good dancer,' I murmur softly, then wonder why I said that because I've just been in a car accident and this seems like a weird time to want to have sex.

'I – What? Did you hit your head, princess?'

'I don't know,' I say. 'It all happened really fast.'

I look out the window, trying to ignore my body and focus on the tall townhouses that line the street go by. We stop at a light, and I stare at the crosswalk as a woman in heels strides across on her phone, looking like she's on her way somewhere.

'Where are we going?'

'To our house, babe. Hey, could you step on it?'

'Step on what?'

His arm snakes around my shoulders gently. 'I was talking to the driver.'

I close my eyes again. I can't help it, and before I know it, the car is stopping.

Paris pays the fare and helps me out.

'What's happening?' I ask.

'We're just at our place in Metro. We keep a house here, remember?' Paris says slowly.

I nod as he leads me up a short flight of red, brick steps. This place looks like it was built a while ago.

'Was I in a car accident?'

He doesn't answer me but opens the door and I find myself in a lobby with a shining wood floor and a high old-fashioned ceiling. Stairs wind elegantly up in front of me, carpeted in red. Paris doesn't stop, taking my elbow in a firm but gentle grip and leading me down the hallway, past the stairs into a bright room lined with books and comfy places to sit. I scan the shelves and see that they're not the kind of books that were in Vic's study back at their Clubhouse mansion. These are mainstream books like bestsellers and stuff. The kind that aren't for show, just for enjoyment.

Paris' touch leaves me, and I lean into him, wanting it back. Theo and Korban are here, sitting together and speaking in low tones. They stop talking when they notice us.

Korban stands and strides to Paris, giving him a lingering kiss on the lips that makes a zing go straight to my core.

I swallow hard. 'That was so hot,' I breathe.

Korban turns on me with a sneer and suddenly has me by the throat, lifting me up onto my tip-toes.

'It wasn't for you!' he snarls so nastily that I whimper.

Why is he so mad at me?

'Kor, let her go!' Paris commands, but Korban doesn't budge.

'It's about time we found out what this human bitch has been planning. I'm not playing anymore, girl! Who are you working for?'

I'm terrified, but his words make me remember that time he caught me in the woods, the way he held me down and touched me, and I can't help the moan that leaves me. He drops me like I burn him and I catch myself, somehow not falling over.

'Kor, listen to me. She's not right. She's been saying weird stuff in the car.'

Theo pushes past them both. 'What weird things?'

'Just whatever comes into her head and she keeps asking the same questions and then forgetting the answers. She just asked me if she was in a car accident. What's wrong with her?'

'Fuck,' Theo says, looking into my eyes closely. 'Fuck those assholes at the hospital for not doing their jobs.'

I frown. 'What's happening?' I ask, starting to get scared. 'Am I dying?'

'No, sweetheart, you aren't dying,' Theo assures me. 'I think maybe you have a concussion. Did you hit your head in the accident?'

I look over at Korban whose face is unreadable. 'I'm sorry if I said something wrong,' I whisper, my chin wobbling.

He looks at Theo. 'Maybe it would be a good time to question her while she's like this. Might get something useful out of her.'

'She's my patient and there's no fucking way I'm letting you interrogate her when she clearly has a head injury.' Theo rolls his eyes and looks at Paris. 'Do something with him. Now. I'm going to take care of Jane the way they should have at Metro Gen.'

Paris takes Korban's arm and then cups his cheek with his large hand, making Korban look at him. 'There's nothing in the fridge and we need to eat some real food. Come with me to get take-out. She'll still be here to question later when Vic's awake.'

Korban heaves a sigh.

'Fine,' he growls. 'Now. Later. I guess it doesn't make much difference. I *will* be making her tell me what I want to know though.'

Korban and Paris leave the room and I hear them go out the door a minute later. Theo surveys me like he's looking for something.

'How are you feeling?' he asks.

'Not really sure,' I say. 'Why was Korban so angry with me?'

I rub my neck where his fingers dug into me and, for some reason, it makes me pulse between my legs.

'Don't worry about him.' Theo's voice sounds strained.

'What's wrong with me? Give it to me straight,' I try a chuckle, but it falls flat.

'Come upstairs. I'll take a look at you.'

'Sure thing, Doc,' I say without a hint of emotion.

He takes my hand and leads me back to the front door where the stairs are. There's geometric wallpaper going all the way up that captures my eyes and refuses to let go.

'Who decorated this place?' I ask quietly, my gaze running along the symmetrical lines with a will of its own.

'That was Paris all the way. He wanted to keep it in 'the traditional style' or something.'

He watches me closely the whole way up the stairs like this is some kind of test.

We reach a landing at the top with a short hallway to the left and right. There's a bathroom in front of me and an elevator. Before I can wonder why we didn't take it, he moves me along.

'The rooms are smaller here,' he says, 'but you can have mine again if you want. I can bunk with one of the others.'

'Doesn't seem fair that I keep taking your bed,' I say, peering through open doorways into bedrooms as we walk past.

He looks back and gives me a once-over. 'You could always let me stay in there with you, princess.'

My cheeks heat. That one was blunt enough for me to understand. The image I get of being in his bed with him as he ... My legs almost buckle with the force of the need that hits me.

What was that? What's wrong with me?

He leads me into a room, and I stop at the threshold when I see it's like an actual doctors' office.

'Do you meet patients in here,' I ask.

'No one from the general public no,' he says, 'but if a member of the Club needs to see a doctor and I'm in the city, they usually come here.'

My eyes fall on the exam table and I close my mouth, remembering the things he said to me about what he likes ... wow, was that only this morning?

I swallow hard and I hope he doesn't notice that I'm suddenly nervous as he draws me into the middle of the room and closes the door.

'Take off your clothes,' he says.

'Excuse me?'

But I want to. I *really* want to. My heart is pounding hard in my chest and my clothes feel constricting.

'Not like that,' he says. 'I need to check you over properly. There's a hospital gown right there. Put it on. I just want to make sure you're okay.'

'How will you do that exactly?' I ask, stomach fluttering.

'Well, I'll have to touch you – with your permission, of course. But don't worry, Miss Mercy, you're in capable hands.'

My eyes widen. He just did *the Doctor Wright voice*. Does he know he did or is that just how he talks to all his patients?

He turns around and pulls a blue curtain across, giving me a little bit of privacy as I take off the clothes that I put on this morning. I slip on the gown. It's the kind that ties at the back, so if I turn around, he'll see my bare ass.

I slide my hands down my body, the cool cotton teasing my skin, my nipples that are rapidly hardening. I need ...

'Doctor?'

'Is everything okay?'

'Can you help me with this, please?'

I turn my body to face the wall, and I hear him pull the curtain open. There's silence and I look over my shoulder innocently to see that he's frozen. His hand is still on the blue material, and he's staring at my naked ass.

I shift on my legs, letting it wiggle a little even as I wonder who this person is who has control of my body because I never do stuff like this. I don't even know *how* to do stuff like this.

He swallows hard. 'What can I help you with?'

'I can't get the ties.'

'That's okay,' he replies, not making a move to touch me. 'Sit on the table.'

I try not to let my disappointment show as I do what he says. The leather feels nice against me, making me shiver.

'This is just like a regular doctor's office,' I mutter as if I've been in one since I was a kid, which I haven't.

'That's the idea. It puts my patients at ease. Can you imagine if it was all dried herbs hanging from the ceiling, incantation books, and potion bottles in a secret cabinet in this day and age? I mean I have that stuff too. I just keep it on the DL.'

'But I saw your Med School diploma,' I say, canting my head at him. 'I thought you were a regular doctor.'

'I am, but I'm qualified to work on supes as well as humans, and that means training in more than one form of medicine.'

'Like what?' I ask, very interested.

'Well, for example, you need a CT scan. It's a great way of assessing internal damage for humans and for supes but getting a supe inside one of those tubes would be a mission and a half. They just don't trust human machines, so a doctor qualified to work with supes has other means of finding out the same information,' Theo explains, producing two gold, button-looking disks. He holds them in his palm.

'What are those?'

'Just a way of me seeing what's going on with that bump on your head without us having to go all the way to the other hospital. They rest on your eyelids. That's it. It won't hurt. All you need to do is lay still and stay awake, Jane. You can do that for me, can't you?'

I nod. 'Yeah, it's just ... I feel so ...' *like I want to tear off this gown and throw myself at you.*

A shudder runs through me at the thought.

'I know you don't feel like yourself. That's why I need to check you out, sweetheart.' He sounds weird and he's definitely doing *the voice*. 'Are you ready?'

'Yeah.'

He shines a small flashlight in my face without warning and I wince.

'Does anything hurt?'

'Yeah, my fucking eyes,' I growl.

He chuckles and puts the light away. 'Sorry.'

'My shoulder,' I say, 'and I feel hot. My head is starting to ache now too.'

I hadn't noticed that before. I touch a spot on the back of my skull and his fingers follow mine, probing the area.

'You've definitely got a bump back here. That would explain it.'

'Explain what?'

'Don't worry, princess. I'll get you all fixed up. Close your eyes.'

I do as I'm told and I feel him place the two disks gently

over my eyes. There's silence for a minute and I'm just opening my mouth to ask him if everything's okay when he removes them.

'All done,' he murmurs. 'Just a little concussion as I suspected. You're going to be fine, I promise. Anything else hurt? Your chest? Your stomach?'

I shake my head.

'You're lucky you weren't hurt worse. I heard the car was pretty banged up.'

'I think Vic made sure I was safe.'

Theo gives me a small smile. 'Sounds like Vic.'

'Why would he do that?' I say half to myself. 'He doesn't even like me.'

Theo doesn't answer.

'Lay back,' he orders and I do what he tells me with a sigh.

'Eyes open,' he reminds me when I close them and I nod, keeping my gaze locked on his face.

There's something there – anticipation maybe – and I'm suddenly nervous again, but I can't help the next thing I ask.

'When you were talking about the exam table before, was this the one you meant?'

He turns away and runs a hand through his hair, pulling it a little like he's frustrated. 'Actually, I was talking about the room similar to this one back at the Clubhouse.'

'Here,' he gets an old-school thermometer out.

'Is that for under my tongue?' I ask.

'Well,' he says, 'I could get my rectal one out if you want.'

My eyes widen, and everything below my waist contracts. He's just playing with me, right?

'No, thanks,' I say quickly, afraid I'm going to blurt out an 'Okay!' instead.

He smiles like he has no idea what's going through my head and I'm sooooo glad he can't read my mind. He puts the thin tube under my tongue and I try to relax as he raises my arm and begins to move it this way and that, making it hurt.

I give a small cry.

'I'm sorry,' he says. 'Looks like it's a little bit sprained. It'll take a few days, but it'll be fine. I'll give you some painkillers. How about your ribs from before? Are they still aching?'

I shake my head. 'No, they didn't really hurt much after that pill you gave me last time. Can I have another one of those?'

He looks rueful. 'No can do. They're a pretty powerful fae concoction. Even supes can only take 'em once in a blue moon. Too much fae stuff has consequences for all of us. Bad ones usually.'

He puts my arm back down and then takes the other one, doing the same thing.

'That one's fine,' I mumble.

He hushes me. 'Just keep that thermometer in your mouth, Miss Mercy.'

His fingers trace my collarbone, down one side and up the other before pressing my sternum over the hospital gown.

'Does that hurt?' he asks.

I shake my head and he moves his fingers down, feeling my stomach, tapping at it here and there. I shake my head again at his inquiring look and he moves down to my lower abdomen.

My thighs squeeze together and I try to keep my breathing level as he goes lower.

Do I really want him to do something now?

Yes. Right now!

Whatever was starting with Vic was interrupted and although I'm hurting and I think I might be in shock or something, I need this like I need to breathe. I've never felt such desire for anything before, never had such a demand flowing through my body. It's like sexual overdrive. How can I want that when my body is killing me from the accident?

Oh.

He's using his supey power on me. Why would he do that to me *now*?

I wince a little and pretend it's from his fingers pushing gently into my stomach, trying to swallow the emotion that's rising up like a spring tide to drown me. Is it right to feel betrayed right now?

If it is, I know that it's stupid to feel this way. I'm an on-call girl now. It makes sense that they'd use me whenever they need to, regardless of whether I'm physically sound. But the feeling doesn't go away even when I apply that logic.

Tears come to my eyes and I blink them away. A whimper pushes its way past my lips though and Theo stops what he's doing like he cares.

'What is it? Did I hurt you?'

Yes, I want to say, but I don't.

'Just my stomach,' I mutter instead, wishing he'd stop touching me now.

'Okay.'

He sits me up and an intense wave of arousal hits me,

making me want to grab him and pull him to me. I swallow hard and watch him do the same.

'You're injured,' he whispers like he's trying to convince himself of something. 'Not in your right mind.'

Then why are you using your voodoo on me?

He takes a step back as my fingers grip his biceps hard. If he doesn't do something first, I'm going to start begging him to fuck me.

He pulls away with a curse and snatches a vial off the table, filling a syringe with the quick and precise movements of a doctor who knows what he's doing.

'What's that?'

'It's something we supes use. It's safe for your concussion and it'll help with the pain,' he sticks my arm with it before I can react, 'and it'll put you out for a little while.'

What?

Panic courses through me.

'But—'

'Don't worry. It'll make you feel better.'

My eyes are already starting to close and I feel him ease me carefully to the exam table so I don't fall as my limbs go limp.

'I'm sorry, Jane.'

∽

Let's Talk Spoilers! Join My Discord!
https://geni.us/KyraSpoilers

∽

NEED MORE DEMONS?

DESIRE AFORETHOUGHT SERIES-

Caught in the clutches of five formidable Incubi bikers, neurodivergent Jane Mercy navigates a treacherous world of dangerous secrets, unyielding passion, and looming threats.

Will she emerge unscathed, or will the sizzling world of demons shatter her, piece by piece?

Succumb to an intoxicating realm where incubi masters awaken dark desires and debts are paid in the throes of passion. (on Kindle Unlimited)

https://geni.us/DesireAforethought

DEMONS AND DEBTS *(AUDIO BOOK NOW AVAILABLE!)*

When debts call for desperate measures, will a deal with demons be the path to salvation or damnation?
https://geni.us/DemonsandDebtsAudio
https://geni.us/DemonsandDebts

🚴 **Hot Monsters/Supernatural Biker Gang**
🧠 **Neurodivergent Strong Heroine**
🏃 **On the Run Mystery**
💚 **Paranormal Romance**
🐺 **Reverse Harem**
😈 **Enemies to Lovers**
🔒 **Dark Past/Secrets**

DEBTS AND DARKNESS

In the darkest corners of desire, will she find freedom or lose herself forever?
https://geni.us/DebtsandDarkness

🔥 Emotion Manipulation by Incubi
🌑 Hidden Secrets & Deceptions
😼 Hate-Love Dynamics
🎭 Dancing to their Tune
😨 Self Preservation vs Demons
👥 Reverse Harem
💚 Enemies to Lovers

DARKNESS AND DEBAUCHERY

Caught in a web of lies, betrayal, and heartache, can she conquer the darkness and reclaim her life?
https://geni.us/DarknessandDebauchery

🕊️ Gilded Cage
🔍 Unknown Enemies
⏳ Race Against Time
🧩 Deciphering the True Self
🕊️ Pursuit of Happiness & Freedom
👥 Reverse Harem
😈 Enemies to Lovers

CHAPTER 2
SOLD TO SERVE
DARK BROTHERS SERIES BOOK ONE

One woman enslaved. Three callous mercenaries. Secrets that could destroy them all ...

Kora ran away to start a new life where she was in control of her own destiny and her own body. Instead, she was captured and auctioned to the highest bidders: Three former mercenaries with black hearts and a dilapidated castle.

Mace is their leader; harsh and unforgiving. Kade lives in the shadows and, if his snarls are anything to go by, may not be a man at all. And cruel Lucian's only delights seem to be drink and terrorizing their new possession until she breaks.

And she might.

Kora has never been a slave and she must keep that secret at all costs. If they learn who she is, she'll be forced to marry a man who terrifies her far more than these lords do.

Can she escape these three dangerous Brothers who have begun to show her that there is more to them than their tragic pasts? And if they find out her secrets, can she trust them not to throw her to the wolves?

Sold to Serve is the first book in the Dark Brothers Series of dark fantasy RH romance. If you like strong FMCs, deliciously dark antiheroes and your love stories with bite, you will adore this book by Kyra Alessy.

It was hot for the time of year. The midmorning sun beat down on her fair skin, making her squirm in the ropes that held her to the wooden slaver's pole. If she survived the day, whatever wasn't covered would be well and truly burnt by this evening. She glanced down at her body. Her robes and shift were long gone, but thankfully some of her smallclothes remained. The wrapping around her hips provided at least some modesty, though her chest was bared to all. A good portion of her was still caked in dried mud from the night before. That might at least help with the sun, she thought.

A bead of sweat trickled down her scalp under her hair, leaving an itch in its wake. She pushed herself up onto her toes, but it was no use. Her wrists were bound too high to reach. The best she could do was to rub her head on her arm, spreading the wetness and dirt alike.

She scanned the busy street of Kingway, a typical market of trinkets and foodstuffs in a bustling town, large enough to get lost in, but certainly nothing like the mammoth cities in the north she'd heard about. She and two others, an unfriendly old man with a nasty cough and an equally hostile youth, were the only slaves for purchase, it seemed. Neither of them had spoken to her since she had found herself chained alongside them in the wagon.

Her lip quivered. Only yesterday evening she was saying the final rites, beginning the three-day ritual that would see her cast off her old life and step happily into the priesthood. Being a Priest of the Mount was – well, if she was honest, it wasn't as if it had been her fondest dream. She admitted to herself that she did not feel the call to serve the way the other novices professed to, though she had never spoken those thoughts aloud. For her, a life in service to the Mount was a means of escape and of safety. Complete and irreversible. Or at least it would have been in three days' time when she said her vows and swapped her grey novice's robes for the black ones of the priests. A tear tracked its way down her dirty cheek. For the thousandth time, she hoped to the gods that this was a dream, just a silly nightmare, and she'd wake up a bit late for morning prayer and be chastised as usual. But as she heard the telltale jingle of the coin purse at the portly slaver's belt, she knew it wasn't so.

She had been stolen last night as she slept in her narrow cot in the long room with the other novices. A tall, cloaked figure hefted her up easily, covered her mouth and threatened to kill her if she struggled. She was frozen; heart thundering, ears roaring. Her life had not prepared her for anything like this. It wasn't until she felt the thud as she landed on the ground outside the walls of the cloister that she finally came to her senses. After her months of hiding, they had found her ... she couldn't go back! She pushed him as hard as she could, but he didn't let go. He grunted in pain and slipped in the mud instead, taking her with him and covering them both in it. He recovered his balance first and slapped her hard.

When she awoke, she was chained in the wagon and her abductor was gone. Her angry demands, questions and, finally, pleas were pointedly ignored by the other slaves and saw her gagged by the slaver; the smelly rag was still tied tightly around her head and jammed between cracked lips she wished she could moisten. She'd realised then that she'd been wrong. He hadn't taken her to bring her back to her family, nor to Blackhale, her betrothed. It had simply been to sell her. She'd never had to worry about this before. She knew it was done, especially here in the south, but the estate had been guarded and no one stole freewomen with property. She had been taken for no other reason than that she was nearest the window in the dormitory and she was no one. A part of her had been relieved – at the time.

Now, the slaver approached her, the wisp of a licentious smile on his face from the attention her semi-naked body was garnering, filthy though it was. He didn't seem interested in her except for the money she would bring him, thank the gods. He looked past her, into the crowd, and she jumped as he bellowed, 'Flesh auction! Midday!'

Flesh auction. She closed her eyes rather than see everyone's on her. She'd heard of such things, but of course never been to one. And now she was to be the main attraction.

She was left to braise, and after a while she couldn't help but drift, half-dozing and pretending she wasn't here, that this wasn't happening. The voices, noise and frenzy of the marketplace melted into the background.

'Is she alive? Looks like a dried-up corpse.'

Her eyes opened just a crack. They felt sore, swollen. She turned her head towards the voice and was ensnared by a man's gaze. He was older than she, with dark hair that was greying at the temples. He was a large man and wore a fine green tunic embroidered with a house sigil that she recognized but couldn't place.

He perused her body slowly from bare feet to chest, where his stare lingered, and she shifted uncomfortably, her face burning from more than the sun, which was now almost overhead. He smirked when his eyes met hers.

'I'll be at the auction,' he called – to the slaver, she assumed – 'but looking at her, the price better be low.' Then he stepped closer and said, for her ears alone, 'You're going to be mine, girl.' His hand darted out and kneaded her breast, pinching her nipple hard. A hoarse cry erupted from her throat, weak and muffled by the gag, and she kicked out at him instinctively. He chuckled and pulled the gag down, taking in her face almost as an afterthought.

'Save your strength,' he muttered. 'You're going to need it before the day is done.' And then he was gone, leaving her shivering at his words even though she was absurdly grateful she could finally moisten her lips.

Looking out into the street, her eyes filled with tears. She wasn't sure what she'd expected, but, perhaps naïvely, it wasn't that. What was going to happen to her? She'd never even kissed a member of the opposite sex nor had the talk that she knew other girls had before their wedding nights. She wished her father hadn't kept her so cosseted. The most she'd seen were servants' stolen moments in stairwells when she'd snuck around at night. She had little idea of what to expect.

She noticed a man standing not far from her. He seemed frozen in the middle of the street – in everyone's way. People tutted as they passed him, but he ignored them. He was staring at her – not at her nakedness like the others, at her. She stared back, taking him in. He looked ... *weathered*.

That was the first word that came to mind to describe him. That and handsome, she supposed, in a brutish sort of way. He looked like a stable hand or a ... *a mercenary*. Yes, that was apt. She'd never met a sell-sword before, but he was what she imagined them to be like. The look in his eyes was hard; dangerous. His hair was the color of wheat, cropped quite short. His shoulders were broad. He was a head taller than anyone else in the street and she guessed she'd barely make it to his chest. He wore black despite the heat of the day, and his dark leather boots were dusty and worn. He was no farmer nor merchant, that was for certain.

The slaver appeared in front of her with a bucket and, before she knew what he was about, she was doused in freezing water. She gasped at the sudden cold on her burning skin and screamed in shock. Then he began to sluice the water down her body, rubbing the worst of the mud and dirt away with his hands like she was a dog or a horse. She twisted and kicked, striking his shin with her foot, and he swore and took a short whip from his belt. He struck her twice in quick succession, and she squealed as it bit into her back and shoulder.

'Please, I beg you. Stop!' she whimpered.

'Shut your mouth, slave,' he growled at her and then, as if only just taking in her words, 'You speak prettily. He didn't tell me where he found you, but you aren't some village lass, eh?' He sounded surprised and then made a deep, horrible sound of satisfaction. 'They're going to be chomping at the bit for you.'

She stopped fighting, not liking the gleam that appeared in his eye. She held her breath as he continued with his ministrations. His impersonal fingers trailed up and down her skin until she could bear it no longer and then he poured another bucket over her head. She gritted her teeth and didn't make a sound, sagging in the ropes that bound her numb hands as he pushed the gag back into her mouth.

He cut the bonds moments later and she fell to her knees. The younger of the other two slaves picked her up at the slaver's direction and they began to walk down the road to the town square. She was glad of it. At least this hid her body somewhat and she didn't have to traipse through the town with everyone watching. Even if she was of a mind to walk, she didn't have the strength to struggle away from his grasp anyway.

She was thrown roughly into the middle of a raised platform. Grit dug into her knees, but she didn't move until the slaver wrapped his meaty hand in her long dark hair and dragged her to her feet. He began to speak loudly for the gathered crowd to hear.

'This slave comes to me from a ruling house. She's a hard worker. She can cook and clean. She can perform any menial tasks set before her. Who will give me five?'

'House slaves go for thrice that in these parts!', yelled someone from the crowd. 'Your words ring false.'

'House slaves are rarely sold,' another added from close by. 'Why has this one been cast out?'

'She was caught stealing,' the slaver replied smoothly, unmoved at being branded a liar. 'But she comes from good stock. Needs a firm hand is all.'

Kora gaped at his lies, looking at the men and women around her whose faces ranged from surprise to outright revulsion. The man was a fool. No one of means would buy such a house slave for their home. Short of killing their master, thievery was one of the worst grievances that a slave of status could have against them. It meant they weren't trustworthy and therefore useless to a noble family of any rank.

'I'll give you three for her,' someone called out, sounding bored.

She recognized the voice as the wealthy man in the green tunic from before and tensed. He didn't want a house slave, he wanted a pleasure one. If she knew anything at all, it was that.

'Five.'

'Seven.' *Green tunic.*

The voices sounded uninterested. This was very much not the frenzy of bidding the slaver had expected. She didn't look up to see who bid on her; she was too busy praying to the gods that this would not be her fate.

She realised dully that the number had stayed at seven. The slaver's hand tightened in her wet hair. She winced in pain as he pulled her head back, displaying her body more blatantly as if just realizing his blunder. His hand reached down to the cloth wrapped around her hips. He meant to pull it off! Here in front of everyone. He wasn't trying to peddle her simply as a house slave anymore. *No!* She twisted away from him with a cry and she felt his grip on her hair loosen, but he pulled her back roughly with a forced laugh that spoke of a nasty beating with that small lash he carried if she was still in his power later.

'Come, come, good people. She's a spirited one is all. Worth ten at least!'

'Twenty.'

The crowd hushed and the slaver's eyes gleamed. He was silent for a moment. 'Can you pay it?' he asked at last.

'I can.'

The voice was hard and gruff. She sighed through the gag

in relief. That wasn't the man in the green tunic's voice. She opened her eyes and dared a look. The man from the street. The mercenary. She swallowed hard, in some ways more terrified. What could he want her for that was any different from the other one? Her eyes flicked to the man who'd been outbid, his crisp lime clothes a beacon in the crowd. He looked gracious, as if he didn't care, but she could see a barely contained fury in his countenance that no one else seemed to notice. He was anything but satisfied with the outcome.

The blond sell-sword came forward. Her new master until she could escape and make her way back to the Temple. She had a week, perhaps, before the moons moved out of alignment. After that it would be too late to begin the rites, and the door to the Mount would be closed to her for good.

The slaver waved him back. 'You can come for her later.' He squeezed her arm hard as he said it, his eyes promising more pain.

She turned her gaze to the mercenary, trying not to let the fear show in her eyes. The slaver wanted time for his revenge. No doubt he'd make up some lie about her trying to escape if asked.

The mercenary's hard expression didn't waver as he threw a bag of coins onto the dais. It landed at the slaver's feet. 'I'll take her now.'

Thank the gods. Her shoulders almost sagged in relief, but she didn't want to give the awful man any satisfaction.

The slaver's lip curled slightly as he maneuvered his body down to pick up the purse. He didn't let go of her, instead using his teeth to open the drawstring. Looking inside, he smiled coldly.

'So be it,' he said and pushed her hard. She yelled as she fell off the platform, but she was caught long before she hit the ground. She didn't need to look up to know it was him, her new master.

But she did look up, and her breath hitched as her eyes caught his. For a moment neither of them moved, but then his gaze flicked down, just a moment before she realised she was in a man's arms all but naked. She began to squirm and he set her down, his face hardening as he looked at her. Someone handed him the Writ of Ownership, which he took and pocketed, not even deigning to look at it.

Then he simply turned and walked away, what was left of the now-dispersing crowd parting before his long stride. Unsure of what to do, and feeling green tunic's eyes on her, she hurried after him, crossing her arms over her chest to conceal herself.

She caught up with him as he neared the outskirts of the small town. He never even looked back to ensure she followed. They came to a stable, where a large horse was tethered outside. He finally turned to her, a length of rope in his fist. He took her hands and looped the rope around her wrists, tying them together in front of her firmly but gently. The other end he tied to the saddle. He took the horse's bridle and began to lead it towards the forest road but hesitated. He turned and her eyes flicked to a knife he now held, wondering what he would do. She was surprised when the gag around her head went slack and fell to the ground. She immediately licked her cracked lips, grateful for this small mercy after the past day.

He mounted his horse in silence and it began to walk slowly, its gait steady. She was pulled forward and she gasped. She took a halting step and then another, wondering where he was taking her. Her skin was on fire, she needed water and she was this man's prisoner, but it was either move forward or be dragged, so walk she did.

They travelled for a time. She wasn't sure how long for, but the forest began to darken and still horse and rider showed no signs of stopping. She focused, as she had all afternoon, on putting one bare foot in front of the other. It was all she could do. Step. Step. Step. On and on and on.

Finally and inevitably, her toes caught a stone and she stumbled, her knees giving way in betrayal. At first he didn't stop, and she was afraid he'd let the horse plod on, dragging her behind like a felled deer.

'Please. Stop. I beg you.' Her voice broke and she hated the sound of it.

The horse drew to a standstill. She tried to stand up as he dismounted and approached, but it was no use. Her legs just wouldn't hold her any longer. She fell back to the ground with a low cry.

'I can go no further. Please let me rest,' she implored, raising her eyes to his.

He looked surprised at her weakness, as if he hadn't even considered she might tire. She saw no kindness in his face, and for a horrible moment she thought he might simply continue, whether she was on her feet or not.

But he let out a long-suffering sigh. 'Very well. We'll camp nearby for the night.' He scanned the forest path ahead of them. 'But not on the road.'

She gave a squeak as he picked her up and set her on his horse's back. His eyes narrowed at her. 'He's a war horse. He won't obey you, so don't even try,' he ground out.

She nodded as she gripped the saddle with her bound hands and he led them into the forest. Soon she heard the trickle of water and they came upon a small clearing with a shallow stream running beside it. She looked around her. The trees here were old; thick and foreboding. She shivered and then inwardly chastised herself. When had she become so foolish? *They're just trees.* It didn't matter that the closest thing to a forest that she'd ever been in before today was a small hunting wood on her family's land. She'd spent time in nature as a novice during her training, after all. Though she'd never camped outside overnight.

The mercenary took her from the horse and set her on the mossy ground, pushing her down to sit with a heavy hand on her shoulder. She frowned at his back while he busied himself with his horse, ignoring her once more. She looked out into the forest and then at the stream. After the ride, she was feeling a bit better. Should she try to run while his back was turned or slake her thirst? Shaking her head at the thought of attempting to get away in her current state, she half crawled to the bank, gulping the cool, clear water until she felt sick. She wouldn't have got far anyway, she reasoned, and there would be other opportunities.

When she looked up, he was lighting a fire in the middle of the clearing. She inched closer to it. Her skin still felt hot, but her teeth chattered. Soon he had a small blaze going, and he turned his attention to her. He didn't speak, just watched her as she sat. She stared back at him, drawing her knees up so he couldn't see her nakedness. He'd had all afternoon to look at her breasts, of course, but he hadn't. To sit in front of him now like this made her feel helpless, and she didn't like it one bit.

He leant back against the tree behind him. 'What's your name?'

'Kora. What's yours?' she fired back.

His lip twitched. 'Master, I suppose.'

She tried to keep the sneer off her face, but she knew she'd failed when he raised an eyebrow at her. She wrapped her arms around herself, still shivering despite being quite close to the fire.

His eyes narrowed. 'How long did he have you staked out in the sun?'

'All morning until the ... the auction.'

He was silent, as if waiting for something more.

She gritted her teeth. '*Master*,' she choked out.

He snorted. 'My name is Mace.' He grabbed one of his bags and dug around inside for a moment. Then he tossed her a small pot. She fumbled, only just catching it. 'Your skin is burnt. Use the salve and drink more water or you'll get sun sick.'

'Why do you care?', she snapped and wondered where she'd found the gall to speak to him in such a way.

She saw his jaw clench. 'You were expensive,' he said coldly. Then he stood and walked over to where she sat, towering over her like a giant. She swallowed hard and made herself crane her neck to look him in the eye. She would not be cowed.

He leant down and she couldn't help but flinch. Would he beat her for her insolence? But instead he seemed to be inspecting the marks the slaver had given her earlier in the day. 'Use the salve on those lashes too,' he muttered, untying her wrists. When she was free, he straightened and marched into the undergrowth. She stared after him as he melted into the twilight.

For a while she watched the forest where he'd disappeared, wondering if this was a trick of some sort, but he didn't return. She used up the small pot of salve over the worst of her burnt skin and the ridges the lash had made and found that her body immediately began to feel better. There was none left for her feet though and she belatedly realised she should have tended to those first.

She went back to the stream, biting her lip as she looked out into the night beyond the dancing shadows cast by the fire. She should run now while he was gone, she knew, but the more she gazed into the darkness, the more she feared. There were noises coming from beyond the clearing and she didn't know enough to identify what animals made them. There were wolves out there at the very least. She went back to the fire, stoked it and fed it with some sticks the mercenary had left before lying on the soft moss and closing her eyes.

She woke groggy the next day. The fire smoldered next to her and she was covered in a blanket she hadn't had the night before. She sat up and looked around the clearing. The mercenary – *Mace* – was standing with his horse.

'Get up. It's almost time to go.'

A thick, dry biscuit landed in the moss in front of her. It wasn't much, but she hadn't eaten in two days, so it was a veritable feast as far as she was concerned. She gobbled it quickly and stood, keeping the blanket carefully around her. He turned away from her as he smothered the fire, so she quickly saw to her morning needs while he wasn't watching. Then she drank deeply from the stream again. She did feel better today despite sleeping on the ground. The salve he'd given her had done wonders. Her skin was still a bit red, but it didn't hurt anymore. Even the welts from the slaver's lash no longer felt swollen.

Her bare feet were a different story, however. They already hurt, though she was only walking on the soft moss of the clearing, and she knew that if she looked, they'd be a mess of cuts and blisters from the day before. She hoped they didn't have far to go today.

She clasped the blanket around her shoulders tightly as he beckoned her – as if that would offer her any real protection. 'Where are we going?'

Mace said nothing at first, and she thought perhaps he wasn't going to tell her. He gave one of his sighs.

'To the keep,' he said finally as he snatched the blanket from her.

She gasped, but he ignored her, rolling it up and stowing it on the horse without another word. He tied her hands as he had the day before and lashed her to his horse. He took them back to the road.

'Is it far?'

He muttered something about indulged house slaves. 'Walk quickly and we'll get there faster.'

She stared at his back with a frown as he mounted his horse and they began the trek anew. Before long, her feet were in agony as they travelled over the rough stones and sand of the thoroughfare. She took to trying to walk on the edge in the grass and moss whenever she could. She also began to pick at the knot in the rope. She knew something about knots; not the names or anything so involved, but her seafaring Uncle Royce had taught her some, and Mace had used one that was similar. She'd be able to get it undone eventually.

She didn't make a sound as they travelled and, again, he never once looked back. After a while, her deft fingers slowly but surely began loosening the rope around her wrists, but when it suddenly and very abruptly fell to the ground, she tensed, sure he would notice. She'd meant to hold on until the last moment, but now the rope was being dragged along the ground sans prisoner.

Her eyes darted to him, but he hadn't looked away from the road ahead. Without a second thought, she dashed into the undergrowth, trying to be as quiet but as quick as she could be. Ignoring the pain in her feet, she dodged trees and stumps.

DEMONS AND DEBTS

∼

MACE

Mace wasn't sure what prompted him to look back when he hadn't all morning. Perhaps he heard something and his finely tuned senses put him on alert, or perhaps it was just luck that he turned his head at just the right moment to see his newly bought and very expensive slave running into the undergrowth and the end of the rope trailing along the ground behind the horse. He gave an annoyed, rasping groan from deep in his throat. He should have known after what the slaver had said that she'd be trouble. And how had she gotten his knot undone so quickly?

He leapt from his mount and sprinted quickly through the trees, the horse's easy canter ceasing immediately. He knew this stretch of road well. The river wasn't far and it would slow her down. He moved much faster than her. There was no need for him to rush, though for some reason he did.

He hadn't been himself since Kingway when he'd seen her bound in the sun, skin burning, covered in mud. Ordinarily he wouldn't have looked twice, but instead he found himself staring at her, unable to tear his gaze away. Her bearing was not that of an owned girl. It made more sense when the slaver said she was a house slave, but he'd have known it at once by the lilt of her voice as soon as he'd heard it on the road. They always sounded like they were part of the noble families they served and were typically a bit above their station because of it, in his experience.

So he'd paid a ridiculous amount of coin for a potentially useless slave girl; one so intractable that, though he'd been a picture of respectability last evening despite wanting to give her a good hard fucking to put her in her place, she still ran at the first opportunity. She'd learn soon enough that he and the others were not like the noble family her kin served. Thieving and any other mischiefs would be punished harshly.

At least she'd be well-versed from birth in the needs of a large estate though. A house slave's domestic skills were valuable, after all. He grinned, remembering other female house slaves he'd come into contact with. Such helpful little things usually and always up for a bit of bed play in exchange for less work. Kora could try to seduce them if she liked. Gods, she'd probably succeed, but she'd get no special treatment for the effort.

His brow furrowed as he remembered how she'd felt in his arms when he'd caught her after the slaver had thrown her off the dais. Warm and perfect as if she fit him somehow, as if something was moving into place. It had been a curious sensation and not something he'd felt before. Perhaps ... No. He steeled himself against these odd thoughts. She was an untrustworthy house slave that would be useful in their endeavors with the estate they'd bought after leaving the Dark Army – well, as long as they kept her on a short leash anyway. She would be useful to them and the keep so long as she was watched closely. That was all.

He caught sight of her up ahead, her shorter legs no match for his. He let out a slow breath. Gods, even now he was tempted. He shook his head as he got closer and reminded himself that she was a slave who had been cast out. She would be devious and disloyal. They couldn't let their guard down around her. He had to remember that a slave who stole could never be reliable no matter where she came from and the only way he'd earn back even half of what she'd cost him was by ensuring well that she was never idle.

As he neared, he heard her labored breathing and sneered cruelly. Pampered little thing. They'd enjoy putting her to work in the keep; show her what it was to be a true slave.

~

Kora had been running for ages, branches tearing at her arms and legs, when the trees gave way to open space. A river. She skidded to a halt at the edge of a short stone cliff, wondering if she should run along it or jump in. But before she was able to decide, much less act, something hit her hard between her shoulders, plunging her into the surging water. Her cry was cut short as she went under. She flailed and kicked in the current, her head breaking the surface as she finally remembered to keep her fingers together as she paddled. She coughed and spluttered, trying to get her bearings. Then she heard someone clear their throat and looked up. Mace stood where she had been. She thought he looked amused at first, but his expression rapidly darkened and she cursed inwardly. She wouldn't get another chance before they arrived at this keep, wherever it was.

He pointed downstream, his order clear, though he said nothing, and she made her way to a shallow bank. He was waiting there, and as she clambered out of the water, he took hold of her dark, tangled hair and dragged her up onto the shore. Still he said nothing, but pushed her through the forest, using his grip to steer her in the direction he wanted her to go. She clenched her jaw and let him simply because there was nothing else she could do, but she hated every moment of it.

When they arrived at the road, he practically threw her onto the ground beside his horse that seemed to be awaiting him patiently. Her knees and hands slid agonizingly on the gravel. She turned over to find his hulking form a hair's breadth away, a length of knotted rope in his hand.

'My patience is at an end. You'll get no more kindness from me,' he growled, and she scrambled back in fear. Quick as a snake, he grabbed her ankles and, when she kicked out at him, he swung the rope. One of the knots hit her hard in the thigh and she cried out.

'You need a good whipping, slave. Shall I do it here in the road?'

Kora shook her head and ceased her struggle, tears rolling down her cheeks.

He made a sound of anger that had her shuffling away clumsily, afraid he'd make good on his threat, but he merely grabbed one of her injured feet and peered down at the mess of cuts and scrapes.

'You foolish girl!' he growled. 'Why didn't you tell me?'

She didn't answer him, unsure of what to say that wouldn't get her a cuff on the ear at the very least. Had he not realised she wore no shoes? Why did he even care?

With a shake of his head, he tied her ankles and wrists together quickly and swung her like a sack of grain over his horse's back. She landed with a grunt and they started on their way once more, his arm reaching behind to grab hold of her so she wouldn't slide off.

They travelled like this until the sun was high, the mercenary and his horse plodding along while she bounced around upon the demon beast's back, her stomach rolling despite its emptiness. At least her feet were being spared. *Small mercies.*

She was just beginning to wonder if he was going to

keep her like this the whole way when they passed under something. She twisted her neck to see what was happening. It was a great stone archway and beyond it was a large and imposing fortress. *The keep.* It was grey and stark against the green of the valley behind. There were two towers and a moat as well as a thick defensive outer wall complete with ramparts, though parts looked as if they were crumbling from years of neglect.

They went over a bridge and under a raised portcullis into a bustling courtyard. She could hear the blacksmith's hammer close by and a thousand other sounds that reminded her of home. She wondered if her mother even knew she was gone and felt a sudden pang of sadness that brought tears to her eyes. Mama was probably sitting in her chair looking at nothing, as she did every waking moment. She never spoke, never did anything except stare at the wall and occasionally wander off. She'd been that way as long as she could remember.

She turned her thoughts away from *before* and steeled herself. It wasn't over. She would find a way to escape. She had to. She had less than six days, but she could still become a priest and, once she had pledged herself to the gods, neither her father nor Blackhale could gainsay it. She could visit her home without fear if she ever wished to. Provided she could find a way out of here within four nights, she could make it back to the Temple before it was too late.

NEWSLETTER AND DISCORD

SIGN UP TO MY NEWSLETTER AND DISCORD AND STAY IN THE KNOW!

Members also receive exclusive content, free books, access to giveaways and contests as well as the latest information on new books and projects that I'm working on!

It's completely free to sign up, you will never be spammed by me, and it's very easy to unsubscribe:

www.kyraalessy.com

https://geni.us/KyraAlessyDiscord

facebook.com/kyraalessy
instagram.com/kyraalessy

Acknowledgements

For my kids, who will hopefully never read this book. I hope this series saves our house from the increased mortgage rates because I'd hate to have to go get another job.

For my grandkids, who I hope do read this and recognise how fucking epic their granny was when she was young and fun.

For me as an old woman. (If I've survived his kooky, fucked up planet). OMFG, stop being so fucking OLD and go tear some shit up!

xx 2023 Kyra

ABOUT THE AUTHOR

Kyra was almost 20 when she read her first romance. From Norsemen to Regency and Romcom to Dubcon, tales of love and adventure filled a void in her she didn't know existed. She lives in the UK with her family, but misses NJ where she grew up.

Kyra LOVES interacting with her readers so please join us in the Portal to the Dark Realm, her private Facebook group, because she is literally ALWAYS online unless she's asleep – much to her husband's annoyance!

Take a look at her website for info on how to stay updated on release dates, exclusive content and other general awesomeness from the worlds and characters she's created – where the road to happily ever after might be rough, but it's worth the journey!

- facebook.com/kyraalessy
- x.com/evylempryss
- instagram.com/kyraalessy
- goodreads.com/evylempryss
- bookbub.com/profile/kyra-alessy
- tiktok.com/@evylempryss